PRAISE FOR *THE LOST PRAYERS OF RICKY GRAVES*

"In *The Lost Prayers of Ricky Graves*, six intertwining narratives form a blistering tapestry of love, loss, and tragedy, reminding us that sexual identity remains a ferocious struggle for many small-town youths. In his remarkable debut, James Han Mattson both enthralls and horrifies, using the backdrop of a high school shooting to illustrate grief and longing in the age of digital communication."

—T. Geronimo Johnson, author of *Welcome to Braggsville*

"*The Lost Prayers of Ricky Graves* is wrenching and hilarious, frightening and deeply propulsive. With keen insight and virtuosic prose, Mattson conjures a Greek chorus of voices to illuminate a thoroughly modern tragedy. An exhilarating debut."

—Jennifer duBois, author of *Cartwheel*

"James Han Mattson's *The Lost Prayers of Ricky Graves* is a deeply felt and deeply moving meditation on the way our more tender emotions—longing, empathy, compassion—have simultaneously changed and remained steady in a world ever more maddeningly mediated through technology. It is a gripping story about the inescapable dangers of love."

—Benjamin Hale, author of *The Evolution of Bruno Littlemore*

"*The Lost Prayers of Ricky Graves* is comic and tragic storytelling that slowly, ingeniously reveals the nature of adolescence, identity, and the complex politics of small-town communities. This artful narrative builds to poignant truths on the ways we love and hurt on another."

—Krys Lee, author of *Drifting House* and *How I Became a North Korean*

"The Lost Prayers of Ricky Graves is a compelling, suspenseful, expertly told narrative that manages to have sympathy for even the worst of its characters. It's a brilliant performance. I couldn't put it down."

— Ron Hansen, author of *A Wild Surge of Guilty Passion* and *The Kid*

"James Han Mattson's enthralling debut deftly explores the messy complications of technology in modern life. Big-hearted and devastating, generous and probing, *The Lost Prayers of Ricky Graves* is a compulsively readable tale of finding forgiveness in the midst of cruelty, and wresting love from the wreckage of violence."

— Matthew Griffin, author of *Hide*

"The Lost Prayers of Ricky Graves is an immensely wise and big-hearted and fiercely smart novel—a heartbreaking autopsy of the current social moment. It's a darkly funny, brilliantly constructed book about technology and violence and love and the loneliness that binds us all together. Put simply: James Han Mattson is a ridiculously talented writer. This is a great, great debut."

— Stuart Nadler, author of *The Inseparables* and *Wise Men*

THE
LOST
PRAYERS
of
RICKY
GRAVES

JAMES HAN MATTSON

Text copyright © 2017 by James Han Mattson

Published by Little A, New York

www.apub.com

Amazon, the Amazon logo, and Little A are trademarks of Amazon.com, Inc., or its affiliates.

ISBN-13: 9781503942486 (hardcover)
ISBN-10: 1503942481 (hardcover)
ISBN-13: 9781503942479 (paperback)
ISBN-10: 1503942473 (paperback)

Cover design by Joan Wong

Printed in the United States of America

First edition

In memory of
Gerald Shapiro and James Alan McPherson

They will make it possible to live really anywhere we like. Any businessman, any executive, could live almost anywhere on Earth and still do his business through a device like this.

—*Arthur C. Clarke, on computers, 1974*

A thousand fibres connect you with your fellow-men, and along those fibres, as along sympathetic threads, run your actions as causes, and return to you as effects.

—*Henry Melvill*

A VISITOR

ALYSSA GRAVES

So I didn't come back for my brother's funeral because I had to work and I was newly pregnant and there were reporters and seeing Ricky dead and pieced together by some amateur embalmer-type person would've seriously pushed me over the edge, I know this. But I did come back afterward, and that should've meant something because look: I wasn't abandoning my mom or purposely leaving her all alone with those cameras shoved in her face; I just needed to work a few more shifts, save up for my return trip, figure my shit out before I went back to the Springs for god knew how long.

So anyway.

I came back after it all blew over—coward move, sure, but whatever—and I was huge, eight months in, waddled like a duck, and even though I hadn't really been the best at communicating with my mother, mostly because, as she put it so abruptly, "You're no good, Alyssa," I still needed to be there for her, because who else did she have? Everyone was blaming her for Ricky's craziness, and Ricky's craziness wasn't her fault. It wasn't anybody's fault, but still, people were whispering and making all these assumptions about how terrible and neglectful and mean and abusive she was, and she wasn't any of those things—the opposite, actually—and it wasn't fair that people judged her on Ricky's actions, because she had nothing to do with them.

But still, that "You're no good" stung, because of anyone in the world, I expected her to always have my back, to understand me. I mean, she understood when I was thirteen and I drunk-drove Mr. Lessard's car, and she understood when I was sixteen and got pregnant the first time, and she understood when I announced to both her and Ricky that I was gonna have an abortion. She held my hand through it all. Didn't judge me one bit. When I cried and screamed and apologized over and over and over, she got a cool cloth for my head and said, "Shhh, baby. It's okay." But then—so weird—she just snapped. Like two days after I turned nineteen, she just stared at me with her big green eyes and said in the most hateful way, "You're no good, Alyssa," and I suppose a lot of people wouldn't take it so harshly, you know, would probably just be like, *She's obviously on her period,* but my mother had never *ever* said anything like that to me in my life, and there were times when she should've—should've said that and a lot more—but then, at nineteen, working two jobs, at Kohl's and the Green Room, and basically holding my own in every way imaginable, well, that wasn't the time to go telling me about being "no good."

"What do you mean, no good?" I asked her. I was helping her cook something or other. Pasta, I think. "What're you talking about?"

"Never mind," she said.

"What?" I said. "You can't just say I'm no good, then tell me to never mind."

She sighed, and yes, she'd definitely done that to me before, that sighing. She'd sometimes just look over at me from wherever it was, sometimes even across a big room like our living room, and sigh. It was annoying, but nothing I wasn't used to. I wasn't easy, I admit. But by then, at nineteen, I'd gotten my shit together, working those jobs, helping around the house, babysitting Ricky, hanging out with Corky less and less.

"I'm just tired, I guess," she said. She was stirring something that didn't need stirring. She was doing something to do something.

"Is it the rent thing?" I asked. "'Cause I'll pay. You just tell me how much. I'll pay."

4

"It's not that."

"Well?"

"It's just . . ."

"It's just what?"

"Never mind."

"No."

"Please, Alyssa. Never mind."

And we went on like that for like ten full minutes, her telling me it was nothing, and me pressing, pressing, pressing, her trying to talk about the food, and me telling her to stop avoiding the issue.

"Alyssa," she said. "Please."

"Tell me," I said.

"Forget it," she said.

"Don't tell me to forget it."

"Can you get the basil out of the fridge?"

"Don't do that."

"Alyssa. Jesus."

"Tell me."

And then, finally, after I just stood in front of the refrigerator, blocking her way, she said, "Fine! Fine!"

"Fine what?"

She balled her fists by her sides. Her face went red. "Why haven't you cleaned your bathroom?" she said.

"*That's* why I'm no good?"

"I go up there, it's a mess. It's gross. You can't even respect your living quarters."

"Christ. I'll clean it," I said.

"I mean, what kind of example are you to Ricky?"

"Ricky? He doesn't need an example."

"What you are is trouble," she said. "You're trouble for him. And I'm worried, him growing up, seeing how you do things."

"How I clean my bathroom?"

5

"I worry about that. What kind of model his big sister has been. I worry all the time."

"You're serious? I'm busting my ass."

"Couldn't even graduate high school." She shook her head and stirred.

"I'll clean my damn bathroom!" I said.

She didn't say anything more, just turned back to her pot and kept stirring, and I knew then that I had to leave, that her silence meant *Get the hell out of my house,* and the more I thought about it, the more it seemed feasible. Like yeah, I probably wasn't the best influence, but I wasn't the worst either. I was a *unique individual,* and unique individuals did things their own way, right? Like, what's that saying—beating your own drum? Anyway, when my mom told me I was no good, I realized that it was a perfect opportunity to just start over, do things my own way, to ignore my mom, and maybe, to a lesser extent, my kid brother.

"I don't need to be an influence on anybody," I told my mom. "Especially on that little shit."

She didn't respond.

Ricky and I didn't really get along much, mostly because I was so much older than him. He was just this kid, this nuisance—eight years younger, so basically an alien. When I told him and my mom that I was having an abortion, he said, "Who's that?" and I cracked up, because my mom was so grave and serious, and here's this kid who knows nothing about what's happening asking who "Borshon" is.

"No, I'm *having* an abortion," I said. "It's when you get preg—"

And my mom stopped me there, as she should have, because eight-year-old kids don't need to know about that kind of thing. But still, late that night, I snuck into his room, found him under the covers with his flashlight playing some video game—sneaking, really—and I felt this wave of pride, because that's exactly what I did when I was his age, except back then we didn't have the digital contraptions; I had to make do with the sleazy romance novels I found in my mom's bedside drawer.

"Psst," I said. And he immediately turned off his flashlight and lay down on his bed and pretended to sleep. "Don't worry, Ricky," I said. "It's just me."

"Lyssa?" he said, leaning up and rubbing his eyes. He always did that, all the time, night or day, rubbed his eyes. It was dark, but he had a yellow night-light, so I saw some shadows on his face. "I was sleeping."

"No, you weren't."

"I'm so tired now."

"Oh, shut up."

I sat on his bed, and he just kinda looked at me the way kids do—you know, innocent, wide-eyed, whatever. Standard kid shit, kinda like everything's a miracle or something. "I just wanted to tell you," I said, or rather, I whispered, "you might've had a niece or nephew. I don't know which. But you might've, if I hadn't decided on this."

"A niece or a nephew?"

"Yeah. Like I was gonna have a kid. But now I'm not."

"You were gonna kid?" he said.

"No," I said. "I was gonna *have* a kid."

"Where?"

"Never mind. Jesus."

"Is Mommy mad at you?"

"I don't think so," I said. "She seems okay with it all."

"But Lyssa, where is the kid going to live?"

"That's just it, Ricky. I'm not having it. It's a process. A bad one. But I just wanted to come in here and tell you that you might've had a niece or a nephew. Would you like that? A baby to play with?"

"A baby?" I could tell, even in the dark, that his eyes were wider. "You're gonna get a baby?"

"Oh, forget it."

"But yes!" he said, clapping his hands. "I want a baby to play with!"

And right then, right as his hands made that tiny clipped sound, I thought, *Of course I'll have this kid. Why the fuck not! Why not give my baby brother the joy of having someone to play with.* And I leaned in and hugged him harder than I'd ever hugged him, and he pushed me away, but I kept on. He felt so good, so little and wonderful, and I thought, *A kid! A kid would feel like this all the time!* So I continued to hold him, even though he squirmed and batted at my shoulder. I continued because he was, at that moment, extremely important.

Of course, the next morning my mind changed, but I never forgot that clap and that revelation, and I wondered, and still wonder to this day, if I'd decided to just go ahead and have the kid, if maybe Ricky wouldn't have flipped out. If he'd had a little niece or nephew, maybe he'd still be alive. But really, who knows. Nobody can tell these things. There's no way.

When I got back to town, my mom stared at my belly for a while; she knew I'd gotten pregnant again, because I was Facebook friends with June Byerly, and June was sorta close to my mom in that way all small-town people are close to each other, I guess, and so it must've slipped, because one day, out of the blue, I got this email from my mother saying, **YOUR PREGNANT AGAIN?!?!** and I noticed how she didn't spell "you're" right, and suddenly I felt this terrible need to go back to school and get my diploma, stop waitressing, maybe work in an office, make a real living. I didn't respond, of course; I just cursed June under my breath, because I knew it was her who told. She was the only Facebook friend I had left from El Monte Springs, and even though I'd thought about unfriending her so many times, I just couldn't bring myself to do it, because even though she was a bad gossip and talked shit about basically everybody, she'd helped me through my major breakup with Corky, and to unfriend someone like that was to commit some sort of horrible Facebook sin, and really, I didn't hate June anyway—she was a good person—but I just wish she would've left the Springs, like I did, so we could've been true friends.

Anyway, a lot of it was my fault too, since I should've thought harder before posting that stupid Facebook status. Me being all discreet about it, clever or whatever, saying, Something's percolating! because I'd just learned that word from my coworker Sandra—"percolating." It's like what coffee does, but she said it could mean a lot of things, like bubbling up, and I thought, *Well, if a baby isn't bubbling up, I don't know what is.* So I posted it, and of course I got all these comments asking me what I meant, and I only responded with, Time will tell, thinking I'd covered my bases and all, but word must've gotten out that the thing percolating was my new baby, and June must've contacted my mother right away, saying, "Oh my god. Alyssa's pregnant!"

I figured I'd try to just get more shifts at the diner, maybe pick up another job somewhere, make things work. I definitely wasn't gonna have another abortion. Even though the kid's dad was long gone—stupid one-night stand. Seriously. Didn't have sex for like almost a year, then the first time I got drunk and did it, I get fucking pregnant. Figures. But whatever. After he was done fucking me, he scrambled into his clothes like he'd just gotten caught diddling an infant or something, then ran out of the room without a word. Douche.

He was good-looking, though. I remember that. I'd just got done with my shift, and Sandra was whining and complaining about how we never went out anymore, so I finally said, "Fine. We'll go out for like two drinks. That's it." Well, two drinks turned to seven, because Sandra just couldn't stop. (That's one reason I didn't go out with her anymore. Alcoholics just suck you in, make you one of them, and I'm not. I mean, I don't even like being drunk that much.) And we were laughing about something or other when this really handsome guy came over to us and asked if he could buy us drinks. Sandra was married and all—though that was really a messed-up situation too—so she flashed her ring and got all indignant, but I said, "Sure. Why not." And Sandra kinda looked at me slyly, squinting a little, because I think she'd always been a bit jealous, not because I was some knockout or anything, but because I was available, and guys kinda sensed that; she would've been available too—I'm sure of it—if she were a little prettier.

Sounds so horrible to say, but I'm just trying to be as honest as possible. I mean, she flashed that ring all over the place mostly because she wanted everyone to know that she *had* someone and she wasn't this horrible wretch who couldn't get a man. And yeah, she had a few unfortunate physical things, like kind of a bobblehead but not really—because her body wasn't small; her head just seemed disproportionate. I mean, she was probably two hundred pounds, and she was only five five or something, and it seemed like so much of that weight was between her bottom lip and her chin. It was like her face hadn't decided when to quit—I know, harsh, but that's reality. Still, she was wicked witty and smart and funny, and so she shouldn't have felt so insecure all the time.

So he came over and I let him buy me a drink, and Sandra kinda smirked, turned to her margarita, slurped it, got all silent, and this guy stared and stared at me, and I wasn't creeped out at all. Maybe it was the alcohol, maybe it was just my horrible dry spell, but I couldn't help but feel like to him I was the only person in the bar, maybe even in the world. He asked the usual questions: where I was from (I never said El Monte Springs, just said, "Oh, around the area"), what I did (which was dumb, 'cause I was still in my uniform), what brought me out, etc., etc., etc. Fifteen minutes in and Sandra was totally looking away, playing with her hair, sighing, and even though I tried to get her in on the conversation, she just smiled her insincere smile, her "work smile," and looked away.

I at least got the guy's name. Roger. I didn't get a last name, but "Roger" was sturdy enough, I suppose. Wasn't gonna name my kid that, but I would tell him or her that Roger was one of the handsomest men I'd seen. He had perfect teeth and a kinda square face and jaw, the kind of face you saw on commercials with model guys trying to be like blue-collar workers—though seriously, construction guys and whatnot did *not* look like how they looked in those commercials, especially not in El Monte Springs—and he looked like he either ran or worked out. You know, the type of body with muscles but not overly developed ones, not the gross bulging kind. In bed, I noticed he had a tuft of hair right at the bottom of his neck—kinda a weird place, since there wasn't any on his back—and I remember I kept pulling on it as he did his thing. Wasn't the best sex, really, but wasn't the worst. But then, afterward, with him leaving so abruptly, I pieced it together. He was married, of course. In town on business. Should've known. He wasn't wearing a ring, but that didn't mean anything. Never did.

Next day, Sandra wouldn't talk to me, just went about her business like we hadn't gotten totally hammered the night before. I tried talking to her, but she pretended she was really busy, even though the diner was completely dead. The day after that, though, she talked like nothing had happened, and we were best friends again. She was so temperamental, that one, but I've learned you've just gotta let people have their emotions, screwed-up or not, and then wait for things to get back to normal. There's no use sitting on things forever.

So I got back to the Springs, and my mom stared at my belly, then she just went on and on about how she was so worried about me this whole time, how I could've at least called once in a while, and I didn't really respond at first, 'cause like *she could've called too*—I mean, she did call right after Ricky, like all the time, but I just couldn't take talking to *anyone* during that time—but after a while just listening, I finally told her that I was sorry, that I should've told her about getting pregnant; she was gonna be a grandma, after all, and I suppose she had a right to know that firsthand from her daughter. She asked about the dad, of course, and I told her that I didn't know, that he just left, and at first I thought she might go on about this too, about my irresponsibility, about my terrible acceptance of casual hookups, about my not using protection, about a bunch of things having to do with me and men and sex and maturity and long-term goals and short-term pleasures and—Well, look: this fear was in my head, because she wasn't *like* that, she never *had* been. She was actually really cool, and my time away had made me change her into something not based in reality.

Anyway.

I guess because she was my mom and not some nonrelation, I didn't see all that awesomeness back as a teen—even at *nine*teen. I just thought she was this presence that was always going to judge or look down on me for some reason or another. But I wasn't nineteen anymore; I was twenty-five—older, wiser, etc., etc., etc.—so as she nodded, kinda furrowing her brow and blinking for a long time, I thought about how good it was for me to come back, to help her out through this Ricky mess, this absolute nightmare of a shitstorm, because if anyone, *she* needed the most support. The public scrutiny alone . . . And so I felt good and useful, even though I didn't know how much I was gonna be able to do for her, me in my engorged state and all, no job, little money, no real friends. But I would try my best.

And besides, there was also me: Ricky was my brother, and I hadn't properly grieved; at least that's what people told me. It was hard to grieve when you were in this constant state of shock, not really knowing how to deal with the fact that you not only have a suicide in the family, but a homicide, which was something that just didn't happen except in the news. And to have strangers dissecting every second of his life—strangers who didn't know shit about him or this town, strangers screaming on the Internet for some sort of justice, as if Ricky had been their brother or son, as if they'd had some relation to Wesley Thompson or Mark McVitry—well, it just became this totally messed-up thing, like impossible to process, and so being around my mom, around my family, was the best thing, I thought; it would help me grieve properly. Of course, I never expected to meet Jeremy, but I guess things happened, and in the end, it was probably for the best, the way things happened.

EMAIL CORRESPONDENCE
SEPTEMBER–DECEMBER 2009

From: **Harriet Graves** <harrietgraves4321@
yahoo.com>

To: Victoria Gorham <Victoria@victoriago-
rham.com>

Date: September 19, 2009 at 5:43 PM

Subject: Your #1 Fan!!

Hi there!

My name is Harriet Graves and I just wanted
to let you know that I've become your #1
fan! I know you probably get tons of email
from fans of your books and maybe you
have someone like an assistant go through
them all so who knows if you'll see this but
I thought why not try, right? Your website is
really great by the way, and I like your photo,
that suit really looks awesome where'd you

get it? Lol. Listen to me, talking about your suit! Your probably thinking, this woman's crazy!

I read The Fem-Core twice and also How To Be Strong twice and I'm halfway through The Nine Habits of Successful Single Mothers, and all your talk about inner strength and deep introspection and finding it through ten minutes a day of "total unfiltered concentration" has really helped me get through so much and find the courage to actually confront my adult child Alyssa. Before I read your books I was pretty weak with her but now I feel like I have the strength to get her moving for her own good. When you said that even adult children need their parents to give them pushes every once in a while, a lightbulb went off in my head and I realized that I hadn't pushed her and that I needed to because she is eight years older than my other child and so is a role model and influence. Well anyway she ended up moving to Boston after my discussion with her and leaving her boyfriend who wasn't really going many places with his life and she's very happy now and I think she owes her happiness to you and your books!

I'm pretty sure you are a genius so it's strange that I can actually write a note to you, just with a few clicks and keystrokes. As you know, growing up we couldn't communicate with celebrities like this. It's awesome! And I know you probably won't respond but just to be able to write you a note is enough.

If you do respond, I have a question, and it's about what I read in The Nine Habits of Successful Single Mothers. It's actually the third habit: Tailoring Conversations. You say that single mothers of more than one child need to make sure to "tailor conversations to individual child needs" but I'm not sure what your saying really. I read the chapter and I like your example of your own children, but I guess I don't really understand how you wouldn't tailor conversations. I mean, you talk to each child differently because as you put it, they "live in different spheres," but I guess I'm confused about the importance of this habit because it seems only normal to do this? Sorry for my ignorance on this, I'm sure your probably thinking I'm the dumbest mother ever but if you have some clarification (and you respond!) I'd really appreciate it.

Anyway, thank you so much for your books!! I think they are truly amazing and inspiring.

Sincerely,
Harriet Graves

From: **Victoria Gorham** <Victoria@victoriagorham.com>

To: Harriet Graves <harrietgraves4321@
yahoo.com>

Date: September 29, 2009 at 12:05 AM

Subject: Re: Your #1 Fan!!

Dear Harriet,

Thank you so much for your kind words! I'm
humbled beyond belief. It's readers like you
who keep me going.

I'm glad your daughter is doing well in Boston
and that my suggestions are really working
for you. And yes, too often when our children
become legal adults, we feel helpless to help,
and like I mention in my book, too many parents just say things like, "Well, they're on their
own now. They make their own decisions."
Parenting, as you know, is a never-ending process. Our children look to us for answers, even
as they age, and as single mothers, we bear
the burden of being, as I call it, "sole sage."

Your question about habit #3 is a good one,
and I'm more than happy to clarify, although
from your email, I think you get the gist of
it already. It's basically saying that if you are
rearing more than one child, you need to
understand how fast times are changing and
that the context surrounding one child might

not be the same as the context surrounding another child. My example of my own children was about technology, about how one of my boys—and all of his friends—spoke in tech terms that my older son didn't. My younger son basically understood Internet stuff from a very early age, so it wasn't ever new to him. For my older son, though, it *was* new, even though he's relatively proficient, and because of this, I adjusted my vocabulary and my tone when talking about computers.

I hope that makes sense! Thanks again for your kind, kind words.

All best,
Victoria Gorham

From: **Harriet Graves** <harrietgraves4321@ yahoo.com>

To: Victoria Gorham <Victoria@victoriago-rham.com>

Date: October 1, 2009 at 2:44 PM

Subject: Re: Your #1 Fan!!

Hi Victoria!

Oh my god I can't believe you replied and that you actually took the time to think about my question!! I am so honored. Thank you so much!! I'll be honest, I'm a little star struck right now. Seriously, you are such an inspiration to me and thousands of women!

So this single motherhood thing is pretty crazy, huh? Like you said in The Fem-Core, nobody should complain about being underpaid until they work for free as a mother. I work in an office and it's not half as hard as trying to do the right thing with my children!

So I know you are totally busy with writing a new book (I think I saw an interview where you said your next book was going to be about something totally different? I can't remember what it was though) so feel free to ignore me if you want (but please don't! hehe) but I was wondering what your take was on friendships, I mean friendships your kids make. My youngest, Ricky, was for a long time really good friends with this boy Mark McVitry, mostly because I'm very good friends with Mark's mom. They hung out all the time. But like overnight, right when Ricky and him went into middle school, they started not hanging out. I am still friends with Mark's mom, and I have never asked her about it, like if they got into a fight, but maybe I should bring it up with her? This probably sounds like a dumb problem, but I get a little worried sometimes because Ricky is starting to be quieter. I know it's normal during adolescence for a kid to withdraw a little, but my daughter never really did, she was always doing stuff with friends, so this is new to me. Do you have any sage advice?

Thank you so much again!!!! I am so appreciative of your time!! I'll totally understand if you don't write back (but please do! haha).

Sincerely,
Harriet Graves

From: **Harriet Graves** <harrietgraves4321@yahoo.com>

To: Victoria Gorham <Victoria@victoriagorham.com>

Date: October 23, 2009 at 11:25 PM

Subject: Re: Your #1 Fan!!

Hi Victoria!

I'm sure you are very busy with writing your new book, so I don't want to bother you or anything. I was wondering if you received my last email though? Sometimes I think my emails don't actually send for some reason. A few of my friends have said they didn't get my messages.

Anyway, to update you, I actually did ask Ricky about his friend Mark McVitry, asked him why he didn't hang out anymore, and he just shrugged and said they didn't have classes together. This didn't make much sense to me but I let it go at that. I also asked him if he missed his sister since she left and he shrugged again. I don't understand all this shrugging! I didn't have this with Alyssa. Maybe I'm not phrasing things the right way? I seriously wish I could pry his little head open and read his thoughts. Other than that though, everything seems peachy. He's an A student, made the honor roll again. I couldn't be more proud!

I hope your writing is going well! I can't wait to read your next book. When will it be out?

Sincerely,
Harriet Graves

From: **Harriet Graves** <harrietgraves4321@yahoo.com>

To: Victoria Gorham <Victoria@victoriagorham.com>

Date: November 17, 2009 at 12:30 PM

Subject: Re: Your #1 Fan!!

Hi Victoria!

Wow, you must be very busy! I assume writing books and researching probably takes up all your time. That and responding to the countless emails you probably receive from people like me!

Anyway, I wanted to say again how much I appreciated your response before. It really helped a lot.

Ricky is doing better, I think! He seems happier and he's still doing well in school. He told me the other day that he hung out with this guy Corky and that it was okay. Corky is my daughter's ex-boyfriend. I don't have too many good feelings about him and I don't think I want Ricky hanging out with him, but I'll be honest, it's better than him hanging out alone in the house. Corky is also Ricky's summer camp counselor, and even though I think he (Corky, not Ricky) is a little rough around the edges, I think he takes that job seriously. So I'm okay with Ricky hanging out with him, I guess. Is that not a good thing? I mean, Corky is 25 years old, maybe 26, I can't remember. Anyway, he's double Ricky's age. I've talked to a few of my friends about it and they all seem to think it's a little strange, but I've noticed that Ricky isn't mopey as much so I'm hesitant to tell him he can't hang out with him.

I hope you have a great Thanksgiving! I hope writing is going well!!

Sincerely,
Harriet Graves

From: **Victoria Gorham** <Victoria@victoriagorham.com>

To: Harriet Graves <harrietgraves4321@yahoo.com>

Date: December 21, 2009 at 11:58 PM

Subject: Re: Your #1 Fan!!

Hi Harriet!

Please accept my apologies for my tardiness in returning your emails! This fall has been *crazy* for me, as maybe you saw. I had all these appearances, and while it might seem glamorous, it's mostly just draining. I'm a writer first and foremost, and as a writer, I'm pretty private. I don't like being in the spotlight. But if I'm helping people, I'll do it, and it seems I've helped a few people!

About Ricky: Children mature differently, and it's not unusual for a tween, especially one from a single-mother household, to seek the approval of a male figure. I think that's probably what's going on with Ricky and Corky. Since you know Corky, and especially since Corky has been Ricky's camp counselor, I don't think you have much to worry about with that relationship. Still, because of the age difference, I'd pay attention to their interactions, just to be on the safe side.

Honestly, it might be good that Ricky has this role model. Withdrawal from parents is very natural in adolescence as peer acceptance overwhelms parental acceptance. If Ricky is withdrawing from peers as well, perhaps Corky is someone he can confide in. I know it sucks being a parent and not being able to be your kid's #1 confidant, but this adolescent stage is very tricky and very nerve-wracking. I wish you the best of luck. It'll go well in the end. I'm sure of it.

Thanks again for your kind words, and have a happy holiday season!

All best,
Victoria Gorham

MAN-DATE CHAT TRANSCRIPT
OCTOBER 18, 2014

Rickyg9999: hey, sup?

Jeremyinsf: not much, u?

Rickyg9999: chillin

Jeremyinsf: cool

Rickyg9999: like your pic

Jeremyinsf: thanks, man

Rickyg9999: you like mine?

Jeremyinsf: sure, man. nice.

Rickyg9999: thought you might

Jeremyinsf: haha why's that?

Rickyg9999: just had a feeling lol

Jeremyinsf: well, your feeling's right

Rickyg9999: cool

Rickyg9999: so what brings you on here?

Jeremyinsf: just lookin around, wasting time I guess

Rickyg9999: cool

Jeremyinsf: and u?

Rickyg9999: same

Jeremyinsf: you're in New Hampshire?

Rickyg9999: yeah sucks

Jeremyinsf: never been to that state

Rickyg9999: well now you got a reason to come lol

Jeremyinsf: haha

Jeremyinsf: so you're 21?

Rickyg9999: yeah

Jeremyinsf: young guy!

Rickyg9999: not that young

Rickyg9999: people always think I'm older

Rickyg9999: I'm in college but some people even think I'm older than that

Jeremyinsf: older than college?

Rickyg9999: yeah

Jeremyinsf: you must be really mature

Rickyg9999: I guess lol

Rickyg9999: so are you from San Francisco?

Jeremyinsf: have lived here a long time, but grew up in the Midwest

Rickyg9999: oh that's a change huh?

Jeremyinsf: yeah

Rickyg9999: your pic is pretty hot

Jeremyinsf: thanks

Rickyg9999: I'm not that muscral

Rickyg9999: muscular

Jeremyinsf: haha you look good though

Rickyg9999: I go to the gym sometimes but mostly work out at home

Rickyg9999: I have a home gym in my own apartment where I live alone

Jeremyinsf: nice. that means you don't have any excuse not to exercise!

Rickyg9999: lol yeah and maybe look like you some day

Jeremyinsf: thanks, bud

Rickyg9999: so you meet a lot of dudes off here?

Jeremyinsf: lol no, not a lot, but nobody ever says they meet a lot of guys off here, right? ;)

Rickyg9999: I haven't really been on here very much, I'll be honest I'm not out or anything, I mean my mom doesn't know and neither does my sister

Jeremyinsf: oh, I see. well, it takes time. it's a process.

Rickyg9999: what process?

Jeremyinsf: coming out

Rickyg9999: oh ya I don't think I'm ready, I mean I don't think my mom will freak out but who knows

Jeremyinsf: well, you should wait until you feel it's right

Rickyg9999: you seem like a real cool dude, other guys on here are so lame, just close their windows right away when they find out that I'm like not their neighbor or something, I mean even if I was I wouldn't jump their bones Jesus lol

Jeremyinsf: why, thank you, Ricky. that's your name, right? I'm Jeremy, obviously ☺

Rickyg9999: yeah that's my name and great to meet you too!

Rickyg9999: so do you ever get to the East Coast?

Jeremyinsf: yeah, sometimes for work, but usually just to New York and DC

Rickyg9999: that's not that far

Jeremyinsf: I'm just in and out usually

Rickyg9999: well you should think of coming up farther north, we could meet in Boston or something

Rickyg9999: u there???

Jeremyinsf: I'll think about it, bud

Jeremyinsf: good luck with your mom and sister

Jeremyinsf: got a meeting soon. ttyl

Rickyg9999: sure man

Rickyg9999: I'll add you to my buddy list

Rickyg9999: ??

Jeremyinsf has closed his chat window.

MAN-DATE CHAT TRANSCRIPT
OCTOBER 25, 2014

Rickyg9999: hey!

Jeremyinsf: hey bud!

Rickyg9999: how's your weekend?

Jeremyinsf: busy as always haha

Rickyg9999: what do you do for work?

Jeremyinsf: I'm a controller

Rickyg9999: lol you control things?

Jeremyinsf: yeah, kind of. accountant who controls things haha

Rickyg9999: oh wow that's cool

Jeremyinsf: it can be

Rickyg9999: I'm studying psychology

Jeremyinsf: always liked those classes in college. interesting

Rickyg9999: yeah I'm very interested in how humans behave

Jeremyinsf: we're a weird bunch, us humans ☺

Rickyg9999: after I graduate from college I'll work for the CIA or something like do profiling stuff for the government

Rickyg9999: or maybe start off at the NYPD like investigating criminals minds

Jeremyinsf: like CSI or something?

Rickyg9999: kinda I guess

Jeremyinsf: sounds interesting

Rickyg9999: yeah I have some leads already, people asking for a specialist, I just need to finish my studies first

Jeremyinsf: of course

Rickyg9999: I'm pretty exite

Rickyg9999: excited

Jeremyinsf: when do you graduate?

Rickyg9999: I have two more years left

Jeremyinsf: cool. what school is it?

Jeremyinsf: ?

Rickyg9999: well right now I'm taking classes online at Harvard

Jeremyinsf: oh, I didn't know you could do that. wow, that's impressive

Rickyg9999: yeah I have to be in New Hampshire cuz of family things but they really wanted me in the program so they said I could just do my classes online for now

Jeremyinsf: oh. well, that's good

Rickyg9999: yeah it's a real competive program so it's hard to get in

Rickyg9999: where did you go to college?

Jeremyinsf: UC Berkeley

Rickyg9999: oh that's a good school

Jeremyinsf: not as good as Harvard ;)

Rickyg9999: well it's still good

Rickyg9999: that's in the Midwest where you grew up?

Jeremyinsf: ?

Rickyg9999: I mean Berkley is in the Midwest right?

Jeremyinsf: no, it's in CA

Rickyg9999: oh for some reason I thought it was in the Midwest I'm not sure why I thought that lol

Rickyg9999: you must really like it in CA going to school there and then working as a controller in San Francisco, must be wicked nice there

Jeremyinsf: so how are things with your mom and sister? still thinking of coming out to them?

Rickyg9999: I really want to especially my sister cuz she's wicked cool but I'm just so nervous. it's like I watch TV and the world is really into the gay rights thing like gay marriage, and my mom is really for it and my sister too and that's so great but then my mom will ask me about girls and I'll feel like if I came out it would just be really bad for her, she had a gay brother who died of AIDS

Jeremyinsf: wow, that's a lot to handle, but it sounds like you have some cool support. and you can chat here with me too. I've been through it, and I can coach you a bit if you want. the internet can be a really great place for support

Rickyg9999: wow were you like a school counselor or something?

Jeremyinsf: haha no, but I know how tough it can be

Rickyg9999: well anyway I knew you were awesome. and hot as hell ;-)

Rickyg9999: so maybe someday when I get a break from studying I'll take a trip out there, maybe next summer or something

Jeremyinsf: it's a great place to visit

Rickyg9999: it would be nice to meet up too

Jeremyinsf: sure man

Rickyg9999: so is all your family still out in the Midwest?

Jeremyinsf: yeah

Rickyg9999: which state?

Jeremyinsf: North Dakota

Rickyg9999: wow that's weird

Jeremyinsf: haha weird?

Rickyg9999: just never hear much people coming from that state

Jeremyinsf: well, there aren't that many people there! haha

Rickyg9999: there aren't that many people here eithee, it's such a small town I hate it

Rickyg9999: either

Jeremyinsf: I hear ya. my town was 1800 people. no joke.

Rickyg9999: holy shit that's super small

Jeremyinsf: yeah

Rickyg9999: but you got out, you moved to San Francisco and everything

Jeremyinsf: you'll get out too. just a matter of time.

Rickyg9999: I wish I could right now but I have some home issues and school and everything

Jeremyinsf: home issues?

Rickyg9999: yeah I have to take care of my mom, my sister's gone now so it's just me and her

Jeremyinsf: where's your sister?

Rickyg9999: she moved to Boston

Jeremyinsf: well, it seems like you two should switch places!

Rickyg9999: yeah but she's got a life there and she

wanted to get away from El Monte Springs as much as me and she's older so that's why she got to leave and I had to stay

Jeremyinsf: well, just wait it out, bud. things will get better before you know it.

Rickyg9999: yeah I keep saying that too, thanks your a real cool guy

Jeremyinsf: aw, thanks

Jeremyinsf: hey I gotta run

Rickyg9999: well have a good day

Rickyg9999: I like your new pic btw

Jeremyinsf: thanks, man. ttyl

Jeremyinsf has closed his chat window.

MAN-DATE CHAT TRANSCRIPT
NOVEMBER 8, 2014

Rickyg9999: hey I missed you last Saturday

Rickyg9999: u there?

Jeremyinsf: last Saturday?

Rickyg9999: yeah u weren't on

Jeremyinsf: oh, I was out of town

Rickyg9999: where did you go?

Jeremyinsf: just down to LA with friends

Rickyg9999: that sounds fun

Jeremyinsf: it was all right. drank too much

Rickyg9999: I don't really drink that much

Rickyg9999: there's this place here called the Meadows

where everyone hangs out and drinks but I don't go there it's dumb

Rickyg9999: it's outside and it's getting too cold to go there anyway

Rickyg9999: and everyone acts stupid cuz there drunk

Rickyg9999: I mean maybe I'll go there once or something I don't know, there's this guy . . .

Jeremyinsf: there is? a guy? ;-)

Rickyg9999: yeah his name is Wesley and he keeps saying I should come down to the Meadows with him like it'll be a blast and I think he might be in the same situation as me, you know like not out

Jeremyinsf: that sounds interesting . . . and promising ☺

Rickyg9999: yeah I mean I really like him and everything but he's kinda part of the cool group and I'll be honest I'm not really part of that group and he's always hanging with this kid Mark McVitry who ignores me even when we had projects together in class and used to hang out when we were kids, but anyway I think Wesley's pretty hot and really awesome and funny

Jeremyinsf: sounds like you've got a crush!

Rickyg9999: I just think we're going through similar things

Jeremyinsf: yeah, it's so difficult

Rickyg9999: so where do you like to drink?

Jeremyinsf: I dunno. different places, bars.

Rickyg9999: you go to gay bars?

Jeremyinsf: sometimes I guess

Rickyg9999: I bet guys think your smoking hot there, must be fun

Jeremyinsf: lol not sure about that

Rickyg9999: you must work out like every day huh?

Jeremyinsf: not at all!

Rickyg9999: maybe you could show me some techniques ☺

Jeremyinsf: I probably wouldn't be the best person for that. I'm not one of those gay guys who lives at the gym.

Rickyg9999: well you got an amazing body

Jeremyinsf: thanks!

Rickyg9999: I'll think about this summer coming out there but kinda poor and everything being a college student lol. maybe you could come here and just hang out sometime since you've never been here. there's not a lot but we did get a few new places downtown and there not so terrible from what I hear

Jeremyinsf: sure thing, bud

Jeremyinsf: have to head out now. take care of yourself!

Rickyg9999: ok just let me know your plans

Jeremyinsf: will do, bud.

Jeremyinsf has closed his chat window.

JEREMY LITTLE

I met Alyssa outside of the Full Monte Motel. She stood by the office—a sliding window, which, from behind, housed a bearded middle-aged man in khaki pants—smacking her gum and rubbing her belly. When she saw me, she furrowed her brow and stopped chewing. I smiled. She didn't smile back. She resumed her chewing and turned her gaze to the horizon, which rolled for miles and ended in a wide sheet of pale-blue sky. It was late morning, and she looked as if she'd just awoken, her brown hair uncombed, her eyes puffy with sleep.

The motel, like most of the buildings in El Monte Springs, looked scuffed and off-center, as if it'd been erected on a series of pitcher's mounds. Its facade suggested years of neglect and misuse—a second-story window broken and covered only in plastic, a splattering of bird shit painting the chipped wood. Alyssa fit perfectly with the motel, her oversize gray sweatshirt like the dull bulb of a welcoming lamppost. She reminded me slightly of my high school girlfriend, Carly, who'd worked at the Dairy Queen in Racketsville and who'd smoked incessantly, sometimes inside the restaurant, spilling her ash into our milkshakes.

"Hey," Alyssa said, turning back toward me, squinting. "I don't work here, in case you were wondering."

"I wasn't wondering," I said.

"Oh, okay. Smart-ass, huh?"

"No."

It was July 20, 2015, about four months after Ricky's death. I'd been there for three days. It hadn't taken me long to find her house: a single-story blue bungalow surrounded by tall, unkempt grass. On the porch was a grisly floral-printed love seat, the kind of furniture that made your hands feel chalky. In the gravel driveway sat her car, the red-and-white Massachusetts license plate glinting brightly against the yard's overgrowth. On my first day in the Springs, I waited across the street in my rental, dipping my head below the window, telling myself that Alyssa Graves was none of my concern, that I was unnecessarily complicating my life, that I'd done nothing wrong and needed no forgiveness.

When she came out and got in her car, I froze, my mind abruptly retreating to Ricky's grainy Man-Date thumbnail, remembering all the times he'd asked me to come to this town, this neighborhood, this house. *I asked you so many times to come out here and you said you couldn't all the time and now I know you won't so it doesn't matter cuz I can't talk to someone in person cuz you won't come out here you understand?* I shuddered.

Alyssa roared out of the driveway and down the street, her belly pressed firmly against the steering wheel. She didn't pass me directly, but I could still make out the side of her face, which was rough and indented, and contained a sharp, pointed nose and a slightly jutted chin. When she got to the end of the block, she took a right.

And I miss her so much all the time cuz I mean she was mean to me a lot, sometimes ignored me with her friends but she was someone I admired and I can't say that for anybody else.

Still shaking, I turned my key in the ignition and sped away.

On day three, I sat outside her house again, slouching as before, except this time, before she came out, I gathered the nerve to scribble a note on a napkin, race to her car, and throw it in the open window. Fifteen minutes later, I watched her waddle out and squeeze into the front seat. Before she drove off, she picked up the napkin, massaged the corners with her thumbs and index fingers, and tossed it onto the passenger seat.

"Hardly any guests today," she said. "You're like one of the only ones."

"Oh," I said.

"Here visiting someone? Like family?"

"No," I said, feeling a spike in my throat.

"So what're you doing in the Springs?"

"You said you don't work here?"

"Not yet, but soon, I think." She scratched her leg and rubbed her eyes. "You're not like on vacation or something, are you? What a place to come to."

"Not on vacation."

"You a reporter?"

"Not a reporter."

"I don't get it." She weaved back and forth, from leg to leg. The spike in my throat enlarged.

"I'm on business," I said.

"What business?"

"Boring stuff. There somewhere good to eat around here?"

"What business?"

"I'm starving."

She sighed and tossed a clump of hair from her shoulder to her back. "Food? I don't know. There's Buster's down on McKinley. Seafood, standard shit."

"Not really looking for seafood," I said.

"What're you lookin' for?"

"I dunno. A burger."

"There's the Red Robin, I guess. But McDonald's is better. Don't know why anyone should pay more for a cheeseburger."

"McDonald's."

"Yeah. Just down the road. You see it? Like two blocks." She squinted.

"Sure."

"I mean, there's Burger King and Wendy's down there too, but McDonald's is closest." A car zoomed past.

"Mmm."

"So why are you here again?" she said.

"Listen, you hungry?"

"Me?"

"Yeah."

"Look at me. I'm always hungry."

"Wanna burger?"

"With you?"

"Why not?"

"Kinda weird."

"I'm not that weird. Promise."

"You could be some psycho."

"Maybe. But we'd be going to *McDonald's*."

She looked down at her hands. "Do you know me? I mean, do you know who I am?"

"We just met."

"Thing is, I got a note. A note that said come down here, to the Full Monte Motel. Only other guests besides you are an old couple from Maine visiting their son."

"I don't know anything about that."

"You sure."

"Yeah. Positive."

"But now you're offering to buy me lunch. Strange coincidence, don't you think?"

"I'm just being friendly."

"So you didn't write the note."

"Swear to god."

"Well, Jesus. That's wicked strange. I already asked Robbie about it, and he said he didn't write it either and, as far as he knows, none of his staff did."

"Who knows."

"People've been fucking with me since I've come back. That's all I'm saying."

"Fucking with you?"

"See, I can't tell if you're playing or if that's real."

"I'm not playing. I don't know you."

"Really." She bit her bottom lip.

"Not at all."

"Well, fine. I'm hungry. So, sure, you can buy me a burger. You can tell me your deal while we eat, I guess."

"I don't—"

"Let's go."

In the greasy yellow haze of the fast-food restaurant, she looked less friendly, less adolescent, more damaged, more worn. Though her body, even in its full state, secreted youth, her eyes contained small flecks of aged, reddened grief. She would become old quickly, I knew. Most people in places like this did.

"I'll be honest with you," she said, biting into her Big Mac. "Robbie hasn't been the nicest to me since I've been back. I don't know why. I mean, we've known each other forever." She set her sandwich down and wiped her cheek with her napkin. She had a small mole on her right middle finger, right below the cuticle, and it grew and shrank with movement. "I thought I'd probably be able to get a job at the motel, but he's just not having it. He's treating me like everyone else here is. You know, like what's the word? Like when people think you have some sort of awful disease and just avoid you all the time?"

"Pariah?"

"Never heard that before, but sure." She tilted her head and chewed slower. "So what's your deal? You're not a reporter?"

"No," I said. "Not a reporter."

"Swear to god?"

"I swear."

"Okay. I think that's good enough. Aren't reporters like cops or something? They need to identify themselves?"

"I don't know."

We ate in silence for a while. At the counter, a blond frizzy-haired woman ordered a large #4 meal. She told the cashier that she didn't want cheese, just extra lettuce. At one of the center tables, a family of six chomped loudly on their burgers. One of the children, a boy about seven years old, smeared ketchup on his cheek and showed his sister; she giggled and opened her mouth and said, "See food!" The dad threw them a stern glance but said nothing.

"You have business here. In El Monte Springs," Alyssa said.

"Is that so weird?"

"There's not a lot of business here."

"There's enough."

"So what's the business?"

"It'd bore you to death. Accounting stuff."

"Oh, I get it," she said. Her face suddenly softened; her eyes grew bright. "Mr. Mysterious. Bet that works with all the ladies. What is it? Like, you keep this air about you, like you can't reveal everything or whatever, right? So the women keep pressing you until they just can't stand it anymore, and that's when you get your hook in them and write them notes, huh? I know how people like you work. Come here wicked cute and city-like. I know your kind of moves." She winked. "So you always invite random strangers to restaurants?"

"Not always. Only sometimes. And this isn't a restaurant."

"Sure." She smiled. "Anyway, I suppose I should thank you, you know, for the *distraction* and all. I've been bored out of my mind—not working, lugging this thing around. Just wanted to make sure you weren't a reporter."

"Not a reporter."

"'Cause there were so many."

"Reporters? For what?"

"Seriously?"

I shrugged.

"I'm just gonna pretend you're telling the truth. Don't know otherwise, I guess. So. Well. It was big for a while. And I was living in Boston, and I didn't . . . and somehow they found out where I was, found out I was pregnant, everything . . . I'm online too . . . coming out of my workplace, all their cameras . . . Whatever. Anyway. I don't wanna talk about it now. You can look me up if you want. Alyssa Graves, but you probably already knew that."

"Alyssa Graves." Her name felt funny on my lips, sharp and metallic, like I'd licked a pair of scissors. I realized, then, that I'd never said her full name out loud.

She sighed, brushed her hair from her cheek, leaned back. "What a fucking mess, huh?"

"What?"

"Ricky," she said, sighing again. She blinked, looked up at the ceiling, and I felt momentarily devastated. "Jesus," she said.

"I'm not sure . . ."

"If you're telling the truth—which you aren't—just look it up. Seriously." Her eyes froze over, retreated.

"Listen, I'm just here on business."

"Whatever."

"I'm sorry if—"

"Look, I said, 'Whatever.'"

We stayed for a little while longer, veering away from further conversation about her brother, and before we parted ways at the motel, I asked her what she was doing the next day, if perhaps she wanted to meet me at the Starbucks across the street.

"What for?" she said.

"Because I have some free time," I replied.

"Look. I'm not really available right now."

"It's okay. Doesn't have to be like *that*."

She stood silently for a while, scratched her face, bit her lip, shuffled from foot to foot, and finally said, "Fine. Got nothing to do anyway. I'll be there at two." She turned around and waddled to the parking lot, and for the hundredth time that day, I envisioned Ricky negotiating El Monte Springs, planning ways to escape, contemplating relationships, texting his sister, falling in love, sitting at his computer, and typing to a man he thought might introduce him to a life he could unequivocally embrace.

So here's how everything started:

In San Francisco, I had a boyfriend named Craig, a professor of sociology at UCSF, and during our second year together, he canceled all his social media accounts and swore off online communication. He'd decided, abruptly, that electronic interaction was toxic, that it downgraded the significance of real human connection, that it resulted in what he called a "digital tapestry of unanswered prayers."

"That sounds so *serious*," I said when he'd first brought this up. We were at a bistro in Nob Hill called Lish. It was 8:30 p.m. I'd ordered the duck confit; he'd ordered the grilled salmon. I was tired from work, and the people next to us—a stately straight couple in robust corporate-wear—were enragingly silent, making me lower my voice and soften my chewing.

"You can think of it as me attempting to be mentally healthier," he said.

"It's not healthy to depart from society," I said.

"It's not a departure. I'm still here. We're still talking, right? If anything, it's a reintegration."

He had dark, steamy facial features, a right eye that sometimes twitched into a quick wink, and shoulders that flared into a surprisingly perfect horizontal line. Sometimes when he ate, he balled his food into one side of his mouth, and when he did, I resisted the urge to reach over and slap his swollen cheek.

"If everyone's digitally connected and you're not, it's a departure," I said.

He sighed and played with his green beans. "It just seems so sad to me," he said. "All of us communicating like this. All of our desires on display on a screen. All of our wants readily available for dissection and derision from strangers."

"You're being melodramatic." I ate a bite of potato. The couple next to us remained unnervingly stoic.

"I've been thinking about this a lot."

"And?"

"I think we all know—somewhere deep inside, somewhere we don't want to explore, somewhere maybe close to the subconscious—that the chances of us living the life we want, the life we've *envisioned*, are very slim. We have to make do. And the digital age has plastered that 'making do' for everyone to see while simultaneously mandating that we be *more*. Achievements become 'likes.' Thoughts become 'shares.' Emotions become comments at the bottom of a video. It's a digital tapestry of unanswered prayers, and if you look really close at it all, you see this enormous wall of human misery."

"But that misery will be there no matter what, even if there *were* no Internet."

"Sure, but the Internet highlights and amplifies it. The minute you plug in, you're assaulted by millions of lonely people desperately seeking validation for their existence."

"Lonely? Really? Millions?"

"I just don't want to be a part of it. Maybe later I'll rejoin, but now I need to be away from it all."

This conversation started our relationship's demise.

The problem was this: Craig's independence from digital communication underscored my dependence on it. For example, when we'd go somewhere, like on a miniature road trip, he typically drove—first, because it was his car, and second, because he liked driving more than I did. Before his analog catharsis, he'd use GPS, like the rest of the country, but now, given his complete disconnection, he didn't, so we got lost. He'd stop for directions, buy bulky maps, scrutinize them, ask *me* to scrutinize them, and I'd feel entirely put-out, partly because he wouldn't allow me to properly—*digitally*—navigate, and partly because it just seemed so uncool to look at an unwieldy piece of paper when smartphones abounded.

Also, our communication with friends changed. I'd tell Craig what was going on with so-and-so, discussing a Facebook post or a recent tweet or an Instagram photo, and he'd just stare blankly back and say something like, "That's cool." When we got together with our friends, large blocks of conversation passed by without a single word from him; he'd just sit there staring dumbly at us, smiling every once in a while and sighing quite often. Eventually, he stopped going out altogether, choosing to spend his weekend nights alone in the living room with a book and some wine, often ignoring me when I came home late at night.

"What's worst about it all," he told me one evening, "is that there's potential with electronic media. There's potential to really help people, to reinvigorate altruism. Someone reaches out, exposes themselves, so to speak, and the person on the other end, knowing only what's on a profile, reaches back and is of human service."

"That happens all the time!" I said. We were in the living room. I'd decided to stay in, to be with my silent partner. He was in the rocking chair, a black comforter wrapped around his legs. "You don't get it at all!" I said. "There are forums for people—people who need advice or help from others struggling with the same thing. Without the Internet, these things wouldn't exist. Real people help real people online. Strangers help strangers. It's the very definition of altruism!"

"But how much can you do with back-and-forth messages?" he asked. "Support groups shouldn't be online. It confounds the very idea of support."

"You're ridiculous!"

"How much support can you get from reading a message on a screen?"

"You wouldn't know, I guess."

"I remember reading on Facebook about the death of a friend's mother. This friend posted this status five minutes after her mother had died. *Five minutes.* Immediately, a flurry of condolence messages. Hundreds, including mine. Do you think those messages did anything for her grief?"

"They could've. You don't know."

"Before, you'd go to the store, buy a card, send it, take time to think about your friend. But now? A few seconds and you've done your duty."

"Your friend's not the norm."

"And my friend? She posted because she was so used to posting about anything that happened to her. Her misery was attached to this electronic validation. She'd posted so much that she no longer understood how egregiously inappropriate it was to announce a death to virtual strangers before she told family members."

"People handle things differently. Seriously. You're being insufferable."

"Besides that, I guess what I'm saying is that if what she'd posted had compelled a stranger, or even an acquaintance, to hop on a plane and go to her, well, it would've worked. Social media would've spurred true altruism."

"I can't deal with this talk anymore."

"I could be wrong, you know," he said.

"I know. And I think you are."

Given my aggravation, I surprised myself that night by leaning over in bed and kissing him as hard as I could. He hesitated momentarily, pulling his tongue safely behind the rigid blockade of his teeth, but my persistence and force eventually beat him out, and soon I was on top of him, sweating and panting, swirling my tongue against the nape of his neck, feeling enormous and formidable, thinking about all-that-he-was and all-that-I-wasn't, and finding the contrast exceptional and arousing. And as he shifted obsequiously beneath me, transforming instantly from intimidating to ingratiating, I thought about validation-necessity-need-trust-love-companionship-fidelity-complement-legacy-faith-argument-power, and these thoughts, in their compressed aggregate, made me come. And after

I came, I kissed his forehead, rolled over, reached for my phone, said good night, and scrolled through forty-five brightly colored photos of my friends holding various cocktails on the shores of Puerto Vallarta.

Back at the Full Monte, I checked my phone; it was blank—no notifications, just a time/date stamp, a keypad, and a picture of a rainy forest. I threw the phone on the bed and went to the small wooden desk. A single black notebook sat on top of it, a cheap, flimsy one-subject whose wire coils threatened to dislodge prematurely. I'd purchased the notebook right before coming out to New Hampshire, figuring that my small instructional to Alyssa should be as personal as possible—a letter instead of an email or a text message, something handwritten instead of typed. But while I'd started the note multiple times, I'd found myself blocked, completely unable to interact with the paper. I felt like I was engaging in a hip, ironic form of communication, an exercise in retro-cool or something, and every time I wrote *Dear Alyssa,* I imagined sending the note not by regular post but by bike messenger, not in an envelope but in a biodegradable sandwich carton, not with a stamp but with a scratch-and-sniff sticker and a sticky piece of vinyl. Simultaneously, I felt grandmotherly, like I should be writing in slanted cursive, peppering the letter with short banal anecdotes about family life and ending it with an overly sincere desire to see her again.

Still, even with these roadblocks, I was determined to write the note by hand, so I sat down again and concentrated on my recipient, Alyssa Graves, comparing her online picture to her in-person persona. In her online photo, uploaded to the personal blog of "DreckKeck," she stood outside a diner in Boston, smoking and talking to a heavyset woman. Though her face was partially obscured by the restaurant awning's shadow, she looked as if she were smiling, the visible, right-side portion of her lips curving dramatically upward. The caption below read: *This is Alyssa Graves, the sister of Ricky Graves, the boy who just murdered a kid and shot himself in New Hampshire. You'd think she'd be slightly less happy about things.* Surrounding the photo was a self-righteous, reductive look at the myriad horrors of the digital age, titled "Digital Media Is Turning Us into Emotional Zombies."

It all enraged me, partly because it made gross assumptions, as most idea-driven blogs did, and partly because a closer look at the photo revealed that the smile wasn't a smile at all but a grimace; Alyssa's eyes didn't match the pronounced lip-curve: they were droopy, lifeless, forlorn, fatigued. When I'd first seen the post, I'd written a scathing reply, lambasting the blogger's obvious hypocrisy and attacking his use of Alyssa Graves as thesis reinforcement. When I'd finished, I'd written a good eight hundred words of insufferable polemic fueled mainly by my recent breakup with Craig, and I would've sent it had I not scrolled through the commentary below and found that every single message encouraged the blogger's assertions. He, the blogger, this DreckKeck, was one of those cowards who discarded critics as soon as they posted, creating a page of unwavering support. He wouldn't get past my first sentence before deleting my reply, so there was no point in posting it.

Still, Alyssa's picture had stayed with me for days. I had difficulty concentrating at work. When I slept, I dreamed of her. I found myself composing short messages in my junk email account, sending them to my regular account, pretending I was her and replying as me. I felt guilty, ashamed, angry, confused, and the whole time, I wondered whether I'd feel anything had I not had that two-year relationship with Craig Martinez. In the end, I decided that he'd been the reason for everything, and this made me feel even more terrible.

In any case, I hadn't expected to like Alyssa so much, and this liking further complicated everything, for if I hadn't liked her, I would've simply written her my instructional letter, made an oblique apology, and left town. As it happened, however, her warmth and candor moved me, and seeing her sitting there at McDonald's, her belly pressed against the edge of the table, the only thing I could think about was when I'd get to see her again.

ALYSSA GRAVES

I'm not sure exactly *what* happened, him asking me to lunch and me really considering and thinking about accepting and—I don't know what it was, but I was like, *Should I?* He seemed real nice and good-looking, and in my head I was like, *God, please let it be him who wrote the note. Please let it be him. Pleeease let it be him,* but I was also thinking, *Alyssa, don't fall for that. You need to learn that guys are guys, and guys will be guys no matter what,* which, of course, meant that guys were scum, dirty abandoners, every one, players and all. But I was so lonely since I'd come back—not working, just lounging around the house all huge, checking my phone every nine seconds, waiting to pop—and when you're not busy, all you do is think, and my thoughts weren't especially positive, if you know what I mean. I guess I just didn't realize how terrible it would be being back, being in the house, seeing all the rooms that Ricky used to be in.

It was really bad for my mom: she couldn't go even a second without saying something like, "Remember when Ricky . . ." and I think for the most part a lot of these rememberings weren't really all that true, just nice memories my mom wanted to have. Like one time, at the dinner table, just her and I, she said, "Remember when Ricky made me a birthday cake? Got up so early, looked through all my cookbooks 'til he found the one he thought I'd like the best, the one with all the chocolate, got all the ingredients together, and just put them in the oven. Oh man, that was a mess, right? You remember how it splattered everywhere?" I said I did, though what she was really remembering, I think, was the time Ricky painted the kitchen walls with a whole bottle of Hershey's Syrup. He wasn't trying to make anything, was just bored, I guess, so he made designs on the walls and the refrigerator, stick figures that melted and ran all over the place, and my mom got so angry she spanked him over and over until he was screaming for her to stop. But I suppose death does weird things to your memory, makes you think of the person in a way that's better than the person actually was.

I caught *myself* doing this from time to time, to be honest. Like one day, as I was in the bathroom putting makeup on, I had this instant memory of him as a kid coming up behind me and tugging at my shirt while I was doing my lashes. It surprised me so much that I poked myself in the eye and for a moment was actually blind, like saw just black with red spots, even though my eyes were both open, and in the memory, after I regained my eyesight, I yelled at him, but not that much, just told him he needed to be more careful when I was doing my makeup, and then, when he looked up at me all cute, I bent down and picked him up and shook him 'til he giggled. But later that day, the memory came back, and it came back for real, like somehow in the bathroom when I'd first remembered it I couldn't actually bring myself to think that I'd been in the least bit abusive to him. What'd actually happened was that I'd leaned down to him, like right close to his face, and screamed, "You little shithead! You don't do that shit when someone's near their eye!" and he started crying, and that didn't do anything for my anger, actually made it worse. I shouted, "Stop crying, you fuckin' baby!" but of course he wouldn't, just got louder, so I slapped him hard across the face. My fingers left a mark, and he'd been only what—seven, eight?—and he instantly stopped crying, like someone had pushed an off switch or something; he just looked at me like, *Oh my god, what did you just do?* And that *still* didn't stop me from being angry. I mean, I had to control it really bad, like take deep, deep breaths, because at that moment I seriously visualized squeezing his neck.

"You hit me," he said, like he was more curious than anything, not upset at all. He was more upset about me shouting at him, which was really a clue to how he was all through life, I guess.

"Yeah," I said, turning back to the mirror. "Sorry." My anger was leaving real fast.

"Should I tell Mommy?"

I shrugged. "Do whatever. I don't care."

"I won't tell."

"Okay."

"It'll be like a secret between us."

"I mean, siblings hit each other all the time," I said. "It's not a big deal."

"But it can still be our secret, right?"

"Sure. If you want it to be." And now I was like totally not-angry. Maybe a little confused. Like why was he so obsessed about keeping my slap a secret? Whenever my friends hit their kid brothers and sisters, the younger ones went bawling to their mom, tattletales all of them, but Ricky, he just wanted to gather up a bunch of these personal times between us—good and bad both—and not tell anyone. Weird little creeper.

"I won't tell," he said, walking away.

"I don't care," I said.

Another time he did this was when I had Jill Tremain over and we were smoking weed in the basement, and he came down in his pajamas, though it was only like six o'clock or something, and said, "That cigarette smells weird." Jill was high as fuck, so she just giggled and giggled and giggled, and then she grabbed Ricky by the cheeks and said, "Oh my *god*, you're like the *cutest thing in the world*!"

"Ricky," I said, "this isn't a cigarette. This is weed. I've told you so many times."

"But they look the same," he said.

"They don't look *anything* alike," I said. I wasn't as giggly as Jill because (a) I just didn't get that way as much and (b) I hadn't taken as many hits as her.

"*So cute!*" Jill screamed.

"Jill," I said. "Shut up. You're too loud."

"Too loud? It's not like anyone's *sleeping*, right? Your mom's not even *home*."

We were listening to this really awesome band called Death Highway Nine. They were local, and we'd gone to a couple of their shows in Portsmouth with our fakes. I had a thing for the drummer, Vernon Miles, but I wouldn't tell anybody, because I didn't want Corky to find out—he could get wicked jealous. Anyway, Ricky picked up the CD case and turned it over, like really scrutinized it, and I felt a little weird, because on the cover was a picture of a naked lady—could see her boobs and some of her vag—and she was just looking lazily out a window smoking a cigarette. Well, he looked hard at it, then looked at the joint in my hand, and he beamed a sort of proud face and said, "We can have this be a secret!"

"A secret?" Jill said. "What secret, buddy boy?"

"He just likes that sort of thing," I said.

"What sort of thing?"

"Secrets."

"Oh. That's weird." She went into another fit of giggles, and Ricky rushed back upstairs.

Anyway. So what I was getting at earlier was that memories aren't always reliable, especially when the person we're thinking about is dead before his time, and I kinda wanted to tell Jeremy this, about my revelation regarding memories, because even though our meeting was maybe high on the creep-o-meter—I'm not stupid; he wrote the note—he was an out-of-towner and therefore safe. And I didn't know what the hell he wanted from me at the time, but that kinda didn't matter then, because he had this smart, quiet quality to him—almost robot-like, but not, more like just strong, stoic—and that made me want to tell him everything I was going through.

Because I was obviously going through a lot. I mean, my mother, dealing with her, that kinda distracted me from a few of my own emotions, but it wasn't like I didn't have them. I was part of a family that now had a history of violence, and in a town like El Monte Springs, that was just really bad news. We were marked, my mother and me, and I knew it: everywhere I went, people looked, whispered, fake-smiled, fake-chatted, and I knew no matter how much they said otherwise, they sort of blamed my family's dysfunction for Ricky's rampage. Even June Byerly, the bitch. I saw her in the grocery store the other day, just looking through the meat section like her life depended on which cut of steak she was gonna buy—really staring, scrutinizing, analyzing, whatever—and I said, "Hey," and she looked up, shocked, then fake-smiled and said, "Hey, Alyssa, glad to see you back." And she weirdly didn't comment on my pregnancy, just started talking about the weather, which was absolute nonsense for a nosy gossip like her. Seriously, until then I'd had no idea she was even capable of small talk. She usually started her sentences like, *Did you hear . . . ?* or *Can you believe . . . ?* and then would be all conspiracy about it, right? Just lean in and whisper, as if all the news she was saying was between us. But this day, in the meat section, she talked about how fucking *hot* it was, and went on and on about some sort of global warming BS, and I just stared at her, because it just sounded so fucking strange coming from her mouth. This was the woman who'd barged into my house when Corky had pulled a knife on me, and who'd threatened to call the cops, and told everyone in town about the incident within a two-day span of it happening, and now she was concerned about global warming?

"June," I said, "the weather's the weather. Who cares?" And she looked at me all indignant and shocked like I'd just told her her kid was retarded, and then she just turned back to the meat and said, "Well, what else am I supposed to talk about with *you*?"

I asked her, "What's that supposed to mean?" but she didn't say anything, just kept on scrutinizing her chops, so I walked away feeling slimy and gross. I guess I should've expected that kind of reaction to me coming back, but expectations and the actual thing are so different; I mean, I really believed that people would be supportive of me and my mother. We'd just lost a member of our family! But see, that's small-town politics for you. Wesley's family was just more important, I guess—they were better known, more popular maybe, had more money, donated to the right places, were elected to city positions and so on—so of course Wesley's death meant more, and besides, he was *murdered* by Ricky, so he was a victim automatically, and even though Ricky died, he shot himself, so everyone just assumed it was a choice, which technically it was. But the more I thought about it, the more I actually believed that *Ricky* believed he didn't have a choice, that killing himself was the only thing he thought he could've done.

Anyway. So Jeremy sat there in McDonald's, and I saw him looking at me like guys do—you know, long eye contact and all—but not like a predator, not gross and meat-pie-like. I mean, people didn't look at me much that way anymore because of the pregnancy, but guys, you know, perverts, in any case. But Jeremy was different, like he didn't strike me as someone who'd fuck and leave. So yeah, I thought about it, thought about getting to know him in a better way—even if I was just this sensational thing to him because of my brother—because, really, think about it, I was about to pop, and because I'd come back to the Springs I didn't have work, and my mother, she wasn't that helpful, so what was I gonna do? I needed someone to help me, if even for a little bit, and that's why I thought about Jeremy, maybe even flirted a bit, because why not. What did I have to lose?

But then, as it always did, the subject shifted to Ricky, and I felt how I usually felt when I talked about it. Like my life just didn't matter anymore, like I didn't own it, even with my baby coming and all, like it now belonged to my dead little brother, and people didn't talk about it, because it was rude or something, but—I don't know, I mean, sometimes they talked about how me and my mom were to blame and everything, and sometimes they talked about how sad I must be, but they never, ever talked about how fucking *angry* it all made me, how Ricky with his psychotic shithead move ruined my goddamn life, made me a part of something I never asked to be a part of. And, really, I refused to feel guilty about being pissed. I had that right.

Well, I knew in the back of my mind that Jeremy wasn't going to really help me out with the kid—I mean, why would he?—so that's why, right after McDonald's I swallowed my pride and called up Corky. I hadn't seen him or talked to him since I'd gotten my restraining order, but I'd heard a few things about him from Ricky when he'd been alive, and from what he'd said, Corky had actually turned out better than I'd expected. He worked full-time at the plastics factory, and I knew that was a hard job, on your feet all day, hauling those big sheets over your shoulders, doing the same shit for twelve hours a day with just a half-hour break. Rough stuff. I didn't think Corky would actually do something like that and stick with it—he'd never been very good at keeping work, if you know what I mean—but I guess he'd been there ever since I'd left town, had even been promoted a couple times, which shocked the hell out of me because of his overall misbehavior.

So I called him up and—coincidence!—he was off work, and he was like, "Well, well, well, Alyssa Graves is callin' *me*. How about that."

"Don't be a jackass," I said.

"Knew you'd come back," he said. "And you're pregnant."

"What's that supposed to mean?"

"Fuck, can't I just congratulate you?"

His voice sounded off. I said, "You chewing again?"

"Don't have much time to chat. Gotta get—"

"I heard you're working full-time now. That's great."

"Yeah. I work. That surprising? Three on, three off, twelve-hour days. And when I'm off, I'm usually lookin' in on Mark."

"Mark?"

"You didn't know?"

"Mark *McVitry*?"

"Kid's still all shell-shocked from gettin' shot. Won't hardly come out of his room. But I coax him, and we go have lunch sometimes, and I try to get him to talk about things." He paused. "Soon as he got out of the hospital, I told his parents I'd help out any way I could, and they were real grateful. They both work, can't just watch him all the time. And I get three in a row off, so perfect, right?"

"You're taking care of Mark? That's *insane*."

He sighed, like I was really too much. "Why'd you call me?"

"I don't know. Honestly."

"Well, when you figure it out, maybe you can call me again. But I gotta jet. See ya round." He hung up.

So being away made me see everything differently, gave me perspective, like they say. I mean, coming back, I kept thinking that I hated Corky, that he was just this dumb loser who'd never leave the Springs and never make anything of his life, and I told myself I'd never contact him again even though we lived close now, 'cause seriously, he was going *nowhere*, but then there I was, calling him almost right away. And talking to him, hearing his voice—which, before, always sounded too smoky and choppy, like he'd swallowed a bunch of rocks, too many cigarettes clearly . . . well, anyhow, I felt like maybe this whole time I'd misjudged him, that whatever he did, he always had good intentions, a heart of gold maybe—no, that's going too far. I dunno. But, I mean, who else would volunteer his days off to spend them with Mark McVitry? From what I'd heard, Mark was a real mess, maybe even worse than my mom. I mean, they say he had PTSD or whatever it was that soldiers had after war, which was kinda stupid if you really thought about it, since he wasn't in anything *that* horrible, but anyway, I guess he woke up screaming and was always sweaty and nervous and couldn't sit still and sometimes attacked people for no reason and said that he saw Ricky's bloody ghost all the time and had lost like a zillion pounds. This when he only got shot in the arm. I mean, getting shot at all is a terrible thing, don't get me wrong, but he didn't *die*, didn't even get that injured really. I mean, he fully healed; it was just his head that got all messed-up—trauma, I guess—and he couldn't really see a shrink, on account of him hardly ever leaving his house. So for Corky to kinda take control like that, well, I guess I couldn't fault him for everything anymore—he always had some good in him, always was very thoughtful even if he wasn't all that ambitious, and . . .

Well, thinking positively about Corky for the first time in a long time suddenly made me think of other positive things, like the time he took me to the state fair on my birthday and we rode the Ferris wheel seventeen times, because he wanted to kiss me at the highest peak in town for every year I was born. Didn't make sense, of course, since we obviously went around more than one time each ride; he ended up kissing me like fifty times or something, but I didn't mind. And the time we went fishing and I caught a fish but didn't want to take it off the hook, and he said he'd do it but then threw the fish at me and said, "Catch!" and I was so scared and grossed-out I screamed and batted the floppy thing back into the water, and he laughed so hard I couldn't help but laugh with him, even though I should've been boiling angry. And the time I had the flu and he just sat by me for hours, holding my hand like I had some deadly disease—like a *pariah*—and kissing me on the mouth, even though I was probably contagious. And just all the time he spent with Ricky, never really judging his weirdness, but always just being there, always listening to the little shit like what he said was important. So yeah, being away gave me a new outlook on Corky as well as everything else about the Springs, and I found, weirdly, that even with all the stuff that had taken place, even with all the drama and sadness and anger, I could sometimes feel real love for things I'd always thought I'd hate forever.

BRAD "CORKY" MEEKS

I'll be honest, her phone call rattled me. I hadn't heard her voice in how long—six, seven years? I wasn't prepared for it, especially for it to sound the same. Not like it shouldn't have, but I thought that if I ever talked to her again, her voice would sound older, maybe less sexy, and I'd kick myself for having feelings for so long. But no—talking to her was like talking to her back before she'd left. And that was the hard part, 'cause then I pictured her, remembered her naked, remembered all the corny shit we did and said together. Well. I'd tried to sound aloof, but she probably saw through it. I dunno. I fuckin' hated that she'd come back. Hated it.

After I got off the phone with her I tried to go to sleep but couldn't. I had a few beers, watched some TV, tried to doze, but my mind kept racing, even with the alcohol. I felt wicked pissed, then felt pissed for feeling pissed, and for some reason, in all that fuckin' pissiness, my mind raced back to Ricky, to hangin' out with him while his sister was gone.

Like for example, a month or so before he shot himself, I saw him in the library at one of the computers, all bundled up in his parka. I went up to him and tapped him on the shoulder. He jumped clear out of his goddamn seat. He closed a chat window and gave me this look like I'd choked his pet hamster.

"What's good, Ricky?" I said. "Haven't talked to you much lately. You good?"

He looked greasy, normal for a teenager. I noticed a new patch of pimples on his forehead.

"I'm good," he said. "My laptop isn't working, so . . ." He had this nasal voice, kinda whiny. World had done him this huge fuckin' disservice by throwin' him into it—that's what his voice sounded like. Still, I could look at him and see him when he was a kid—cutest kid alive—so I tried not to be judgmental, like some of the closed-minded fucks in the Springs.

"You ain't lookin' at porn, are ya?" I said, chuckling.

"No," he said. "I gotta go."

"Wait a minute," I said. "What's the rush? Maybe wanna go for a ride or somethin'?"

He looked at me again like I'd killed something, then he changed, positive-like, even smiled a little. "It's freezing!" he said.

"We'll sit in the car. No biggie," I said.

Going for a ride just meant hangin' out by the water and smoking dope. We did that once in a while when he got to be older, like after his thirteenth birthday. We'd just take my truck to Naper's Creek and sit under the shade, if it was nice out, and smoke up. He needed it, high-strung as he was, and it wasn't like I was doing something so terrible, since everyone smoked weed. Anyway, he was a better person to talk to high. Less of the bitchy defensive crap—drove me batshit. With pot, he was semiadult.

Anyway, this day, after the library, we sat in my truck and listened to WINK, the country station. They were playing newer bands lately, and I didn't know how I felt about that. I turned the music down, and when I did, Ricky told me about Wesley Thompson.

"We're friends now," he said.

I thought, *Shit,* 'cause Wesley Thompson wasn't someone to be friends with a kid like Ricky Graves. Wesley Thompson was just a bad seed, rotten to the core. Not sayin' I was an angel, but I had a conscience, and I felt bad for the things I'd done. But Wesley, he could've stabbed his own grandma in the heart and cracked jokes at her funeral. Still, he was charming as fuck. Dangerous, dangerous combination.

"So what's this?" I said, blowing some smoke and fogging the window. "Wesley Thompson? Why you wanna hang around him for?" Outside, the creek was just a sheet of ice and snow; trees were skeletons. It all looked pretty.

"*He* wants to hang out with *me*, Corky," Ricky said. "Just go to the Meadows sometime, I guess."

"You never been to the Meadows," I said. "That's not . . ."

"What."

"Nothin'."

"No, you tell me."

"I was just gonna say, that's where the fuckin' losers hang out."

"Well, that'd make everyone a loser but me, right?"

"Hey, you're not the only high school kid doesn't hang out there. And besides, it makes you different, man. You don't wanna be like following the herd, 'cause you're a unique one. I swear it."

I wasn't lyin' about this. He *was* unique, in a weird way. But who wasn't weird that's unique? All the great artists were unique, right? Guy who cut his ear off? Gotta be pretty unique to do that kind of shit.

"I think it could be fun," Ricky said, staring out at the frozen water. Breath-smoke came out his nostrils.

"Well then, go for it," I said. "Just don't get too carried away, okay? They tell you to keep drinkin' and you don't feel good, you just say no."

"I'm not a kid," he said, taking another hit.

"Didn't say you were. But I got more experience in this whole department than you. And you never drank before, right? It's different from smokin' up."

"I've drank."

"When?"

"At camp."

"No, you didn't."

"Yeah, I did."

"I was your fuckin' *counselor*. Would've known if you drank."

"I've drank before. That's all I'm saying."

"Listen, I'm just sayin' take it easy."

"I don't need you looking out for me, Corky."

"Not lookin' out for you. Just sayin' take it easy, okay? Don't go overboard."

Couldn't actually imagine the kid drunk. How did those types get when they drank? For some reason, I thought of my boss, Henry Chang, down at the factory. I'd gotten drunk with him a few times after work, and every time he turned into this huge red smiley face, and then he'd start singing. Loud. First few times, I thought it was funny, but then I got embarrassed for him, so I stopped goin' out, made excuses, said, *Sorry, dude. Got shit to do.* He told me once that all he did when he was younger was study hard so he could come to America and make a life, but 'cause he studied so much he didn't really learn how to interact with people. I told him he did just fine—maybe just tone down the singing.

"Alyssa texted me," Ricky said, and just hearing her name made my heart pound. "She asked about you."

Was hard to hold in my excitement, and I hated myself for that. She'd left me; I should've been raging. But the only thing I ever felt was terrible, horrible longing. "Yeah? What'd she ask?"

"Just if I still talked to you."

"And what'd you say?"

"I said no. She hates you."

"She doesn't hate me."

"Thinks you're a bad person."

"No, she doesn't."

"Not just 'cause of the knife thing . . . She really doesn't like us talking to each other."

"You and me have a different relationship. Separate. It's fine. But listen, why were you talkin' about me in the first place?"

"I told you. She wanted to know if we talked."

"But she asked you out of the blue? Like you were talkin' about somethin' else and she was like, 'How's Corky?'"

"She didn't ask how you *were*. She asked if I still talked to you."

"I was on her mind, though, right?"

"I don't know. Not in a good way. Who cares? You still like her?"

"No. Course not."

"Then why do you care?"

"You don't just get over someone that fast."

"It's been *years*."

"Takes a while."

"Then you *do* still like her."

"She's a special girl. You know that. Nobody like her. That mean I wanna be with her? No. But—anyway, whatever. She's doin' okay?"

"Yeah."

"That's good. Let's talk about something else, okay, bud?" My nose and eyes got tight, and that wasn't good—meant I might actually shed a tear. Couldn't believe that after all that time, I could still feel those feelings. Made me think she had some sort of magic spell over me.

"It's okay. I miss her too."

Back in '09, when Alyssa told me she was leaving, going to the city, something snapped in me like it's never snapped before. I just went berserk. We were at her house. She was babysitting Ricky while her mom was out, and we were watching a rerun of *Seinfeld*. Alyssa didn't like the show, thought it was boring. She didn't like New York types, but she suffered through it 'cause she knew I loved it. Whenever there were these long rerun marathons, I'd watch and watch and watch. Those four characters—fuckin' brilliant. Didn't think any other show in the history of shows put people together like that, like some real harmonious shit: when I thought of Jerry and Elaine and George and Kramer, I thought of a gigantic four-piece puzzle, all their little notches connected somehow, all of them coming together to make this perfect little friendship.

Always wished I had something like that in the Springs, but the friends I had in high school all left—better things to do, college mostly. I just stayed alone with Alyssa and my folks and my brothers. So when she told me she was leaving, I felt my head blow up, like splatter all over the goddamn carpet.

"You weren't even gonna talk to me before you decided this?" I said.

"I'm talking to you now," she said.

"You can't just make this decision by yourself."

"I'm breaking up with you, Corky."

Not sure if my experience was unusual, but I don't think so. I'm sure other people when they hear those words "I'm breaking up with you" flip out and go insane, 'cause who wouldn't? You see your girl-friend, you see your life, especially when you're twenty-two. And when she said she wasn't only breakin' up with me but she was moving to the city? Fuck—I lost it. I suddenly had nothin'. I was normal one minute, then suddenly—bam—empty as a fuckin' balloon.

"But why?" I said. "Why would you *move*?"

"Jesus, Corky," she said. "Everyone moves. Everyone but you."

"And you *knew* I wouldn't go with you?"

"Of course I knew. You're gonna be here forever—you said it. That's why we have to break up."

"The Springs is my fucking *home*."

She shrugged. "I want something more."

On impulse I went to the kitchen, picked up a long knife, came back, and pointed it at her like a lightsaber. First, she just blinked, surprised probably, but then she laughed. "Is this how you're gonna keep me here? You're gonna *stab* me?"

"You can't just tell me you're leaving like that. That's not how it's fuckin' done."

"Look at your hand, Corky. It's shaking. Jesus."

"You're not leaving."

"I am. And I'm so sorry. You mean a lot to me, but you're holding me back—you know this, I know this. Now put the knife down, okay, baby?"

"You've been talkin' to your mom. She's finally got to you."

"Ha! My mom? She thinks I'm 'no good.' Her words exactly."

"She said that?"

"Jesus, stop waving that thing around, Corky. You're gonna really hurt someone."

At this point, I was aware of what I was doing, but I felt like someone else was holding the knife. Not like an out-of-body thing, but it was definitely surreal, kind of like I was on a set of a movie. Still, I heard Elaine laughin' on the TV, so I knew that I was still there. I looked at the knife. I looked at Alyssa. I couldn't hold back: I started crying like a fucking baby. "Oh god, please don't go," I said. "Please. You'll kill me."

"You'll pick the Springs over me every time," she said. "And what'll I do? Just sit around and waste my life here?"

"This is a good place to be," I said. "A good fucking place."

"How would *I* know any different? I've never *been* anywhere else!"

"Alyssa. Please. You'll fuckin' kill me, I swear."

"I'm very sorry, Corky."

"Alyssa."

"Maybe sometime we can be friends."

"Friends?"

"Yeah."

I just stood there for a while, tryin' to process that word, "friends," feeling worse than I've ever felt in my life, when someone knocked on the front door. I opened it, and there was June fucking Byerly, looking like someone'd just sucker punched her.

"What?" I said.

"Oh my *gawd*," she said. "Why the hell do you have a *knife*?"

I'd kinda forgotten about the knife. I walked back to the kitchen and put it away, then tried to catch my breath. From the living room, I heard June say in her stupid bird-voice, "Are you *okay*? Wait, did you *tell* him? Oh my god, did he just *flip out* on you? You should get a *restraining order*. Are we even *safe* here?"

"Everything's fine," Alyssa said.

"I'm calling the cops."

"June. No."

"You're *clearly* upset. He *threatened* you, I can tell. He should be in jail."

"June. It's fine. He's fine."

"No. Alyssa. I can't believe you're just so *calm*. This is *serious*."

"I feel sad, June. That's all."

"He's a *monster*. I always knew."

"He's not a monster. He's just upset. Understandably."

"He's *violent*, and not just with guys at the bar. He's a *domestic abuser*."

"He's fine, June."

"He's *not* fine. He's completely *screwy*. I always knew this. Didn't I tell you? All this time, didn't I tell you?"

I came into the living room, but I didn't stop. I didn't look at either of them, just headed for the door.

"Corky," Alyssa said, getting up.

"Don't talk to him," June said. "He's not right."

"Hey, hold up," Alyssa said. "Corky!"

But I was already out the door. I'd forgotten to shut it behind me. No way I was gonna let June Byerly see me emotional. No fucking way.

MAN-DATE CHAT TRANSCRIPT
NOVEMBER 22, 2014

Rickyg9999: did you go to LA again last weekend? haha

Jeremyinsf: ?

Rickyg9999: just didn't see you on last Saturday, was getting worried lol

Jeremyinsf: sorry, bud. was just busy.

Rickyg9999: I'm usually busy on the weekdays and then I try to relax on the weekends

Rickyg9999: so how are you?

Jeremyinsf: good, thanks, and you?

Rickyg9999: remember when I told u about the Meadows, that place where losers just hang out and drink? well I was thinking I might go and check it out, would be cool if u were here we could check it out together

Jeremyinsf: I thought you'd been there before

Rickyg9999: nah just hesitant cuz all the losers in this town. don't wanna be associated

Jeremyinsf: gotcha

Rickyg9999: I knew you'd understand, you from South Dakota and everything, probably like the same situation all the losers who just stay in the town forever go to the same place til their like 50 unless their married or have kids

Jeremyinsf: North

Rickyg9999: ?

Jeremyinsf: you said South

Jeremyinsf: anyway, yeah, I think we had a place like the one you're talking about. I think every small town has it, right?

Rickyg9999: yeah probably, I'm just not that interested and plus I'm really busy with college work and everything but I thought if someone cool were here we could go together, maybe just sit around make fun of it you know

Jeremyinsf: sounds fun ☺

Rickyg9999: I'm about to have my Christmas break if your looking to go somewhere, even though California is probably nicer now lol

Jeremyinsf: haha a bit rainy, but not as cold I imagine

Jeremyinsf: so I have a question

Rickyg9999: yeah dude anythong

Rickyg9999: anything

Jeremyinsf: ok, at first you said that you lived alone, but then you said you were taking care of your mother, so you don't live with her?

Rickyg9999: well I live with her now but I used to live alone

Jeremyinsf: ok, was just curious

Rickyg9999: yeah it kinda sucks she's always on my case about schoolwork

Jeremyinsf: that's how moms are haha

Rickyg9999: she keeps telling me how everything can be accomplished with hard work and sometimes when I wanna be alone she'll just barge into my room and ask me dumb random questions, I get sick of it

Jeremyinsf: what does she do for work?

Rickyg9999: she works at a shipping company, front desk type stuff but she always has other projects like this last project is she's thinking about writing a book. she thinks she can sell it on the internet, she was soooo excited like almost celebrating the idea like nobody's written a book before

Jeremyinsf: that's interesting. what's the book about?

Rickyg9999: not sure, about being a parent I think. she doesn't talk about the details lol

Rickyg9999: anyway she's always saying she's trying to improve herself and her station in life but I don't understand that really lol

Jeremyinsf: what don't you understand?

Rickyg9999: what her station in life is cuz I think it's ok doesn't need improving I mean she's got a house and kids and a job, and some people around here don't even have that

Jeremyinsf: do you live with your dad? sorry if that's too personal

Rickyg9999: no he's not around but that's ok I didn't know him and don't really care that much

Jeremyinsf: do you think she wants to find another?

Rickyg9999: another what?

Jeremyinsf: another man

Rickyg9999: god I don't know maybe but that's not something we talk about, and her station in life isn't about that I'm pretty sure it's more like getting more money or a better job or being discovered or something even though she didn't even go to college

Jeremyinsf: oh, I see

Jeremyinsf: you sound like you don't get along that well?

Rickyg9999: we get along fine I think normal like you said but since my sister left she's kinda smothering me a little, I dunno I think she has a different kind of relationship with Alyssa which is ok I guess

Jeremyinsf: Alyssa is your sister?

Rickyg9999: yup

Rickyg9999: so if you came I couldn't put you up or anything sorry, but there are cheap motels like the Full Monte if your worried about money. but your probably not ;)

Jeremyinsf: everyone is worried about money, no matter how much they have

Rickyg9999: yeah that makes sense

Rickyg9999: so is your family still in North Dakota?

Jeremyinsf: yep. they're never leaving.

Rickyg9999: oh sorry to hear that

Jeremyinsf: haha don't know why you'd be sorry

Rickyg9999: did you like it up there?

Jeremyinsf: I got away as quick as I could lol

Rickyg9999: yeah I can't wait to finish school and get the hell out of here it's so backwards

Rickyg9999: but there's this guy Wesley who lives here and he's been really wanting me to hang out and maybe I think he likes me in a gay way

Jeremyinsf: yeah, I remember you mentioning him before

Jeremyinsf: he's one of the popular kids you said?

Rickyg9999: ya but that's so dumb, popular you know, it's silly but anyway sometimes I catch him staring at me in class and I know it's more than just a glance I can tell

Rickyg9999: he looks at me and smiles

Jeremyinsf: and you're interested in him?

Rickyg9999: I mean he's cute and everything but I'm moving on with my life in bigger ways and I'm pretty sure he's gonna just be here forever like the other losers

Jeremyinsf: I didn't ask if you were gonna marry him ;)

Jeremyinsf: but maybe just fool around?

Rickyg9999: I don't think he's like that and I'm not like that either are you?

Jeremyinsf: like what?

Rickyg9999: like a person who just fools around, I mean if I'm going to be dating someone I want them to be committed to me and me be committed to them

Jeremyinsf: well, if you're single, no point in not having some fun, right?

Rickyg9999: I don't believe in just having sex if that's what your asking

Jeremyinsf: doesn't have to be full on sex, but maybe even just make out a little. have you before?

Rickyg9999: have I what? made out? no how could I here?

Jeremyinsf: it's fun. you should try it ;-)

Rickyg9999: is that all you want, sex?

Jeremyinsf: I don't think I want anything right now. just got out of a difficult relationship. done with that for a bit.

Rickyg9999: abusive?? Like he beat you??

Jeremyinsf: no. nothing like that. just difficult.

Rickyg9999: oh I see, well I'm a kind guy always have been, my mom actually thinks I'm too kind. I see people who need help and it's like an instinct to just help them out

Jeremyinsf: that's a good trait to have

Rickyg9999: so he said a lot of hurtful things to you?

Jeremyinsf: no. it's hard to explain. he was very smart.

Rickyg9999: how long were you with him?

Jeremyinsf: just two years

Rickyg9999: why would you stay with someone for two years if it was difficult?

Jeremyinsf: I was in love I guess

Rickyg9999: doesn't sound like love

Jeremyinsf: it was

Rickyg9999: well I don't think I could ever say anything mean to you I think your wicked cool

Jeremyinsf: thanks ☺

Jeremyinsf: so this guy you think likes you—what's his name again?

Rickyg9999: Wesley

Jeremyinsf: that's a terrible name

Rickyg9999: really? why?

Jeremyinsf: I dunno. I just think it sounds a little skeezy

Rickyg9999: I'm not sure if it sounds like that, I guess I don't have any opinion on the name

Jeremyinsf: as you shouldn't! but I'll be honest, I probably hate the name because it's the name of a co-worker I can't stand.

Rickyg9999: what's wrong with him?

Jeremyinsf: just one of those guys who thinks he knows more than he does. you know the type?

Rickyg9999: lol sounds like my entire town

Jeremyinsf: yeah, dude, you need to get out of there

Rickyg9999: I'm working on it ;)

Rickyg9999: but it might be getting better? there are some cool places opening up like this 80s cafe they're doing it all over trying to make it a hip spot I guess

Rickyg9999: u there?

Jeremyinsf: yeah, gotta run though, meeting up with friends

Jeremyinsf: great chatting, as always

Rickyg9999: ok. well let me know your holiday plans I'm serious about you coming out here if you want, I think we'd have a great time

Jeremyinsf: sure thing

Jeremyinsf: see ya

Rickyg9999: bye

Jeremyinsf has closed his chat window.

MAN-DATE CHAT TRANSCRIPT
DECEMBER 6, 2014

Rickyg9999: have a good Thanksgiving?

Jeremyinsf: yeah, actually went back to Nodak for a bit

Rickyg9999: oh. was it fun?

Jeremyinsf: better than I thought, bud. haven't been back in so long. childhood memories, they came a-rushin back ;)

Rickyg9999: bet that sucked huh?

Jeremyinsf: my childhood wasn't awful. some parts of it, yeah, and I'm glad I'm out of there, but there were some really good times too. like with my cousin Brian.

Rickyg9999: you were close?

Jeremyinsf: wouldn't say close, but there were some good times.

Rickyg9999: like when?

Jeremyinsf: there's this sand pit right across the street from my old house—hasn't changed in 20 years.

Jeremyinsf: well, when we were kids, my cousin and I would have these bike races there. dumbest thing ever since our bikes weren't really made for sand, and this was the sinking kind, not the hard kind, so it was a big chore to move even a foot.

Jeremyinsf: we'd fall like hundreds of times trying to get from one end to the other and by the end we'd be dirty and scratched up but we'd be laughing really hard

Jeremyinsf: sometimes made it a big production too. had his parents and my parents and his brother and sister cheering us on, making bets. sometimes had the other neighbor kids participate, and mostly I won.

Jeremyinsf: my parents always made like it was such a big deal too

Jeremyinsf: would run up to me and hug me like I'd gotten first in a marathon or something

Rickyg9999: that sounds kinda weird

Jeremyinsf: it was, maybe a little, but when I went back, we did it again, you know, as adults, and it took us twice as long and it was cold and there was some snow to deal with, but I won again and that made me feel strangely good

Rickyg9999: I took some more pics

Jeremyinsf: oh yeah?

Rickyg9999: yeah

Rickyg9999: (pic sent)

Rickyg9999: (pic sent)

Rickyg9999: (pic sent)

Rickyg9999: ??

Rickyg9999: I guess you don't like

Rickyg9999: oh well

Rickyg9999 has closed his chat window.

MAN-DATE CHAT TRANSCRIPT
DECEMBER 13, 2014

Rickyg9999: guess you didn't like. it's ok

Rickyg9999: u there?

Rickyg9999: hello????

Rickyg9999: u srsly ignoring me now?? am I that gross to look at??

Rickyg9999: u serious??

Rickyg9999: well fuck you then

Rickyg9999: you should watch out, kiddie porn and all

Rickyg9999: they'll find that shit even if you erase it

Rickyg9999: I'll tell them you made me do it

Rickyg9999: asshole

Rickyg9999 has closed his chat window.

JEREMY LITTLE

"Oh my god," Alyssa said. "Are you like really thirsty or something?"

It was 2 p.m. on day four in the Springs, and we were in Starbucks. We were the only people in the place, and this made the music—some millennial crooner with a thick, milky voice—loud and intrusive.

"Craving sugar," I said, setting my enormous blended drink on the table. It sloshed lazily like thick, multihued mud. Her "tall" drink looked small in comparison.

"Clearly." She looked refreshed—her eyes clear, her hair washed and pulled back into a tight ponytail. She smelled like grocery-store berries and watermelon, and her face was powdered, hiding some of the pockmarks I'd seen the previous day. "So are you gonna just be mysterious all the time?" she said.

"Mysterious?"

"I mean, when're you gonna actually tell me what you're doing here. If it's because of Ricky, I won't be mad. Swear. Just so long as you're not a reporter, like a *news* reporter. But if you're maybe like writing a book or doing some sort of research, it's fine, really. You don't have to hide and pretend shit with me."

"I looked you up last night."

"Huh?"

"Online," I said.

"Did you learn a lot?" She blinked.

"I'm very sorry for your loss. Can't imagine what you're going through."

"Who *are* you?"

I leaned over the table and sipped my drink without holding the cup or the straw.

"Cute," she said. She wiggled in her chair, tried to copy my no-hands move. The cup, unfortunately, was too close to the center of the table, and her belly stopped any sort of grace. She puckered her lips, craned her neck, and sucked air. I laughed and moved her cup closer to her. She picked it up, smiled, and sipped. "Anyway, I couldn't talk about it for a long time. I mean, can you imagine? Strangers everywhere suddenly interested in me and my mom. People who actually knew us didn't want to talk about it *at all*, but strangers, people who didn't give any sort of shit what we were going through, they just couldn't get enough."

"I'm a stranger," I said.

"Yeah. But that's the thing—I think I'm okay to talk about it now. I mean, I *want* to talk about it. There's a ton to get off my chest."

"I imagine."

"And since *nobody* here will talk much to me or Mom, well, maybe you're just the person to, you know, *discuss*. But first—before I do that—you gotta tell me the truth. Why are you here?"

"My name is Jeremy. I'm here on business."

"Gonna stick with that, huh? Well." She sighed and took another sip. "I guess it doesn't matter just so long as you *swear* you're not a news reporter."

"I swear."

"Okay. See, everything's like—oh, I'm not sure—it's like very confusing for me in my head. I got my mom on one hand, who just can't seem to get her shit together. I mean, she lost her son, so that can't be easy, especially with the circumstances and all, but, man, it's like she doesn't even see me, and I'm really trying to help her with everything, you know? And then I've got this kid inside me, which is *enough* drama, if you ask me. And then, well, I've got the other thing. So it's a lot for one person." She sipped. "And I can't read another article on gun control. Not another single one. I mean, I told him where my mom hid hers. Of course I did. I don't believe in having a gun in the house without everyone knowing where it is. Just seems wrong. But you know how it makes me *feel*? I mean, can you *imagine*?"

"I'm sure it'd all be overwhelming."

"Listen to you. All composed. I bet it'd take a lot to rattle you."

"I get rattled. Easily, actually."

"Okay. Name one time then. One time you got really rattled."

"One time?"

"Don't think too hard." She winked.

Some of the staff behind the counter watched us. One girl in particular, a round-faced broad-shouldered teenager, glanced at us every few minutes. Her black polo stretched tight across her meaty arms.

"So are you excited about being a mother?" I slurped the last of my beverage.

"Don't change the subject," she said.

"I don't know. When I was twenty-two, I got into a car accident, went into a ditch, actually, thought I was gonna die. That definitely rattled me."

"That doesn't count."

"Why not?"

"Because it was a *car accident*, dummy."

"And?"

"Never mind." She sipped her drink and furrowed her brow. "Excited? I don't know. Yeah, I guess. More worried than anything, though. I mean, people assume you're excited because, well, it's motherhood, and motherhood is supposed to be so great, but nobody but the mother—if she's single—nobody but her thinks about all the expenses and all that."

"You're worried about expenses."

"Of course."

"And the father?"

"Who knows."

"I'm sorry."

"It's okay. Just not in the picture, if you know what I mean." A few small hills of frozen ice and sugar rested at the bottom of her cup. She moved her straw around and tried to pierce them. "I'll be fine, though," she said.

"Fine?"

"Yeah. Of course."

"Fine."

"That a weird word or something?"

"No, not weird. You'll get that job at the motel."

"Yeah. Hopefully. If not that, something else. It'll work out."

"I'm sure. It usually does."

"Yeah."

We didn't talk about much else, which was strange, given that she'd prefaced our conversation with a desire to talk about Ricky. When she'd finished slurping up the final crystallized sugar-water remnants from her cup, she stood up and asked if I was ready to leave.

In the parking lot, I hugged her, and she held on tight. Her belly felt cool against my hip, and for a second, I imagined myself staying in El Monte Springs, helping her raise her baby, adopting a father-figure role, providing as much as I could for a kid whose uncle I'd only known online.

It wouldn't be so bad, I thought; after all, what would I miss about my life in San Francisco? The weather? Maybe. My friends? A little at first, but I'd get over them and they'd definitely get over me. My job? Accountants were needed everywhere. Culture? Progressive politics? Ethnic food? My Nob Hill apartment? Sure, but all that I could discard for the sake of a distinct and meaningful purpose. The only thing pulling me back was my pathetic and repressed hope that one day Craig and I would be together again, and this made me deeply anxious, so before I went to the motel, I went to the liquor store, bought a bottle of wine, and drank it alone in my room.

I'd first met him at a video bar in the Castro called the Midnight Sun. It was Friday night, and my friends were boring me: Derek was getting huffy about some scam he'd bought into, and Kyle was trying to placate him in his usual sober manner. The music videos were all '80s, which I usually liked, but that night the bright, zooming images made me feel old. I was about to tell my friends that I was going home, when I felt my phone vibrate against my leg. I took it out and saw that I had a new message on my mobile Man-Date app.

"Oh my god, you're not even paying *attention*," Derek said to me. "You're checking Man-Date? Jeremy, I lost two thousand dollars. *Two thousand dollars.*"

The man messaging me was twenty-five feet away. His screen name was Crusher. I looked around but couldn't locate him. We proceeded to have a conversation.

Crusher: can't stop lookin at you

Jeremyinsf: haha wish I could say the same. where u at?

Crusher: your pic doesn't do you justice

Jeremyinsf: thanks

Crusher: buy you a drink?

Jeremyinsf: ok

And then there he was, in front of me, smiling—the beautiful dark-haired man I'd spend the next two years with.

"So what're you drinkin'?" he said.

"Vodka soda," I said. From my left, I felt the stares of my friends, simultaneously judgmental and envious.

"Kinda figured something like that," he said. "Be right back."

He wasn't tall, but he seemed it as he walked away. He had an imperiousness that I found both sexy and intimidating. Before he got back with my drink, Derek leaned into me and said, "I guess I'll forgive you this time."

"I'm Craig," he said when he returned.

"I'm Jeremy," I said.

Two hours later, we were in my bed, his head a large ball of bouncing black hair between my legs. The next day, we were intertwined, our clothes on the floor, our mouths whispering ironclad promises to each other through fluttering bedsheets. Two months later, we were domestic partners.

That we'd actually met on an app wasn't lost on me as he cut himself off from everything online. In our final few months, as he continued to withdraw from the life I understood, I couldn't help but wonder if he found me irrelevant, a poor schmuck with a bunch of unanswered prayers, seeking meaningful life answers through a variety of pixelated screens. I also wondered if he felt conflicted about how we'd met.

"Am I one of those lonely people you were talking about?" We were in bed. He was reading, of course. I had my tablet on my lap. It was summer, so the whir of the fan made us talk louder than normal.

He removed his reading glasses, rubbed his eyes, put his book on the end table. "I think I'm too tired for this conversation," he said.

"I just need to know."

"We need to talk about this now?"

"Yes."

"Okay." He pushed himself up on the bed and sighed. "Fine. The answer is, I don't know."

"We met on Man-Date," I said. "Without technology, we wouldn't be here. How do you justify that?"

He shrugged. "I don't. I didn't feel the same way then as I do now."

"But doesn't it change anything? Doesn't that change us?"

"I don't see why it would."

"How am I supposed to do anything online without feeling that weight?"

"I don't know. Does a vegetarian put a judgment on a meat-eater? Perhaps. But do they coexist? Certainly. And do some meat-eaters end up marrying vegetarians? Absolutely. And perhaps every time a meat-eater eats meat, they feel self-conscious around their vegetarian spouse. What does that mean? Perhaps it means that the meat-eater thinks the vegetarian has some merit in his or her lifestyle choice."

"Oh *god*."

"You asked. You started this."

"So you want me to join you?"

"I want you to do whatever you wanna do. Would it be nice? Yeah. But honestly? I don't think you can. I don't think you can just be. You're too attached."

"I can."

"Then try."

"Maybe I will."

"It'd be nice."

I started with Facebook; I deleted my account and sent a final status update telling my friends I'd be gone for a while. After that, I waded through the entire digital gamut, erasing accounts that instantly begged me to come back. Within a week, I no longer had social media: no Pinterest, no Instagram, no Twitter, no LinkedIn, no Tumblr. Within two weeks, I'd erased my video-chatting software and most of my apps; I'd also told my friends to stop texting, to call if they needed anything.

"Who the fuck *calls* people?" my friend Kyle asked.

"You do now."

"Sorry, man."

He never called.

Week three, I disabled our Wi-Fi.

Week four, I had a breakdown.

"This is not a way to live!" I told Craig one night. We were in the kitchen. He was making a sandwich, carefully cutting the crusts off the bread.

"Less than a week without Wi-Fi and you're freaking out," he said, dipping a knife into a mayonnaise jar. "I told you."

"Because I'm *normal!*" I said. "I live in an advanced society! I *participate* in an advanced society!"

I'd been unable to sleep that week; I'd been too busy planning how to go about daily tasks without the Internet. I had to actually *go* to the bank, then *go* to the post office, then *go* to the bookstore. My bills had to be paid by post, by *check*, and I had to subscribe to the actual paper if I wanted to know what was going on in the world. At work, I only used email, and found that I had immense stretches of dead time on my hands, time I normally spent doing nonwork things.

In North Dakota, my parents assumed I'd succumbed to some gay disease and, as a last resort, they called in a panic.

"What's *happening*?" my mother said. "You're not *anywhere*."

"I'm here," I said. "Just not online."

"But that doesn't make any sense!"

"Just call if you want to chat," I said.

"What? Who calls anymore?"

What pushed me back to technology wasn't the communication or logistical inefficiencies, though they certainly added to the speed of my reunion, but rather the malignant sense of missing out on the world.

Without social media, I'd become erased and uninvited, defriended and devalued, ostracized from an insistently mobile society; I was the guy everyone avoided, for fear he discover that he hadn't been asked to the party, and this constant disconnection felt like an unreachable itch in the middle of my back.

My days of total online death amounted to a little less than a week. After the sixth day, I reconnected our Internet, reinstalled my apps, reinstalled my video-chatting software, and rejoined all the social media sites.

"It's about living," I told Craig. "It's not about validation for me. It's not about putting myself out there for the world to see. It's not about any of the shit you were talking about. My emotions are intact. My thoughts are intact. I have real connections with real people, and the Internet facilitates that. What you're doing? It's silly. A stupid statement. It'd be the same if people refused to use cars when cars were invented. You're isolating yourself, and it's not hip or cool. It's just dumb."

Shortly after this conversation, we broke up. And shortly after we broke up, I started texting him over and over and over and over, and when he didn't respond, I started chatting voraciously with whoever would chat on Man-Date, seeking out a person to help, a person in obvious need, a person to prove my previous point about the reality of online altruism.

This was how I met Ricky Graves.

BRAD "CORKY" MEEKS

So I went to the Starbucks during my break, and there she was, lookin' ready to pop. She was still pretty, but it was hard to concentrate on that, 'cause she was having coffee with some dude with shiny fucking hair. I stood near the door and watched for a while, saw her blink heavy, saw him smile, and when I couldn't take it anymore, I left with no coffee, sat in my truck, and breathed deep like I was always telling Mark to do.

I called work, told Henry I just got sick—really bad diarrhea and vomiting. Said I needed to take a half day. Henry was cool, just said, "Get better soon," and after he hung up, I noticed my heart pounding, like it was struggling to get out of my chest. I'd had this feeling before, like right after Alyssa left for Boston, and I swore to the doc that I was having small heart attacks but he said I was fine, said I was experiencing panic, and he gave me this CD, some soothing woman's voice giving me instructions on how to breathe. First, I thought it was bullshit; I was actually getting mad that the doctor wasn't treating this thing I thought was obviously deadly. But after a bit, I gave the CD a try, and weird enough, it worked, and whenever I felt that shit creeping in, I just heard this soothing woman's voice and remembered my breaths.

So I'd tried to get Mark McVitry to listen to the CD, but he said he couldn't listen, couldn't do anything with any sort of electronic device anymore. And I said that that was dumb, because it wasn't a video, just sound; his hallucination-Ricky couldn't pop out at him, 'cause there wouldn't be a screen. But he wouldn't budge. He wouldn't budge on pretty much anything, really, especially at the beginning. He was always just wondering why I was hanging out with him, "babysitting" as he put it. *Why are you here? Why are you here? Why are you here?* Shit. Like a broken record.

Well, I had a difficult time answering him, because he made a few good points: First, I was much closer to the Graveses than to the McVitrys, had wanted to marry Alyssa from the get-go, and Ricky— well, I'd always helped him out a bit in life, and like I said before, we sometimes smoked up together. Second, I thought the picture Mark and Wesley and those other dumbfucks had posted of Ricky with Scooter's dog was really fucking cruel. And third, Mark was pretty much right when he kept saying that I'd always taken Ricky's side at camp—I'd only done that, though, 'cause, well, who else would've? If not me, who?

So when Mark asked me why I checked in on him, took an interest, I couldn't really answer him that good, because the reason I was doing it was not really that explainable to a teenager. The reason I was doing it was because I loved my town; I loved El Monte Springs, would never leave, even for Alyssa. I knew the Springs had its problems and its faults, but what town didn't? I loved it, felt a duty to my town, so when one of my townspeople was in true need, especially one who I knew really well, because he was my camper at Burroway, well I felt that by helping that person, I was helping mend the town. But how did you explain that to a fuckin' seventeen-year-old who's suffering from PTSD 'cause he got shot by your ex-girlfriend's brother? You couldn't. It just didn't make sense. And honestly, it didn't make 100 percent sense to me either, but it was truth, clean and simple. I knew and loved every inch of the Springs, from downtown to the Meadows. It was where I learned pretty much everything I knew, and even though I spent some time in other places, like Florida and Virginia and Western Mass (mostly as a kid, but still), nothing ever compared to home.

So as soon as my heart got normal again, I called Mark, made sure he hadn't seen a Ricky-ghost, and he said he was fine, so I just sat and waited some more. Then I saw Alyssa and the dude come out, and she gave him a hug. I analyzed the hug close, like how long it was, where the hands went, if he tapped her back or rubbed it. I noticed there was a lingering, but not with him, with her, like she kept her hands on him after he backed off. *Charming city fucker,* I thought. She went back to her car and he went to his Corolla, and neither of them saw me, so I followed him and saw that he was staying at the Full Monte Motel. He got out of his car, allowing me to get a good look. I noticed he probably had some money. Nice clothes. Hair slick. Shiny shoes. Professional-looking overall. Definitely not the type to stay at the Full Monte. Made me think he had some very ulterior motives. Maybe a fetish for pregnant chicks. Probably married with a few kids back where he was from.

"Hey," I said out my window. But he was already in his motel room; he couldn't hear me. So I just sat for a while, then turned the radio to 98.7. Nitty Gritty Dirt Band came on, of course. "Fishin' in the Dark." Always made me think of camp—mostly 'cause I used to have my group of kids sing it for the talent show. They liked it. Well, some of 'em did. Some of 'em thought it was way too country. Like Ricky. But back then, Ricky didn't like anything. Was like pullin' teeth to get him to do stuff.

Once in a while, though, I saw hope. Like this one day, he was just sitting in the cabin and playing on his little gadget, and I told him he needed to pick an activity, wasn't allowed to just sit around. He just ignored me, but I was a lot bigger, so I picked him up from his bunk, and he was surprised as fuck, so he started yellin', and I tossed him—not hard—out of the cabin and told him he could do crafts if he wanted but he couldn't just be alone in the cabin. Well, he didn't do crafts, but he began walking directly for the archery field.

First, I was confused, 'cause no fuckin' way he was gonna do archery, and Bryan Musgrove, who was in charge of that station, gave me a look when Ricky approached. I said, "What? Give the guy a bow and arrow." So Bryan went to get the equipment, and Ricky just stood there staring down at the hay bale. His arms were limp, and his back was a little hunched, and his mouth was open. There was this breeze that kinda moved his hair over his forehead, and, man, I swear to god, right then it was like lookin' at a really fucked-up but beautiful painting. Like this kid with the green grass and blue sky and the wind and his fuckin' hair moving a little and him staring down at the hay bale should've been *framed*.

So Bryan handed Ricky a bow, and Ricky just looked at it like it was some sort of wild animal. Bryan went through the coaching motions, but he just wasn't good with kids like Ricky, so I said, "Listen, Bryan. Why don't you go help Kelsey over there. I'll teach Ricky."

First of all, Ricky was holding the thing like a harp. I turned it right in his hands, threaded the arrow into the nocking point, stabilized it into the rest, told him just to pull back as hard as he could. Course he didn't pull that hard, 'cause when I said let go, the arrow just fell on the ground. He looked confused and nervous, but I told him it was okay, it happened all the time, and I told him to do it again, this time try to pull harder.

"Hurts my fingers," he said.

"Cut that negative attitude shit," I said. We weren't supposed to swear, but we knew each other, so it was okay. "You'll never do anything if you think that way."

He sulked, pulled back, let go, and it fell again.

"You're not letting go the whole way," I said. "You still have one finger on it. You've gotta release totally."

"What do you mean?" he said. "I'm letting go."

"Here. Lemme show you." I took his arrow, threaded it, pulled back, let go. *Phwaap!* I hit the hay but not the target. "See? See how I let go totally?"

"That's what I did."

"No, you didn't. You just let go a little, like you're hesitating. Here." I threaded again. "Pull back. Then when you let go, spread all your fingers out like this. See?" *Phwaap!* This time I hit the target. Not a bull's-eye but close. "You gotta believe you can do things," I said. "You'll never do nothin' unless you believe you can do it. Confidence is the most important thing. And girls love it."

He looked down and depressed, and for a second I thought he was just gonna throw the bow and arrow on the ground and head back to the cabin. I was ready to walk away. *Fuck him,* I thought. But after a bit, he threaded again and pulled back and did what I showed him. Arrow didn't hit the hay—not even close—but went about halfway there, so at least he was letting go right. I told him he had to pull back more and he said he couldn't, and I looked at him and said, "What'd I just say? Confidence?" And it didn't sink in, 'cause the next two fell flat. So I grabbed the bow, demonstrated again, and the little shit actually looked away.

Tipped off my rage something fierce. I grabbed him by the shoulders and shook him. He looked at me wide-eyed, like I was actually gonna pop him one. "Thread the fuckin' bow," I said, and he did it, pulled back, didn't let go properly, let the arrow fall, and I said, "Again," and he did it and failed, and I said, "Again," and "Again," and "Again," and "Again," and maybe the rhythm of this shit made him try a bit harder each time. By the time I got to the tenth "Again," he was makin' that arrow soar. By the fifteenth, he was hitting the hay bale. By the twentieth, he was hitting the target, and when he did this, he made his top lip snarl and then he threw the bow on the ground and ran back to the cabin. I felt real proud then, like he was my kid and he'd put his mind to something and had accomplished that thing. I let him sit in the cabin the rest of the day.

In my truck the music was bothering me, so I turned the radio off. Too much country wasn't good. I was starting to regret my decision to call off work when—surprise, surprise—Alyssa came rolling into the Full Monte parking lot. I got a bit nervous—didn't have much of a story to tell her why I was there—but I had no reason to worry. Motel shared a lot with the laundromat. She didn't even notice me. She parked and waddled first to the front desk window, then over to his room. At that point, I was just like, *Fuck, it's her life. Whatever.* But I was still a little cut up about it, so I stayed, hoping to see her rush out of the place, calling him all sorts of names. But, whaddya know, it was *him* that came out. Went to her car like he owned it—unlocked it and everything. Dug through some shit on her front seat, got a pair of sunglasses, put 'em on, and went back to the room. And seeing him in her car, in her *property*, well, that made another wave of emotion go through me. Not sure if it was anger or sadness or whatever, but it was definitely negative, like a combination of everything bad. Anyway, it left me paralyzed, like I couldn't fuckin' move. I just sat there completely still, like a statue, and I thought maybe something was wrong with me, like in a medical sense. But then she came out of the room alone, calm and smiling, and I got control of my senses again, and I realized I was okay, just maybe a little shocked. Who wouldn't be, seeing your pregnant ex with a dude like that?

ALYSSA GRAVES

Seriously, like right after I got in my car, Joy Demivo came knocking on my window looking all serious, like she was about to tell me someone died right there in the Starbucks parking lot. So I rolled down my window and said, "What?"

She was like, "Your boyfriend left these on the table," and she handed me some ugly sunglasses.

"My boyfriend?" I said.

"Yeah," she said.

I mean, I didn't have anything against Joy—she was in my brother's class, and I think one time she was Starbucks employee of the month or something—but she sounded so sarcastic with that "boyfriend" shit. "He's not my boyfriend, Joy," I said.

"Well then, your friend." She was judging me, I could tell—looking at my belly, probably thinking that she was so glad she had a job and wasn't pregnant like me—so I just looked at her and shook my head and went to hand the sunglasses back, but she'd already left, so I was just dangling my hand out my window.

Anyway.

So I sat in the parking lot for a while, just looking at the glasses—they were just cheap plastic things, maybe from 7-Eleven or something—and I thought maybe they were a sign. Sounds dumb, but still, I knew that Jeremy and I were meant to meet again. Something inside me told me he was supposed to be part of my life somehow, because—

Look: I didn't get these feelings that much, these intuition feelings, but back in Boston, Sandra would sometimes talk about how I needed to really get in touch with that side of myself, said I needed to recognize when things were supposed to happen, and pursue them or whatever. She was real into all that mystical shit, like crystal stuff and cards with pictures of goddesses, and astrological charts, and at first I thought it was a bunch of crap, but I never told her that, because she was really convincing, like she'd *studied* this stuff, so sometimes I listened to her, and by the end of my time at the diner, I didn't think it was all wrong—just most of it. What stuck with me most was when she said that we all have this energy sense that we don't use enough, that it's just like feeling and seeing and hearing except it's more like intuition, but stronger, like we know how things are supposed to be, or when someone comes into our life who's very important to our overall path.

"It's not even astrology," she said. "It's more like science. Like our brains have this extra energy that we don't recognize because we're too busy using it for the more everyday things, like thinking about our families and boyfriends and work and stuff. But you just need to turn it on, that recognition, so you don't miss out on what you're supposed to do and who you're supposed to be."

I told her it didn't make a whole lot of sense, because if you're supposed to do or be something, you'll do or be it, and she just chuckled at me like I was some amateur. She said, "Seriously, Alyssa? Think about it. You're supposed to do things all the time and you don't do them because you get lazy or whatever. Then you have bad consequences and you have regrets. If you become in tune with this other sense, you'll have less regrets."

Well, that sounded pretty good to me, less regrets, so I thought about it a bit and eventually decided that, yeah, I'd try to turn that part of me on, recognize signs like she said, better my intuition and all. And Jeremy leaving his sunglasses on the table and me seeing the sign, that was obviously the intuition thing kicking in, so I wasn't going to ignore it.

Before I went to his motel, though, I went home to check on my mom, and—weird, but not that weird, actually—I found her in the living room staring at the television with the sound off. It was some sort of infomercial for jewelry, the kind of ad that looks so white, and the sellers were these has-been famous people who wore white to match the background. Mom seemed so into it, even though there was no sound: she was leaning forward and biting her nails, like the infomercial was the most suspenseful thing in the world, and when I said hi, she shushed me with a finger. So I sat on the couch next to her and watched the most boring thing I'd ever seen—seriously, the only things on the screen were two old blond ladies and a gold necklace and a blinking $299.95!—and it took like five whole minutes before she even took her eyes from the TV.

At that point, I was over feeling sorry for my mom, because I just didn't have enough energy for it. She just got so *weird*, like supernonsensical but also kinda like a zombie? And you could only really feel bad for someone for so long before they just got tiresome. I mean, I'd only been home a month or so, but still, a month with my mom in that state was like a year, honest to god. Lots of maintenance, if you know what I mean.

Anyway, she finally looked at me and asked how I was, but not in a regular normal way like people did when they greeted each other, but with the stress on the "are," like, *How* are *you?* As if I'd been the one totally separated from the real world for the last few months.

"I'm fine," I said.

"You know," she said, "I thought about you a lot today. Thought about you as a kid. You were a good kid, Alyssa. Everyone here thought it."

"And now?" I said.

"And now," she said, looking far away, "you're okay." She smiled and rubbed my belly.

When you're away, you have time to really think about your family and why they did the things they did, and I'm not talking about Ricky here—I'm not sure if anyone will ever really know why he did what he did—but about my mom. I think I've said before that she was the cool mom growing up, the one who let us stay up late and do illegal things. Sometimes she swore and drank, but she never really intruded or tried really hard to be friends with my friends or anything. But then when I was around eighteen, she sorta changed. Like she was still cool and lenient, I guess, but she also started thinking of herself as this really wise and insightful person, and I'm not talking just normal smart, I'm talking ultrasmart, like she suddenly knew what was best for everyone and she always felt the need to give advice in this really annoying way. Like this one time, I had some friends over, and we were in the basement listening to music and hanging out and kinda deciding if we wanted to go to a movie, when she came down with some cookies (which was totally weird, because she never did that sorta thing—brought us snacks and stuff), and my friends looked at her weird but accepted a few Oreos and then looked at me like, *What's up with her?* And instead of leaving the cookies and going back upstairs, she sat down on one of the beanbags and just smiled for a little while.

"How are you girls doing?" she said.

"We're fine," I said.

"That's good," she said.

We just sat there for a while, and my friends kept looking at me like, *Uhh, what do we do?*

She sighed but kept smiling. "Life is so *interesting*, isn't it?" she said.

"Are you drunk?" I asked.

She laughed. "Seriously, girls, you'll blink and be my age." She had the plate of cookies on her lap, and she took one and bit into it. "But my life is great. I've got two great kids, a great job, this house—what more could I ask for?"

"It's really great," Shelly LaFarge said. I shot her a death glare.

"That doesn't mean I'll settle," she said. "I've got so much more to offer—I know it. And so do you girls! You just really need to concentrate on your future," she said, like totally sudden. "I'll tell you, it's not easy to get places in this life, and you have to start early as you can."

"Mom, we're about to go," I said.

"But when you find your way, your path," she said, "it's the most rewarding thing ever."

"How did you find *your* path, Mrs. Graves?" Shelly said.

"Shelly," I said.

"It was a process, Shelly," my mom said. "It's called introspection. Looking inside yourself. Seeing what you're meant to do. I've made all these mistakes along the way, but since I have this gift of introspection, I've been able to become so much stronger because of them." She sat up and looked out at us like we were her congregation.

"That's *so* cool," Shelly said. "Introspection. I've never even heard of that!"

"You'll understand more when you get a little older," my mom said. "But what I was saying is that you have to really envision yourself ten years from now, 'cause it'll happen so fast. And when you envision yourself, you need to envision yourself as a strong, independent woman, a woman who can take care of herself in any situation. Maybe you'll have kids. Maybe you'll have a husband. Who knows. In any case, you need to see yourself *being* something."

"Oh *god,*" I said.

"Alyssa," my mom said, "why are you being so negative?"

It wasn't like she'd found Jesus or something, but it was kinda similar, like suddenly some heavenly creature or whatever had told her that she needed to spread her amazing smarts or something. It was *so annoying*, and she became so *chirpy*, like overly friendly, even fake sometimes, and it got to the point where I didn't even want to invite people over because I was afraid of her coming down and trying to be wise or whatever. When I asked her about it, kinda confronted her, she just said that she'd been reading things, and that these things were very enlightening, and didn't I want her to be a more well-rounded person? Didn't I want her to strengthen herself, work on her inner fem-core?

"Your inner what?" I said.

Didn't I see her as a smart, capable woman who was successfully raising two children on her own? Didn't she believe in constant improvement? *Of course, of course, of course,* I said, but I was still a little confused, and she never did answer what "fem-core" meant, so one day I went into her bedroom and snooped around and found all these books in the little compartment below her nightstand, and they all were by this woman Victoria Gorham; they had to do with finding your purpose in life, mostly from a feminism perspective, and how you keep this purpose alive while you were raising kids. Some of the sentences were underlined, especially the things about *empowerment* and *strong female role models* and *introspection* (so *much* about introspection), and she'd written notes all over the margins, like *ABSOLUTELY!* and *Makes sense!* and *BRILLIANT!*

I felt sorta bad for snooping, so I came clean with her, told her I found the books, and instead of getting mad that I'd gone through her things, she just looked at me all bright and smiley and said, "Well, do you wanna borrow one?"

I said, "No, of course not."

"Well, if you ever do, just let me know," she said. "She's fabulous."

I didn't know what else to say, so I walked away.

But anyway.

It wasn't like she was that way every day. Mostly she was normal, and after a bit, I just let her sometimes-weirdness go. After seeing those books, I kinda figured some of her change had to do with her not being in a relationship with a man for a long time, and just maybe her suspicion of men in general. I mean, she went on dates and stuff, though they were never serious, but I think she still resented my dad for leaving and Corky for taking up my time and her brother for dying in her arms . . .

Yeah, Uncle Joe. That was maybe the most difficult for her.

The story could seriously take days to talk about, but the gist of it was that she had one brother, and when he was only like twenty, he got AIDS, and since nobody in her family was actually around or alive anymore and since he didn't have medical insurance, she had to take care of him. Of course this caused my dad to go nuts—he *hated* my uncle, sick or not, called him a whiny little faggot over and over, told him he deserved his misery and so on—and my mom was working full-time and taking care of a baby (me), so this was all really stressful for her.

Anyway, the way she told it, Uncle Joe wasn't the easiest person either; he was demanding and bitchy up 'til the day he died, telling her how he hated her, how it was her fault that he was sick, how their family was a bunch of hypocrite redneck morons. And my mom just tried her best to ignore all his hateful shit, and continued to clean up his *literal* shit like it was any regular thing. (I guess he couldn't control his bowels or something.) But it all just blew up one day, and she was like, "Mike's right! You deserve what you got! What, did you think sleeping with hundreds of guys was gonna make you *healthy?*" He died like a couple weeks later while she was bathing him, and she swore that he'd waited 'til she was touching him to go, just to spite her. And it'd worked, 'cause whenever she told me this story, she teared up and said it was the worst thing she'd ever said to anyone in her life.

Between her brother and my dad, she didn't really have stellar males in her life, so it made sense that she was so hesitant to like Corky. I mean, him and me were serious for a long time, even talked about marriage, especially after he got me pregnant. So maybe she panicked a little, told me I was "no good" to get me to move out of the Springs and start a new life without him. It obviously worked, 'cause that's exactly what I did—packed up, broke up, skedaddled. And not a moment too soon, 'cause it was then that she started *obsessing* about that whack-job author Victoria Gorham, talking about her nonstop and starting her sentences with *Victoria says . . .* as if she were on a first-name basis with the woman, as if they were close friends or something, as if they spent hours together in cafés or on the phone or whatever. Poor Ricky had to deal with that for quite a while.

Victoria thinks you made a great decision moving to Boston, she wrote me in an early email.

Victoria? I replied.

Yep! she wrote.

I didn't respond to that. Fifteen minutes later, I got a text from Ricky, saying HELP! MOM IS INSANE!! And that made me chuckle a little, 'cause I knew exactly what he was talking about.

So after I ate a sandwich, I told Mom that I was going out for a bit, and she was like, "Out? Honey, you just got home. You need to rest. You can't be running around like that." And she was right, 'cause I was exhausted. Every movement was getting real hard for me, and a lot of the time I just wanted to sleep for hours. But something inside me— that intuition thing, no doubt, not the baby—kept telling me that I had to return Jeremy's sunglasses that afternoon, that if I waited, the whole reason-for-everything shit would be over. Besides, I'd just come to check on her, not to like hang out with her, and she was fine for the most part, just sitting there, not crying in her bed like she sometimes did.

"I'll be fine," I said.

"Where are you going?" she asked.

"I just need to return something."

She crossed her arms over her chest and looked back at the screen, which hadn't really changed. I swear those infomercials are just all the same—all that white, enough to drive a crazy person even crazier. "Turn the sound on at least," I told her, but she ignored me.

When I got to Jeremy's room, he was talking on his phone, but he motioned me to come in anyway, and I took that as a good sign, since he could've just stopped his conversation and said something rude like, "What do you want?" Well, he sounded pretty heated, so I took a seat on one of those ripped-up pink chairs and pretended not to listen, though it was impossible, since he was in the same room with me. It was clear that the other person was not happy that he was extending his stay, and I thought, *Girlfriend? Wife?* Just had that kind of ring to it, I guess, but then he mentioned something about a spreadsheet, and I knew it was about work. Still, I sat back and closed my eyes for a bit and imagined that he was actually confessing to his wife how he'd met this pregnant girl and how she was like the one and he couldn't control his feelings, and that he was sorry but he was leaving California and moving to New Hampshire right away so he could spend the rest of his life with her and he could help raise her kid. When I opened my eyes, he was just looking at me, and his face was sorta red. I sat up in the chair as best I could.

"What's up?" he asked, and I realized I left the sunglasses in my car.

"You left your sunglasses at Starbucks," I said.

"Yeah?"

"Sorry. I brought 'em, but I left them in my car."

"You left what?"

"Your sunglasses."

"Oh. They're in your car? I can get them if you want."

I liked that he was thinking of me, my state anyway—you know, not wanting me to move if I didn't have to—and plus, that meant he wanted me to stay a little bit, which was a good sign. So I threw him my keys and told him what my car looked like, and he went outside and returned with the sunglasses on.

"Hey," he said, "you think it's pretentious wearing shades indoors?"

I wasn't sure what he meant, but I didn't wanna make like I was stupid, so I said, "No."

"Really? I can't think of anything more pretentious."

"I think they look good on you."

He took them off and kinda gave me a sideways glance. "I don't know if you heard, but I'm extending my stay. There's more work than I thought."

"At the financial company?"

"Yeah," he said, and he smiled. It was such a great smile—all teeth—and I had that fantasy for a second again of him and me, and it all seemed real perfect.

"I'm glad you're staying," I said.

"Yeah," he said. "Not much longer. Just a couple days maybe."

"Things not so great back in California?"

"It's not that. Just—"

"None of my business, I know."

"Just a few things to take care of before I go back."

"Gotcha."

So he sat on the chair at the desk and put his notebook or whatever away and said, "Hey, feel like playing a card game or something?"

"Seriously?" I said, 'cause that was such a weird thing to do, like not watch TV or even make out, but play a game. "Like gambling?"

"No," he said. "I don't have much of a poker face."

"Then what?"

"Well, what games do you know? I got a stack of cards, and I have a little extra time."

"Hmm," I said. "Well, the only real card game I know is gin rummy."

"Gin rummy, eh? I know that one too. Wanna play?"

So I agreed, even though I thought it was really weird, a girl coming to a guy's motel room to play cards. But seriously, Jeremy was a different kind of person—I knew it—not like a lot of the other perverts around town, so it was actually a little refreshing, just sitting there across from him and playing a game I hadn't played for like a really long time.

"You're really weird, you know that?" I said. "Who plays card games except on the computer or something?"

"Well, you must," he said, dealing. "You know how at least."

"I mean, I used to play card games, like years ago. Not anymore. Not even at the diner when it's dead."

"So I'll tell you a little secret," he said, discarding and smiling. "When I was a kid, like in elementary school, I dreamed about being a blackjack dealer at a huge casino. I'd just watched *Rain Man*, and for some reason, the casino scenes stuck. All the flashiness and money and noise and winning and all that. Well, for years afterward, every time someone asked me what I wanted to be when I grew up—and people asked a lot—well, I'd say I was moving to Las Vegas to deal cards. Hearing a kid say that threw a lot of people off, and I loved that. I loved seeing their expression change."

"That's weird," I said.

"Of course I didn't move to Vegas and deal blackjack, but I still bring a pack of cards with me wherever I go. Sometimes I just sit and shuffle. Calms me a little."

"I guess everyone's got their thing."

"Your brother," he said, blinking hard, "did he ever talk to you about what he wanted to be? What he wanted to do? Just curious."

"Ha! Is that your segue? That's kinda funny."

He didn't say anything, so I just sighed and said, "To me? No, not really."

I drew. Almost a set.

"He was wicked smart," I said. "Like a straight-A student who didn't really even try. He did all the advanced classes too, like the nerd classes that prepared you for college or whatever, but, I dunno, he never seemed to be that interested in any of them, if you know what I mean. They were just classes."

But then—that wasn't true. Talking about it, I remembered this string of texts he'd sent me, like maybe at the end of his sophomore year. It started with him saying, out of the blue, **I'm gonna study crime scene work I think, like lab work and forensics at college**, and I responded by just saying, **Cool.** 'Cause what was I supposed to say? He obviously watched too much television—that shit like *CSI* wasn't real life. I'd seen a documentary on it, and for the most part all those people who actually did it for a living just talked about how tedious their job was and how television had made it wicked glamorous but totally fake.

Still, the little shit surprised me, with a bunch of other texts that contained all these statistics and case studies, and I was impressed, 'cause seriously? It wasn't like he had an iPhone yet, just a little flip phone, so he was taking the time to key in all this stuff from his little keyboard, transferring all the info from a library computer, and it was actually pretty interesting, like stuff about tampered evidence in murder cases and how DNA testing changed court processes, and the number of nonwhite incarcerations versus white and etc., etc., etc. And the texts just kept coming and coming, so many of them that I just turned my ringer off for a while, 'cause it was getting to be too much. I never ended up reading all of them, but when he was finally done sending—like seriously, days later—I sent him a text saying, **Wow Ricky!**

"I read a few articles about him, your brother," Jeremy said, giving me serious side-eye. "All his teachers said how good a student he was, especially in the sciences."

"Yeah," I said, my throat suddenly dry. "Who knows what he could've been?"

"I'm sorry."

"No," I said. "Just hadn't thought about that, I guess—about his chopped-off future. When something like that happens, most people are just thinking of the past, like really analyzing everything about the kid's family life, his social life, his school life, etc., you know? It's not like he was in a car accident or something else that wasn't really newsworthy. If that'd been the case, people would've talked about his shortened future or whatever, but in this case? No. They just wanted to place blame somewhere. Guns. Parents. Education. Technology. Small-town life. Homophobia. High school politics. You name it."

"Yeah."

"It's like all of us, Ricky included, stopped being people when it all happened. We became causes, things to blame. It sucked. 'Cause, again, if it'd been a car accident, Ricky'd be a *person who died too soon* instead of a *person to figure out*."

"It has to be so difficult."

"Everything's difficult."

"Not everything."

"Gin."

"Seriously?"

"Yup." I showed him my cards.

"Damn. That was quick."

"Sorry. I'm good." I smiled.

We played like four more hands before I started feeling real tired, like fall-on-my-face tired, so I told him I had to get going. He seemed like deeply troubled about it, kept saying, "One more hand, one more hand. You sure?" and I just looked at him and smiled and made some comment about falling asleep in the middle of the game and not wanting him to see me drool (he laughed), but still, I thought it was wicked sweet of him to want me to stay around—this when I'd only come over to return his sunglasses—so I said I'd see him again sometime before he left, and he seemed okay with that.

So I got up and he gave me a hug, and I thought it was a lingering one, but I couldn't be sure. Definitely no pat, which was good. Corky used to tell me how to analyze hugs. He said that if there was a pat, it was just a friendly thing—kinda like how guys did with each other, you know, to make sure it wasn't anything gay. And if there was no pat, it still might not mean anything, especially if the hug was short, but if you counted to three and there was still some contact, that meant the other person was into touching you, so it was safe to say that they'd like to get in your pants (unless it was like at a funeral or something). Well, I counted to four with Jeremy, so I thought it was safe to say that he liked me in some way, even in my pregnant state, and just thinking about it made me feel pretty nice all over—warm and maybe less tired. Guess I had Sandra to thank for that.

MAN-DATE CHAT TRANSCRIPT
DECEMBER 27, 2014

Rickyg9999: hey man, how've you been?

Rickyg9999: u there?

Rickyg9999: have a good Xmas?

Jeremyinsf: yes

Rickyg9999: ur alive!!

Rickyg9999: I wondered there for a bit

Jeremyinsf: I'm alive, yes

Rickyg9999: hey sorry about going off like that before

Rickyg9999: just sorting through some shit, you know?

Jeremyinsf: I don't know if I should be chatting with you

Rickyg9999: I was joking about the kiddie porn thing

haha. I'm 21, remember?

Jeremyinsf: made me really uncomfortable

Rickyg9999: I know, I'm sorry shouldn't have gone off like that sorry

Jeremyinsf: really have to watch what you say

Rickyg9999: I know I know sorry

Rickyg9999: i just thought you thought I was ugly cuz you didn't reply to my pics so I got pissed, but it's all good

Jeremyinsf: you're not ugly. I just didn't know how to respond.

Rickyg9999: it's cool

Jeremyinsf: do you have friends there?

Rickyg9999: what's that supposed to mean? yeah I got friends, a lot of them but I can't talk to everyone like I can talk to you

Jeremyinsf: we've never actually talked

Rickyg9999: we could if you want. I can give you my number

Jeremyinsf: I don't think I can talk right now, but maybe some other time though

Rickyg9999: that's cool

Rickyg9999: so you go back home again for Christmas?

Rickyg9999: ??

Jeremyinsf: no, I stayed here. was with friends.

Rickyg9999: down in Los Angeles again? lol

Jeremyinsf: no, here in San Francisco

Rickyg9999: it doesn't snow there right?

Jeremyinsf: right

Rickyg9999: would be really weird to have winter with no snow

Jeremyinsf: happens in a lot of places

Rickyg9999: lol yeah I guess your right

Rickyg9999: so you were just with friends? you exchanged gifts and everything?

Jeremyinsf: we did. ate, drank, the usual.

Rickyg9999: are they all gay?

Jeremyinsf: who?

Rickyg9999: your friends

Jeremyinsf: no

Rickyg9999: ok look I'm very sorry I can tell your being a little hesitant to chat like before and I know I just lost my head there but I'll be honest, I think your wicked cool and smart and awesome and I shouldn't have sent those pictures cuz they weren't appropriate I know but is it ok if we forget that?

Rickyg9999: hello??

Jeremyinsf: ok, bud. but can you just be up front with me? are you 21?

Rickyg9999: sorry I lied about that too I'm actually 18, still legal though lol

Jeremyinsf: and you're not in college, are you?

Rickyg9999: I'm in high school sorry

Jeremyinsf: ok. you really, really made me nervous there.

Rickyg9999: I know, I'm so sorry

Jeremyinsf: well, all right then. just be honest from now on, ok? I think you're a good kid and, to be honest, I kinda think of myself as a mentor of sorts. I keep remembering how difficult it was for me growing up. if I'd had the internet, I probably would've reached out too.

Rickyg9999: I basically didn't have the internet til now cuz I just got a computer!!! I was using the library before but now I have my own, it's so awesome

Rickyg9999: but you didn't have the internet at all growing up?

Jeremyinsf: haha nothing like it is now. I'm old

Jeremyinsf: and things are so different for gay kids these days

Rickyg9999: if you mean like accepting yeah kinda but not totally cuz i mean I know this kid in class he said if he ever had a gay kid he'd tell him to leave and come back when he's straight

Rickyg9999: anyway he was real serious about it even though everyone was calling him a homophobe and thinking he was really messed up. My friend Claire said that he's probably gay himself

Jeremyinsf: people still say shit like that? about throwing their kids out?

Rickyg9999: yeah it's small town stuff you know

Jeremyinsf: Jesus

Rickyg9999: yeah messed up

Rickyg9999: so I'm off school now

Rickyg9999: just kinda lazing around helping my mom out

Rickyg9999: if you wanted to come see how we live out here ;) lol

Jeremyinsf: bet it's cold

Rickyg9999: not as bad as you'd think. people still even go to the Meadows, like they have bonfires in the middle of the winter

Jeremyinsf: what's the Meadows?

Rickyg9999: you forgot?? lol anyway remember I told you how it's this place where a bunch of people from town go and get drunk?

Rickyg9999: lots of high schoolers but some older people too, just this big field and forest with a bonfire pit

Jeremyinsf: sounds fun

Rickyg9999: yeah remember Wesley? The boy I talked about? he's like dying to have me come out there and hang out but it's always seemed kinda lame to me

Rickyg9999: but I'm thinking of going cuz I don't have a lot else going on now lol

Rickyg9999: if you were out here we could go together

Jeremyinsf: yeah, sounds cool, and I'd definitely go out there if I weren't so swamped with work

Jeremyinsf: plus we don't even know each other really haha

Rickyg9999: we kinda do, just haven't met. I mean we chat, that's getting to know each other right?

Jeremyinsf: I guess, but you know what I mean

Rickyg9999: I will be honest I really like you

Jeremyinsf: cool. I like you too, bud

Rickyg9999: I mean I felt real bad about how I reacted that time before and it's ok if you don't like my pics, I understand I'm not everyone's cup of tea but I enjoy these conversations and I look forward to them on Saturdays so that's why I was so angry that you weren't responding

Jeremyinsf: let's just keep this G-rated, ok?

Rickyg9999: oh that's fine it's not like I take X-pics all the time or anything but it seems like other guys do on here so I thought I'd try

Rickyg9999: but I see what your saying

Rickyg9999: I didn't think you were gonna chat with me anymore

Rickyg9999: anyway, you got big New Year's plans?

Jeremyinsf: nah, I hate New Year's

Jeremyinsf: bunch of amateur drunks. every year I just stay in and go to bed.

Jeremyinsf: I know . . . I'm old haha

Jeremyinsf: but the crowds aren't my thing

Jeremyinsf: I mean I might have a few drinks here, but that's it

Jeremyinsf: i actually got trampled once

Rickyg9999: what? srsly??

Jeremyinsf: I was out on New Year's Eve, someone pulled the fire alarm, everyone raced for the door, someone pushed me over. fractured two bones in my hand.

Rickyg9999: wow

Jeremyinsf: yep. haven't gone out since

Jeremyinsf: no big loss for me anyway. some of my friends usually get together on New Year's Eve, but I'd just rather not even leave my apartment.

Rickyg9999: yeah it gets kinda crazy here too, lots of fights for some reason

Rickyg9999: every year this guy Corky ends up starting some fight, I don't even know why he goes out on New Year's Eve if that's what he's gonna do and he's my sister's ex-boyfriend and my old summer camp counselor

Rickyg9999: we kinda have a weird relationship now that my sister's in Boston.

Jeremyinsf: weird how?

Rickyg9999: like my sister would kill me if she knew I talked to him as much as I do but he's one of the only people here who understands me I guess

Rickyg9999: I suppose that's cuz he's known me forever

Jeremyinsf: are you out to him?

Rickyg9999: out?

Rickyg9999: I'm not out to anyone.

Rickyg9999: if I told Corky he'd probably be wicked surprised but he'd eventually be ok with it cuz he's like a redneck but he's kinda different in a way

Rickyg9999: or maybe I just think that cuz we talk a lot

Jeremyinsf: it's important you have someone to talk to

Rickyg9999: yeah I got friends

Jeremyinsf: sounds like this Corky guy is a good friend.

Rickyg9999: I wouldn't really think of him as a friend cuz he's old and everything

Jeremyinsf: haha I'm old!

Rickyg9999: no your not that old but even though your older than me we have a different friendship than me and Corky. it's just different

Jeremyinsf: ok, you're close to your sister though, right?

Rickyg9999: I mean she lives in Boston now and she's older but she's wicked cool, we text sometimes

Rickyg9999: actually I was thinking about her the other time we chatted when you were talking about biking and your cousins in the sand or whatever and I wondered if we did anything like that

Rickyg9999: the only thing I can think of is when she taught me how to play this card game gin rummy, I guess our grandma taught her.

Rickyg9999: I never knew our grandma so it was special in a way

Rickyg9999: anyway we used to play it sometimes when I was a kid and she'd beat me all the time but a few times I beat her and she thought that was awesome, wasn't a sore loser at all

Jeremyinsf: sounds like a good big sister!

Rickyg9999: well she ignored me most of the time but that's ok cuz she was older but I really liked those gin rummy games cuz she was real nice to me then and she liked the game and talked about Grandma

Rickyg9999: anyway I gotta go but I'm off til January 15th if you wanna come out here

Jeremyinsf: I'll think about it, bud

Rickyg9999: don't think about it too hard ;)

Jeremyinsf: ok man

Rickyg9999: my number's 603-201-1234 easy to remember cuz 1234 lol

Jeremyinsf: thanks

Rickyg9999: call whenever

Jeremyinsf: will do. take care.

Rickyg9999: see ya

Rickyg9999 has closed his chat window.

JEREMY LITTLE

The Full Monte Motel was set up such that the office was simply a small cube of space cut out of an actual motel room. The manager, Robbie Sisco, was only on duty four or five times per week, and when he wasn't at the desk, he didn't stick around. He was technically "on call," but I quickly learned that "calls" were rarely answered, meaning that the person behind the desk had to take on all the managerial duties with no formal support. George Winwood, the guy who'd been working the day I'd met Alyssa, told me that Robbie "managed" by leaving a stack of passive-aggressive Post-it notes on the desk after one of his shifts, then assuming everyone would understand his intentions.

"Worst fucking person I've ever worked for. Pardon my language," he told me.

George was a middle-aged guy, maybe fifty, who constantly wore his pants too high, adding years to his age. Most of his long, sallow face was covered by a big unkempt beard, and he had a habit of scratching his right cheek until small red lines erupted. On day four, after I'd called work and told them I wouldn't be back for another few days, and after I'd played four rounds of gin rummy with Alyssa, I went down to the office, rapped on the window, and found him with crumbs in his beard.

"Well, howdy, mister," he said. Behind him, a thirteen-inch TV/VCR combo played a black-and-white movie. The heroine was someone I should've known, a perfectly coiffed movie star relegated, unfortunately, to my Generation X amnesia. She walked down an elaborate winding staircase in a sparkly evening gown, looking coyly into the camera.

"God, I haven't seen one of those things in forever," I said.

"One of what things?" He scratched at his face and released a few crumbs.

"A VCR. Much less a TV/VCR combo."

"Yeah. Pretty much the only place you're gonna find one." He smiled. I thought, then, that if he just dressed better, perhaps shaved, maybe stood up straight, he could pull off an adjective like "dashing" or "sophisticated." He had a nice smile: it stretched from ear to ear and revealed a straight set of slightly yellowed teeth.

"You guys always this slow?" I said.

"Nah. But this isn't a summer tourist town, you know? We get busy during the school year, 'specially over the holidays. We only got twenty rooms."

"Yeah," I said. "I saw Robbie yesterday. Kinda a stout guy, right? Italian, I'm guessing?"

"Yeah."

"A bit standoffish."

"Moody, I'd say. But Robbie's Robbie, you know? He doesn't know how to run a business. He gets pissed at the smallest problem, thinks everything should go smooth all the time. In the service industry, he thinks this. What shit."

"You hate working for him, right?"

"'Hate' is a strong word, buddy. Don't think I *hate* anything. Do I think he's got some *unorthodox* ways of managing? Yeah, sure." He had a thick New England accent, pronouncing "unorthodox" as *un-ah-tha-dox*. I found it simultaneously charming and disconcerting.

"You said he was the worst manager you'd worked for."

"I guess. But I haven't worked that many places. I've been here twenty years, and yeah, of all the managers, he's the worst so far." *Yee-uhs. Man-a-juhs. Fa.* "Sheila, when she ran the place, she was on top of everything, even did extra advertising. We were *busy* in the summer when she was here. And she treated us well too. Brought everyone out to dinner once a month to show appreciation."

"What happened to her?"

"What happens to everyone who doesn't belong in El Monte Springs. She left."

"I see."

George grabbed the remote off the desk and turned the movie volume down. As his back was to me, he said, "I saw you with Alyssa Graves."

"Yeah?"

"Yeah. You some sort of reporter?"

"Not a reporter."

"I didn't think so." He turned back toward me. His eyes narrowed, then softened. "None of my business really. Shame what happened. Kinda threw this town for a loop. We're not used to that sort of thing here."

"So have you talked much to her?" I said. "Alyssa, I mean. Has she told you how she wants to work here?"

He shrugged. "She's hung out here some, yeah. Robbie pretty much ignores her. Says he doesn't wanna bring that sort of drama here."

"The drama of her brother? Or her pregnancy?"

"Her *brother*. Nobody cares about her pregnancy. Half the women in this town are pregnant. Like all the time."

"How would she be bringing the drama of her brother here?"

"Don't ask me. Just what he said. I wouldn't care if she worked here. Never had a problem with her or her family. Not that I know them at all really, but still."

"So maybe you could help her get a job then."

He rapped his knuckles against the window and scratched his face. "I'm curious," he said.

"Yeah?"

"I mean, you come here, hang out with Alyssa, ask me if I can get her a *job*, but you're just here on business? Wasn't born yesterday, bud."

"You got me."

"So what're you doing here?"

"I'm a graduate student," I said.

"A student? Aren't you a bit old to be in college?"

"Not college. Working on my PhD. Doing my dissertation on school shootings."

"What kind of topic is that—school shootings? And our *shooting* didn't happen in a *school*. You know that."

"My paper focuses on the siblings of the perpetrators."

"Ah. That's why."

"I didn't want to seem intrusive."

"There were reporters everywhere before. All over the place with their cameras. A zoo."

"Yeah, that's why—"

"But a student? That's not so bad. Doing stuff for a university, nothing wrong with that."

"So you could maybe convince Robbie? I mean, try and convince him anyway? Of hiring Alyssa?"

"Why would I want to do that?" He leaned into the window. I smelled tuna. When he smiled, I saw dark between his front two teeth. It dampened his smile's original radiance.

"Listen," I said, stepping back. "I get a stipend from the university. To do research."

"A stipend?"

"Yeah. Not a lot. But I could pay you for your troubles."

"Pay me?"

"Yeah. Let's say . . . hmm . . . three thousand?"

"You wanna pay me three thousand dollars to get Robbie to hire her?"

"Whaddya say?"

"Seriously? And how the hell will her working here help your school research?"

"Listen, offer's on the table." I turned around. "You feel like talking about it, just call my room. I'm beat. Gonna turn in soon."

"You're absolutely serious."

"Have a good night," I said. "Call me later if you want." I walked away. I felt cold, clammy. I sat on the pink chair and watched the phone. It didn't ring. I looked at my cell phone—nothing. I turned the TV on—nothing interesting. I turned it off. I'd never felt so shady, so *ridiculous*, as I did then. I paced a bit, grabbed my deck of cards, shuffled.

An hour passed before the phone rang. George said, "Well, if this helps your academic research . . ." And instead of feeling relief for doing a job well done, I felt immensely tired. I lay on my bed, let myself doze, and was awoken abruptly a few minutes later by a loud pounding on my door.

BRAD "CORKY" MEEKS

I sat there frozen, sure she was gonna see my truck, but she didn't even look in my direction, not once. *What the hell is going on?* I wondered. She tore outta the lot, didn't even look when she went onto the road. Almost ran into this blue jeep. Guy's face said, *Fuck you!* from his window. Had to suppress an urge to follow her home. Definitely wanted to talk to her, ask her what the deal was with that shiny-haired dude. But I couldn't do that in front of her mom, so I just left and went to see Mark.

His mom was there, and Mark—surprise, surprise—was in his bedroom. She said I could go on down. At first, he didn't answer the door, but I knew he was in there, so I knocked a little louder and finally he opened it up. I said, "What the hell, bud. It's just me." He let me in, and he closed the door behind me. "Smells like a goddamn locker room in here," I said. "You showering?"

"I've been drawing," he said.

"Drawing what?"

"Drawing pictures."

"Well, that's good, doin' art," I said. "I've heard good things about that for therapy."

"Wanna see?"

"Sure, man." Guessing it wasn't a good idea to fixate on the smell, but still.

He pulled out a bunch of loose-leaf papers and unfolded them, and damn! The pictures were all just pencil sketches, but they looked real as shit. Still, these things weren't what you wanted to sit and stare at. Talkin' some real disturbing shit: guns, blood, death, brains, the whole works. So as I was lookin' through them, I was thinkin', *Man oh man oh man.*

He said, "I don't wanna keep them. I just did it because it felt okay. But you can take them. I don't wanna see them after I'm done."

Fuck if I wanted a bunch of drawings of a bloody Ricky Graves, but I took 'em anyway, 'cause what else was I gonna do? Just say, *No, Mark, you keep 'em. I don't wanna look at that shit?* Couldn't do that, so I took 'em. And as soon as I did, he looked relieved, as he should've, 'cause I was sure anybody but me would've said, *No, thanks. Good-bye, freak. So long.*

So I took the pictures, folded 'em up, put 'em in my pocket, and then I asked how he was doin', and he said, "A little better. The drawing helps."

"Well, keep it up, then," I said. "If you want, I could collect 'em every week, take 'em off your hands, since you don't wanna keep 'em." Creeped me out something fierce—having a whole booklet of murder-suicide pictures at my place was kinda fucked—but he never said I had to keep 'em, so I could probably burn 'em or, at the least, throw 'em away.

"So your parents say you might start therapy." He nodded but looked at the floor. "It'll be like the drawing," I said, "but just through talkin'. You gotta get all this out of you before you can be . . ." I wasn't sure what the word was. Normal? Sane? Happy? Always had to be careful with Mark. Didn't wanna offend him, 'cause he was goin' through a bunch of shit I couldn't relate to.

Anyhow, I sat on Mark's bed and said, "Listen, be straight up with me, yeah?" And he looked at me like I'd asked him to sit on my fuckin' *lap.* "Be honest," I said. "If you could go back to bein' the same person you were before the whole thing, before everything. You know, back to when you posted the video of Ricky and . . . well, you're different from that now, 'cause, you know . . . so I'm askin', if you could go back to bein' that guy, would you? Answer me straight up."

And he didn't hesitate, just blurted out, "Yes! Obviously! You think I like being like this?"

"No, course not. But—and I'm not judging here—what I'm sayin' is you would be *exactly* like you were. Like a shithead who posts pictures of a kid makin' out with a dog."

"God, you're just like everyone else, like I deserve this." He turned away from me and looked out the window. Kinda felt sorry for him then. He'd gotten so skinny. Not like he wasn't before, but now he was starting to look sick. Was the complete opposite of what I remembered from camp. Back then, he was the star of every sport, one of those dudes the girls whispered about, totally comfortable in his skin but without the fucked-up arrogance of Wesley Thompson. One time—kid was only in seventh grade—I caught him in the woods making out with Bridget Sorenson. They were really goin' at it too. Not like innocent preteen shit, but full-on tongue, hands, etc. I watched them for a sec, not 'cause I was a perv, but because it was just kinda shocking. Both Mark and Ricky'd been in my cabin every summer since fourth grade, and I'd always seen them as the same, like little kids, and Ricky, I *still* saw him like that, couldn't even imagine he'd ever do something as bold as take a girl to the woods. But maybe it wasn't 'cause he didn't want to or wasn't curious about it but because it wasn't an option for him. Mark was different: he was living in a world where making out was a possibility, and watching him and Bridget, I realized that him and Ricky weren't gonna be friends anymore.

"I have a question," I said, feeling suddenly wise and older.

"Okay," Mark said, not looking at me still.

"What's it mean to be a Facebook friend of someone?"

"Huh?"

"I mean, that word, 'friend.' It's different nowadays."

"You talk like you're really old."

"I don't have Facebook. I don't like it."

"Well, if you don't like it, you know what it's about enough not to fuckin' like it."

"Just that word, to me—'friend.' Seems messed-up. Like would you do what you did to Ricky if he was a real friend?"

"I'm tired. Go away."

"Would he have done that to you if you were a real friend? I mean. No. Just seems like the word 'friend' is different now."

Course I was thinking about *Seinfeld* again, that perfect and fuckin' hilarious four-piece friend group. *Could a show like that exist today?* I wondered. *Or was friendship something different, like maybe something less tight?* I wondered about friendship a lot, because all I saw anymore were groups of people together on their phones, like they always wanted to be somewhere else or with someone else. It was creepy to me sometimes, even at work, seeing random coworkers stopped in different places throughout the factory staring at their phones. Like these things had some sort of alien force we couldn't look away from for even a few minutes. Was one reason I never got an iPhone myself. Also, I just didn't care about enough people's lives that much to look them up on the Internet. If I was gonna help someone in the Springs, I was gonna do it in person, not online.

"I can't look at any screens now anyway," Mark said. "I don't give a shit about Facebook friends."

Before I left, I told his mom I thought he was doing better and that I was glad he'd finally agreed to therapy. She was very appreciative—real sweet woman.

"We're really thankful to you," she said by the door. She always dressed like a mom—jeans, sweater, you know. Always had a snack available. "He looks up to you," she said. "And I think he's kinda afraid of you too. It's a good combination for him."

"He's a good kid. Maybe confused a little."

"Well, we appreciate you," she said. She always looked tired. Media was brutal to her. They always blamed mothers.

After, I drove by the Full Monte motel, hoping to get a glimpse of the intruder. I saw a little light from his room—hardly a speck, but something showing me he was there—so I idled in the parking lot and thought of what to do. The guy shouldn't bother me so much, I knew, and Alyssa had her own life to live, and if she wanted to hang out with city visitors, well, I shouldn't be involved. But something about him and that hug gave me the creeps. Plus, Alyssa was all up on hormones due to bein' so pregnant—probably not in the right frame of mind, shouldn't be messed with. So . . .

Truth is, when I thought of her, I got that small feeling in my gut like I did way back when. Not wicked strong or anything, but it was there, like some sort of living animal under my skin. I remembered it being really fuckin' bad when we first met, like so much that I thought for sure she'd think I was some freak; I kept pulling at my shirt and scratching my head like some loony. I'd seen her around before—couldn't help but notice that sorta beauty—but she was just a kid at the time, like fourteen, so I looked from a distance, never really talked, 'til one Saturday night when I was at the Meadows with my good buddy Mason, and we were drinkin' and talkin' and stayin' in our "older" section of the field, which was basically the north section. She was with some friends in the south section, and I didn't usually wander that direction, but that night, Mason had to go talk to his little brother about something, so I followed him.

Turned out his little brother was in Alyssa's friend group, so while Mason was saying some older-brother shit to Benny, I turned to her and said, "Hey, Alyssa." Right away, when her eyes locked on mine, I felt hot all over, like burning up, feverish. That's why I kept pullin' at my shirt. Always thought I was smooth with the ladies, but then? What a goddamn joke I was, and her only being fourteen. Fuckin' pathetic.

"Hi, Corky," she said, brushing her hair with her fingers and taking a sip from her cup.

"Nice night out, eh?" I said.

"Whatever. I guess yeah."

"You havin' fun in school?"

"What?"

"I mean . . ."

"School sucks."

"Yeah, haha. I'm glad I'm done."

"Well, lucky you."

She turned to her friend Cassie, and I thought it was over, like I'd made such a fuckin' fool of myself she'd never talk to me again, but then, like just a minute later, she turned back to me and said, "Hey, you got any weed?" So we ended up back at my apartment—me, her, Cassie, Mason, and Benny. The others, they just huddled around the TV and laughed a whole bunch, but me and her, we talked all night about shit, mostly about what we wanted to do with our lives. She said she wanted to be a nurse, and I was like, fuck yeah, she was the perfect person to take care of people, bein' so warm and considerate and shit, and at like 3 a.m., when everyone else was passed out, I got the courage to kiss her, and she kissed me back, and it was like really fuckin' incredible.

I still felt that hotness all over my body, and it was wicked uncomfortable, but not in the way you'd think, not in like a sickness kinda way, but in a way that made me know that this was something very different from anything I'd ever experienced with any chick before. It was fuckin' *nervousness*, and I, Corky Meeks, didn't *get* nervous. Maybe on edge sometimes, but never nervous. But Alyssa, she made my heart skip a beat every time, so I knew, just *knew*, that I couldn't fuck anything up with her. So I tried real hard to be the perfect boyfriend—catered to her every goddamn need, took care of her brother, her mother, was even nice to her idiot friends. But still, in the end, she left. And I won't lie—her leaving destroyed me.

So I decided in the parking lot that the best course of action was to try to get this dude out of town. If she still wanted to see him after the kid was born, that'd be fine, but not now. Not when she was so pregnant.

So I went to his door, knocked soft for a bit, stopped, listened, heard nothing, then started knocking louder and louder and louder, aggressively. I felt angry, just suddenly outta the blue. So I kept pounding, and then I listened again, feeling sweaty, and I heard footsteps, so I raced back to my truck and got the fuck out. Perfect timing too, 'cause right then that geezer George Winwood came hobbling out of the office, looking to see what's up.

"Get outta town!" I screamed as I peeled out of the lot. Didn't know why I said this since the only person who heard was George, and that wouldn't make any sense.

Anyway, as I was driving down the road, I looked in my rearview mirror and saw the guy's room door open. I could barely make him out, but I thought I saw him shaking a little.

I dunno. I just have a thing about intruders, people coming to the Springs and messing shit up with their total lack of knowledge. For example, this one time, like the day after Ricky killed Wesley and himself, there was this guy all decked out in a shirt and tie—from the city obviously—and he came by my apartment and said, "Brad Meeks?" And I knew he was trouble from the start, 'cause nobody called me Brad but my grandma and maybe some older teachers.

I said, "Who the hell are you?" knowing full well who he was, some news guy wanting to talk to me about Ricky. Fuckin' vulture.

"You were Ricky's camp counselor, right? And his sister's ex-boyfriend?"

And I wanted to ask how some dipwad like him knew that, but then I thought of how everything spread rapid-fire these days.

"I'm busy," I said, and started to shut the door, but he had the nerve to put his hand out, stop me midshut.

"I just wanted to ask a few questions," he said.

So there was the anger, boiling fierce, 'cause he was an outsider trying to infiltrate the Springs, like he knew a damn thing about it. I started pushing him—pushing him hard, pushing him down the hall of my apartment building—and he was stony-faced, no doubt dealing with people who hated him all the time, and he kept asking me questions as I was pushing, like, "Did you see signs of disturbance?" and "Have you been in touch with Alyssa?" and "What was Ricky's relationship with Wesley Thompson?" And we were almost to the stairs and I kept pushing, and I could suddenly see that he was starting to sweat. In my building there was nowhere to escape once you got to the stairwell, and we were at the stairwell. Few more pushes and he'd fall down and crack his neck. Still, he kept facing me—brave fucker—and when we got to the stairs, it took everything I had not to shove his puny ass as hard as I could, watch him split himself down those steps. He looked at me like, *Seriously?* then just shut up. One word and I'd push. One word. But he didn't say anything, so I turned around and went back to my apartment. "Don't fuckin' come back," I said. And when I looked back, he was still there, just staring out at me.

Day after that little incident, I went to see Mrs. Graves. When I got to her house, I had to swim through the reporters. They were everywhere. Vans. People in front of cameras. People pointing. A true circus. One lady all dressed up rushed up to me with a microphone. "Corky Meeks!" she said. "Corky Meeks!" And I didn't care what anybody said: you never got used to strangers knowing your name. I batted her away, felt like pushing her like I did the dude at my apartment, but I stopped myself, because she was a lady. She kept screeching, "Corky! Corky!" so I started running.

I got to the front stoop and knocked real hard on the door. Got nothing for a long time. But then from behind, Mrs. Graves's voice said, "Go away!"

"It's Corky!" I said.

"Corky?"

"Yes. Please open up. They're gonna come up here and try to film me if you don't."

"Corky?"

"Yeah, it's me!"

She opened the door, and I bust in, and goddamn! Looked like a fuckin' *tornado* ripped through the living room. Papers and plates and god-knows-what-else all over the floor. Coffee table turned over. Rocking chair upside-down. Scratches on the sofa, stuffing coming out. And it was dark. Shades were pulled all around the house. Everything was shadowy and creepy.

And Mrs. Graves—I expected bad, but that? She looked eighty. Nightgown totally full of stains, some I didn't wanna know what they were. Hair was sticking up everywhere—looked like she'd just gotten outta the electric chair. When she saw me, she hugged me, and I just held her for a while as she cried and cried and cried, and I'll admit: I shed a few tears too. Who wouldn't? This was my past all around me, unraveled and dirty as fuck, and Mrs. Graves? Seriously, before Ricky's shit, she would've never let herself go like that. That woman had too much pride.

"Corky!" she said, sniffing, holding tight. "Alyssa won't talk to me! I've called her every minute! And she doesn't answer. She won't answer!"

"She'll answer. She will."

"What if she doesn't?"

"She'll answer. Just keep trying."

"She won't! I keep trying!"

"Just keep at it," I said.

Then she stepped back, and it was like everything changed. She got dark, like she remembered something about me. "Oh god," she said. "Why are you here?"

"You shouldn't be alone," I said.

Her face crinkled, and even with the light being so dim, I could see that she wasn't herself; something real bad had taken over. Probably typical of anyone in her situation, but it was still unsettling. She turned away and went to the kitchen, and I followed her. It was even darker there. She was like a silhouette.

"Go away," she said. Hardly saw her mouth moving—it was that dark.

"You need to rest," I said.

"I don't need you here," she said.

"You can't do this alone."

"Do what? There's nothing to do. Go away."

"I understand you haven't cared for me in the past, Mrs. Graves. But I'm honest when I say I wanna be here."

"Jesus, go away, Corky. I don't wanna look at you." She moved to the window and peeked out the curtain. Gray light made her face look kinda claylike, like she was some art molding or something. I had to look away—it was too much.

"I just wanna help."

"Help what? Go."

"I don't want to."

"I don't give a fuck what you want," she said. She closed the curtain, and she became that silhouette again. Kinda creeped me out, so I walked toward the living room, where there was more light.

"Listen," I said. "You need some rest. It looks like you haven't slept."

She sighed and hung her head, didn't say nothing more, just stood there rocking from foot to foot and lookin' down. After a while, she sat down on the floor, leaned up against the cupboard, and crossed her arms over her knees. I went to her and sat down. Her silhouette-head disappeared in her arms. Her hair kinda fell all over the place, so I moved it away from her face.

"I'm waiting for the shock to wear off, Corky," she said into her knees. "It's so fucked, waiting for it, knowing you're in it, the shock. It's so fucked."

I put my hand on her shoulder. It moved a little, like a little jerk, like my hand was cold or something.

"Like everything's a movie or something," she said. "Not real. I can't feel much right now. But I'm trying. I thought Alyssa was gonna help me with . . . but she's not answering. It's just all so fucked." She scratched her knee. "I wrecked my house 'cause I thought it'd make me feel something. Didn't. The fuck is wrong with me. Ricky . . . With my brother, all I did was fucking feel. The whole time. But with Ricky . . ." She looked up.

"You need rest," I said. "You're right. You're in shock. Me too."

"But what if I'm always just in shock? What if I'm in shock forever?"

Couldn't answer that. I didn't know what this was all supposed to feel like or how long it was supposed to last.

"Oh god, just get out," she said.

"Look—"

"Jesus, Corky. Just go."

"I can help out. I'm here to help out."

"Christ. Look at me. You think anything'd help me right now? Just leave. I wanna be alone."

"Whatever you need, I can—"

"I need you to get out."

"Call me later?"

"No."

"I'll be around."

"Please. Just go."

I didn't go. I put my hand on her shoulder again. She brushed it off. So I just sat there with her in the dark for a really long time, listening to her breathe through her mouth. I think she fell asleep at one point, but I'm not sure. When the streetlights came on, she stood up, went to her bedroom, and closed the door. I stayed.

EMAIL CORRESPONDENCE
JULY–AUGUST 2012

From: **Harriet Graves** <harrietgraves4321@ yahoo.com>

To: Victoria Gorham <Victoria@victoriago-rham.com>

Date: July 9, 2012 at 3:52 PM

Subject: Your new book!

Hi Victoria!

It's been so long since I wrote you last, but I was in the grocery store the other day and I saw a copy of your new book right in the check-out aisle! My grocery store doesn't really put books there, so obviously it was something special. I bought it right away. I'm about a quarter of the way through, and seriously it's brilliant. I don't know how one person can have so much wisdom about life! And your only 45? That's what I read on the internet. Wow! You must feel very accomplished.

Like I said I'm only about a quarter of the way through but I really like what you said about goal-driven purposes in life. I like that you aren't just someone who says things like "Chase your dreams." You actually have real suggestions for real people! I'll be honest, now that my son is getting older I'm thinking more about what I want to do with the rest of my life because he'll be gone soon, to college for sure because he's so smart, and then I'll just have this empty house. So I thought maybe I would try to write like you! I mean, I love to write even though I might not be that great at it (forgive my typos!!), and I have experience with raising children, plus raising children with a big gap in their age, AND I haven't really found books that address this issue specifically. So what do you think? You think I have a shot? I think I could help the world with my experiences.

How are things going with you and your children? My daughter is still in Boston, working away and living her life. My son is away at camp. I think the last time I wrote to you I was a little concerned about him, but now I've just accepted how different he is from his sister and I've treated him, like you write about, in his "context." He still hangs out with Corky sometimes, and now a lot of times because he's at camp and Corky's his counselor (I can't remember if I told you that??). He spends a lot of time on the computer nowadays, and since we don't have one at home (I use the computer at work, he thinks it's stupid that we live in a house without a computer, but I think it works out fine right now), he goes to the library. The library is a good place for a kid to be, I think.

Oh, I just can't wait for this adolescence to be over though! I know in Fem-Core you call adolescence some of the most traumatic years not just for the kid but for the parent, and I kind of didn't believe you because Alyssa wasn't so bad. I mean, I'll be honest, she had an abortion and kind of got into trouble sometimes (mostly just drinking though, standard stuff) but I understood her more, I guess. With Ricky it just seems like I reach out and reach out and try and try but hit a brick wall every time. I'm still doing my ten minute head clearing every day, and I keep thinking of his "context," but some days I just want to throw my hands up and say, "Fine, you win!"

I think what bothers me most is that I don't really know if he realizes how much I think about him, how much I love him. I say it a lot and he grunts or says nothing and then just goes into his room or goes to the library. He doesn't really hang out with friends, and when I bring this up he gets very defensive and says how could he have friends in a town like El Monte Springs? I think he finds inner peace when he goes to the library and uses the internet, like he feels connection or something, so I'm saving up to buy him a laptop. It will be a big chunk of money, but it would keep him home more and maybe make him happy. I'm getting with the times, Victoria! I realize that face-to-face stuff isn't cherished as much as it was when I was growing up, hell, even when my daughter was growing up, and even though I think it's not really a good thing, I know I need to adapt (and yes, that is taken directly from The Nine Habits!!!).

So write back when you get a chance. I know your so so busy, probably doing some sort of book tour. I feel a connection to you, seriously, and I love that I can write this and send it to you instantly. I appreciate you and your work so much. It has helped me through a lot.

I hope your summer is going good!

Sincerely,
Harriet Graves

From: **Victoria Gorham** <Victoria@victoriagorham.com>

To: Harriet Graves <harrietgraves4321@ yahoo.com>

Date: July 15, 2012 at 1:22 AM

Subject: Re: Your new book!

Hi Harriet!

It's so great to hear from you! It *has* been a long time! I remember your emails, and I remember our discussion about Corky. It's weird: I *do* get tons of emails (I've hired an assistant to go through a lot of them), but once in a while I find a kindred spirit on here. I know that sounds weird since we haven't exchanged *that* many messages, but when I saw your name in my inbox, my heart did a little happy dance! Strange how connections work!

Your son sounds like a typical teen, although I know in Fem-Core I say there's no such thing. I think I've evolved since then, as evidenced in my new book. I'm not afraid of saying how sometimes clichés contain nuggets of truth. I think when I was younger and just starting out, I was trying to just be so original, and now I'm just more comfortable as both a writer and an experiencer of life and a parent.

I think you should absolutely write! I encourage anyone who wants to write to do it! You seem to have a very unique perception of life and motherhood, and I'd definitely read about it! Who knows? Maybe we'll do a signing somewhere together sometime!

And yes, I, too, have struggled with the technology divide. I love it and I hate it, but the fact is that it's the reality of the world we live in, so how I feel about it isn't going to make it any different. I have mixed feelings about people, especially my children, connecting with strangers online—I know how predatory people can be, especially when they're anonymous—but then again, I think sometimes real, beneficial connections happen! It definitely makes it easier to *find* people with similar interests. Just type a few words, and there you are! Thousands of people who like the same things you do. It's incredible.

I'm sure things will go better with you and your son. Hormones are weird. They'll stabilize soon enough.

So great to hear from you!

All best,
Victoria Gorham

From: **Harriet Graves** <harrietgraves4321@yahoo.com>

To: Victoria Gorham <Victoria@victoriago-rham.com>

Date: July 16, 2012 at 12:25 PM

Subject: Re: Your new book!

Wow, it's so wonderful to hear from you!!! I'm so flattered that you take the time out of your hectic life to write little ol' me an email! And yes, I feel that connection as well! Like I told you, ever since I started reading your books, I just knew we were like you put it, "kindred spirits" (honestly, writing that makes me shiver! I never thought I'd hear from you let alone have you call me something like that!!!).

So this morning I got a phone call from my son (he's at camp remember) and he actually sounded happy. I don't remember the last time he seemed that way! He was telling me about how things were actually going good for him, and how maybe when he got home he'd like to take an archery class or something. He's never been big into sports or anything, but he actually sounded excited about this. This made me excited and so as soon as I got off the phone with him I looked for archery classes in the area. I couldn't really find much but I'm going to keep looking. It's amazing how just that little positivity can make your day!

So like almost right after I hung up with Ricky, my daughter Alyssa called me! We had this really great heart-to-heart, and she of course asked about Ricky, about how he was doing, if he was behaving himself. She's older of course so she has that protective instinct towards him even if she doesn't really stay in contact with him much. Well I told her about my conversation with Ricky and she said it was great and that she really couldn't believe that Corky stayed doing that camp counselor thing but that maybe he was good at it if he could get Ricky to be happy about things. She's a little sour about how much I didn't like Corky when they were dating, but I'm over that now and I told her that and sometimes, I told her, I actually even like him now. She just went silent when I said that.

Anyway, thank you for your encouragement with my writing!! I've seriously given it lots of thought and maybe I'll start on it soon. I want it to be a sort of guide for parents who have kids who are very different in age. I think that situation presents issues that other parenting books don't really address. Do you think it'll be hard to get a publisher? I think maybe I will have to get some professional people to edit for me because of typos and grammar. I'm excited to start!!

I hope your good! Write back whenever you get a chance. I'd love to hear how things are going for you on your tour.

Sincerely,
Harriet Graves

From: **Harriet Graves** <harrietgraves4321@yahoo.com>

To: Victoria Gorham <Victoria@victoriagorham.com>

Date: August 1, 2012 at 2:23 PM

Subject: Re: Your new book!

Hey Victoria!

I hope your not too busy from your tour or anything, but I can imagine it might be pretty hectic. I haven't started my writing yet, but I plan to very soon. You said you would want to read it? Would you let me know what you think if I showed you some of it when I start? I just want to know if I'm on the right track.

So one reason I haven't started writing is because Ricky came back home a week ago and remember when I told you he sounded so happy on the phone at camp? And that I was looking for an archery class? Well, I found one and I told him about it thinking he'd be overjoyed but he scowled and said he wasn't interested and went to his room! Well, I figured something must've happened at camp so I knocked on his door and he didn't open it, but he left it unlocked so I went in and he was on his bed staring at the ceiling with his hands folded across his stomach not listening to music or nothing and when I sat on his bed next to him he didn't move, he was like a statue. I asked him if he was all right like I'd asked him so many times and he didn't say anything, just kept staring at the ceiling. Again, like I've told you before, there's that brick wall, but anyway, this time I felt something different, I don't know, it's hard to explain, like maybe something more than just hormones. It was an awful feeling, like not only was there a brick wall but there was something trying to get through that brick wall and not something nice. Maybe it was how he was grinding his teeth? I don't remember him ever doing that, not when he was a kid, not ever. And his eyes were totally glazed, not like with drugs but with I don't know, like nothing, like no feeling at all, like dead. It gives me shivers just to think about and write about.

Anyway, are these just signs of stress? I know in The Nine Habits you talk about knowing the difference between normal teen angst and something more damaging and you said sometimes it was hard to tell but that periods of long-term isolation were a sign, but I was wondering if it's still a sign even with technology today? I mean, isn't everyone isolated because they just look at their phones and computers? Isn't that pretty normal now?

So I let him be for a bit, and he seemed better after a couple days. He always seemed better after his trips to the library, and that kind of got me to ask for a raise at work. I'm aiming to get him a laptop by Christmas. It's just a little hard because of all the bills and everything, but I think I can make it happen. I've been doing research, and I don't want to get him a cheap one but one that'll last and one that's "cool." I'm leaning toward a Macbook Pro. Do you have any thoughts on that?

So haha I know it's probably nothing but that feeling I just can't shake it, that awful feeling, and I was wondering if you, as the expert, had anything to say about that. I know I didn't describe it very well, the feeling, that is, but I think if you've experienced it you'd probably know.

I hope everything's good for you, kindred spirit!

Sincerely,
Harriet Graves

From: Harriet Graves <harrietgraves4321@
yahoo.com>

To: Victoria Gorham <Victoria@victoriago-
rham.com>

Date: August 12, 2012 at 12:52 PM

Subject: Re: Your new book!

Hey there!

Hope I'm not bugging you with all my emails!
I'm finding that even just writing to you serves
as an inspiration. It's the little things, I guess.
Even if I don't get a response right away, I'm
finding it like therapy to write about some
things in my life this way.

So as you probably guessed from my last
email, my son Ricky has been quite a handful.
Honestly it's a different kind of handful than
Alyssa was. It's not like he gets in trouble at
school. It's more that he just won't talk to me.
For a week now he hasn't said hardly anything
to me, and I keep asking him why he's so mad
but he just shakes his head! I'm also noticing
that maybe he doesn't shower as much as he
should. I think you mentioned in The Nine
Habits that personal hygiene was one of the
most important things for teens, that they
always needed that boost of self-confidence

that comes with looking and feeling clean. Well, he doesn't seem to need it? I work all day, and he's 14. I can't just throw him in the shower! I'm thinking of getting Corky to drop some hints. Do you think that's a good idea?

He's spending more and more time at the library too. He wakes up, maybe eats a little breakfast, and goes there. It's walking distance, so he can walk, and thank god they are on summer hours so he can't be there when I get home from work. But he might as well be since like I said he's mute at home.

Last Saturday I told him I wanted to go with him and he just looked at me with real wide eyes. Then he said that he didn't want me to go, that he liked going alone, and I said I needed to check some books out too so why not go together and he stared some more and said he didn't actually wanna go and went to his room instead. I ended up going by myself not to check out books but to ask one of the librarians, Susan DeVance, about him. I've known her for a bit and she's not really the nicest lady but she's always been okay to me. But anyway, she said that mostly Ricky just sat on the computer and surfed the internet, sometimes wrote things in a little notebook, sometimes actually read books. I asked if she knew what kinds of websites he was surfing and she gave me a hard look and said, "We have parental security blocks, Harriet." Just like that. Rude, don't you think? I didn't even ask about parental security blocks, just what websites he visited. Maybe I was curious what he was looking up for school. She didn't have to assume I was thinking about him looking at porn (though of course that's what I was thinking).

As rude as she was, though, it did put my mind to rest to think that he wasn't looking at sex stuff. But still, I don't know if those parental blocks are 100%. Do you know anything about that? I think when I get Ricky his laptop, I'll have to think about that sort of thing. There are some creepy people out there.

Well, look at me, going on. How's everything going with you? Are you working on something new? I haven't made it through your newest yet just because I've been so busy, but what I've read I've loved!

Sincerely,
Harriet Graves

From: **Victoria Gorham** <Victoria@victoriagorham.com>

To: Harriet Graves <harrietgraves4321@yahoo.com>

Date: August 12, 2012 at 12:53 PM

Subject: Automated Response: Re: Your new book!

I am currently out of the country and will have only limited access to email. If you have questions on bookings or signings, please contact my assistant at Rachel@victoriagorham.com.

Thanks, and happy living!

All best,
Victoria

From: **Harriet Graves** <harrietgraves4321@yahoo.com>

To: Victoria Gorham <Victoria@victoriagorham.com>

Date: August 16, 2012 at 3:45 PM

Subject: Hello!

Hi there! I know your out of the country (you must be doing some research abroad!! Exciting!!) but your automated message didn't say when you'd return, so maybe your back already? Anyway, I just wanted to let you know that I started writing! I'm so excited. I wrote about seven pages. It was a very enlightening experience. I have attached them here. I know it isn't very much, but I just wondered if you thought I was on the right track.

By the way, Ricky's doing better just over the last few days. He's started talking to me again. I asked him if anything happened at camp this year, and he said no. He said he was upset just because he was sick of having to go all the way to the library to do stuff online. I didn't tell him what I had in store for him for Christmas, but I seriously can't wait to see his face in a few months. He's going to be so happy.

I also asked him about Mark McVitry. I don't know if you remember, but he's the kid who Ricky used to play with when he was younger. I just asked why he didn't invite him over anymore, and he shrugged and said he didn't feel like it. My instinct was to pry further, but then I remembered what you said in The Nine Habits and realized that some conversations just didn't need a lot of discussion. I mean, if I thought about it, a lot of my friends from high school aren't my friends now, so it makes sense that friends from elementary wouldn't always carry over. Anyway, I left it alone after that and it seems fine now.

Hope you are having fun in whatever exotic country your in!! Hope to hear from you soon!

From: **Victoria Gorham** <Victoria@victoriagorham.com>

To: Harriet Graves <harrietgraves4321@yahoo.com>

Date: August 16, 2012 at 3:46 PM

Subject: Automated Response: Re: Hello!

I am currently out of the country and will have only limited access to email. If you have questions on bookings or signings, please contact my assistant at Rachel@victoriagorham.com.

Thanks, and happy living!

All best,
Victoria

HALLUCINATIONS, CONQUERORS, AND THE UNRAVELING OF MARK MCVITRY

MARK MCVITRY

It's totally real, this disease, 'cause Mrs. V, she doesn't lie. It's like when something really fuckin' bad happens to you, you can't stop being paranoid about everything, like things are truly lurking around every corner ready to shoot and attack.

Weird thing is, right after, like after I was done with the painkillers and my arm started working right again, I felt fine, like I thought I'd be able to live my life normally. School was canceled for a week, of course, but when it reopened, I went back, and people actually called me a hero; all my teachers gave me good grades on tests, and girls, they wanted to touch my arm. Scooter and Bryan and Grant, they laid off the dick-punching. The weather was perfect, and my parents seemed really proud of my quick recovery. Even the reporters were nice to me, not mentioning the Ricky-Maggie picture at all, so I obviously felt amazing, like indestructible and heroic. I even remember thinking, *Damn. Maybe I should go into the military. Just for this!*

Well, that feeling lasted two weeks. After that, the bathroom incident happened, and from there, everything just got fucked.

So my demise: I was going to the bathroom at school, just standing there at the urinal, when I heard this cough from one of the stalls. I didn't think about it that much, just thought someone was taking a dump or something, but then the cough got louder, and I got chilled, because I knew, just *knew*—I mean, something in my brain *told* me— that it wasn't just some random kid with the runs but *Ricky fuckin'*

Graves. And I stopped peeing, like in the middle, just held it, and ran out of the bathroom, dribbling a bit on my pants. I got out to the front lawn and peed right out in the open, and when I looked up, I saw a whole bunch of faces staring out at me from the school windows.

The principal sent me to Mrs. V's office, and I told her I was fine, that there'd been a line for the urinals and I couldn't hold it. She seemed okay with this answer and I went on with my day, but then, in fifth-period English, while Mrs. Brummer was talking about some boring dead poet, I actually *saw* him. Ricky, I mean. He was standing right behind her, staring wide-eyed at her back while she made all her hand gestures. His face was white and dead. His eyes were these huge black saucers. And he was fuckin' *smiling*. In his hand he had a gun. He pointed it at me and dribbled blood from his mouth. I got so freaked-out I ran out of the classroom and vomited in the hallway.

From then on, everything sucked.

Mrs. V called it "post-traumatic stress"; she said other kids had it too, other kids who'd been at the Meadows, but my case, of course, was way more severe. She said I should stay home from school for a while, try to get some better sleep. She told my parents, and they didn't like the idea, because they had to work; they were both concerned about me being alone in the house when I was obviously suffering from something mental. So they talked about it alone for a little bit and, in the end, decided that Corky Meeks, my old camp counselor at Burroway, would check in on me every once in a while, because he'd, like, *offered*—which was a bit messed-up, since he was Alyssa's ex-boyfriend and heavily connected to the Graveses and used to always take Ricky's side in everything at camp, of course. But none of that seemed to bother my parents, because one day, there he was, like a fuckin' babysitter. I told my mom how I felt, and she just looked at me and said, "He's not a babysitter. Just think of it as someone to help you when you're sick. If you had the flu, we'd do the same thing." I left it at that, 'cause my mom had been through a lot, and people online were still attacking her for some unknown reason.

Well, the first day Corky came over, like in May, two months after I was shot, I didn't really come out of my room, partly because I was pissed that he was around but mostly because my room seemed like a safe enough place. I never heard or saw the Ricky-zombie-thing there. Just everywhere else. I couldn't get him outta my head, and every time I looked out the window, or at the TV, or at my phone, there he was, bloody and smiling and holding his fuckin' gun.

Around noon on that first day, Corky knocked on my door and asked if I needed some food, which I did, but I said, "No," and nothing else. I was always hungry, but food made me sick.

"You gotta eat," he said. "I'll make us some sandwiches." Ten minutes later he knocked on my door again and said, "I'll just leave it out here, okay, bud?" By that time, I was starving, so when he left, I opened the door and took the plate. I only ate like three bites before I started feeling queasy. I left the rest of the sandwich on the plate outside my door and just lay on my bed and listened to some Avenged Sevenfold.

The next day I was a little more restless, having spent all of the previous day in my room, so I went to the living room and sat on the couch and looked out the sliding glass door. I couldn't watch TV or play games, look at my phone, or do pretty much anything because of the Ricky-zombies, so I just stared outside onto our porch, watched a reddish-black bird fly around, tried to clear my head, and prayed Ricky wouldn't pop up in our backyard.

After a few minutes I heard the toilet flush, and then Corky was there with me, sitting in the chair, smiling.

"How you doin'?" he said.

"I'm fine," I said.

"Glad you came out. You hungry?"

I nodded but didn't look at him.

He went to the kitchen and came back with some sandwiches—the same thing he'd made the day before: turkey and Swiss, with some lettuce and tomato and lots of mayo. I took four bites and put the plate on the coffee table.

"Stomach upset?" Corky said.

"Why are you here?" I said.

"You gotta eat."

"I get sick."

"Well, you want coffee?"

I nodded. He went to the kitchen and started the coffeemaker.

"You doin' your schoolwork down there in your room?" he asked.

"Why are you here?" I said.

"Schoolwork? You got some?"

"This is some sort of sick joke, you being here."

It was fuckin' *weird* being with Corky, because of how close he was to the Graveses. And, like I said, whenever shit went down at camp, like when someone played a joke on Ricky, Corky had always assumed I was in on it and gave me hell. I remember one time, he took me aside, like in the woods behind the cabins. This after someone—Louis McGovern, I think—did something dumb like put a dead frog in Ricky's bed or something, and Corky said, "What's wrong with you?"

"Me?" I said. "What do you mean, me? I didn't do anything."

"You and Ricky were tight," Corky said.

"Huh?"

"Just a bit ago, right? Like last year?" he said. His breath came down on me like fuckin' smoke clouds. "You and him were friends. And now?"

"I didn't *do* anything," I said.

"You were laughin' like a guilty person."

"Christ," I said. "You always take his side 'cause of Alyssa."

"I'm not taking any side. I'm just saying, I think as a friend you need to help cut this shit out. You know Ricky's sensitive."

I didn't say anything, just stared at him, angry. He didn't have a right to tell me that I needed to defend Ricky. Ricky'd turned into this total fuckin' weirdo. And yeah, so what if we'd played as kids. We were fuckin' *kids*.

So anyway. I knew Corky really liked the Graveses, took their side on everything, so I couldn't help but think that everything he said to me was kinda hateful, even the "You gotta eat" shit. My head came up with all these ideas, made me wicked paranoid. I kept thinking he was gonna murder me, you know, to get vengeance and finish what Ricky hadn't been able to do. These thoughts freaked me out, so before Corky could set the coffee down, I raced back to my room and stayed there until my parents came home.

Obviously, he didn't murder me. He kept coming over on his days off, and after a while, I kinda looked forward to it. School only had a few more weeks left, and my teachers and Mrs. V said that it wouldn't be worth it for me to go back. This was good, 'cause I couldn't have handled it anyway, but still, I was wicked bored, even with my fucked-up illness. For the most part, I stayed in my room, drew my drawings and hung out, but on the days Corky came over, I came out and we talked. He made coffee, and for some reason I could drink that and not feel queasy. Sandwiches were another fuckin' beast though: I could only eat just a few bites without feeling sick. He kept making 'em, though. Guess it was his babysitting duty or something.

Sometimes we talked about nothing—sports, weather, etc.—and sometimes we just sat. He was always on the rocking chair, and I was always on the couch, looking out onto our patio, thinking about how warm it was getting. Wasn't really exciting, but it beat just sitting around by myself, waiting for the day to end.

"I don't really get this," I said one day. "You keep avoiding my question."

"What question?" he said.

"Why the fuck are you *here*?"

"Why wouldn't I be?"

"Uhh. Duh."

"You don't know anything about me, Mark," he said. "If you did, you wouldn't have to ask such a dumb question."

"You always took Ricky's side."

"I don't take *any* sides," he said. "*You* were in my cabin just as long as Ricky was." He looked away from me. "And Ricky's gone. You're not."

"But you always liked him more!"

"Not true. He just needed more attention. Now let's switch subjects."

The day after this conversation, he didn't make coffee; instead, he said that we should go to the Starbucks on McKinley Road. I totally cramped up, felt like vomiting.

"What, you want me to freak out in public again?" I said.

"Isn't healthy just cooping up in here," he said. I noticed then how ugly the tattoo on his forearm was. It was just these two motorcycles surrounded by red lightning bolts. Lame.

"I'm not *supposed* to leave," I said.

"Who said that? You're seventeen, right? Nearly a full-grown man."

"My parents . . ."

"Your parents don't care if you go to the damn Starbucks for a mocha."

"Why do you wanna go anyway?"

"Just told you. Feeling a bit cooped."

"Well, I feel fine."

"You can't stay in the house forever."

"Dude, who said anything about forever? I just don't wanna go."

"Come on."

"I'm getting tired."

"It's one in the afternoon."

"So? I'm getting tired."

He threw his hands in the air. "Fine."

"Fine what?"

"Go back to your goddamn room. Hide out some more."

"I just said I'm tired."

"You're not fuckin' tired," he said.

And I wasn't tired, but I went to my room anyway. Wasn't about to get bullied into going to the Starbucks. Wouldn't give him the pleasure of a fuckin' freak show. I didn't even *like* Starbucks, hadn't even liked coffee 'til Corky started making me drink it with him. And who knew—maybe he'd gotten me addicted. Maybe he was like a pusher, except with coffee. He was trying to get me hooked, first on just the Folgers shit we had in the house, then on the more upscale Starbucks. Before you knew it, there I was, all strung out, needing my caffeine fix, looking like some homeless dude all dirty and crazy, just hanging out in Starbucks 24/7.

But then the next day—ha!—he got me to go. I just gave in like some spineless fuckin' baby. He said, "Let's go," and I said, "Fine." Just like that. Jesus!

The first steps were pretty bad. Just leaving the house, closing the door behind me, I felt like I was at this place where I couldn't go back, like the door would just lock forever.

"Fuck. I can't," I said. But Corky was already to his truck, and the front door was closed behind me, so what was I gonna do? I half closed my eyes because I didn't want to look at the trees. Then I walked.

The drive itself didn't do much because I closed my eyes the whole time. I told Corky I was tired, and he just grunted. My head was all sweaty. I told him five times to turn around and go back. He said I'd be fine.

When we actually got to the Starbucks, I started thinking I'd be okay. Nothing bad had happened yet—my eyes had been closed, sure, but I was still outside, wasn't I?—and I really did want some coffee. So when Corky opened the door for me, escorted me in, I thought,

I'm okay now. I'm not nuts anymore. I thought about going back to school, getting that hero's welcome again, everyone loving me and being proud—what a fucking comeback! Two in a row! School was almost out, so it'd be a huge surprise for everyone to see me well. No mental shit, no cast, nothing. Would probably get me laid. A nice thought.

But then, of course, as soon as I walked in and looked behind the counter, there was Ricky—eyes and forehead dripping in blood, staring like a corpse at all the customers. I blinked real hard, shook my head real fast, told myself, *Not real not real not real.* But when I opened my eyes again, he was still there, staring at me. There was even more blood than usual, blood not only on him but on all the other workers, and he looked at me through all the blood, some of it going into his mouth, and smiled. His teeth were black, and his eyes were red. He lifted his arm and showed me the gun, and then he raced around the counter while all the other workers just moved like zombies, and then he rushed toward me like a speed freak, and I saw the worms in his mouth and the skull bones in his hair and the blood in his eyes, and I just acted on instinct: I grabbed his neck and squeezed as hard as I could.

Well, turned out I was choking this sophomore kid I actually knew, Larry Levine, and Corky was pushing us apart, and everyone in the Starbucks was staring. When Ricky disappeared and I saw it was Larry, I just gaped at him for a long-ass time. What else could I do? Finally, I said, "Sorry," then I looked at Corky, whose mouth was wide open. I aimed for his jaw, but missed and punched his shoulder instead. Then I ran back to his truck and closed my eyes, thought about being dead.

A little over a month later, like in July, I told my parents I'd see a shrink, because my mom started bawling and she never bawled. We were having dinner silently, like usual, and she suddenly couldn't control herself, wept right there into her chicken, and didn't leave or try to hide it, and my dad just stared at her for a while, then put a hand on her back. I asked her what was wrong, and she didn't say anything, just kept bawling, shaking her head. I didn't know what to do, so I just said, "I'm sorry, I'm sorry, I'm sorry," and she didn't respond, just kept crying.

"I'll go see Dr. Huntington," I said, and though this didn't really stop her crying, it made it calmer.

My dad shook his head and stood up. Before he left, he put a hand on my shoulder and squeezed.

So I decided before I went in to see the shrink that I'd only tell him about certain things: (1) my hallucinations, (2) my dreams, and (3) my episode in Starbucks. I wouldn't tell him about my drawings—he didn't need to know about them. Thing was, they were all I'd been doing down in my room and they made me feel good. But in a bad kind of way, like a wrong way maybe, because I could draw Ricky however I wanted, with whatever combo of bones and blood and intestines, and I usually went the brutal route, because I hated him so fuckin' much. And I knew the doc would want to know why I drew *him* of all people when I kept hallucinating him, and it was just something I didn't feel like explaining, especially to a serious professional dude. Basically, the drawings made me feel kinda powerful, in control of shit finally, and I guess since Ricky was the one who'd taken everything away, they allowed me to destroy him over and over and over.

It took a while to get my first appointment, and it ended up being on the day after I gave Corky a bunch of my drawings, so I was thinking about them hard, wondering what he'd done with them. When I got into Huntington's office, then, I was really nervous, 'cause they were all I was thinking about, and I couldn't really answer his questions at first, because I was obsessed with not revealing anything about them.

I tried to focus on the room, which was kinda plush, not what I expected. The big-ass chair I was in was actually comfortable, cushiony: my arms were resting a little above where they normally would, because

I was sinking down into the seat. His chair didn't look as comfortable, but more formal. Leather and wheels. Like a big office chair. The room was a perfect temperature, which made me think that someone constantly monitored the AC to make sure that everyone who came in was comfortable. And there was a lot of space, just floor with grayish carpeting, and this made the room look a lot bigger. I liked it there. Could see myself sleeping there if it came down to it. Plus, Ricky was nowhere in sight.

"You can feel free to tell me whatever you want," he said. "You don't have to say anything you don't want to."

I'd known Dr. Huntington since I was in elementary school. Him and my dad went to high school together, and once in a while they went out and played golf or had beers. He'd always seemed like a good enough guy, not like some of my parents' other friends, who always socked me in the shoulder and teased me about girls. Hated that shit.

"I saw him twice on the way here," I told him.

"Saw who?"

"Ricky."

"You saw Ricky."

"Yes. I see him every day."

"Where do you see him?"

"Wherever. Not in my house, but when I look outside sometimes, he's poking his head out from behind trees. I'll be honest—it was hard to even come here. Haven't been out since Starbucks with Corky."

"When you hallucinated Ricky behind the counter."

"Yeah."

"That must've been really difficult for you."

"Wasn't fun."

"But you're here now, so you got out again, and from what I can tell, you're not hallucinating."

"I'm okay right now."

"But you're afraid he might show up."

170

"Sure. I'm always afraid of that."

I suppose since he dealt with loonies all the time, nothing really surprised him. Plus, everyone knew I hallucinated Ricky. Since my time in Starbucks, the whole town knew I was a fuckin' freak. Sometimes if my parents had friends over—which was rare, after everything—they'd look at me with this I'm-so-sorry look, their faces trying so fuckin' hard to not be judgy. And I hated it, 'cause I didn't need anyone's pity; I just needed to get rid of all this shit and get back to how things were.

"So what does he look like," he asked, "when you see him?"

"Bloody. Freaky," I said.

"Anything else? Like can you perhaps read an emotion on his face?"

"I try not to look too hard."

"That's understandable."

"The few times I did, though, he looked upset."

"Upset?"

"Pissed."

"Angry."

"Yeah."

He tapped his pen on his notebook and looked past me toward the wall. He was a weird-looking dude, really pointy—like his nose and cheeks and chin were all trying to form isosceles angles or something. He didn't wear glasses, but he looked like he should, just to complete the shrink look. He wasn't that tall, but he had these wicked long legs, so I guess that made him seem taller, especially when he was sitting.

So he talked a little about PTSD and said I needed to think of *that day*—as if I hadn't thought about it every fuckin' day since. Basically, he said that there was no real way to cure it, that he didn't want to prescribe me meds either, but that he hoped our sessions would help me get through it. Understandably, I was like, *WTF? No real way to cure it?* What was *that* bullshit? What was the point of talking to him if he wasn't gonna help me get rid of it? I asked him if it'd end, and he said that everything eventually ends, and I didn't like that, 'cause it was like he was saying that it'd end when I was dead, and I didn't plan on dying any time soon.

So since my first freak-out, my friends just dropped off the face of the earth. Not like they were total jackasses or anything, but they didn't even fuckin' *visit*. And whenever I tried calling Bryan or Grant, I'd just get voice mail. It was fuckin' *enraging*.

When I got home after the first Dr. Huntington session, then, I was really surprised to get a call from Claire Chang. She's this sorta hot Asian girl who sometimes hung out at the Meadows but mostly hung out with people I wasn't friends with. She said she was calling because she'd been thinking about me, hoping I was okay. Which was weird shit—it wasn't like we were ever tight. We had fourth-period Algebra II together, and she sat next to me, and I guess I saw her down at the Meadows a few times, but mostly, like I said, she hung out with other people.

"I'm okay," I told her.

"I've heard you've been out more," she said, and I kinda dug the way she talked. It sounded happy.

"Yeah. Not a whole lot, but some."

She didn't talk for a while, and I wondered if she just put the phone down. (She was a bit crazy herself. Like one time in Algebra II, she finished her test, then cut each of the corners off her paper, and with those four little triangles she made this pointy-shaped thing, kinda like a puffball, but spikier and littler.) Then I heard her sigh, and she said, "I know it's probably a little weird, me calling you, but I'm serious about thinking about you and everything. Those last weeks in algebra with you gone, it was like *weird*. And I know how weird that sounds, and this is gonna sound even weirder, but you missing actually affected me more than the whole shooting itself. I mean, I guess it's all connected, but you know what I mean. So for a long time, I wondered why it affected me so much, like was it just a reminder? Maybe. But anyway, it literally took me this long to call you because I was just trying to process it. But I'm glad I called and I'm glad you're doing better, and if you need anything, I'm pretty free this summer, only working part-time."

So here was the other crazy thing: Claire was really grossed-out by the Ricky-Maggie picture. I remembered, right after it was posted, she didn't even look at me for a week, and sometimes she even looked away, like she was disgusted by my fuckin' presence. I asked her about it and told her it wasn't a big deal—just a guy kissing a dog, saw it all the time on the Internet—but she didn't respond, just shook her head, like I was the biggest asshole she'd met. I mean, a lot of girls thought it was gross, but for some reason I thought Claire would think it was funny. Wrong about that!

When I hung up, I took out my sketch pad and drew Claire instead of Ricky. I gave her hoop earrings, though she didn't wear them. I also made her wear a dress, and I'd never seen her in anything but jeans or shorts. She had long black hair, kinda fat lips, skinny eyes, small tits. She was thin, but not anorexic. Her skin looked really soft, and I made it look soft in the drawing with different shading. She was sexy, but I guess until I drew her I didn't realize how sexy.

When I was done, I held her picture next to one of a bloody Ricky and thought, *I like the one of her better.* So I drew her again, this time putting Ricky in the background behind a tree, looking out, bleeding.

CLAIRE CHANG

Okay—I was only ever friends with Ricky on Facebook. So sue me, right? I mean, it wasn't even *that much* of a Facebook friendship. Like we never posted shit on each other's walls or even commented on each other's statuses, but we messaged once in a while, like private-messaged, and sometimes we "liked" each other's stuff—mostly him liking *my* stuff, but every once in a while, I'd think some inspirational meme or pet video he posted was kinda awesome and I'd "like" it. Poor guy never really got that many likes on things, so I helped him out once in a while, and I think he appreciated it, 'cause he'd message me to thank me for liking something.

But whatever.

I mean, our messages to each other were literally the most boring things you could think of. Like once in a while he'd say, What's up? and I'd just be like, Uh I'm in class obvi cuz so are you, and he'd respond, Haha yeah I know. I mean, that was seriously his idea of a good convo, I think, and I guess other people'd be annoyed by it, but I wasn't. It was just him being his dork self, so whatever—what did I care? I wasn't gonna be *mean* about it, like so many other kids at school, calling him all those really cruel names. I was evolved, you know? I could be friendly with *anyone*.

But then, I guess he thought our Facebook messages were like real life, because one time he sat with me and my friends at lunch and acted like we were besties or something, and my friends, especially Julie

Emerson, snickered and outright turned away from him, like he literally had some disease you could catch from his breath. And even though it was wicked rude of them, my mind was spinning, because, I mean, I wanted to be with my friends without him there, but I didn't know how to tell him that. Anyway, that lunch thing only happened once, 'cause he got the idea after that and didn't sit with us again, which made me feel bad, so I Facebook-messaged him and said, **Hey sorry about Julie and them they're assholes sometimes,** and he responded, **Its cool.** But I knew it *wasn't* cool, because he kinda looked away from me in the halls for a few days after that. I didn't know why he'd wanna sit by a bunch of dumb girls anyway; it wasn't like we had the best conversations or whatever. Mostly we spent a lot of our lunch on our phones, catching up on posts and tweets and pics and selfies, 'cause we weren't supposed to have phones out in class (even though we did, obv.) And there were some times when we didn't even exchange any sort of words to each other, just ate and typed, and sometimes we didn't even eat but just typed, 'cause that's how things were.

Well, after a while, Ricky got back to normal with messaging me, got over the little lunchtime shit, but the messages were different, like not just the normal **What's up?** but maybe a little more deep? Like about love? Which was soooooo weird because—WTF?? Love? I thought maybe he was like trying to tell me he liked me at first, but then Julie reassured me that wasn't the case, 'cause everyone knew he was gay.

Well then why would he wanna talk about love shit???? I texted her.

I dunno maybe he's like gonna come out to you or something tell you he likes to butt fuck lol, she texted back.

Gross, I texted.

But still, she got me thinking that maybe I *was* the person Ricky was gonna come out to, and I guess for a hot minute I felt honored? Like that's a huge deal, and for him to pick me, even though I wasn't really much of a friend in real life . . .

So anyway, his messages were like asking advice or whatever. Like how did someone know if they were in love, like what actually happened? And I responded as best I could, even though I wasn't sure if my answers were correct. I could just go on the experience I had with John Bloom.

John Bloom. He was this new kid from somewhere in Western Mass. Only at our school for a year before he went back to living with his dad out there. Quiet, played guitar, kinda scraggly hair, skinny, beautiful beautiful beautiful beautiful beautiful beautiful!!!!! Brown eyes that looked both sad and alive. Never saw anything like them in my life. Every time I saw him, it was like all my organs literally flipped over, kinda like flipping an egg in a frying pan. And since we passed each other in the halls all the time, by the end of the day I was literally depleted.

He smiled at me all the time too, like we both shared this incredibly secret secret of my insides flipping around (stomach, lungs, kidneys, liver, intestines <ew>, *heart*) but we didn't talk for most of the year, just passed each other and smiled. I didn't really see him with many people. He must've thought that because he was only going to be there for a year it wasn't worth getting a group of friends. (And seriously, who'd want a bunch of El Monte Springs friends anyway? Soooo lame.)

But one time I saw him walking with Chris Winters, and Chris and I had been friends since god knows when, so I texted him—Chris—one day and I said, **U WERE WITH JOHN BLOOM?!?!** And he responded, **Yeah so?** Of course he was trying to play it cool, 'cause he knew how much I was into John, but I could see through him—always could. He was actually one of the only people I told about my crush. (I didn't tell a lot of that shit to my girlfriends anymore, 'cause they were so quick to post shit and embarrass me.) So I told him he had to come to my house after school and tell me everything. He replied that he was busy and that we'd just have to meet another time. I was pretty sure it was a lie, a cover-up, because he hated coming over, thought it was weird my mom and dad collected so much stuff (literal hoarders, my parents), so instead I suggested we go to the diner for dinner, my treat. He liked that idea and was suddenly not busy. The way to Chris Winters was through his stomach.

So we went to the diner, and he ordered, seriously, like three meals—a salad, soup, *and* a burger—and I had to check my wallet just to make sure I actually had enough money on me, 'cause my debit card had like ten bucks on it. Well, I had like forty dollars cash, so I was good, since I only got a slice of apple pie. So on his second course—the salad, which wasn't like a normal side salad but seriously *overflowing* with chicken and bacon—I was like, "So? What's he like to hang out with?"

He just stuffed his face more and chewed really loudly and didn't say anything, so I told him I'd leave right then, make him pay for everything if he didn't start spilling. So then he was like, "What do you even wanna know, Chang? He's just a dude. Normal enough. Wicked good at guitar."

"You jammed with him?"

"Yeah, just a bit. He's been taking lessons since he was like five or something. Was in a band before, but quit it when he moved up here."

"What kind of band?"

"Rock band. Sometimes did Zeppelin covers, I guess."

"That's amazing."

"What's amazing about it? Everyone's in a fucking band."

"What? Seriously, nobody's in bands nowadays."

"Well, it seems that way anyway."

"God, Chris, you don't know anything about anything."

People *always* asked us why we weren't a couple, me and Chris, and, god knows, if I'd let him, we'd've been screwing every night. At the Meadows when he was drunk, he sometimes said how much he was into me, but then the next day he was back to being like my brother, and that was fine. Was never ever gonna cross that line. Chris just wasn't my type, and he knew it. I didn't like pudge or even stocky. Muscles weren't my thing. I liked tall. Skinny. Mysterious. JOHN BLOOM.

"You shouldn't eat so fast," I said, 'cause like watching him eat his burger was literally making me queasy. He had zero manners, and during one bite all this ketchup spilled out onto his shirt and he didn't even wipe it, so I leaned over and did it for him, like his fucking *mom*.

"I'm hungry," he said.

"So what else about him?" I said. "He's in a band? And what else?"

"I dunno. His mom's up here, but he's only gonna live with her for a year then go back to Mass."

"And he doesn't have a girlfriend down there, right?"

"Not that I know of. We didn't talk much about that."

"Well, get the scoop."

"You want me to tell him you like him?"

"No! Don't you dare."

"Well, what's this about then?"

"I'm just asking questions, that's all."

"I don't know why you can't just be honest."

"Well, maybe you can slip me into the convo sometime."

"Like what?"

"I dunno. Whatever. You're not *that* dumb. You can figure out a way."

He shrugged and said, "Fine."

So like a whole week went by and I was crapping my pants, because I didn't hear anything from Chris. But then *finally* I got a text saying that he talked to John about me, and I felt like I was having a heart attack (!), like I was sweaty and I could hardly hold my phone still. *This is what love is!* I kept thinking. *Madness! Madness! Madness!* By then, I was seriously writing love notes to John every night, closing my eyes and imagining us on a date—him leaning in to kiss me and not caring about what everyone else saw, and then, after the most amazing kiss *ever*, him ASKING ME TO MOVE WITH HIM TO MASS!!! saying, "We'll just graduate there. It'll be great."

Anyway, I seriously should've left it all alone, 'cause I just wasn't ready for the response. Chris texted, U sure u wanna know? And I was like, Of course duh, my heart literally in my throat. Then he texted, He says he's just not into the whole Asian girl thing. I told him he's a fuckin loser to say that.

And how the fuck was I supposed to respond to that???? I just kept staring at my phone, thinking, *This is a joke. This is a nasty, nasty joke.* Sure, people liked to make fun of my Asian-ness—it happened in a town so white—but I never, ever pegged John to be a person who would ever say anything about it; he just seemed so *beyond* it. And meanwhile, I was still in love!! Meanwhile, I was still thinking about rushing home and writing him another letter! Meanwhile, I was still picturing me away from my dumb family, going to high school in Mass!

After a long time, I texted, He's making a dumb joke obvi. Chris didn't text back, but I saw him after school—worst day of my *life*—and he pulled me aside in the parking lot and said that I should just leave it alone.

"Leave what alone?" I said. "It's not like we're even together. We haven't even really talked, except maybe a couple times."

"Just . . . he's not what you think he is. I don't think he's that nice of a person, if you know what I mean."

"Well, whatever."

I walked away, trying to look confident in my rejection, but inside, my heart was a complete and utter mess, sometimes splitting in two (maybe even three) and other times still soaring and flipping in joy, like there was still a chance.

Time happened, of course, and over the next few days I changed, got so sad I just didn't talk to anyone. And after that sadness left, I got angry, and then I was angry like *24/7*, and I lashed out at my parents and my friends, and especially Chris—who eventually just stopped texting and talking to me, and I had all these terrible, terrible thoughts every time I saw John Bloom in the hallways, but still, the thing was, mad as I was, I WAS STILL IN LOVE.

All that messed-up emotion, of course, led me to Conquerors.com and Alexandra B, and that ultimately led me to my Mark McVitry plan. But first, before that, before Ricky's shooting, I messaged Ricky and just spilled everything about John Bloom and how love was literally the most evil emotion and that he was better off not thinking about it, because it'd just hurt. He just said, I totally understand I feel the same emotions and I think it's from the other side too. And at first, I didn't understand what he meant by "from the other side," but then I thought about it and realized he meant it was reciprocated, like whoever it was loved him too, which made me real curious, because honestly, this was Ricky Graves. I mean, like I hated to be mean, but . . .

I asked him if he'd be willing to tell me who the "other side" was, and it literally took him like two days to respond, but he did respond. And when he did, it like totally made my stomach drop to the floor.

WESLEY THOMPSON, was his message.

Now look: Everyone knew Wesley Thompson was this raging asshole, like a dude who actually made fun of a girl for having *cancer*, but for some reason, he had like a tight-knit group of friends, and they followed him around like fuckin' *puppies*. This group was always up to something, like playing practical jokes at other people's expense, and Wesley, he was just rotten, rotten, rotten, and I didn't understand how Ricky couldn't see that. Like seriously? Did he think Wesley was being real about anything he might've said? But then, the guy did have that wicked charm streak, like totally got girls and everything, but anyone with half a brain knew he was just a player in that regard too.

Anyway. First, Ricky had come out to me!!! This was pretty outstanding, but to be totally honest, I didn't feel as honored as I thought I would—maybe because of Wesley Thompson being involved—but for a little while I *was* able to think of myself as pretty special in someone's life, even if it was Ricky Graves's life. But whatever—it was still a huge deal. So I messaged, You're gay? As if it was some big shock or something, even though everyone basically knew. He didn't respond for a while, but finally I heard my phone vibrate, and his message said, I guess so.

And when he said that, I seriously wanted to throw him some sort of coming-out party. Like didn't that happen sometimes? I mean, not like I'd ever have done it, but it crossed my mind right away, 'cause it seemed like it'd be fun. But anyway, after it sank in that he'd told me like literally the most intimate thing about himself, I thought about Wesley Thompson and was just like, *This is not good.* Obviously, Wesley was playing him, and who knew what he was going to do. Like who knew what kind of sick, cruel prank he was gonna play. So I wrote Ricky back and said, I don't think Wesley is gay, and he responded, He's having a difficult time with it like me.

So that was the angle Wesley was taking: pretending that he was struggling with his sexuality. Which was completely and utterly WRONG when there was *actually* a person struggling with it. But then, this was Wesley we were talking about. Jesus.

I kinda wanted to tell Ricky to wake the fuck up, like seriously, hadn't he been around the last three years? Hadn't he *seen* what that fucktard had done? But I didn't, because part of me just thought it was up to Ricky to learn this shit for himself. So I said, Just be careful k? And he didn't like respond for three whole days, and when he did it was just a K, which basically meant he was pissed at me for even thinking it could be anything but true love or whatever.

So after that, I did a little Facebook/Twitter stalking and looked at what both Wesley and Ricky had posted, and it wasn't really anything that exciting, just some dumb videos: Wesley's of the *Jackass* variety, of course, and Ricky's more like pets and animals or whatever—nothing special. But what I did notice was that Wesley had "liked" a ton of Ricky's stuff, like within the past month, so I was guessing the prank thing had been thought of about a month before, "conceptualized," as Mr. Briggs liked to say in social studies class.

Well, whatever. I mean who the fuck knew what was going on in Wesley's dumbass head. I didn't think I could actually stop anything, because, well, I just couldn't. I didn't have that sort of power or influence in school. And plus, I had my own shit to deal with—mostly my anger, which was literally growing by the minute.

See, I was mostly a laid-back chick, right? Like I didn't rock the boat, make waves or whatever, did all right in classes, paid attention for the most part. But that whole thing with John Bloom, him saying that he just wasn't into "the Asian girl thing," that really got me going—like really, REALLY got me going. Because, like I said earlier, I'd had that kind of comment before, I guess, but it'd never been from someone I COMPLETELY AND UTTERLY LOVED!! So it was devastating, and just fueled this hatred, anger. Like I started seeing things in a different light, like in a light that was really fucking unfair to people who weren't white. That privilege shit that Mr. Briggs talked about in class, well, it started to make sense, and my eyes, they opened to all the goddamn injustice in the world, and I started paying attention to the news and seeing it firsthand like *everywhere,* and all of it just felt so awful and disgusting that I needed some sort of outlet to voice my frustration. So I did a search online for social justice groups and found Conquerors.com, a group that said it was "dedicated to broad social justice awareness." They wanted to "conquer" racism, sexism, xenophobia, transphobia, and homophobia, and I thought that was really good (though I wasn't really sure what "xenophobia" meant), so I contacted them and said I wanted to get involved somehow.

Well, how they did it was if you wanted to volunteer, you had to first go through this mentorship thing, like you had to have these discussions with a "seasoned" person, whatever that meant. They basically wanted to get the lowdown on why you were interested in the organization, which was a little dumb, because, um, obviously: conquer racism?

Pretty simple. But anyway, they paired me with this woman Alexandra B, and she was wicked cool. She'd gone through all this hardship with really shitty men but had literally overcome it all and had found a really great home with the Conquerors. I asked what she meant by "home," since as far as I knew the Conquerors was just online or whatever, and she responded, via email:

> *I have developed my most lasting relation-*
> *ships online, and sometimes, when I'm*
> *in the same location as a mentee, I meet*
> *face-to-face.*

She was in Seattle, so I didn't think I was gonna meet face-to-face with her any time soon, but she said she came east sometimes and there were rallies everywhere, so maybe in the future . . .

Well, anyway, I downloaded the Conquerors app to my phone so I could chat with Alexandra B whenever, and we swapped photos, and it was then that I saw that she was black and had this really nasty-looking scar that ran from her right eye all the way down to her lip. And of course I didn't ask about it right away, but thank *god* she brought it up, because I was literally screaming inside, wanting to know how she got it. Anyway, apparently it was from an old boyfriend (!). He'd gotten drunk a lot and was usually pretty nice, even intoxicated, but one day he just flipped and sliced her fucking *face*! Needless to say they weren't together anymore, and he went to jail for a while.

I still have feelings for him, she texted. Isn't that something?

I told her it wasn't that weird to me, given my situation with John Bloom, and she said she thought we'd have a great working relationship together. I said, Yeah, but I was all hesitant, 'cause I didn't know what she meant by "working relationship"—since I wasn't getting paid or anything and I didn't really even know what I was getting into with the Conquerors, only knew that I believed in their mission and I wanted to be involved. I also admired everything on their Twitter feed. Like they had some awesome true statements about oppression and fighting white supremacy and ending straight white cis patriarchy. (I had to ask what "cis" and "patriarchy" meant, so good thing Alexandra B was good at explaining and being patient.) And for the first time in my life, I felt like something, like a part of something big, like *involved in a cause*, and there's something very amazing about that feeling. It's like, suddenly, you make a difference. Suddenly, you matter.

So anyway, Alexandra B was such a sweetheart to me, always telling me I looked so pretty in my pics and just complimenting my smartness all the time, and she had these terrific insights about the world, about seeing the world from the eyes of the "marginalized," as she put it. I loved how she wrote, so smart and educated, and when we talked on the phone, her voice was like a really sweet mother's, like a mother who's constantly rocking her kid to sleep or something. And seriously, I literally went on and on and on about John Bloom, and she listened to everything I said and came back with really nice responses, saying everything I felt was normal and that time would eventually heal me, but time takes time. And I thought that was so smart that I posted it as a status—Time takes time—and got like thirty likes.

She also was *very interested* in my situation—like what it was like being a Chinese girl in El Monte Springs, like what sort of "microaggressions" I regularly faced. And she'd give me these tasks—like go through the day and just count all the times I felt I was treated different because of my race; it could be as small as someone staring or as big as someone calling me some racist name, but they all mattered. And one day I came up with over fifty, and I immediately texted her and was like, Some of them come from people I call friends!!! Well, noticing all that, I started to pull away more from everyone, because I just kept seeing it everywhere—like the way Julie Emerson said she wished she could have "such straight Asian hair" and how Kaley Gordon said "Asian food" wasn't her thing, like there was only one kind of Asian food. Even my guy bestie, Chris Winters, said things about my body, making it racialized. It was just so much!

Wow! I texted. My eyes have been opened!!

A big thing after we talked about microaggressions was this idea that we needed to not just be so tunnel-visioned with our own oppression that we didn't see the oppression of others, meaning that it was so, so important, according to Alexandra B, that we were *cohesive*, that we weren't blind to the struggles of other marginalized groups. And it was all this talk—talk of looking *outside* myself to others—that brought me back to the subject of Ricky Graves.

MARK MCVITRY

After Claire's call and after I drew her, I felt better. Not totally, but better than I had in a long fuckin' time. I guess that needs some clarifying. Before I started drawing her, I didn't feel sick, just nervous all the time. Kinda like when you're watching some creepy horror movie and you know the killer's gonna strike, but only music is playing, or maybe it's just dead silence. Or if you're on a roller coaster and you're going up real slow, you know, the anticipation shit. Well, before Claire's call, I was feeling that all the time, scared of the next time I'd see the ghost-Ricky again. The drawing helped a little bit, but just a little. Maybe like when you're at the very top of the roller coaster but haven't gone down yet. It was like Claire's call was the killer jumping out or the plummet down the coaster, and afterward I was still terrified but felt okay, like it wasn't all completely unknown anymore.

So during my next appointment with Dr. Huntington, I told him about her. First, I told him that she was never a big part of my life to begin with. Then I told him it was strange that she'd called and made me feel better. After that, I told him about the roller coaster–slash–horror movie thing, and he nodded, said it was interesting. After that, he told me I needed to start thinking about the incident more, that I was *avoiding*. And that made me wicked pissed, 'cause I'd just told him about a breakthrough, this after just one day of seeing him, and all he cared about was me reliving that night, which was stupid. Like was that some sort of thing in psychology? Like if you had something that affected you so bad you were supposed to relive it? Seemed to me that if you were trying to get over something, you should do the opposite, like forget it. But he pressed on and on, so what could I do.

"I've gone over it a million times," I told him.

"Make it a million and one then," he said.

"You know what happened."

"You need to discuss specifically. Close your eyes."

I felt like he was really impatient, but I had no idea why. We'd only had that one session, and he'd told me I didn't have to say anything I didn't want. But whatever. I closed my eyes.

"It's February," he said. "Unseasonably warm, yes?"

"What? It happened in Mar—"

"It's February 28," he said, and his voice was stern, like my dad's. "It's unseasonably warm. It's Saturday night. You're at the Meadows."

Oh fuck. *That*. I opened my eyes.

"Close your eyes," Dr. Huntington said.

"What for? *You* wanna blame me for it all too?"

"Let's just do this. Humor me."

"Humor you?"

"It may not seem like it, but I'm trying to help."

"I thought I just talk about whatever here. I wanna talk about Claire."

"After," he said. "Let's just try this. Yes?"

"I really don't wanna talk about that."

"Just for a bit, okay? Just a little while. Not extensive."

"And what if I don't?"

"I guess I can't make you. But I'd be disappointed."

"Would you tell my parents?"

"I can't tell your parents much of anything."

"So you wanna talk about that."

"I would."

"There's not much to talk about."

"Well, let's try. Shall we?"

"It's not that great of a story, as you know."

"Humor me."

"Jesus."

So I decided to "humor" him. I don't know why. I guess part of me thought that if I didn't, my parents would find out, and even though that wouldn't be so terrible, I'd already disappointed them enough. So I closed my eyes again.

Anyway, it was widely known that Ricky Graves was a fag—I mean, that he was gay—and that he had a huge fuckin' crush on Wesley. He never hid it. Everyone knew, and everyone made fun of Wesley for it. Sometimes a group of us would be over at his house and we'd take turns pretending we were Ricky, saying things like, "Oh, Wesley, you're *so* big," and kinda bending over in front of him and wiggling our asses like a girl. It was all a joke, you know. Guys being stupid. No harm really.

Well, anyway, Wesley always laughed about it, and one day he got this idea to, you know, play a practical joke. We'd already invited Ricky down to the Meadows a few times, and he'd said no. But then one day—February 28, to be exact—Wes called him up, and he laid it on thick.

"It'd really mean a lot to me if you came to the Meadows," Wes told him. "I've been having thoughts about you. Confusing thoughts."

And Ricky said yes.

I mean, we had nothing against him. He was a weirdo, but none of us hated him or were homophobic. I mean, we were all Facebook friends and followed each other on Twitter and Instagram, and, seriously, I couldn't really be homophobic, since my uncle was gay and he was like my favorite guy. We were just gonna mess with him a bit, nothing huge. Also, I basically grew *up* with Ricky. His mom and my mom were like good friends, and so we were together a lot as kids. He was into video games back then, so we'd just play for hours. He wasn't much good at any of them, not even this wicked simple *Simpsons* game, where all you did was run around as Homer and eat donuts. But he was a good sport about losing, and playing with him stroked my ego, I guess. Well, in seventh grade, he just got weird and whiny and stopped playing video games, so I distanced myself. Anyone would've.

Anyway, it was Saturday. The Meadows was kinda packed. Cold, since it was February, but warm enough to be outside. Most of the people were around the bonfire or kinda close to it. A few of the girls were dancing, tearing shit up. The music was this techno garbage I've never heard before. Not really into it—kinda faggy. The plan was for me and Scooter and Bryan and Grant to hide in the back woods with Scooter's dog, Maggie, far away from the bonfire, and Wesley, he was gonna have this fake heart-to-heart with Ricky, was gonna tell him that he was thinking about him a lot and that he thought he wanted to explore, maybe make out a little in the back woods. He'd only be able to do it if it was totally dark, he said.

So of course Ricky took the bait. And we heard them coming and tried to hold in our giggles, but I was scared as hell we were gonna be seen. We were just behind the old outhouse, after all, four guys crammed as fuck. Then Ricky said, "Here? That's kinda gross," and it was really hard not to bust out laughing. It wasn't like the outhouse had been used in years and years, but he was still thinking like that. Anyway, Maggie was about to whine, and you could still hear her through the muzzle, so we were all hoping it wasn't gonna fall through.

"This is as good a spot as any," Wesley said, and he moved closer to us. By now we could probably touch. I was wicked nervous. "You ready?" he said.

"I can't see you," Ricky said. "It's too dark."

"I'm over here," Wesley said. "Just follow my voice."

"Can't we go where it's a little lighter?"

"Nah, man. I can't do it like that."

"Okay," Ricky said.

There was some shuffling, leaves crunching or some shit, and I tapped Scooter's shoulder, and he took the muzzle off and just kept his hands around Maggie's mouth.

"No touching, okay?" Wesley said. "Just lean in."

"No touching?"

"Yeah. Just lean in. Over here. You shaved your lip like I asked, right?"

"Yeah."

"Okay, over here, man."

"It's so dark."

"Over here. Just lean in. Just don't try any touching. Any touching and it's off."

"Okay," Ricky said.

And so Scooter went where Wesley was standing, and I kinda shuffled around them and it was perfect: Ricky leaned in, Scooter let go of his dog's mouth, and I got the pic of Maggie and Ricky's tongues touching.

How could we not post it? We orchestrated it so perfectly. I mean, we took the pic down almost right away, but still, people saw. I think people were more shocked by Ricky's method of kissing than the fact that it was a fuckin' *dog*. I mean, Ricky's mouth was wide open, and his tongue was straight out. Like did he really think that was how you kissed a person, dude or otherwise?

Well, when the flash went off, he saw everything and, of course, ran off, and we were laughing. It was a fucking joke, after all. Nobody was hurt. A fuckin' *joke*. Afterward I felt a little bad, but I mean, just because you were the butt of a joke doesn't give you the right to shoot people. If that were the case, nobody'd be alive, because everyone's been in that position before. For example, I remember one time Wesley and Scooter planned this birthday prank on me. Like, they got me a gift, wrapped all nicely, and I was surprised, because I'd never gotten anything from them, except maybe when I was like five. Anyway, it was this nice box, and no way did *they* fuckin' wrap it, so I figured Wesley's mom made him get me something. I was turning sixteen, after all; it was a big deal to me. Well, I started opening it, tearing away the bow and paper and shit, and was trying to hide my excitement, because even though I didn't wanna admit it, it was wicked nice of them to think of me like that.

Anyway, I was just kinda joking around, you know, calling them names like I always did, but, man, I was really fuckin' excited, was thinking it was a new Xbox game—maybe *Grand Theft Auto V*, 'cause I'd hinted at it so many times. Not like they would get it, but maybe. So I was imagining us all playing the game, laughing and having just a real good time, when I finally got all the wrapping paper off and looked inside, and saw a big pile of hardened shit—from Maggie, no doubt.

Well, they were laughing so hard, and in between breaths, Wesley said, "You said we weren't gonna get you shit for your birthday! We proved you wrong! We proved you wrong!" And it was just not a very funny joke, especially for me at that time. Because, I'll be honest, I was suddenly very sad and upset. I thought things would be different. I thought maybe for once they'd be cool and genuine and nice and whatever. Don't know why I actually thought that'd fuckin' happen, but I was hoping. And I was disappointed, yeah, but after a while, I could laugh with them, because it was a joke. *It was a joke.* I would never even *think* of *shooting* them over a goddamn joke. You have to be crazy to do that.

Dr. Huntington said, "So the joke you played on Ricky, you think it's the same level of jokery that your friends played on you?"

"Of course not. I mean, we posted it online, and we shouldn't have."

"That's it? Just the posting is different?"

"They were both jokes. We obviously handled them differently."

"There may be a difference between jokes your friends played on you and jokes played on you by nonfriend types you admire."

"Admire? Ricky didn't admire us."

"I think he did."

"Nah. He was just into Wesley. Like sexually."

"I have a feeling it goes deeper than that."

"I don't know."

"I think you understand what I'm saying."

"Huh?"

"Why do you think you have these hallucinations, these dreams of Ricky?"

"Isn't that your job to figure out?"

"Perhaps. But I'd like you to tell me what you think."

"I already know. I have PTSD. Both you and Mrs. V told me."

"Certainly. PTSD. But let me ask you this: Do you feel guilty?"

I didn't want to talk anymore. I hated this line of discussion. Blaming the victim. Telling me that I was at fault for someone shooting *me*. I'd fuckin' heard it all before. And I didn't know what else to do. *Fuck the world, man,* I thought. *Seriously. Fuck it.*

Dr. Huntington finally got a clue. He understood that I didn't want to talk about that, so he switched the conversation over to Claire Chang, asking me what I thought it was about her that made me feel better. I told him I didn't know, of course, and why was he always asking me my professional opinion on things when he was the doctor? He chuckled and said he needed to get my perceptions on things. He said he wasn't there to cure me but to guide me through a rough patch.

"I didn't know I had a crush on her until now," I said.

"You have a crush on her?"

"Yeah. I mean, I always thought she was smokin' but didn't think of her more than that. I know that sounds weird. I mean, now I think of her as like smokin' and maybe someone I'd like to date."

"Just from that one call?"

"We're gonna meet up tomorrow."

"Not at Starbucks, I presume."

"No."

"Where then?"

"My house."

"A bit of a rush, don't you think?"

"We're not gonna do anything—at least I don't think so. But I just said it'd probably be good if I wasn't out in public with just her. Don't want to make any scene. I mean, I've only been out with my parents and Corky. Who knows what could happen with her. I don't wanna ruin it."

"Your parents will be around?"

"Nah. But don't worry. I'm not even thinking about sex yet. Can't imagine it. But it'll be good to talk to someone other than Corky and my parents."

The truth was, I wouldn't have minded sex. I mean, I wanted a date, like a real date, with dinner and stuff, but I didn't think I was ready for that. It was almost like I was more ready for sex than a regular date, because at least sex was in my house. I wasn't going to pressure her, of course, but hey, she was the one who suggested she come over when my parents were at work, like during the time Corky usually hung out. (I made sure he wasn't coming that day.) So why wouldn't I think she might be up for it. In any case, I was thinking I might be in love with her. Like why not. Who actually knew what love felt like? Who said it couldn't happen suddenly like that, like a fuckin' realization? I'd never felt about my exes like I felt about her. So it was definitely a possibility.

After my therapy session that day, I went home and drew her again. It made me feel really happy.

CLAIRE CHANG

Before I even decided to do what I did with Mark, before Ricky shot him and Wesley and then shot himself, and, well, before that, I really, really tried to reach out to Ricky. I sent him a bunch of Facebook messages, literally apologizing like a zillion times for being out of touch, and he seemed okay at first, but then—ugh!—there was the posting of him with Maggie, Scooter's dog, and after that: total silence.

I told Alexandra B all about it—about how he'd come out to me in a chat, and how he was struggling, and how the Wesley Thompson dumbfucks used that struggling to humiliate the poor guy, and how I was really concerned, because he, Ricky, wasn't responding to my messages.

And she was great as usual, texting, I really admire your empathy, Claire. We need more people like you in the world.

That made me feel good, obviously, but I told her that it was all because of her and our chats and discussions that I felt all this stuff.

Nonsense, she texted. It's inside of you. You are a genuinely good person.

But even so, even if that was for real, me being "good" and all, I still couldn't seem to get through to Ricky, and I was literally not sleeping, because I was concerned and feeling really, really guilty. Like maybe, somehow, I could've stopped Wesley and his stupid followers, because I'd *known* that Ricky liked him and that he'd thought . . . Well, I could've-should've done something, and I kept telling Alexandra B that, but she said that I could only move forward, couldn't change the past. So I literally upped my efforts like 1,000 percent, even called Ricky, but he never answered, never picked up his phone, and he deleted his Facebook account, so I had no way of getting to him except in person at school. And at school he wouldn't even look at me; he wouldn't look at *anyone*. And then, just a couple weeks later—a couple fucking weeks (!)—he was dead!

I was devastated. I didn't know how Alexandra B could call me a "genuinely good person," because—ohmygod!—I wasn't there for him when he'd needed me! He'd been a part of a terribly marginalized group, and I'd failed him! I told Alexandra B this and cried and cried and cried, and she cried with me, because it was the saddest fucking thing ever in the whole fucking world, and she kept saying in her soothing mom-voice, *You couldn't help it. It's not your fault. You couldn't help it. It's not your fault.*

Well, what happened was that my sadness eventually turned to anger, and my anger was channeled toward Mark McVitry, because, well, when he came back to school? Seriously, people cheered. They fucking *cheered*. Yeah, he got shot, and that was wrong and all, but everyone seemed to conveniently forget that he'd literally destroyed Ricky's life with his little prank. Like because he was a *survivor* of a shooting, he automatically got off scot-free and literally *nobody*—not even my parents or my sister or anybody—thought he needed to change, that he needed to really try and understand what life had actually been like for a person like Ricky. And then he started freaking out, like literally went *insane*, had to leave school and everything, and I thought, *Well, this is his conscience, for sure, his guilt,* and maybe he needed just a little push to make this all come together for him. Maybe, I thought, to get him to heal and at the same time make justice a real thing, he needed to experience what Ricky experienced. On a smaller scale, of course, but still . . .

Alexandra B told me it was healthy to get angry at injustice but that it was *not* healthy to "exact revenge." But this was sort of where we weren't, you know, on the same page, and we actually argued sometimes.

Like I told her that nobody would ever learn what it was like to be us if they never had to experience the *humiliation* of being us—things would literally never change! She kept saying that *conversation* was the way, that it was the only way, but I was so angry and upset that I couldn't listen to that. Conversation didn't do shit! People needed to feel what it was like—*that* was justice, I told her.

So I brainstormed ways to publicly humiliate Mark like he'd publicly humiliated Ricky. And honestly? Once I got real deep into this? That sadness and anger once again turned into *purpose*. Who *cared* if Mark was going through whatever with his mental state! It all seemed like a sham to me, a way for more people to feel sympathy for him, and, I dunno, I just needed more from him, I guess, a real change. Alexandra B said I must keep my emotions in check, that my situation involved a "huge amount of suffering" and that I should never "add to suffering," and I guess it made sense, but I just didn't want to listen to that sort of reasoning then, so I stopped contact with her. I didn't need the Conquerors anyway, I thought. I could "exact justice" on my own.

Well, it took me a while to come up with a plan. I thought of a bunch of things, all involving Facebook, of course, but none of them seemed really *good*. I mean, maybe humiliating, but just not quite the same as Ricky's humiliation, I guess.

But then at work—like *divine intervention*—Vera Mahoney came up to me with her phone, and at first I was like, *Oh god, Vera, I'm not in the mood to see pics of your new apartment. Seriously.* But she didn't show me that. Instead, she showed me a picture of her cute little nephew all dressed up as a cheetah.

"This was last Halloween!" she said. "I can't stop looking at it. Isn't he *adorable*?" I must not have answered right away, because she said, "Claire? Earth to Claire. Come in, Claire."

"Oh yeah. Real cute," I said, but in my head, I was like, *Animal. That's it. Animal! Animal! Animal! Animal! Just like Maggie was an animal! But what animal for Mark?*

"Anyway," Vera said, "I know it's way past Halloween and everything, but I don't think I ever showed you that pic. It's just so cute, and I was doing that thing where you just scroll through everything? And that came up, and I was like, *I've never shown Claire that!*"

Maybe a rat, I thought. *Or a snake.*

"Every year, he's a different animal," Vera said. She sighed. "God, I wish they didn't have to grow up. It's so fun to see what he's gonna be the next year."

Something gross, I thought. *Beetle? Roach? Skunk?*

"Are you there, Claire? Seriously, you zone out more than anyone I know . . ."

No rat. No snake. No beetle-roach-skunk.

Pig.

Of course.

Pig.

I looked at Vera and was suddenly filled with all this joy, like I felt like I'd solved some huge life mystery or something. I smiled real big and threw my arms around her and said, "You're the best! You're the best coworker ever!" She didn't hug back.

"What?" she said, pushing me away. "What's wrong with you?"

"Oh, nothing. Just happy. Just feeling *innovative.*"

"Well, we got customers," she said, getting kinda cold. "So I guess you'll have to put that feeling on hold."

I could feel her looking at me weird when I went to the register, but I didn't care, 'cause I felt SO GOOD. I even sang a few lines of the Katy Perry song that came on, and when some guy came up to me with his mountain of yogurt and toppings, I gave him a 10 percent discount, just because.

I'll be honest, I was literally shaking when I called Mark up. I didn't know *what* to expect—like would he freak out? Would he just not answer? Would he be all zombified and drooling on the phone? I mean, I was sure I was the *last* person he expected to hear from, since we were basically just Facebook friends and sat next to each other in math. So what would he think? Well, I shouldn't have been so nervous, because he was like *really excited* to hear from me, and we talked for a bit and I laid it on thick, told him how much I was concerned and that I was only working part-time if he ever wanted to hang. My luck he *did* want to hang, so we arranged a time at his house when his parents were gone and Corky Meeks, who'd become like his *babysitter* or something, wasn't looking after him, and this was a little nerve-wracking since, I mean, this was real. Me and him alone in a house—who knew what would happen.

Anyway, when I got there, he greeted me with this real happy-eyed look. I'd seen it on tons of guys who came into the Yolo. Older guys mostly. Not the skeeze-buckets who said things like *Damn, girl! You fine!* <vomit> but like the guys who maybe didn't get much? Like the guys who were lonely and who I was nice to. The guys who kept coming back to see me. Like Dan. He was like sixty or something, came in every couple days, literally had chocolate and vanilla with rainbow sprinkles every time, and just sat at one of the tables and looked at me while he ate. It wasn't creepy, because he had the happy-eyed look. Something totally innocent about it. And he'd lost his wife a few years back to cancer, so for some reason that made him harmless too; I'm not sure why.

So Mark brought me a cup of coffee, even though I didn't like coffee, and we sat down in his living room. No TV or music or anything— just us. I was still wicked nervous, because all I kept thinking was, *What if he goes psycho on me?* I'd heard all the stories. Him freaking out in Starbucks, choking a guy. Him hallucinating Ricky's bloody ghost. Him in *therapy*. And even though I thought it was all a big plot to get more sympathy, sitting next to him, like *in the flesh*, made those stories a little more real, you know? It made me imagine more—him spazzing out, him trying to kill me, him screaming, crying, just literally losing control. So I took a few breaths and reminded myself that the door was right there and he had neighbors and I had my phone. Besides, he really wasn't that big. I could've probably taken him if it came down to it.

"So how were the last weeks of school?" he asked. We were on the couch only like a few inches away from each other. He was staring out at the lawn, but I could tell he was wanting to look at me, so I backed away a little and he turned his head.

"Boring. The usual, you know. I *really* missed you in algebra. It was *so strange* just having that empty seat there."

"Well, I'm sure Mr. Koppy didn't miss me."

"Sure he did! He even mentioned you a few times. Said that if anyone talked to you they should tell you that he sends his best."

"He said that?"

"Yeah."

"But nobody told me."

"Well, you didn't talk to anybody then, so nobody could relay the message."

"Oh."

So I wasn't some sort of stellar actress—like I wouldn't be nominated for a Golden Globe anytime soon—but I wasn't stupid either. I was a girl, and as a girl, I knew my whole *life* was an act. I was supposed to make people feel *comfortable* even when I was unhappy. I was supposed to pretend I didn't fart or shit. I was supposed to make boys feel like they were *supersmart* all the time, and I was supposed to act like a virgin no matter how many guys I'd screwed. As a girl, I knew how to be fake, because all I was expected to *be* was fake. The world got handed to people like Mark McVitry just for being born, but for us, for me, for Alexandra B, for Ricky—we had to work. We had to perform.

"Well, that was a nice thing for him to say," he said.

"Everyone missed you."

"Really?"

"Yeah."

I wouldn't say I was a *boy expert* or anything, but I'd learned a few things. Mostly because I had Chris Winters as a friend, and he'd literally tell me *anything* I wanted to know about dudes. Like one day—and this was like *months* after the John Bloom ordeal—I was over at his place watching TV, and he just blurted, "Guys get scared of you sometimes. You gotta tone that shit down."

"What?" I said. "Random much?"

"I'm just saying, there are guys who like you, but you got this, I don't know, *energy*. Like almost dominating."

"Dominating?"

"Guys don't like that, you know? I mean, I guess they don't mind it once in a while, but mostly, they like to think they're in charge, you know?"

"Where did this even *come* from?"

"Look: guys are pretty simple. They wanna feel necessary. They wanna feel accomplished. They wanna feel like they're totally great at something. And, seriously, if some hot chick can make him feel these three things, plus give him sex, well, he's hooked, you get it?"

"I don't think all guys are that simple."

"Like John Bloom?"

"Shut up." I felt myself go red.

"He's actually the *worst*, like a prime example. Dude, when we jammed he'd always give me fuckin' tips—like I needed 'em, like he was my teacher. Then when Joe Vinton joined us, he got worse, like saying all this shit about what a big fuckin' deal he was down in Mass, like people were somehow hurting musically without him there. He even told us he played with Neil fucking Young once. Yeah, total tool. But just goes to show my theory: necessary, accomplished, great. That's what dudes need to feel, and that's all."

"I don't get it."

"One: necessary. People in Mass needed him. Two: accomplished. Played with Neil Young. Three: great. Had to *teach* me and Joe, 'cause he was so goddamn talented."

"Okay?"

"My point is that if one of us were some hot chick and we just kept giving him all these compliments about his necessary-ness and his accomplishments and his greatness, we'd have him wrapped around our fucking finger."

"I don't care about John Bloom anymore."

"Are you even listening?"

"He's totally off my radar."

"You're an impossible fucking chick," he said. "Im-poss-i-ble."

"I'll do better," I said. "I know I can."

So sitting there with Mark, I couldn't help but think, *Necessary, accomplished, great. Necessary, accomplished, great. Necessary, accomplished, great.* I also thought about all the conversations I'd had with Alexandra B about white male privilege and how that led to so many messes and problems in society. She'd really awakened me to so many things, and that made it even more difficult to sit next to Mark, because, well, I kept feeling bits of anger rise up.

"I'm real glad you called," he said, looking straight at me. His eyes were still happy. "I haven't had company really since . . ."

"I miss your posts," I said. "They were always wicked funny."

"Oh," he said. "I don't really go online much anymore. Because . . ."

"I mean, are you okay? I've heard stuff."

"I'm okay," he said.

I pulled out my phone and saw I had like six text messages from Chris Winters. He was *so* needy and annoying sometimes. Like seriously? Three of the texts were just question marks, like he expected me to answer right away all the time. I logged onto Twitter and scrolled through my feed. I was still following the Conquerors, and they literally seemed to post like every six seconds, like news articles about injustice with a small tweet about how we needed to mobilize. I switched to Facebook and saw a bunch of graduation pictures from my senior friends. Anna DeWitt was going to BU in the fall, and that was literally all she posted about. I can't believe in just a few weeks I'll be living in Boston!! Fifty-seven likes for that dumb shit.

"I feel sorta disconnected since I haven't been on my phone," Mark said.

"You're seriously not missing much," I said. "Just a bunch of graduation pictures. They're all the same."

"My feed's different maybe. Don't have that many senior friends."

"Doesn't matter. They all just pop up anyway."

"Yeah, I guess."

Chris Winters texted another question mark. I responded: Uh busy.

"I didn't think you really liked me," Mark said.

"What?" I said, "Of course I like you. Everyone likes you. People cheered, remember?" I bit my tongue after that, 'cause I didn't want him to hear the sarcasm in my voice. Like, I didn't want to give myself away so early. But he didn't seem to notice, only clung on to the fact that I said I liked him—you know, typical dude.

"You like me?" he said.

"Yeah," I said, feeling hot. I read Chris's new text: Stop ignoring ur not busy. "Sure," I said.

"I'm glad you called," Mark said.

"Of course," I said. I put my phone away then, even though it kept vibrating. I looked at Mark, and he was pale and sweaty on his forehead, and his breathing was quick—I mean his chest was literally *heaving.* "Are you okay?" I said, because seriously? He looked like he was having a heart attack or something. "You look—"

"I'm fine."

So at that point I noticed that even though he was looking at the lawn, he'd put his hand on the couch between us, like real convenient for me or whatever. So I thought, *Well, here goes,* and I took it—his hand—and squeezed it. He turned to me, and I saw sweat running down his cheek, like a *river*, I swear. That's like the only thing I saw for a bit—sweat, sweat, sweat—but after I got control of myself and saw him and his happy-slash-crazed face, I had this little moment of joy, like *ecstasy*. He was wicked nervous, and that meant either (a) he liked me or (b) he was worried about a major freak-out. But I didn't think it was (b), because I just had this instinct, this feeling; I mean, I could tell if a dude was into me. (Except John Bloom, obvi.)

"So there's no medication?" I said, holding tight.

"Huh?"

"Medication? They can't give you some pills?"

"Pills?"

"For your . . . condition."

"I don't have a condition. I have PTSD."

"That's not a condition?"

"I dunno."

I guess some girls would've called Mark cute, but those girls, like Camille St. John and Tina Bristol and Christie Best, they were like *really stupid*, like the kind of girls who literally grew up and married the washed-up high school jock and spent their days tanning and having plastic surgery consultations they couldn't afford, and then when they were like middle-aged, they looked ancient, 'cause nothing in their lives went the way they'd dreamed and all the disappointment just showed on their face. None of those girls ever visited Mark after the whole Ricky thing happened. It was like when he was fine and playing football and not sick, they were like, *Ohmygod, Mark is soooo hot,* but when something happened, when *life* happened, they were *nowhere to be found.* Not that I thought Mark deserved visitors, but you'd think I, of all people, wouldn't be the first person from school to come see him. I mean—god! Not even Grant or Scooter came.

So on the couch, I scooted closer to Mark, and I still had my hand in his, so I was like, *Fuck it. Here goes.* He turned to me, and I smelled the coffee on his breath as he said, "You're amazing." I laughed and touched his shoulder, and then . . . WE WERE KISSING!!

But for literally just a split second, because when I moved closer, he felt my phone vibrating constantly and said, "You gonna get that?" And I just stared for a bit, then sighed and pulled out my phone and looked, and saw like twenty question marks from Chris Winters. I texted back, WTF what is your problem??? and he was like, I am bored come over, and I was like, Ugh. And then I turned my phone completely off, which was something I never did, like ever, not even in movie theaters.

"Do you have to go?" Mark said.

"No, not at all," I said, seriously wondering if I'd totally lost him or turned him off or whatever. "Just friend stuff."

"Oh, okay," he said. Then he leaned in and kissed me again, and I'll admit—it was nice. I mean, I was still thinking, *Pig, pig, pig,* of course, and I couldn't seem to get Alexandra B's voice out of my head: *Conversation is key. Exacting revenge hurts your cause.* But for the first few seconds or so—maybe even a minute—I let myself get into it. Because he was good—not all tonguey, like Drew, my last boyfriend, but soft and considerate and just a little clumsy, which I liked.

"Was that okay?" he said when I pulled back.

"Um, yeah," I said, smiling. It wasn't like I was lying either. It *was* pretty good.

"Can I do it again?"

"Sure."

Who *knew* that the dumb prankster was such a romantic. Never would've guessed from sitting next to him in algebra and seeing him drunk at the Meadows, singing all those god-awful songs with Wesley really loud. Not like I'd ever pictured us hooking up, but if I had, I would've totally pictured it really sloppy and gross, like *nasty.* Like I'd've had to be 150 percent drunk to even begin to think of it. But there I was, 100 percent sober, and his hand was moving down, and I was letting it this time. Not that I wasn't still thinking about my *cause*, but I figured, *Hey, this isn't so bad.*

"You wanna go to my room?" he asked, panting.

That brought me to reality: *Pig.*

"Seriously?" I said. "I'm not like a slut or something."

"Oh, no, no. I didn't . . . I mean, I just thought it might be more comfortable. I . . . Oh, forget it."

"It's okay," I said, smiling bigger, putting my hand on my leg, feeling proud of myself. "I should get going anyway."

"You don't have to. I mean, my parents won't be back for a while. We could just hang out."

"Sounds fun, but, sorry, I have a few things I have to do before my shift."

"At the Yolo, right?"

"Yeah."

"I've seen you there before."

"Yup."

"Maybe we could go out sometime?"

"Yeah. Sure."

"Like tonight? After your shift?"

"Seriously? Are you okay to do that?"

"I'm fine. Really. I'm fine. I feel so much better. I feel amazing."

"I don't get off 'til nine."

"Fine with me."

And that was the first interaction! Went well, I thought. Better than expected maybe. The best thing about it was that it was *obvious* that he wanted to screw. I mean, really? Go to his room just to be more comfortable? Jesus. But anyway. It was good, 'cause I was worried about that. Like if he didn't like me—I mean, physically—if he found me repulsive, I wouldn't have been able to go through with my original plan, would've had to change everything up, and I wasn't sure how that would've worked in the end. But I hadn't had to think about that, thank god!

MARK MCVITRY

Dude, I'd never really been one to dig kissing—always made me nervous, for some reason. But kissing Claire? Totally fucking intense. I mean, drawing her and talking to her was one thing, but kissing her—it was like something other than our bodies was at work. I know that sounds fuckin' corny as shit, but it was absolutely true. After we kissed, something in my head changed, like I felt it physically in my brain, like a big crackling wire had snapped or something. And yeah, Ricky was still there, in my head, but he was so much smaller, and I just knew that if I went out that night with her and I got to kiss her again, he would never, ever, *ever* show up again.

So maybe this was *love*, I thought. I'd never felt for any of my other girlfriends what I felt for Claire in just one day, because, well, she was so fuckin' beautiful. Her lips, her eyes, her skin . . . I mean, I'd known that before; I'd checked her out in math class, for sure. But up close, kissing—totally different story. It was like she became this fuckin' *angel*.

Of course, my parents didn't approve of me going out at night. Since the incident, I'd never been out of the house after sundown; I'd never even asked them before, because night-Ricky was bound to be much scarier than day-Ricky, and who the fuck would I go out with anyway? I didn't seem to have any friends anymore. But now . . .

I told them that I had to do it sometime, that I was feeling better and that I had my phone if anything happened. Of course, my mom wondered about Claire. She said, "Why would she suddenly want to be friends with you now?" A legit question, I guess, since we never were that close, but I wasn't in my right mind, wasn't thinking straight, so I got mad.

"Why?" I said. "I can't have friends now because I'm such a freak?"

That got to her, because she started crying, just a little.

My dad said, "Just be home by midnight," and he gave me the car keys. But before I left, he said in this very concerned voice, "Mark, if you feel *anything*, you call us. Right away. If you're driving, you pull over, no matter where. You pull over and you call us, okay? And if for some reason we don't answer right away, you call Corky. Okay? You promise me that."

I promised him.

"Okay then."

It was really hard to read my dad. He had this stony face all the time, like he didn't show any expression unless someone really pushed his buttons. After everything, he did what he was supposed to as a dad, I guess; he supported with his silence. He was just there, and my mom was the one who talked. And I knew that was how it was with a lot of moms and dads, but sometimes I just wished he talked more, wasn't so fuckin' *mysterious*. For a long time, I didn't know if he thought I was to blame, if he was just holding that in, or if he thought I really *had* turned into a freak.

We only ever talked about it all once. It was about a month after. I was doing schoolwork, or at least trying to, in my room. I couldn't hardly concentrate, because back then the ghost-Ricky was everywhere, both in real life and in my dreams, so I had a book open in front of me and was looking at it, but I wasn't really registering anything. My dad, then, he knocked on the door and came in. He looked at my arm in the sling and asked if I felt okay, and I said, "Yeah." I thought he was gonna leave, 'cause that's what he did back then when he did the checkups instead of Mom—just came in, asked about my arm, and left. But this time he stayed. He actually just stood over me by my bed, and I thought, *WTF?*

"You're okay, right?" he said, and he had this really strange expression. I'd never seen it on him before. It looked both confused and nervous.

"Yeah," I said. "I'm fine."

"You know," he said, then took a deep breath. "This whole thing. It's hard to process. It's confusing to me. I don't know if you know that."

"I'm sorry," I said. I felt awkward, so I looked really hard at my hands and didn't say anything, hoping he'd go away. He didn't. He just stood there, making everything real uncomfortable.

After a while, he kinda tapped his fingers against his cheek and said, "I see a lot of myself in you. And I keep wondering, I keep asking myself—if all this had gone down when I was your age, would I have handled it the same? Would I have done what you did? Handled it the way you did?" He sighed, this time for a long time. Then he said, "I just don't know. Different times. You have different things to deal with. Internet, all that. So I don't know."

I thought he was blaming me for the posting and Ricky's psycho behavior, and I started to feel really fuckin' upset. Because of everyone, I thought *he* would get it. From what I'd heard, he'd played a shit-ton of jokes on his frat brothers in college—some not so nice. "Dad . . ." I said. But he held up his hand.

"I'm not proud, is what I'm saying," he said. "But it has nothing to do with you. What I'm saying is that I'm not proud of myself. I just want you to know that, okay, bud? I'm doing my best. And I just know you'll get better very soon and everything will go back to normal."

He left right after that. Didn't look at me, just left. And that was the only conversation we ever had about it.

So driving a car was totally against the rules, especially because of my previous state, but my dad must've seen something in me, must've noticed that I felt a fuckload better, or that I'd been able to control myself more lately. I just kept my eyes completely on the road, didn't look at anything but cars and pavement, and even though I was nervous as fuck, I made it to the Yolo fine. Not one fucking sighting.

Claire was just getting off her shift, closing up, and she was there with only one other chick, a chubby girl, someone I thought I knew but who was younger, maybe a sophomore. The sophomore smiled at me as she swept.

"I honestly didn't know if you were gonna come," Claire said. She looked a little greasy. It was hot, so I imagined it was a busy night.

"Of course," I said, trying to sound confident.

"Well, I'm gonna change quick," she said. "Then we can go out for a little while."

The only place to go was the Stoney's Drive-In for slushes or burgers, unless we went to McDonald's, but who the fuck wanted to go there? Besides, I thought it'd be better if we sat in the car instead of in a public building where something might happen and I'd be fuckin' embarrassed. So I ordered a Grape Refresher and she ordered a Blue Raspberry Refresher, and we parked and just looked at the passing traffic. There were like six cars parked, so not too bad. And it was dark enough out so even if I'd seen ghost-Ricky, I wouldn't have been that scared. I rolled down our windows, and a breeze came through; it felt nice.

She slurped loud and she looked kinda tired, so I felt bad for dragging her out, but I also felt really fuckin' good, just being around her. Like her energy—she was giving *me* some energy. Seriously, just by sitting there. I actually *felt* myself getting healthier in my head. It was amazing. I felt right then that I wanted to be with her all the time, and I wanted to tell everyone I knew about us; I wanted to post a Facebook status and tweet and take a bunch of selfies of us doing fun shit. People would probably comment. Say things like, What a great couple! and You look awesome together!!

"Everything all right?" she said.

"Yeah. Great. Why?"

"Just wondering."

We sat for a while longer. I didn't know what to say. I was nervous about boring her. She took out her phone and scrolled through some feeds. Then she started texting somebody. I looked over her shoulder. She wrote, I dunno maybe but I'm tired will call tmrrw or something

"This is real cool," I said. "First time I've been out at night." She didn't look up from her phone, but that was fine. I hadn't looked at my phone since the first day I saw the Ricky-ghost, but I knew it was important for people with normal lives to keep up with shit going on. "Thanks for coming out."

"Sorry," she said, putting her phone in her purse. "Had to answer that text."

"No problem."

"So . . ." she said, taking a sip.

"So . . ." I said.

"So it was nice this afternoon," she said, but I heard something else in her voice. Hesitation? I don't know. It just didn't sound that enthusiastic, and that made me nervous.

"I loved it," I said.

"Yeah." She just stared out the window. The traffic zoomed by. The breeze got stronger and rustled her hair.

"I'd love to do it again," I said.

"What, sit on the couch?"

"No . . . You know . . ."

"Oh," she said. "Yeah, but now I feel gross. Sorry. You know. Work."

"I don't mind."

"But I do." She smiled. It lit up her whole fuckin' face. I wanted to take a picture of her so bad right then, with the streetlight comin' down on her, making her partly in the shadows. I wanted to post that shit for everyone to see. It'd be therapeutic, I was sure.

I tried to move closer, but it was hard to do that in a car. There was the emergency brake and the wheel in the way. So I slid back to my spot and just made myself content by looking at her. She pretended not to notice, just ran her hands through her hair and leaned against the window.

"Can I tell you something?" I said.

"Yeah, sure," she said.

"This is the best I've felt ever. I mean today. And I don't mean just the best I've felt since, well, you know, but the best in my life."

"That's literally crazy talk. In your whole life?"

"I'm not lying to you."

"But in your whole *life*?"

"You know when you're sick with the flu for a long time, maybe like two weeks or something? Then you're better? Or maybe not even a long time. Maybe you just have a real shitty hangover. Vomiting and everything. You just wanna die. But then you're better, and you're like, *Wow. This is how normal feels. Wow.* And it's normal to everyone else, but to you it's like superincredible because of what you went through? That's what today's like."

"Well, I'm glad you feel like that."

Her phone vibrated. She took it from her purse, looked at it, and sighed.

"Everything okay?" I said.

"It's nothing," she said. I looked over her shoulder for a split second and saw the name **Alexandra B** at the top of the text screen. I didn't know who that was. Maybe a sophomore or something.

Whoever it was, the message sorta changed her. She threw her phone back in her purse, then turned directly to me. She said, "I seriously don't know how any of us put up with ourselves. This world is so fucked."

I couldn't help myself then. I kissed her again, and she didn't flinch; at least I didn't think she did. It wasn't like the kiss at home, not at all, but it was still sweet as fuck, and I kept going until I was out of breath.

"Wow," she said afterward.

"Yeah," I said.

"Didn't expect *that*."

"You're amazing."

"Well . . ."

We sat for a while longer, looking out at the cars. It was a little surreal.

"Can you talk about it yet?" she said after a bit. "I mean, I know you've talked about it to the cops and everything, but can you actually talk about it normally yet?"

"You don't talk about that shit normally."

"You don't have to."

"It's okay."

"I just never knew what happened, exactly. I mean, I read . . ."

"It's like a dream anyway now. A nightmare. Recurring."

"Well. You don't have to talk about it. I wouldn't expect you to."

"I'm glad you weren't there," I said. "Wouldn't want you to have seen . . ." I could feel myself shaking inside.

"We can change subjects."

"If you want."

"I'm sure you're sick of talking about it."

"Sick? I dunno."

"Old news now anyway, right?"

"For me, I don't think it'll ever be old news. That's the worst part."

"I understand."

"I know you do," I said.

God, it was nice to just have her there, even if we weren't touching. This was how people were supposed to be with each other, I thought. It wasn't always about making out and sex—even though my dick was hard. But that wasn't everything. That was just biology. This was more. This was *being there*. She knew that. She was the only one who knew that, and that's why she was so important.

◆　◆　◆

But she wanted to know about *that night*, and I thought if I was gonna talk about it with anyone at that point, it might as well be with her. So I told her about it. I said:

On March 14, we're at the Meadows, of course. We're drunk. It's not a busy night, but there are enough people there. We're on the outskirts of the field, maybe twenty yards from the main cluster of people. We like it there, 'cause it's chill.

I didn't expect to see Ricky, but he comes, and he comes alone. Wesley socks him in the shoulder and says, "Ricky, man! Good to see ya!"

And maybe if Wes'd just left it at that, he'd still be alive. But he doesn't. He says—and he's slurring because he's drunk—"Old Maggie sure misses ya. Been whimpering in Scooter's garage since you two, you know. Sounds like love to me!"

And I think this is funny, so I laugh. I shouldn't have laughed, maybe. I should've just told Wesley to cool it. I should've taken Ricky aside and apologized. I should've . . . But what's the point now? It doesn't matter.

"Hey, Wesley," Ricky says. He's only wearing a T-shirt and jeans. It's too cold for just that, I think. The T-shirt has a picture of an alligator on it. The alligator has its mouth wide open. It's a weird shirt. It's just white and green.

"Yeah, bud?" Wesley says.

"I'm not gonna be embarrassed again," Ricky says.

"What's that?"

"I said, 'I'm not. Going. To be. Embarrassed. Again.'"

And I should've fuckin' *known* then what was about to happen, 'cause Ricky's eyes are *dead*. He's like a fuckin' corpse standing there. I move away just a bit.

"It's over," Ricky says. Then he digs in his pants, pulls out a gun, shows it to Wesley. And Wesley says, "Holy shit" and backs up. "Ricky, Jesus." Wesley puts his hands up. "What the fuck," he says.

Ricky points it. "You're crying," Ricky says.

"Ricky," Wesley says. "God. What the fuck." And Wesley *is* crying. Like sobbing suddenly. He still has his hands up, so he can't wipe the snot from his nose. "Oh god, I'm sorry, okay?" Wesley says. "I didn't mean—"

And then there's a bang. Or BANG! Or actually, BANG! BANG! BANG! Three shots. Wesley's on the ground. Everyone's screaming. Happens so quickly. The moonlight makes his blood black. It's all over, that blood. And so are little chunks of his skull. But I refuse to believe it. I think it's a joke. I go over to Wesley, shake his body. Blood sprays when I move it, goes on my chin. My feet crunch on some of his bones. It's not a joke. *No. Oh no. Oh no oh no oh no oh no,* I think. Everyone's running away, shouting, but it's like their voices are on mute. Ricky turns the gun to me. I don't hear it go off, but I'm on the ground suddenly, a few feet from Wesley's body. I think I'm dead. But then I open my eyes, and I see the black outline of trees, the shadows, the moonlight. I think of beating Ricky at the *Simpsons* game. I think of eating chips and cookies with him at his house. I think of his mom—she was the nicest. I look up. My vision is blurry. *I'm still alive?*

Ricky's standing above me.

"Please, no," I say. "Oh, please, no. Oh, please, no."

Ricky doesn't point the gun at me, but at his own head.

"No!" I say. "Oh god, no!" *So much moonlight,* I think.

And then he screams, *"Not gonna be embarrassed again!"* and there's another bang, and his blood is all over my face. A few seconds later, a bunch of people are above me shouting. I pass out.

"Some people think you're really brave," Claire said, looking out the window. "Lots of people think that."

"Yeah, I know," I said. "Wounds turn people into heroes. Like automatically. But then, after, like when I wasn't feeling good, they all left. All my friends. Just not around anymore."

"Awful."

"Yeah," I said.

"I was friends with Ricky, you know," she said.

"I didn't know that."

"I mean, not *good* friends. More like Facebook friends who chatted a lot. I mean, he didn't like my friends, so he couldn't be a real like in-person friend, I guess. I dunno. But we sent each other messages."

"I didn't know . . ."

"Whatever. It's all over now. All of it . . ."

"I had a good time," I said. I wanted to change the subject. It was making me nervous, and I could sense the Ricky-ghost clawing through my brain. I needed to go home.

"Yeah," she said.

"I hope we can do this again real soon?"

"Of course."

"'Cause I think you're wicked cool. Seriously. I thought so before too, but it's different now. More intense maybe."

"I'll call you soon."

"I'm getting better. I can feel it. Just a matter of time now."

She yawned. "I'm tired."

"I just wanted you to know."

"I'm glad." I was so fuckin' scared of making her upset. I was terrified of her going away. "I'm pretty much free all the time," I said.

"I know," she said.

"So if you want . . ."

"I'll call you soon."

We sat for a little longer, silently. She pulled out her phone and typed out a few messages. I finally put the car in drive and headed out.

CLAIRE CHANG

So off Route 6 there was this really creepy shack. Like you'd probably think people were *murdered* there, like in *Texas Chainsaw* or *The Hills Have Eyes*, but it was funny, 'cause it was like the opposite. It was a *porno* shop. Like it had actual DVDs of porn, as if anyone *bought* that shit anymore. But besides that, it had sex toys, like tons of 'em. And once, after we'd been day-drinking on a Saturday, Chris drove me there, and I couldn't stop laughing. 'Cause some of the toys—seriously? Like who would even *think* of this stuff?! We kept saying, "Hey, which hole is this supposed to go into?" then laughing *hysterically*. I put a few big black dildos by my face, and Chris threatened to take pictures, but he couldn't, because I swatted his phone away with the monster cocks. There was also like this weird plastic pussy-shaped thing that got wet or something the more you fucked it. Chris took it down from the rack and humped the box. Then he whipped his arm around like a cowboy with a lasso, and I lost it again.

The best thing we saw that day was this curly pig's tail.

"What the fuck *is* this?" I said, turning the box around and around.

"You put it in your butt!"

"Like you stick that curly thing up there? Wouldn't it like tear shit up inside you?"

"Chang! Look at the goddamn picture! You don't put the *tail* inside you. There's an actual butt-plug! Like regular-shaped."

"Oh! The tail juts out!"

"Duh."

Chris took the box from me and put it by his ass and squealed real loud. I literally thought I was gonna pee myself.

"Ohmygod," I kept shouting. "Ohmygod!" I really wanted to take a pic, but I refrained.

Well, the store clerk got pissed at us and said, *"Buy something or get out!"* Which was kinda fucked, since literally *nobody* in the store was buying anything—just looking.

"Sure, sir," Chris said. "I'll take three of these dildos over here—the brown, the black, and the white, 'cause I'm equal opportunity. But just a side note? I don't think you should have brown dildos, because, well, they kinda look like . . . And yeah. Hmm. This Slide-n-Slip rainbow lubricant—a jug of that, for sure. Might need two, actually. And how about a copy of this award-nominated flick. *Hairy Squatter*, it's called? Lovely! And what else? Oh, yes, those spiked tit clamps. You know, just in case my lady here feels *naughty*."

Well, we got thrown out, but it was 100 percent worth it, because I couldn't stop laughing like all day. Sometimes I absolutely *love* Chris. Maybe nobody else in the world makes me laugh as hard.

So fast-forward a few months and I was in the porn-shack place again, this time by *myself*. It was the day after my date with Mark, and I was feeling *super*-self-conscious. It wasn't like I was a prude, really, but being alone surrounded by horny old dudes looking at porn, well, it didn't make a teenage girl feel the *safest*. Plus, since I wasn't wasted this time, I noticed how absolutely gross the place was. Like *filthy*, and I wasn't talking about their products. The floors were literally *sticky*!! GROSS. I tried to tell myself that maybe it was just one of those gallon jugs of lube that fell over or something, but—ugh—just *thinking* about it was literally making my stomach upset.

I tried as best I could to make a straight shot to the toys, but in order to get there you needed to walk through a couple aisles of DVDs. So I couldn't help but see a cover with this woman's face all messed-up: running black mascara, her mouth seriously *full* of cocks (I don't even know how she could stretch her lips that far!), and, of course, cum all over her face. It was good that I hadn't eaten anything yet, 'cause it probably would've come up. I mean, why did boys *like* that stuff? It was 100 percent DISGUSTING! Not just a little even, but DISTURBING DISGUSTING! God! There was something wrong with the male brain, I thought. Something *real* wrong.

So when I got to the butt-plug wall, I panicked a little, because I thought it wasn't there. I scanned through literally *dozens* of different shapes and sizes (seriously, I was like, people need a *variety* of things to shove up there?) and I didn't see it! I was trying real hard not to let myself think too hard about what I was doing, but it was tough because I felt people looking. Like there was this stringy-haired guy with as many tattoos as Corky Meeks, and he was browsing through the DVDs like he was some expert, like they seriously weren't all the same, and I noticed he was inching closer and closer to me. I thought, *Could someone actually get raped in one of these places? I mean, would it happen 'cause the guys are all horned-up?* I was fidgeting, and that made it worse, because THE FLOOR MADE SQUISHY SOUNDS!!!

Ohmygod. So I was about to just bolt, but then I saw it. It was hidden behind one of the plugs that advertised "self-lubrication" (!!). So I grabbed it and took it to the counter, and that was a whole 'nother ordeal, because I was sure the guy was gonna card me, 'cause you were supposed to be eighteen just to be *in* there. But he didn't, thank god. He just stared at me the whole time. Not creepy. Just suspicious. Then after he put the pig-plug in a bag, he said, "Have a good day."

"Thanks," I said.

What a job! To say, "Have a good day!" as you're handing some-body something they're gonna shove inside their bunghole!! Crazy, crazy world we live in!!

Okay, so rewind. The *date*.

It was weird, 'cause the whole time I was sitting in his car, my phone was literally going *crazy* with messages from Alexandra B. The timing wasn't good, obviously, but more than that, it was *eerie*. Like did she *know* I was with Mark right then and there? Had I somehow gotten involved in some sort of spy cult that was able to trace computer and phone locations? I'd heard of that sort of thing happening. Like Jessica Lohr said that she knew someone whose life was totally ruined because he joined some online group, and even though they seemed nice, they slowly got all his personal information and basically wiped his identity clean.

I mean, I hadn't shared any personal info except my Facebook and email and phone number and Twitter with Alexandra B, but none of that could actually let her know where I was, right? I mean, I hadn't shared my *address*. And why would they wanna follow me anyway? To make sure I was doing their social justice work the right way?

Well—her texts were friendly enough, just said that she missed our chats and that she wished we could talk about my feelings with regards to Ricky, and that she knew how upset I was and how guilty I felt but that I needed to forgive myself and not let it all overwhelm me or turn me angry. I got a little paranoid at all the messages, because maybe there were ways to find my location. Who knew. When she asked if I could talk right then, I texted her that I couldn't but maybe tomorrow. Then I tried my best to turn my attention to Mark. You know, *focus*.

I thought about Chris's outline of dudes—necessary, accomplished, great—and decided it was just too much work to think about doing all that shit, that the guy clearly liked me and that I should just be as normal as possible, I guess. But even thinking that, I literally couldn't think of anything to talk about, so I just let him make out with me a little, then decided to ask him about *that night*, like he literally hadn't talked about it a zillion times already. Anyway, hearing him talk about it made it all more real, really gave me the chills. He just went somewhere far away when he was talking, like his eyes were all cloudy, and it freaked me out a little, and Alexandra B's constant texts weren't helping.

At the end, he just said he hoped we could do it again soon, and I pretended to be tired, yawned kinda loud—hinting, I guess—and he picked up on it and drove me home. And that was that. I got out of his car feeling pretty damn good about myself.

When I got to my room, I ignored all the Alexandra B texts and called Chris Winters. When he answered, he sounded all groggy, like I'd woken him or something, and I told him to stop fronting.

"Guess who I just made out with?" I said.

"Wait, you *cheated* on me?"

"Mark!"

"Mark *who*?"

"Mark McVitry, you idiot!"

"Mark *McVitry*?" he said, and I could truly register the shock in his voice, which made me feel real good.

"Yup," I said. "We went to Stoney's after my shift."

"He can actually *drive*?" Chris said.

"Yup. He was totally okay."

"And you went to *Stoney's*?"

"Yeah, that's not so weird. I mean, not a lot of other places open, I guess."

"But why would you make out with *Mark*? Is this like another one of your *charity cases*?"

Typical of Chris to say that. Ever since I tutored Ralph Redding in math last year, he thought everything I fucking *did* was a charity case. I kept telling him I wasn't really that charitable, whatever that meant, but he kept saying it, and it was just another irritant, to be honest.

Anyway, I didn't tell Chris this, but the real reason I tutored Ralph Redding was because his dad worked with my dad, and I guess one day his dad had said something about Ralph not doing so hot in school, and my dad was like, *Claire can help*. Ugh. It was just *like* my dad to volunteer my time to help someone I seriously didn't even know that well. But whatever. My dad didn't make these sort of demands all the time, so I said, "Sure, why not." Not like I had a choice.

Well, after a month of tutoring, I literally wanted to claw my eyes out: I was *way* too frustrated, because this guy was just *hopeless*. Like he just couldn't get *basic* concepts. One time we even stayed up 'til midnight doing one stupid problem—something as simple as *graphing a fucking line*—but he just kept getting confused about what "slope" meant. Like he'd ask, "Is there a reason a slope starts with *m* in that equation?" and I could only just shake my head, 'cause it was just unanswerable. In the end, he was like, "This shit just isn't for me, you know?" And I knew he was talking more about school in general than math.

Thing is, he was wicked good at cooking, would sometimes bring over a whole bunch of ingredients from the store and cook for all of us. My parents—rude as ever—didn't ever eat any of it, even though my dad kept saying nice things about Ralph's dad all the time, how he was one of the best workers and all, but . . . I mean, I ate everything and was seriously *dumbfounded* at how he knew exactly which ingredients went with what. Like he literally could turn just regular spaghetti into something totally unexpected. Like putting coffee or something weird into a mix, and it would be AMAZING.

"You should definitely become a chef," I told him after like a few weeks of tutoring. He just shook his head and said no.

"When I finish school, I'm gonna be the first in my family to go to college," he said.

That was his goal. Didn't happen, of course. He dropped out of high school a week after I stopped tutoring him, and then he went to prison for armed robbery somewhere outside Boston. So that's why everyone thought he was a charity case—because everyone thought he was hopeless—and I just found that sort of thinking really, really nasty, even if it was kinda true.

"He just asked me, so I said yes," I told Chris.

"Mark McVitry asked you to *Stoney's*?"

"Yes! It's not that weird."

"That kid hasn't left his house in *months*! It *is* weird!"

"Well, he did. And he was fine. He was a perfect gentleman."

"This *is* one of your charity cases, Chang! God, what do I have to do to be one of those? Get shot and turn psycho? Drop out of school and rob a convenience store? Please, tell me."

"You already *are* one of those."

"Ha. Ha."

"My biggest project."

"Be serious, Chang."

"I *am* serious."

"What're you doing with Mark? Is this something I need to be a part of?"

"What? No. I'm just telling you."

"Just watch your back. My number one girl and all that."

"It was fun."

"But you *hate* him. You've said it so many times. So there's something else."

"Think what you will, Chrissy."

"I don't like it," he said.

"Well, I don't like *you*."

Like I mentioned, people asked like a hundred million times why Chris and I didn't just get together. Even my parents. Like when we first started hanging out nonstop, my mom came up to me and said,

"Chris. Your boyfriend?" And I said, "No, just friends." But she literally couldn't *fathom* the idea of boys and girls being friends. Like the few times that Chris came to my house when my parents were home, they just gave him this confused look, probably thinking, *What* is *he?* Like, if he wasn't my boyfriend what could he *possibly* be?

It was weird, 'cause they were soooooo old-school on things like that, but then on other things they were totally liberal. Like gay marriage, for instance. When anyone asked my dad about it, he got wicked mad and said, "Why not? Why can't everyone marry? Who cares?" Though I think he had that stance because of this wicked cool lesbian coworker of his, Rea Van Dorn. Well, he'd gone out for drinks with her and her girlfriend (who was seriously like this tall blond model—you'd never guess she liked girls), and he talked about them a lot. So much that one day my mom actually got a little pissed, told my dad that he was talking too much about her. And he just looked at her real surprised, like, *How could anyone talk too much about Rea?*

"Just be careful," Chris said. "I mean it. You're dealing with a bona fide loony."

"I'll be fine."

"That's what you say."

"That's what I know."

"I'm serious."

"Yeah, okay."

"You don't wanna get messed up with that shit."

"I heard you already. God."

"I'm just saying."

"Fine," I said.

I mean, sometimes we *did* talk like we were a couple—like our little arguments and everything—and I loved it, actually, like it was amazing that we could be so close and not let the sex stuff get in the way. But honestly? Even *that* relationship started feeling off, different, after my time chatting with Alexandra B. I mean, Chris'd always been good to me, but I did notice how he could joke a little too much, be microaggressive, make me "othered." And I was hypersensitive to all those things now, saw injustice in everything, and I was sure I was right about the world, so . . .

After I got off the phone with Chris, I scrolled through Alexandra B's texts, and they were all very nice, just wanting to reconnect. She called this a *volatile* time for me, said that it was *imperative* that I talked to someone and not *internalize* my guilt, or, worse, use it as a force for destruction. And yeah, it all seemed sensible, because Alexandra B was a sensible, sensible person, but she was also a different generation, so maybe not in touch with how my generation was? My generation just didn't actually *get* shit unless we experienced it, so all her ideas of justice and just talking about it? Well, they didn't work anymore. People needed more than that.

So I shut her text window down and called Mark and told him I had a good time. He sounded overjoyed, of course. I told him I wanted to see him again, like soon—maybe tomorrow—and of course he was all over that. So we made plans, and as we did so, I was like, *Oh god oh god oh god. I have to go into that gross porn place by myself. Oh god oh god oh god.* But I guess you've gotta just suck it up sometimes, you know, bite the bullet, so that's exactly what I did.

MARK MCVITRY

We always had these kickball tournaments at Camp Burroway, like every summer, and they were fun as hell, just 'cause the kids all got real competitive. Each cabin was usually a team, but my last year there, for some unknown reason, they decided to mix it up, let us pick our own teams. They said it was 'cause the guy cabins had more of an advantage—'cause of our strength or whatever—but that was bullshit, 'cause a few years in a row a girl cabin won. But whatever. Picking our teams was this huge fuckin' thing, because there were these rules, like gender rules and age rules, and it got more confusing than it was worth. Well, summer after eighth grade, like the night before the start of the tournament (it took like five days . . . five days, ten games), I was sitting by Ricky around the campfire, 'cause I didn't have any problem sitting next to him—I wasn't some sort of asshole like Corky made me out to be. Well, he was sitting there with his black hoodie, grabbing his knees and rocking back and forth, and I was like, "Dude, you cold? It's still like eighty degrees out."

He shook his head and looked away. I just shrugged, 'cause that's just how he was—weird and antisocial. Couldn't hardly say more than two words to him without him just shaking his head or being mute. So I started talking to some other kids about teams and shit. We had 'til the next morning at ten to figure out what they were gonna be. Had to have our sign-up sheets all done by then. Well, we needed one more guy, our grade, and we couldn't think of who was left. Like everyone seemed to be taken, all the good ones anyway. And then, like to my right, I heard this little squeak—seriously sounded like a fuckin' mouse—and then I remembered that Ricky was sitting there. So I looked over, and he was staring at me with these really wide eyes, almost like he was frightened of something.

"What?" I said.

"You need another guy?" he said.

I looked over at my teammates. I saw Danielle Torrance kinda shake her head. "Uhh," I said, "I think we're actually good, Ricky."

"Oh," Ricky said, still grabbing his knees.

"But I think Jimmy Garfield is still looking for his team," I said.

"It's cool," he said.

"Thought you were already on a team," I said.

"It's cool." He looked away, and I'll be honest, I felt bad for a minute. I mean, it couldn't be easy to have nobody want you on their team, and I didn't hate him or anything—I was just thinking of the best way to win, the best odds. 'Cause whichever team won got to be served this wicked awesome six-course dinner by all the losing teams. It was a fuckin' *riot*, 'cause we basically got to order everyone else around for a few hours and they had to wear aprons and look real stupid. So there were some high stakes, for sure, and that's why I didn't ask Ricky to be on the team. Thing was, Ricky was probably an *okay* person to have on your team, but he was fuckin' unreliable. Seriously, there were times when he refused to even participate, would just sit in the cabin and read or whatever, and since Corky always took his side, he didn't get into trouble. Which was bullshit, 'cause if any of the rest of us just skipped out like that? Well, we'd have to eat dinner in the cabin alone for the next couple days.

Well, what happened that year was that we lost, like big-time, like got seventh place. (And I call bullshit on this, 'cause when we were up against Jimmy's team, I caught one of their balls, which should've given them an out, but I accidentally dropped it and Corky said it didn't count. Thing was, I dropped it, like *two full seconds* after I caught it! But whatever.) And Ricky was placed on Jimmy's team, and they fuckin' *won*, so Ricky ended up getting the six-course dinner, and I ended up serving him his goddamn drink. When I did, he moved that fuckin' glass of Coke away and looked up at me with these slitted eyes and said, "There's not enough ice." And I could've decked him, I really could've, but I didn't. I just went back and got him some more fucking ice. But then when I set it back in front of him, the cup literally overflowing with ice, he said, "Too much. Dump some out." I was so fuckin' outraged, and I didn't actually know why. 'Cause that was the whole deal, that the winning team got to be total assholes to the losers, and I'd done it before, and it was usually just funny, but for some reason, that year, waiting on Ricky, I just got pissed, and from then on, I really didn't talk to him much ever again.

That was summer before freshman year. Kinda turned out that freshman year was also the year I started hangin' out with Wesley Thompson. Before then, me and Wes saw each other, but we hung out with different people. I mean, we talked, but only in social situations, like during sports events, and even then we didn't talk that much. We were just people who knew each other. That's it.

But ninth grade, we were both JV track, so we saw each other every day in the spring. That and for some reason we had almost every fucking class together that year, like periods one through five; it was like the counselors *wanted* us to be good friends or something. So, really, not my fault that we became close. I mean, we were always together.

You'd think we would've started hanging out because of track, but that wasn't the case. Thing was, during practice, he hardly said a fuckin' word. Like he just sulked in the background, probably pouting because he just wasn't very good. Like I could run the 200-meter in 23.6 seconds, and him? He was like 28.2—worse than some of the fuckin' *girls*—and this had to have made him wicked sore. So I guess he just made up for it in classes, where he wouldn't ever shut the fuck up. He annoyed all the teachers, annoyed most of the students, and since I usually sat next to him, I always got roped in.

Like this one day in physical science class, we had to do team experiments, and even though Mr. Murphy paired me with Todd Jasper, and Wesley with Fred Madreau, Wesley went against his instructions and grabbed me for his teammate. This was all right with me, because Todd Jasper was a really awkward dude with dandruff, and I didn't want to spend *any* time with him, let alone experiment time. And Mr. Murphy didn't give a shit, always treated us like we were such a nuisance.

Anyway, that day Wesley was really excited about this one movie called *Orphan*, which sounded stupid at first. I mean, who cared about a crazy little kid and her adopted family? Boring as fuck, and it was on Netflix, which I didn't have anyway.

"No, dude," he said, "you don't get it. This orphan is *whack*. She's fuckin' *cray-zee*. The things she does, you wouldn't *believe*."

We were supposed to be doing something with liquids and these little colored strips of paper. Something about acidity—not really sure. To look like we were doing something, I took one of the strips and played with it, got it a little wet. I looked up at Mr. Murphy. He was just sitting at his desk reading something, so I put the paper strip down.

"Dude, come over. We'll watch it," Wesley said.

"Huh?"

"You'll be blown away, I swear."

"Isn't it like an older movie?"

"Just a couple years, but it's fuckin' good. My new favorite."

"Well, okay."

And that's pretty much how we officially became friends. *Orphan*. A movie about a girl who's actually a full-grown woman who basically wants to fuck her adoptive dad. Fuckin' weird, and I told him so. 'Cause like seriously, I didn't wanna see that shit.

"I told you it was messed-up!" he said.

"It was fuckin' *gross*."

From then on, we hung out constantly, and I'd be lying if I didn't say it was some of the most fun I'd ever had. We'd go to the mall, go to movies, go to the Meadows, play basketball, drink, smoke, talk about chicks we wanted to bang, just relax and be dudes, and it was pretty awesome. I mean, I had a bunch of friends, but never like a best bud, and suddenly I had one, and it felt real good. Also, Wesley was funny as fuck. If I wanted to laugh, I'd just call him up, 'cause he always had jokes, like *sick* jokes, and no matter how bad I was feeling, they'd always cheer me up, make my stomach hurt and my eyes water from laughing so much. It wasn't until junior year that he started getting kinda mean-spirited about things. Like pranks. Before junior year, we did 'em all the time. No big deal—small shit really. Started off like crushing pumpkins in people's yards on Halloween; getting ahold of people's Facebook pages when they left them on a computer screen, posting funny things about their shitting habits; kicking each other in the nuts unexpectedly; writing on people's faces when they passed out; creating fake email accounts and emailing people about how they were in trouble at school. Standard shit.

But junior year, Wes started getting really anxious, like the little stuff we were doing wasn't working for him anymore, like he was addicted and needed a better fix. Like the thing with Breanna Mills, the girl with cancer who was bald because of chemo. Well, he knew that she was a member of this one support website, because she made this speech in English class about how it had helped her get through. Said that without all the supporting comments, she didn't know if she'd be able to make it, and blah blah blah. Well, Wesley found the site, then he found her *name* on the site, and he replied to one of her posts saying, **BALD CHICKS GIVE GREAT HEAD.** Once he showed us the post, we just busted out laughing, 'cause this chick was seriously *annoying* about her cancer. Was all she could ever talk about, as if we didn't know about it, her being bald and all. But after, I did feel a little bad. It wasn't the nicest thing to do. Chick had *cancer*, after all.

So after Breanna's thing, every fucking thing he did and every fucking thing he suggested was about somebody's deep emotional shit. Like that was his drug, finding out what made people really messed-up and making fun of it. And it just kept getting more and more out of control until, well, Ricky. But I'll be honest. Ricky? Dude, his prank was one of the *tamest*. Seriously. Like it wasn't even all that mean. Wasn't nice, obviously, but it wasn't the worst, by a long shot, and if anyone were to shoot us, it sure shouldn't have been him; on a scale of one to ten, with ten being the worst, that prank was like a four.

Anyway.

Something really fucked-up? Not that. Not the Maggie-Ricky picture. No. Something really fucked-up was the night we were all in Wesley's basement, drinking Bud Light, talking about Camille St. John's tits. It was the regular group—me, Wesley, Grant, Scooter, and Bryan—and we'd basically been drinking and playing video games all day. I was at that point where I was about to fucking pass out, could hardly even concentrate on the conversation, when all of a sudden, Wesley stood up and whipped his dick out.

"Know what I'm thinkin'?" he said.

"Jesus Christ. Put that shit away," I said.

"I'm thinkin' I'd fuck Camille in the ass, then make her lick it clean."

He reached into his pocket, brought out his phone, and showed us a picture of a pair of legs sitting at a desk. "You look close, you can see her fuckin' pussy. Look at that shit. She doesn't wear underwear!"

"You took that?" Scooter said.

"Fuck yeah, I did."

Soon we were all crowding around his phone, trying to get a better look at her snatch.

"Jesus, that's bio class," Scooter said. "I didn't know she was that much of a slut."

"She's just one of those you'd never think was. The best fuckin' kind," Wesley said.

"Damn. She's got some nice legs," Bryan said.

"What the fuck you looking at her *legs* for, homo?" Wesley said.

"I like every part. Equal opportunity, you know."

"You're a fuckin' faggot," Wesley said.

I was having a hard time actually seeing her cunt. It was too dark. I thought maybe I could see like a fold, but I couldn't be sure; I had to look closer.

"Look at McVit," Wesley said. "Really scrutinizing."

"She's not even naked," I finally said. "Look, you can see the outline of—

He dropped the phone on the ground. On impulse, I leaned over to pick it up, and when I did, I felt something soft on my ear.

"What the—?"

Of course I'd forgotten, in my state, that he still had his fucking cock out. Soon as I figured out what he was doing, I pushed him as hard as I could. He fell down, laughing, his dick just flopping out of his shorts.

"No homo," he said.

"You dumbfuck," I said.

"Cool it, man. It's just a dick. We all got 'em."

"Fuckin' asshole."

"Maybe you liked it too much, eh, McVit?"

And I was too drunk to reply, so I raced up the stairs, went out the door, hopped in my car, and drove the fuck home.

Okay, so Claire's suggestion for the next day after our date was to go to the Full Monte Motel. Yep—I didn't think I'd heard her right.

"The Full Monte?" I said on the phone. "Are you serious?"

"Sure," she said. "My parents have all this boxed wine, like *tons* of it. Never drink it, so it just sits there. They literally won't miss it if I take one. So why not just go there and drink? I mean, can't really drink here. Or at your place. The Meadows is . . . Well, I just don't wanna go there. Sure you don't either. So why not there?"

"But . . ."

"Hey—I know it sounds *forward*. But it's really not like that. It's just us hanging out in a room, drinking wine. Can you drink?"

"I haven't since . . ."

"Well, cool. You'll get buzzed quicker, 'cause your tolerance is down."

"I'm not sure."

"It'll seriously be like *so good* for you. You need to be a social person again. And what better way to do that than be in a *safe environment*?"

"The Full Monte?"

"No, with *me*, silly! *I'm* your safe environment! I'll make sure you're totally good, okay?"

"But what if—"

"We both have phones. Anything happens? Just a dial away, okay? Come *on*. I think this'll be really good for your recovery overall. And we spent the *entire day* together basically, and you were completely fine! I must have a calming effect on you!"

"You do. I've actually drawn . . . I'm just saying, I really like you."

"Good! I like you too! So let's do this. It'll be great."

"Okay."

"Perfect!"

"Okay."

"See you then."

"Okay."

This was all so surprising. Like never would've thought it was the same person I went to Stoney's with. I mean, what kind of girl was that forward anyway? Wasn't like chicks had the urge to bone every five seconds like guys did—at least I didn't think they did. Funny thing was, even though she *was* that forward, I didn't immediately think of Claire as a slut. Before the shooting, I would've. Probably would've met her at the motel and messed around, but I would've never talked to her again. I'd do the Marcy O'Malley thing, which meant I'd let her blow me on the DL but wouldn't ever acknowledge her in public. But with Claire? Even though she suggested a *motel* on our second date, I wasn't thinking that way. I still thought I was in love.

And since I thought that, I told myself I wouldn't have sex with her yet. I'd hold off like a fucking *girl*, because that's how much I liked her. It didn't seem right that our first time would be in a motel. It had to be something better, something special. So I'd go, drink from her boxed wine, and just hang out. I'd *talk*. 'Cause it was what people in love did. I was sure of it.

CLAIRE CHANG

So Mark picked me up, and he was wicked nervous, like literally shaking with his hands on the wheel. And I nearly backed out then, because that state could NOT be good for his condition. But then before he pulled out of my driveway, I saw him calm down a bit—like his hands gripped the wheel without moving, and his voice seemed normal—so I was like, *Okay, we're doing this.*

Before he'd rolled into my driveway, I had a short text convo with Alexandra B. She was hurt that I hadn't replied earlier, and I was like, *Uh, you're a grown woman. Why are you hurt that some teenage girl didn't reply to your texts?* But I didn't say that, was just really nice and polite, and said I'd just been so busy lately. She, of course, wanted to know if I was upset with how we'd ended things a while back—like us having our disagreement about revenge versus just talking—and I said I was so over that.

I think about our conversations a lot, she wrote. You are such a bright, interesting young person and I can't even imagine how everyone is struggling in your hometown.

I thought about this for a bit, about how she *couldn't imagine* this total shit—the shit going on in El Monte Springs, and maybe the shit going on in my head—and I thought, *Why not?* Why *couldn't* she imagine it? It wasn't that difficult to close your eyes and just picture other people's lives and towns and whatever. That's what I did all the fucking time—imagined what it was like to live in a city where people were, like, everywhere and there were tons of things to do besides hang out in the woods by some bonfire and drink.

. And wasn't that the whole point of the Conquerors? Like, to conquer racism and sexism and homophobia, wasn't the first step to imagine what it was like to be, as she said, *marginalized*? 'Cause how could you work toward real change if you didn't *imagine* first? I dunno. Maybe I was thinking too hard about it, but I just didn't like that she said that. Because if she'd actually tried to imagine what I was going through in my head, she'd understand that all that talk-talk-talk-things-through bullshit just wasn't really an option.

I am imagining Ricky's struggle every day and I think we need to conquer things in a different way than you, I wrote. It's no biggie.

Just remember that you are not at fault for what happened. Nobody is, she wrote.

I dunno maybe nobody is and everybody is, I texted. All I know is straight white males and their privilege get people killed and nobody should stand for it.

She didn't write back for a while, and I thought maybe it was because I was being harsh, but then, like five minutes later, she directed me to their website and said that the Conquerors New England chapter was having a rally in Boston and that I should seriously consider attending. I said it was hard for me to just go somewhere like Boston by myself—like I drove my parents' car, not my own—and asked why they hadn't paired me up with someone from that chapter anyway. It was literally so close.

They thought we'd be the best fit, she said. And I think they were right, don't you?

Well, then it was *my* turn to be silent for a while, because even though we'd literally connected really well right away, I wasn't sure about now. Kinda like relationships, maybe? Like you think right away that you're meant for each other, and then time happens and you realize certain things, and it just goes downhill. Anyway, I didn't want to start an argument over text, so I just told her, yeah, I thought we were a good fit and left it at that.

"Are you sure you wanna go there?" Mark said in his car. "We could just go out of town, to the country or something."

"Like on some smelly *farm*?"

"Maybe there's a park."

"In the summer? It's gonna be packed with kids. No. Let's go to the Full Monte. I already booked."

"You booked? With a credit card?"

"Yeah. They took my debit card."

"Well . . ."

As we were driving, I felt *myself* getting nervous. Like WHAT THE HELL WAS I DOING? Seriously, in my purse was a PIG'S TAIL BUTT-PLUG and A BOTTLE OF LOTION! If we got pulled over and a cop wanted to check inside, they'd think I was some *deranged predator*, and they'd ask about the boxed wine in my lap, knowing we were both literally underage. Jail time! So at every red light I was like, *Oh please please please please hurry up and turn green!* 'Cause it was taking forever to get there, and the longer it took, the more likely it was we'd get pulled over.

Well, finally we pulled into the parking lot. After he parked, we just kinda sat there for a while.

"This'll be good," I said.

"Yeah," he said.

So after more awkward silence, I got out of the car and went to the front desk, which was actually just this sliding window thing. There was this guy standing outside the window, talking to the desk clerk, and at first I thought he was checking in, but he stepped aside when I got there. He was obviously from out of town. He was wearing expensive clothes, like the type that were literally tailored for your exact body, and I guess that worked for him. His body was pretty nice, like totally fit, but a bit too muscle-y for me. And anyway, he was *old*, like maybe in his thirties.

I'd never actually met the desk clerk before, but he still looked familiar, 'cause everyone in the Springs looked familiar, and he gave me a suspicious eye when I told him all my information. He looked at my driver's license a long time, and I got a little panicky, because maybe he was fucking *memorizing* it! Maybe he was going to call my parents! Maybe he was going to call the cops! And then, the whole search-through-the-purse/wine-box thing! *Predator! Predator! Predator!* But whatever—he didn't. He just gave me the keys. Still, I tried to play it cool and said, "God, I just have *so much* summer school homework! Thank *god* there's a quiet place to do it!" He just shook his head. He'd probably had like *hundreds* of check-ins by horny teens. Who knows.

The room smelled wet, like someone'd left the shower on for a full week. The bed was a little soggy, and the chairs were this hideous pink color; they totally didn't go with the green carpeting.

"What a *dump*," Mark said.

"I think it's *perfect*," I said. "Like the *best* way to spend a lazy after-noon." There were these plastic cups by the sink, so I took a couple, filled them up with the boxed wine, and gave one to Mark. "Let's *do* this," I said. I threw it back in one gulp, which was obviously regret-table, since it was wine. After some serious coughs and a ridiculous red face, I said, "Maybe a little slower."

He was laughing his ass off, though, and that was good. Eased him in and everything. He sipped after he was done laughing, then took a seat on one of the chairs.

"Actually," he said, "this was a good idea. I was a little weirded-out at first, but I think you're right. A safe space for me to see if drinking is cool yet."

"Glad you approve," I said, pouring myself another cup, and making sure to sip it this time.

"And you're the perfect person for me to do it with."

"I'm glad you think that," I said.

So we drank cup after cup and ended up watching some middle-aged blond woman named Victoria Gorham on this talk show. She was talking about raising healthy kids—like techniques and stuff. It was boring, so I changed it to a reality tattoo contest marathon on Spike TV. The contestants literally looked like they spent all their time riding motorcycles and beating people up, but when they had their one-on-one interviews, it was weird, because some of them actually went to *college* and some of them actually sounded *smart*, and that was NOT what you'd expect from that group of people.

"Art is really great," Mark said. I could tell he was buzzed, because his eyes were a little slitted. "I can't imagine drawing your art on people's bodies, though. That'd be wicked hard."

"Do you draw?" I asked.

"I do a little."

"What do you draw?"

"Just pictures. I got the idea from Mrs. V. She said something about me getting such high grades in art. She said that art can be a therapy, so after a while I tried it."

"And does it work?"

"Sometimes."

"Like when?"

"Well, like I carry this one picture I did around with me wherever I go. It kinda helps me feel okay, just remembering it's there. I know, sounds dumb."

"Do you have it with you now?"

"Yeah."

"Can I see?"

"I don't really wanna look at it right now, if that's okay."

"Sure. No problem."

We drank some more, and he seemed fine, like not psycho. I checked my phone a lot and was surprised to see that Alexandra B hadn't responded. I checked the Conquerors on Facebook and Twitter. For some reason, I thought maybe she'd post about me, like tell everyone in the group to send their thoughts and prayers to a brand-new Conqueror, an Asian American girl in El Monte Springs, New Hampshire, who was trying to make sense of a brutal shooting that'd occurred in her town. But, of course, there was nothing like that. The only new thing was something about the Boston rally that was happening the next weekend, the rally she'd texted me about.

"Who're you texting?" Mark said. He was kinda slumped on the bed, sipping the wine.

"Oh, not texting anyone. Just checking shit, you know."

"Anything cool happening?"

"Nope, not at all."

Well, the tattoo show marathon went on for like two hours, and by the fourth episode, I was feeling both pretty good from the wine and also like full of anticipation, because Mark was *clearly* a lightweight having not had even *one* drink for like a *really long time*, and I could tell he was on the brink of passing out soon.

"This is real great, Claire," he said. "I should thank you for doing this for me. It's real great. You're real great."

"Well, I think you're real great too," I said. Seriously? I vomited a little in my mouth. Cheesy-ass shit.

"I've been thinking a lot about my life," he said. "Just a lot. Just. Well. You know. How it's changed. And you're the best change. *Real—* the best."

"Well, I'm not really a *change*."

"Yes, you are! You're the *best* change! Don't say you're not!" He leaned into me and gave me a small kiss.

"You want more wine?" I asked.

"Hell yeah, I do!"

"Cool."

For some reason, even though it was almost like *showtime*, I couldn't stop thinking of Alexandra B and feeling real bad about her not responding. Not like I'd asked her a question or anything, but I just assumed she'd continue the convo. But anyway.

I guess the wine got to me, 'cause I was just remembering our chats from before and how they had literally transformed me, how *she* had literally transformed me and my outlook, and how she'd helped me through my John Bloom crush and how I wanted to stay in touch with her. I finally took out my phone and typed, Hey u there? and waited for like six minutes pretending to listen to Mark talk about how his life had changed so much.

"I feel so fucking great!" Mark said. He was standing up now, swaying back and forth in front of the TV, just staring. After a while, he turned to me and said, "I used to see *him* in there. Like I couldn't have any screen around me because he'd always be in there."

"Huh?"

"I'd see Ricky!"

"Oh."

He looked back at the screen. "But I've been watching this TV for what—three hours?—and he hasn't shown himself *once*. That's a *cure*. Because of *you*."

"Maybe you should lay down."

I tried to look at him and get angry like I had before, but for some reason—maybe the wine?—I just couldn't feel much of anything for him but pity. Like, he just seemed so pathetic, swaying in front of the TV, talking about seeing Ricky Graves on the screen.

Meanwhile, I was getting *wicked* stressed about Alexandra B not replying. I mean, maybe she was busy, but she'd *never* taken that long to respond to me before. I went through all these scenarios in my head.

Like maybe she actually *had* given up on me, like knew I could never become a real Conqueror, because—

"Claire, I know we only went on like that one date," Mark said. "But . . ."

Did I *want* to become a real Conqueror? I didn't even know what it meant, really. I mean, after I got through this phase of talky-talky, after I passed to the next level (I think that's how they phrased it—*passed*, like it was a real test or something), what then? I'd get to go to rallies, wear pins, shout in crowds? I could do that without becoming a part of a club.

"I think I love you," Mark said.

Thinking about it, I realized I didn't give a flying fuck about the Conquerors anymore—they were just a name, just some online group of people—but I *did* care about Alexandra B. 'Cause she was a person, a *real* person, someone I'd talked to and gotten to know, and even though we hadn't communicated that long, I felt something deep, a connection, and I genuinely liked her, and she'd been so kind to me, and she'd taught me things, opened my eyes, made me see the world . . .

"I'm sorry," Mark said. He sat on the edge of the bed and put his hands in his lap. His eyes were closing. He was way drunk. Looking at him, I knew I couldn't go through with my pig-tail plan. It sounded so stupid. What was I gonna do? Just wait 'til he passed out, then take his clothes off and stick it in? Ew. And like he wouldn't wake up. I'd be in jail for sure.

"Mark—"

"I know it sounds *crazy*. We didn't even . . . I mean . . . You must hate me."

"I don't hate you. God, you're drunk."

"What we did . . ."

"Shhh. It's okay."

"Claire. What we did. How can anyone forgive me? What we did. God . . . Everyone left me. Nobody wanted to . . . Only you. You. And Corky. You and Corky. And I love you."

"Mark. Shhh."

"And what we did to Ricky. What we did . . . I deserved . . ."

"You didn't deserve anything."

He lay down on the bed and closed his eyes. My phone vibrated. I looked at it and—*Yes, Yes, yes! Alexandra B!* She said, I'm here.

"Claire, just don't hate me," Mark said.

I will check out the Boston rally for sure, I typed. Sounds awesome maybe we can talk tonight?

She said, Sure. I'd like that.

"I was close to Ricky once too, you know," Mark said. His eyes like kept opening and closing, and I wondered if he even knew what he was saying. Honestly? He looked kinda cute like that—semiconscious, I guess. "I'll try to be a better dude," he said. "I promise."

And that was it: he kinda turned around on the bed and passed out, his mouth wide open. He snored, but not that loud. I shook him a little, but he didn't wake up.

I got up, got the pig's tail from my purse, opened the box, and sat in the chair. I just wanted to look at it and imagine getting revenge with a humiliating pic. I wanted to see if there was any of that left in me. 'Cause at the beginning, right when we'd gotten to the motel, it'd been there, that rage. I couldn't wait to humiliate him, beat down his fuckin' privilege some. But then, holding it in my hand as he snored, I felt gross all over, and not only that, but the tail looked really fucked-up, like something *medieval.* And the more I stared, the more I was like, *Why the hell had this thing ever been invented? What fucked-up brain had thought it was a good idea to have this thing sticking out of your ass?*

I dropped it in my lap. I felt tired and sad, and all I wanted was to talk to Alexandra B and tell her that she'd changed my life and that my anger wasn't that bad anymore, but that I felt really, really sad that

I hadn't helped Ricky more and that some people's lives just overall sucked more because of societal problems, and that even straight white boys like Mark McVitry had these awful demons lurking everywhere in their heads, and I guess the only thing that mattered in the end was that we tried our best not to hurt people and also tried to imagine everybody's pain, 'cause that was the only way toward some sort of peace.

I started crying, clutching my phone. I typed I really appreciate you, Alexandra.

She responded: ♥

I closed my eyes.

An hour later, I woke up. My face was crackly. Mark was grabbing my shoulder, shaking me. "Claire," he said. "Claire, wake up."

"What?" I forgot where I was for a second. Then. Oh yeah. My head hurt.

"Something's happening next door. Someone's in trouble, I think."

"In trouble?"

"We should go help, see if we need to call the police."

I noticed that the pig's tail wasn't in my lap anymore. It was back in its box and tucked neatly into my purse. I looked at him. "Mark," I said. "Did you—?"

"We gotta get going," he said. "Come on."

"Mark—"

"Let's go."

"Mark . . ."

But he was already out the door.

JEREMY LITTLE
REACHES OUT

MAN-DATE CHAT TRANSCRIPT
JANUARY 17, 2015

Rickyg9999: hey man

Jeremyinsf: hey, how you been?

Rickyg9999: so I missed you last week

Jeremyinsf: yeah, sorry. was out of town again

Rickyg9999: down in Los Angeles?

Jeremyinsf: nah. up in Napa Valley. some of my friends have a winery up there.

Rickyg9999: they own a winery? wow that's real cool. I've never seen a winery before except on TV and they always look wicked nice like perfect, like its where you'd want to go and just chill and be one with nature lol

Jeremyinsf: haha I guess it was something like that. how are you?

Rickyg9999: I had to start school again and I hate it

Jeremyinsf: can't be all that bad, right?

Rickyg9999: like I said, people up here are lame

Jeremyinsf: you ok?

Rickyg9999: yeah I guess, just hate it here so much and now it's freezing, makes it all the worst

Jeremyinsf: but you're almost finished with school. that should be exciting. what are you gonna do afterward?

Rickyg9999: dunno. maybe come out there ;)

Jeremyinsf: sure, it's a nice place to be

Rickyg9999: so you'd help me out??

Jeremyinsf: help you out?

Rickyg9999: I dunno it sounds like you have a lot of friends and people who own winerys and that kind of thing so if I came out there I would have to find a job and a place to live unless your gonna let me live with you lol

Jeremyinsf: hmm

Rickyg9999: ok I understand

Jeremyinsf: I mean, we haven't even met

Rickyg9999: that's why you should come out here

Rickyg9999: we can meet properly and get to know one another face to face and you can see what kind of misery I'm living in, and when you see that I'm 100% sure you'll tell me to get the hell out of here lol

Rickyg9999: you'll sweep me off my feet

Jeremyinsf: haha

Rickyg9999: I'll be honest, sometimes I watch chick flicks, not like all the time or anything

Rickyg9999: but sometimes I have to admit I like the idea of being in love

Rickyg9999: like being swept off my feet

Rickyg9999: I just wanna feel something that special, seems like everyone else gets to feel it except me haha

Rickyg9999: if you come out here I can guarantee that I'll make sure you see what you want to see

Rickyg9999: you said you've never been to New Hampshire, there are lots of trails and forests and stuff and we can go hiking and I'd even go out in the winter if you wanted lol

Jeremyinsf: I'm sure it's beautiful

Rickyg9999: or I think there are some winerys somewhere

here too I'm sure

Rickyg9999: not as nice as in California but maybe ok, I mean New Hampshire isn't the worst state or anything

Jeremyinsf: you go back and forth! haha

Rickyg9999: no, I love the state for real cuz its my home but just the people here in El Monte Springs are so stupid

Jeremyinsf: there are stupid people everywhere. lot of stupid people here too.

Rickyg9999: I guess your right but probably less

Jeremyinsf: people are stupid in different ways no matter where you are. they are also remarkable in different ways too.

Rickyg9999: yeah I guess! your incredibly smart, like genius level I'm sure. that's why I like chatting with you we have a real connection

Jeremyinsf: I'm not that smart

Rickyg9999: see that proves you are, my history teacher says people who are real smart don't ever think there smart and people who are stupid think there real smart

Jeremyinsf: haha well, your teacher has a point, I think

Rickyg9999: everyone around here thinks there soooooo smart

Rickyg9999: Like Corky, I told you about him before, my sister's ex

Rickyg9999: he's always saying things like he's the smartest person in the world, giving me advice on how to live and stuff when he doesn't really know shit

Rickyg9999: I mean he's a plastics factory worker

Rickyg9999: Jesus

Jeremyinsf: I guess it might be easier to find traditionally intelligent people in cities, but that doesn't mean they're necessarily "smart."

Rickyg9999: I'm not sure what you mean traditional smart but I'm sure out there people don't go around spitting in the street and yelling at each other in their trailer parks at 3am

Jeremyinsf: haha I think that happens everywhere

Rickyg9999: well you got out of your little town so I will too

Jeremyinsf: good. It'll be a good experience I'm sure.

Jeremyinsf: so you said before that you like chick flicks?

Rickyg9999: lol no just sometimes if there's nothing else on TV, not like I sit and watch Sex and the City every day lol

Jeremyinsf: haha I'm not sure how much Sex and the City anyone can take

Jeremyinsf: but what did you mean when you said that you'd want to be swept off your feet?

Rickyg9999: oh I just mean that you know in those movies everyone gets to be in love, even though they lose it then win it again they always end up happy with the person they want or should be with

Rickyg9999: I know it's bullshit and everything but sometimes I look around school and like everyone has someone and they don't even deserve them or whatever and I don't have anyone and I want it so bad

Jeremyinsf: what's your favorite chick flick?

Rickyg9999: hmm probably The Proposal with Sandra Bullock cuz it's real funny and she just hates Ryan Reynolds at first, doesn't see his true inner heart or whatever, but then she goes and visits his family and she falls for him

Jeremyinsf: do you see yourself like her or him?

Rickyg9999: oh definitely like him, I mean I have lots to offer but people can be real cold and not take time to get to know who I am especially around here

Rickyg9999: if they came and saw me (hint hint) they'd see that I can be awesome ;)

Jeremyinsf: so you see yourself in a long term relationship

Rickyg9999: of course, isn't that what everyone wants? and seriously if you were here I know I'd probably be into you, sorry not a creeper or anything we just connect great ;)

Jeremyinsf: relationships can be very, very painful

Rickyg9999: oh I get it but I haven't even had anything so I wouldn't know

Rickyg9999: so if I came out there I could stay with you for a little while?

Rickyg9999: ?

Rickyg9999: maybe even just a few days to check out the city

Rickyg9999: I think I have enough money to buy a plane ticket

Rickyg9999: it's like maybe $200 or something?

Jeremyinsf: I'm guessing it's a bit more than $200

Rickyg9999: well I have some money I saved from this summer job I had last year working the concession stand and I haven't spent any of it, cuz what am I gonna buy here?

Jeremyinsf: well, let me know

Rickyg9999: I could just leave on the weekend sometime. and maybe you and me could look for jobs for me or something if your up for that lol

Jeremyinsf: it's hard to look for jobs on the weekend. your best bet is the internet.

Rickyg9999: well maybe you could talk to some of your friends, maybe they need an assistant or something? I can use Excel I used it in my intro to business class and I'm wicked good with doing online research since I did a 10-page English paper and had to look all the facts up about Shakespeare

Rickyg9999: plus I'm always on time for work sometimes even early, like last summer when I worked concessions I was always the first one there and my boss said I was the ideal employee

Rickyg9999: plus I type wicked fast as I'm sure your aware of since my messages come up so quickly, I think I type like 90 words per minute or something like that. anyway everyone is always amazed at how fast I can type

Rickyg9999: you got quiet

Jeremyinsf: just thinking

Rickyg9999: about what?

Jeremyinsf: just about when I left my hometown

Rickyg9999: I bet it was great, fantastic

Jeremyinsf: circumstances weren't so great

Rickyg9999: why?

Jeremyinsf: can't really go into it now

Rickyg9999: oh ok bad memories I get it

Jeremyinsf: gotta run, bud. ttyl

Rickyg9999: ok. I'll let you know when I can get a plane ticket

Rickyg9999: probably in March or something? I have spring break maybe come out then instead of just the weekend. who knows maybe I'll find a job and end up staying lol

Rickyg9999: ok man talk to you later

Jeremyinsf: bye

Rickyg9999: bye

Jeremyinsf has closed his chat window.

JEREMY LITTLE

In Racketsville, North Dakota, I had a girlfriend named Carly Sims, a nervously pretty, small-boned brunette who'd dropped out of school our sophomore year to work full-time at the Dairy Queen. We'd known each other since childhood, had hung out at each other's houses through our prepubescent and teen years. When she dropped out, I saw her less frequently, and by our junior year, I'd forgotten about her, or rather, I'd forgotten about our consistent camaraderie, for I saw her at the Dairy Queen every once in a while, and we were generally amicable.

On the day I asked her to prom, she was very busy; the sun had blasted a constant near-tropical heat all over town, and people who'd stayed cooped in air-conditioned buildings all day ventured out to the one place certain to cool their palate. Carly raced around her soft-serve workstation, taking orders without her casual smile, and I could tell by her glistening forehead and swollen eyes that she'd worked a double shift. Two customers before me, she wiped her forehead, said, "I'll be right back," ran to the small kitchen alcove, lit a cigarette, took three enormous drags, blew smoke from her nostrils, and snuffed the butt on a small glass plate. When she returned, she reeked of tobacco.

Back then, I didn't quite understand my sexuality. I had an idea, but I'd never really had a chance to explore, just assumed my compulsions and desires hadn't fully manifested and were therefore unverifiable. I knew I had crushes (I thought Tom Selleck was one of the handsomest men I'd ever seen) but nothing to warrant a distinctly labeled orientation, and because I was still in that terrible rebellious stage of adolescence, and because I knew my mother didn't really like the chain-smoking Carly Sims, when it was my turn at the counter, instead of asking Carly for a grape Mr. Misty Float, I asked if she wanted to go with me to my junior prom.

"What?" she said, her eyes cloudy.

"The prom," I said. "Wanna go?"

"Okay," she said, shrugging.

Of course, my mother was livid, but it didn't really matter, because I was very, very happy. I'd never thought of Carly as anything but a friend—a casual one at that—but the more I thought of her, the more I thought of her in the long-term. I saw us married, with children, with professional jobs and middle-class lives and middle-class attachments. She would manage a Dairy Queen while I analyzed financial data. She would raise our kids while I brought home the money. She would do the laundry while I cooked the meals. We would be a unit, a team, and I would never have to spend another night alone with my parents, playing video games against the computer and reading books about dragons in the dark.

After prom, instead of going to the after-party, which was held at Saint Mark's Church and boasted 100 percent dryness, we went to the park and made out for an hour, her arid, nicotined tongue thrusting in and out of my mouth with a sharp, metronomic constancy. When we finished, we looked at each other, giggled, drank a few beers, and drove up and down County Road 64, a gravel expanse that connected the park to Highway 22, the main drag of Racketsville. I felt happy, and she felt happy, and as the pebbles hurtled away from and around my mother's Dodge Intrepid and the gravel crunched and exploded beneath the wheels and the night encased us in a youthful, star-filled euphoria, I asked her if she'd be my girlfriend, and she said yes, and with my hand still on the wheel, I leaned over and kissed her long and deep. Instead of worrying about the road or my driving, she accepted my kiss and reached down and grabbed my leg.

After a month or so, we had sex. She was closing the DQ by herself, and I was busy doing homework there, trying hard to keep my notebook from sliding into a patch of sticky red residue on the top of the table. From the kitchen she said, "Hey, Jeremy, could you come help me with something?" And when I got there, she was dressed in just an apron and a cigarette, the frying baskets hanging like miniature medieval torture devices behind her. Before I could protest, she threw the cigarette on the ground and jumped in my arms, kissing me hard, numbing my lips. I'd never liked the idea of sex in any room but a bedroom, and I'd certainly never pictured losing my virginity in a place laden with ground beef and lard, but she was insistent. And so, being a man and a virgin and a person hungry for validation, I fucked her over the dishwashing counter, the entire time thinking not of her ass or her vagina or her pendulous globular breasts, but of a mustachioed Tom Selleck leaning out of a red convertible, winking and smiling and saying, *Do me, Jeremy. Do me.*

I knew, then, after my first sexual encounter, that I had moved from the questioning category to full-fledged homosexual, and though over the next few months I tried to focus all my attention on Carly, I couldn't help but envision men, many men—short men, tall men, round men, bald men, hairy men, smooth men—all naked, all beneath me, all begging and groaning.

It was around this time, the summer between my junior and senior year, that Stan Newsome started coming into the Dairy Queen with some regularity. He was a quiet but amicable kid, a C-average student, a guy everyone liked, because he never really made much of a scene and agreed with nearly everything anybody said. He was thin and wiry and usually laughed in the halls alongside the jocks. I'd never had much interaction with him, but I liked him, and when I started seeing him more frequently at my girlfriend's workplace, I didn't, at first, think much of it. As time passed, however, I noticed that he not only talked with Carly but also touched her—on the shoulder, on the neck, on the arm—and she touched him back. This enraged me.

Though I was finally coming to terms with my sexuality, I wasn't comfortable enough to let go of Carly. With her around, I didn't have to admit anything, could just continue living a life in which everyone looked at me as just another guy from Racketsville—someone perhaps less gruff and sturdy and emotionally opaque than most of the men around, but someone who belonged, someone who would marry a Racketsville woman and produce Racketsville babies. It was very seductive, this belonging. It injected its allure right into my heart, spreading warmth like alcohol. So one day—a day I'd caught his hand sliding boldly up her triceps—after he and all the other customers were gone, I went up to her and said, "Stan Newsome," and she said, "Yeah? What about him?"

And I could tell by the tiny quaver in her voice that it was true, that she did like him, that she'd perhaps liked him for a long time, and that should I not be her boyfriend, she might allow his masculine stoicism to woo her. And I felt rage and envy and a terrible ballooning hollowness in my chest.

"I don't like it," I told her. "I don't like him coming around here. I don't want you to see him anymore. I don't want him to come in here."

"I can't forbid someone from coming in here, Jeremy," she said, her eyes small.

"No. But you don't have to talk to him like you do. Right in front of me. Flirting. How do you think that makes me feel?"

"I'm not *flirting*."

"Yes, you are."

"Okay. Whatever."

"Okay? What do you mean? You'll stop?"

"Stop what?"

"Flirting!"

"I'll stop talking to him, if that's what you want. It's stupid, you know. But whatever."

But they didn't need to talk for me to know that something was still happening, some sort of unspoken complicity, and the more I saw it, the more jealous I became. And this jealousy served two functions: first, it solidified my sexuality, for I realized, over time, that I wasn't envious of him per se, but of what proved possible for them should I just fizzle away, and second, it gave me an excuse not to have sex with her; I was too upset, I said. I couldn't get him and her out of my head, couldn't even perform because of how I felt about them. And despite my obtuseness, she didn't break up with me, but rather, became a lovelier creature, trying as much as she could to appease my rampant, outrageous illogic. She mistook my jealous outbursts for real, legitimate caring, and as time passed, she stopped giving Stan any sort of encouragement. When he came in, she turned around, asked coworkers to serve him, fell silent when he called her name. Soon he stopped coming in, and I breathed easier.

After graduation, Stan joined the marines. 9/11 happened, and he was deployed to Afghanistan, where he was killed in Operation Enduring Freedom. Racketsville mourned, and the Newsome family was visited by the then-governor of North Dakota, John Hoeven. Stan's obituary called him kind and quiet, always willing to help somebody less fortunate, and his funeral was attended by every single person in Racketsville but me. I was busy, I told my parents. I just couldn't go. I had things to do. They objected, of course, made me feel guilty, told me how un-American it was to stay at home. They said, "You knew him! How could you? You *knew* him." My father said, "He died for you, and this is the respect you show?" My mother said, "That poor family. You should feel ashamed." My father said, "Disgusting, Jeremy. I'm embarrassed." In the end, however, they left me seated at the kitchen table with a glass of water, staring at the wall, blinking away a flood of toxic, guilty tears.

Carly, at first, refused to talk about it, though I told her time and again that it was okay, that I wouldn't be mad, that I knew she and Stan had been close. Finally, after so much pestering, she put her hands to her face and said, "I'm sorry."

We sat in her car at the park off County Road 64. We hadn't been there since prom night, the night we'd confirmed our romantic dedication to one another, and though it all looked the same, I couldn't help but attach a chilly, unprocessed bleakness to everything. A park, I thought, should be filled with life, both man-made and natural: it should contain waterways, vegetation, benches, sidewalks, vendors. A park should be a place where people congregated on weekends, where multicolored blankets speckled rolling hills and girls in bikinis came to tan. A park should intersect nature and humanity; it should illustrate symbiosis and serve as a place for long-term memory formation. A park, in short, should be a place people wanted to be. It should not, in my estimation, be an empty flat stretch of farmland containing two picnic tables under a weeping willow tree. What I looked at, while Carly shook her head next to me, was lonely and desolate, a vast, unyielding nothing that stretched and roiled for uncountable miles.

"You loved him," I said.

She said nothing. She dug through her jeans pocket, brought out a pack of cigarettes, and lit one. She rested her wrist on the top of the steering wheel.

"You were in love with him," I said.

She blew a cylindrical gray stream out the window.

"You can tell me."

The sun peeked just above the horizon, pasting long, curved willow-shadows on the floor of the field. They crept onto the hood of her car.

"I told him not to go," she finally said.

"You told him not to go overseas? He didn't have much choice."

"I told him not to go into the *military*. You know me. I don't believe in all that shit. Killing. Fighting. Really, what's it for?" She looked out the window. An oval of sunlight dotted her forehead.

"Well . . ."

"He said it would pay for school. He said that once he got back, he would go back to school, get a real job. Then he could marry me."

"Marry you?"

"I said no, of course." She rested her elbow on the edge of the window and threw her cigarette out onto the grass. "You know that."

"Marry you," I said.

"I was never going to break up with you," she said, turning to me. The bottoms of her eyes sagged, adding age to the smoke. "You're the one for me, Jeremy. I know that. But still."

"You loved him too."

"It's different. It's a feeling."

"But you were in love with him."

"Maybe. I don't know. But long-term, I saw *you*. Every night. Even when . . . So I'm sorry," she said. "But you're my soul mate. You're like everything."

And as she said those words, as she told me how she'd picked me over him, had sent Stan to his death to save our relationship, in my head I planned my escape from Racketsville, from her, from the aggressive offensiveness of a park with no waterway. And over the next few days, pondering my life, my decisions, my relationships, I came into my own wretchedness, thrusting Carly into the cobwebbed recesses of the part of my psyche reserved for trauma repression and sexual deviance and psychopathic schadenfreude. And after I'd officially obliterated her as a caring, loving, beautiful woman, I left, moved cross-country without even a note, and I've never seen her since.

◆ ◆ ◆

In El Monte Springs, in my musty motel room, I felt nostalgic and weepy. I wasn't one to yearn for the past, and I certainly preferred complication and complexity over simplicity and pastoralism, but thinking about those years in North Dakota—even with all the emotional turmoil I'd undergone—pleasantly unburdened me. I looked at my phone. No messages. No missed calls. I threw it on the bed.

Craig had broken up with me in our living room, him reading, me trying to. It was late afternoon, and the sun threw a small spotlight onto our couch, brightening his left knee. I remember staring at his knee while he delivered his final sermon, wondering if later he might end up with a square of darker skin.

"Listen, Jeremy," he said, putting his book in his lap. "We need to talk."

I'd known it was coming, had felt it for weeks; it was the small things: him turning away in bed, him leaving the house before I woke up, him staying at work late, him leaving the room when I entered. It was like he couldn't stand the sight of me, like my very presence nauseated him. That we were in the living room at the same time on the same day meant only one thing: everything was finished.

"I just got a text from Donnie," I said, deflecting. "He wishes we'd hang out more."

"Jeremy."

"Maybe this weekend, if you're not too busy."

"Please. Don't make this harder than it has to be."

"It's cool if you are, though. Another weekend."

"Jeremy, this isn't gonna work. We both know that."

"Craig. Jesus."

"You've known for a while. We just haven't discussed it yet."

"I've known?"

"Yes. We've both known."

"That's interesting. That I've known."

"We've hardly talked this whole month."

"That's not true. I've talked. You've avoided me."

"No. We've both acted like the other wasn't even there. This isn't how relationships work."

I'd thought, over the past few excruciating weeks, that he'd known how much his evasiveness tore at me; I'd assumed he was trying to punish me for my inability to keep up with his new technologyless lifestyle. So the fact that he thought I was in on it too, that I was actually approaching an amicable split, enraged me, because it meant that throughout our years together he'd never been able to read me.

My desperation over that month had been as explicit as anything: When he exited a room upon my arrival, I'd call out to him, shout things from the kitchen, the bedroom, the living room, attempting a ridiculous high-decibel pseudoconversation. When he stayed late at work, I'd send takeout to his office. When he turned away from me in bed, I'd ignore his squirms and hold him from behind, if for just a few seconds, kissing the nape of his neck before flipping over and falling asleep. These things, to me at least, were not indicative of a man who wanted anything to end, who saw a split-up as a healthy, organic thing, who'd walk away sad but silent, knowing that while things hurt then, things would end up working out for the best in the end. No. These were the actions of a frenzied man, obsequious to his partner's every desire for fear of this exact conversation, willing to face humiliation for the sake of a frigid semblance of companionship. These were the actions of a man craving connection from the one person unwilling to give it to him. This was a man on the precipice of devastation.

"I've been here this whole time," I said, feeling my voice tremble. "You've been gone, but I've been here."

"Oh, man. Jeremy." The light on his knee lengthened, engulfing the top portion of his calf. "It's been a long time coming."

"You can't do this to me," I said.

"Jeremy—"

"No, no, no."

His face darkened. "I didn't think you were gonna . . ."

"What? You didn't think I was gonna care?"

"We've grown apart," he said.

"No. *You've* grown apart from *me*. I'm still in the same place. But now I have to—oh god. It's because I couldn't do without technology? Is that it? It's because—" I hated myself. I was crying.

"No, that's not . . . I mean . . . it's partly, but no, it's just . . . we grew apart, Jeremy."

"I'll try again, okay? I wasn't giving it my best shot last time. I can do it, I swear. My head just wasn't into it. I know I can do it. I'll show you."

"I don't care about that anymore," he said. "In fact, I'm going back. Gonna start texting again, maybe use a few apps."

"What?"

"I'm okay with it all now. I've come to peace with it."

"Breaking up with me gives you peace enough to go back to technology? You're kidding."

"It has nothing to do with you."

"Fuck. I can't be here right now."

"Jeremy, I'm sorry. I'm really sorry. I didn't think you'd react like this. I'm truly shocked. I thought—"

"I can't," I said. "Not now. I gotta get outta here. You're fucking suffocating me."

"Okay," he said.

While I'd always considered postbreakup drunkenness a Hollywood cliché, I went directly to the closest bar and proceeded to fulfill the stereotype. I wasn't much of a drinker—my friends taunted me mercilessly for my three-drink limit—but that afternoon, I downed four shots and five cocktails in a matter of two hours. The bartender—a skinny bearded guy in red-and-black plaid who I'd seen prancing around town with his similarly dressed comrades—cut me off, said he'd never seen anyone drink as fast as me, which I'm sure was a lie. I promptly cursed at him and called him a stupid hipster douchebag, and he kicked me out, told me never to come back. Apparently, he owned the place.

I wandered the streets until I felt sick and dizzy, climbing steep hills in the hopes of sweating out some of the alcohol. When I got back home, I went straight to the bathroom and vomited until there was nothing left.

"Jeremy?" Craig said, knocking on the door. "You okay?"

I didn't respond. Even in my state—my head pounding, my limbs weak, my stomach gurgling—his voice paralyzed me.

"Do you need anything?" he asked.

I swallowed, then tasted hot vomit. My voice was somewhere in my chest. I had to cough it up. "I can't talk right now," I said.

"Are you okay? Sick?"

"Yeah, I'm sick. Go away."

"I'm staying with my sister tonight," he said.

"Good."

"Hey."

"Please go away."

"I'll call you tomorrow."

"Don't bother."

"Good night."

"Fuck off," I said.

And that was it. I was alone. When I heard the front door close, I leaned over the toilet and dry-heaved. When I was finished, I took my phone out and stomped on it until it was nothing but shards of black circuitry and white plastic. Panting and sweating, I stared at the remnants for a while, then sat down and leaned against the wall. After a few minutes of contemplating the mess—my life—I passed out.

The next day, I went to the Apple store and upgraded.

◆　◆　◆

On day five of my time in El Monte Springs, July 22, I found Alyssa hanging out at the motel office again. It was like she'd carved a spot out in the pavement a few feet away from the service window, a white-and-brown spray of cigarette butts circling her feet. Behind the window, George Winwood sat in his chair, watching another black-and-white movie on the TV/VCR combo. He looked up when I approached, nodded, then went back to his movie.

"You just hang out here?" I said to Alyssa.

"You gotta be persistent to get jobs," she said, smiling. "I come here every day."

"But Robbie's not here."

"He comes every once in a while, just to check up."

"Oh, and I thought you were here to see me."

"Ha. You wish." She winked.

"Hot out, huh?" I said.

She shrugged. "I guess."

"Feel like watching a movie?"

"Like in the theater?"

"No, like in my room. I rented one from room service, but I haven't actually watched it yet."

"You can do that here?"

"Yeah, I was surprised too. Everything else but the TV is pretty low-tech. Funny that they have *that* thing in the office."

"So what movie did you rent?"

"Rom-com. *The Proposal.*"

"Um, seriously?"

"Have you seen it?"

"Like two years ago."

"Well, watch it with me again."

I'm not a movie snob, by any means, but the formula of romantic comedies tends to irritate me. I hate that the leads are always white with a gay and/or black sidekick. I hate that characters are able to afford nice Manhattan apartments on intern salaries. I hate that the male and female leads hold no physical attraction for each other until one of them does something impressive and/or selfless, and I hate that secondary characters are always whittled down to a quirk or two, making them more like props than people. Watching *The Proposal* with Alyssa, however, I felt none of these annoyances; I found it very entertaining. When Sandra Bullock danced with Betty White in the Alaskan forest, I laughed so hard my stomach hurt, and I ended up clutching Alyssa's arm for support, wiping tears from my eyes.

The thing was, for a moment, while watching that movie, a movie Ricky had mentioned by name, Ricky's sad, omnipresent specter evaporated, leaving behind the wondrous possibility of genuine, raucous laughter. And I knew I only had a short window of time before he materialized again, coating my room and the motel and the town with his thick, sulfurous misery, so I took advantage of those few moments and laughed as hard as I could. I laughed and I laughed and I laughed.

"You really liked that movie," Alyssa said after the first credits appeared. We were on the bed, propped up against the headboard. The room was dark except for the TV glow. I'd closed the curtains before starting the movie. I got up, opened them, and introduced a spear of sunlight to the room. I shaded my face. I was still laughing.

"It was funny," I said.

"It wasn't *that* funny."

"Yeah, it was."

"Whatever you say."

I let my laughs finally dissipate, and when I did, the image of Ricky sitting in front of a television watching that movie, laughing and dreaming, assaulted me. I breathed deep.

"Lemme ask you something," I said, sitting back down on the bed. "Do you think movies like that are actually harmful?"

"Harmful?" she said.

"Like do you think they influence people to think that that's how real life is?"

"Um, no. Everyone knows that that's not how real life is. It's a *movie*."

"But some people might think that that's how their life *should* be."

"If they do, they're dumb as shit." She grabbed a pillow and hugged it close.

"But maybe if you watch enough of them, you start believing."

"So if you watch enough horror movies, you start believing that there are guys in masks everywhere killing people with chainsaws and machetes?"

"There *are* guys in masks who kill people with chainsaws and machetes."

"Not that many," she said. "Seriously."

She moved closer to the edge of the bed. I narrowed the space between us. I wanted to be near her. I put a hand on her belly. She looked at it for a while, then said, "Anyway, do I think that movies can influence people? I suppose. I dunno, I haven't thought about it that much, to be honest. But I guess there are real stupid people out there who watch these things and think, 'Oh, that should be my life' and then get hurt over and over and over 'cause it doesn't happen. I mean, I had this friend in Boston, Sandra, my only friend really, and she was married but, I dunno, there was something wrong with the marriage. She didn't go into that much detail or whatever, but I just knew from some of the things she said that it wasn't that great. Well, anyway, she loved these types of romantic comedies and would always be telling me that my one guy was out there and that it was just a matter of time before he showed up and swept me off my feet. And when I said I didn't care about that shit, she'd give me these really weird looks, like I was some sort of alien, like every woman in the world was supposed to care about that romantic shit, like what was wrong with me? I mean, I'll be honest, I think about it sometimes, but not a whole lot. Mostly these days I just think about how I'm gonna take care of this kid." She pushed herself up. My hand fell off her belly.

"But it's safe to say that many people aren't like you, right?" I said.

She shrugged. "I dunno. Maybe."

"Like it's safe to say that most people want to be in love," I said. "Like they want it bad. And when they watch this stuff, well . . ."

"Yeah, I guess. Now that you say it like that, it makes sense that people watch this shit and they think love is like how it's shown. I mean, these kinds of movies don't really go into all the really horrible garbage that comes with love and everything, so maybe they've made us less accepting of faults? Like more demanding? Like we won't settle for anything but the absolute best? And maybe that's why a lot of people my age just aren't able to keep relationships very long. 'Cause people in general are all full of garbage, and if you can't accept other people's garbage, you'll just never be with anybody. I dunno. This conversation is kinda deep right now, especially after watching a movie like *that*."

I laughed. "Well, you're a deep person."

She laughed. "Not really. I just let life happen, I guess."

"Not from what I gather. You're anything but submissive to life's challenges."

"You're weird," she said.

"I could learn a thing or two from you," I said.

Instinctually, I wrapped my arm around her shoulder. She was closer to the edge of the bed, so I had to reach a bit. She recoiled slightly at first, but then, after a few hesitant moments, she came closer and rested her head on my chest. I hadn't been in that position with a woman since dating Carly Sims, and while I'd expected to feel slightly repulsed by her hair's fruit scent, her breasts' softness, her fingers' daintiness, I wound up feeling the opposite—an instant, blistering longing. And after just a couple minutes in this position, letting the longing expand inside me, I tilted her head toward mine, closed my eyes, and kissed her.

ALYSSA GRAVES

You know how when you explain and explain and explain to people what's happening in your head and, even though they nod and everything, you know they just don't get it? It's like people have this automatic-response thing, like there's something in our brain that makes that head movement not in our control, and even though I'm not good at a lot of things—judgment being one of them, because look: pregnant!—I think I'm good at controlling shit like that. Back in school, if I didn't understand something, and I didn't understand a lot—seriously terrible teachers, especially in math—I'd never nod. I'd make myself *not* nod even when I knew they wanted it. I'd be like, nope, not getting it from me, never, no way, no how, and then in my thoughts, *Keep your head very, very still, Alyssa. Very, very still,* and that was actually pretty hard because of all that ingrained stuff.

Anyway, this was how it was with my mother, and granted, she wasn't in her right mind—I get that—but she kept nodding, and that pissed me the fuck off. 'Cause she didn't get it; she didn't get any of it. None of it registered with her—my pregnancy, Ricky's death, our entire situation. She was just retreating to somewhere else, somewhere in her dream-head, so her nodding was just a tic, a complete nothing response.

I mean.

I get it: things take a while to sink in, and really traumatic things that happen to you suspend you in a state of shock or whatever; there's evidence of it everywhere. I'm a perfect example. My state of shock lasted months and months, and it wasn't until I was at home, nearly ready to pop, that it sunk in—that the fact that my brother had killed a guy and injured another and shot himself had actually happened, and that I was living with a woman with such bad denial issues that she'd spend entire days watching the fucking Home Shopping Network and commenting on diamond pendants and earrings and bracelets and toe rings as if they had these magical Harry Potter powers—powers that'd take away my baby and bring back Ricky. This being the same woman who'd told my friends all about *introspection* and *purpose*, and who'd once announced to Ricky that she knew, deep down, that she was a full-fledged genius waiting to be discovered.

Well. It came to a head the day Jeremy kissed me. After I got back from the motel, I found my mom sitting there, staring at the TV, her mouth wide open, and I saw a little bit of drool come down her lip, and I wanted to slap her real bad.

"Listen!" I said to her, and she looked up and wiped her mouth like I'd just woken her up.

"You've gotta get up," I said. "You can't just sit there all day!"

She looked shocked that I'd raised my voice, because so far I'd just been pretty quiet—doing the dishes and cooking and just picking up around her—but like I said, there's this point, this sinking-in point, and it was there, just around the corner. So I sat on the couch next to her, took her hand like she was my kid, and said, "I didn't mean to yell, but I don't think you get how hard this is for me."

She nodded.

"I know I should've come back earlier to help out. I should've come for the funeral. I know that. But you gotta realize that I'm here now, and I'm going through a whole bunch of shit, okay? I'm pregnant. See? You're gonna be a grandma. Do you get that?"

She nodded.

"And I can't hardly deal with anything. Anything. Like Ricky, and . . . I can't deal with that! I can't think about it! If I think about it too long, I get too overwhelmed. Because this!" I pointed to my belly.

She nodded.

"If I think about it, it's too much! Do you get it? I'm having a baby!"

She nodded.

"But I *have* to deal with it, because it happened, you see? I can't ignore it. It's there all the time, and you can't just push that shit away. You see? I should've been there for him more. You see?"

She nodded.

"I was gone. He texted me, but I didn't reply a lot of the time. I just didn't think about him much until . . . Don't you see? Oh god."

She nodded.

"Family, we're supposed to be there for each other. All the time, right? No matter what? Well, I wasn't thinking about . . . I wasn't thinking about him at all! He'd send me messages, and I wouldn't reply! Sometimes he'd say he was depressed. Sometimes he'd write me and tell me how depressed he was, and I wouldn't reply! You understand that that happened?"

She nodded.

"And then . . . I couldn't come back right after. I just couldn't. Not just because of the reporters. I just couldn't. I know you kept telling me to come back, to please come back. I know you did and I should've, but I couldn't! I said I needed to make money for the baby, couldn't just take time off, but I should've come back. I should've been there for you then, and I should've . . . I should've done so many things different. But it's over now, right? What more can I do?"

She nodded.

"And the worst thing—the worst fucking thing about all this—and it's so embarrassing, but I'll tell you, Mom—the worst thing about everything is that I haven't been able to have one single drink since it all happened, and you know I don't drink that much, never have, but it's all I've wanted since Ricky died."

She nodded.

"You don't get it at all!" I said. "You're just nodding, but you don't get it! This didn't happen to *just you*! You can't be so selfish. This happened to *me* too! And this is happening to me still!"

She nodded.

"Mother!" I said. "Stop fucking nodding!"

So before everything, as I've said, my mom and I had a rocky relationship. Not abusive really, but definitely rocky, starting with her telling me how I was "no good." But looking at our relationship as a whole, it was pretty fucking good—like she was my best friend—and yeah, all those parenting books and magazines said that you had to be a parent first and foremost and that you shouldn't try to be all chummy with your kids. Like there had to be a distance, there had to be discipline, coaching, tough love, etc., etc., etc. And that made sense for sure, but it was all on a case-by-case basis, because not every kid was the same, and not every kid had the same needs, like me and Ricky, for example. Me, I needed and wanted that friend, and it worked out; Mom and me helped each other in that respect. But Ricky? He needed more of a real "mom." Like sometimes she'd try to be friendly with him, like "cool," and he just didn't like it, kinda shunned her actually. I thought it was really rude at the time, but now I just think it was his way of telling her, *Stop it. I'm not Alyssa.* He was different. He needed structure—a role model or whatever—and even though she had all these grand ideas about all these big life-things, she just didn't know how to *be* with him.

Like I remember this one time when I was like seventeen and he was nine and my mom wanted to take us to see the movie *28 Weeks Later,* that sequel zombie movie with that guy who's now like one of the Avengers. My brother, though, he was only nine, right? And the movie was rated R, and he didn't even want to see it, wasn't one of those kids who bragged about seeing rated R movies—just didn't care at that point, I guess; I mean, he was only nine—but my mom didn't get that he didn't care about that. She was so used to dealing with me and—yeah, I was pretty stoked, would brag to my friends about seeing it in that offhanded way like: *Oh, yeah, I saw that. Kinda good but totally not that scary* (though it kinda was)—but with him, at that time he'd probably rather have gone to watch *Harry Potter*, because, again, he was only nine.

"I hate this, Mommy!" he said in the theater, and I was wicked embarrassed, because he wasn't really whispering and the people next to us kept giving us death glares.

"Shhh," she said.

"I hate this!" he said again, and this time the guy next to us, this kinda scrawny-looking glasses-faced guy, does the *Shhh* thing for my mom.

"Hey," I said. "He's just a kid."

"What's a kid doing in here?" he asked.

And this made a whole bunch of people in the front do the *Shhh* thing, and at this point I got mad, because I didn't think it was so horrible for a kid to say he hated something—especially when it was blood and guts on a big screen—so I was like, "Shhh yourself!" and this made the usher come to our row and ask if there was a problem, and everyone in the theater did this loud groan, but my mom just sat there chomping on her popcorn, looking at the screen, pretending nothing was happening.

"Mommy!" Ricky said.

"God, Ricky," she finally said, and the usher was just standing there all awkward, probably wondering what the hell he was supposed to do all by himself. It wasn't like movie ushers could call in for backup, like police.

"Ma'am?" he said, and of course my mom ignored him. "Ma'am?" he said again. And at this point, a few people were actually leaving the theater—demanding their money back, I'm sure. "Ma'am?" he said a little louder.

"*What?*" she said.

The manager came a minute later and escorted us out, and Mom wouldn't talk to Ricky for the rest of the day. Completely childish on her part, but so typical.

Not like she was like that all the time. I mean, sometimes she really *did* get him, I think. Like a few Christmases ago, for example, I wasn't there or anything, but Ricky told me all about it. Apparently, Mom made this big to-do, like she'd bought us real gifts because she'd gotten a raise at work like the month before. She shipped mine, obviously (some awesome shit, like really nice jewelry and this cool Kings of Leon T-shirt, and a pair of red sandals and a hoodie and a coffee press), and she just gave Ricky's to him. It was just one gift, but it was a fucking doozy. It was a laptop! I guess my mom thought her low-tech home was pretty much expired, so she'd finally allowed Ricky to join the real world. She'd also bought Wi-Fi.

Well, Ricky was ecstatic. He actually called and I answered, and I could just hear him going *nuts* with happiness, and that was really great because he hardly ever seemed that way those days.

"Mom said there'll be restrictions on the times of day I can use it," he told me, "but I mean, it'll be in my room, so how will she know?"

"I think she can find out," I said.

"I feel like a real person!" he said. "Maybe next year she'll let me have an iPhone."

"Most likely."

"It's so awesome."

"Yeah. Well. So what're you gonna do with it?"

"Well, for one I can finally do my homework at home and not at the library."

"Just don't get too distracted with stuff, okay?"

"Seriously, what family doesn't have at least one computer in their house?"

"I'm just saying. Focus on school, okay?"

"Okay, *Mom*," he said.

When I talked to my mom later, I asked her about the laptop, and she repeated her reasoning for not having Internet in her house all those years, even though I'd never asked that question. She said, "It's like letting a whole bunch of strangers into your goddamn living room, Alyssa. I didn't want that. But I understand now that Ricky needs Internet for school and other things, so I'm moving forward. I can't say I'm totally thrilled about it all, but I thought it was time."

I told her she was doing the right thing and she said thank you, and we moved on to the topic of my gifts, which I loved.

So.

Speaking of strangers—well, in a sense, not totally or anything—a lot of kids from my high school ended up going to UNH, and that's cool, but if I went away to college, I'd go *away*, if you know what I mean. Somewhere I wouldn't happen to run into anyone I knew. I mean, Boston was good, but it was still close. I mean, I occasionally saw people from El Monte Springs, and that sucked. One time, this kid like two years below me in school recognized me at the diner, and he was drunk with a bunch of his bros, and thank god I didn't have to wait on him—not in my section or anything—but he still shouted out my name and, since we weren't busy, I kinda felt obligated to go talk to them at their booth. So he told me all about college and parties and homework and whatever, said he was majoring in business, said he was gonna work on Wall Street, make tons of money as a financial something-or-other— probably like what Jeremy Little did—but I knew even then that he was a lot of talk, 'cause I'd heard through the grapevine that he'd actually dropped out and was working at some hotel in Portsmouth. But I let him talk, and his floppy-haired bro-friends were all nodding their heads kinda seriously, even though it was obvious they were wasted.

And then after he was done talking so highly of himself, he asked, "So, you plan on staying here forever?"

And at first, I thought he meant Boston, so I said, "I don't know."

"Yeah, I waited tables in high school," he said. "Guess it's something you grow out of."

And I was like, wow. Pissed off. Like, *Who the fuck are* you? Even if I *didn't* know his secret story, like the truth of his dropout, even if he *was* getting his business degree, who the fuck was he to act like that. Him being younger and stupider, telling me you "grow out of" waiting tables, like it was something he did as a kid for fun. Trying to sound above me.

"Rudeness is something *you* didn't grow out of," I said, and his bros were all like, "Oooooo."

"Hey," he said, "didn't mean to be rude. Was just sayin'. Don't know how anyone could wanna wait on shitty customers like me for very long."

And that scored him a few positive points, I guess, calling himself a shitty customer, and so we dropped the subject and just talked about El Monte Springs for a while—the people mostly—and after a bit he said, "You still talk to Corky Meeks?" and I felt this really heavy thing in my chest, like a dumbbell weight just dug inside my skin and plopped somewhere in my rib cage, because I hadn't talked about Corky in so long.

"No," I said.

"I always liked the dude. Seriously a nice guy when you talk to him one-on-one. He was my counselor at Burroway. Could hardly tell that he was the same guy who gave Greg Vincent that black eye. Just a cool-mannered dude."

"Yeah," I said. "I guess everyone's got more than one side, right?"

"Hey, how's your brother doin'?" he said. "He come out of the closet yet?"

And all his bros snorted at this, and I just stared at him hard, like seriously willing my eyes to have lasers shoot out of them, because what a fuckin' asshole. I mean, I knew everyone talked about it, about Ricky being gay, and I knew deep down it was true, but the way I saw it, Ricky had to discover that for himself; it wasn't anyone's place to make fun of something someone was truly struggling with, because look: everyone has something very sensitive beneath their outside selves, something they won't talk about to anyone. Secrets.

Take me, for instance. Maybe on the outside I seem okay, put together even, for a waitress, and I think I seem confident and feel confident in most things, but in all honesty, ever since I can remember I've had this terrible fear of having a child who hates me, like some devilish kid who really, really wants the worst for me, and I know that sounds like a weird fear to have as a kid, but ever since I can remember, I've thought about it, because your kids don't *have* to love or even like you, right? Just because they came from you? They can grow up with their own mind and their own brain and just kinda say, *So long, sucker.* I knew this early on. I knew you could just pop this thing out and they could turn around and *murder* you, or maybe just leave you and never talk to you again; it happens. And I know it's rare, but it's something that I think about all the time, such as: I have this recurring nightmare where I have a kid and I see it grow up, like really quick, like maybe a movie montage? And when it's eighteen, it just looks at me with really dead eyes and says, *Good-bye. I hate you,* and then turns around and runs away and disappears.

So what I'm trying to say is that everyone has these thoughts that they keep away, don't tell anyone—not even their wife or husband—and some of these thoughts turn into behavior and struggles and whatever, and it's just not right to judge people based on what you see.

Anyway. So I didn't say anything to this kid whose name I couldn't even remember. I just stood up and accidentally knocked his water glass onto his lap—wish it'd been something more staining—and he got up and shouted, "What the hell!" But I didn't reply, just walked away; I didn't wanna say anything that'd get me fired. And when he'd dried himself and Sandra came back behind the counter after dropping their food off, I heard them snicker, like they were looking at her ass or something, and she walked up to me with a really terrible face, like a combination of tired and sick and sad and angry, and she said, "Friends of yours?" and I just said, "I knew one of them in high school."

And she just sighed, because she had to deal with those kinds of snickers a lot from stupid boys like him, those awful boys who thought every damn woman in the world was impressed by money talk, guys who thought overweight women should always be laughed at as if they had no feelings. What scum.

But then. They had secrets too. Things hidden, just like everyone else. So as much as I hated them, I tried not to judge too harshly.

So back to my mom and her total inability to deal.

After all her nodding and my sermon, I felt really tired, so I just said, "I'm sorry," and I squeezed her hand. "I didn't mean to yell again. It's just that . . . I don't think you get what all this is doing to me."

She just blinked away a few tears. She cried a lot, but those tears right then seemed more real, if that makes sense, mostly because she was trying hard to blink them away. She said, "I'm here for you, Alyssa. I am." It came out like a croak, like something the old Harriet would've said with this uberconfidence but the new Harriet said because it was just left over. It was the saddest thing. Anyway. She hugged me, and it wasn't like the first hug we'd shared since I'd come back, but it was definitely the most memorable, because she was kinda clawing at me. And I felt like I was dangling her over some really steep cliff and she was holding on for dear life, so I just held her like that for a long time, and she kept clawing away, making marks on my back, I'm sure. But I didn't really mind—about the marks, I mean—because she needed it and I did too, because I realized, after a bit, that my nails were leaving marks on her as well.

I guess I was also having this reaction to my mom because I was feeling all weird after Jeremy kissed me. I was trying hard not to think about it, because, seriously, he was leaving, and the last thing I needed was to like some guy thousands of miles away. Strange thing was, even though I'd flirted with him before and was totally into him really early on, after the kiss, I felt something really flat. Not that I didn't like him anymore—I did—but because I knew I *shouldn't* like him, I didn't feel that boy-crazy shit I used to feel. I dunno, could've been because I was older too, more mature. I'd had experiences with men that weren't so good, my baby's father being the prime example. Still, it confused me, and I'd left the motel in a mood that wasn't really suitable for dealing with my mom.

And then—crazy!—after a few hours just hanging out at home, taking a nap, eating some eggs, talking a little with my mom, I got a call from Robbie Sisco—said he wanted to interview me for a job! At first I was like, *I've been trying to talk to you forever, and you keep ignoring me,* but I thought better of saying it, because maybe he really was just busy—busy for a whole month. So I went back to the Full Monte that night (seriously was like I lived there), and he let me into the office and said, "Have a seat," even though there was only one chair, so he had to stand. Well, he decided not to stand, just kinda sat on the counter in front of the little TV, and I thought this was the weirdest interview I'd ever had. Anyway, I was glad for the chair, 'cause it was hard to be on my feet for very long.

"Thing is," he said, "I think you'd be perfect here. And I got an opening—Friday and Saturday night shift, Sunday and Monday three to eleven p.m. What do you think?"

"That'd be so great," I said, even though I was kinda confused, since I was prepared to answer questions like *Why do you think you'll be good for this job?* (*I'm very detail-oriented and love to work with people*) and *Tell me about yourself* (*Well, you've known me since I was a kid, but if you must know, I went to high school . . .*) and *What would you do if you had an angry customer?* (*Well, I've had plenty of experience with that working at the diner. This one time . . .*). I didn't expect him to just say I had a job straight-out. "Wow, I really appreciate this," I said.

"Well, I think you'd do a great job. You're dependable, considerate, trustworthy, honest. Always have been."

"Well, thank you, Robbie."

"My pleasure." He paused and scratched his cheek, which had some stubble—kinda patchy and weird-shaped, not like the sexy five o'clock shadow thing. "Now we gotta talk a little about the obvious thing."

And at first I thought he was talking about Ricky, and I felt suddenly defensive, like, *God, not now, why?* But then I saw him looking at my belly, and I was like, *Oh, of course.* "I shouldn't need that much time," I said. "I've heard of women giving birth and going to work like the next day."

"Well, I wouldn't expect you to come in *that* soon," he said.

"Maybe just a week or so then?"

"A week or so? Yeah, that'd work."

I felt this sudden warmness toward him right then. I mean, before I was really hating on him, like cursing him under my breath all the time because he wouldn't answer my calls or emails or texts, but right then, I thought, *What an understanding guy.* And then it was like I remembered him as an understanding guy all the time. He was a few years ahead of me in high school, but I remember seeing him at the Meadows, and I remember him being extra nice to me even though I was so lowly, like a freshman or something. Back then, everyone called him Guido, because he was Italian—not like there weren't plenty of those around, but whatever—and he really hyped it up, with the greased-back hair and the cologne and the chains and all that stereotypical stuff, but in reality, he was a nice guy who was just proud of his roots. (Though I should say neither of his parents dressed like that and as far as I know nobody in his family did, and so this was all a weird thing made up in his head about how Italians were supposed to look from the movies. But still, it was okay that he was trying to be in touch with his heritage. Good for him.)

"This is such great news," I said. I was brimming. It felt so good, especially after the weirdness with Jeremy and yelling at my mom.

"Can you start tomorrow?" he said.

"Tomorrow?" I said, looking at my belly. I'd just assumed he'd wanna wait 'til I had the baby, since obviously I was due any moment.

"Yeah, just to train. I'll give you the keys. We don't keep them here. Everyone gets their own."

"Like to every room?"

"Well, yeah. A master card, haha. Like the credit card name."

And then—and I knew this was wrong—I thought, *I could sneak into Jeremy's room.* With a master card key I could surprise him, maybe bring him lunch unexpectedly. He was going to leave soon, I knew, and I felt this terrible sadness about it, like as much as it was weird and maybe awkward, I wanted to stay in contact with him, maybe meet up with him if he was ever in New Hampshire again. I still didn't know what he was doing in El Monte Springs, wasn't entirely convinced that it had nothing to do with Ricky, but at that point I was so happy I didn't care. I just wanted to let him know that whatever it was he was doing, I approved, because he just seemed like a good guy overall, a real awesome person. He was wicked cute too, and a decent kisser, even if it'd only lasted like two seconds, and maybe that flat feeling could go away with time?

"See you tomorrow then," Robbie said. "I'll be here at three thirty. Come at four?"

"Perfect."

"Great."

Before I left, I snuck a glance at Jeremy's door. There was a light on, so I thought, *Why not.* Wasn't like I was that tired or anything.

MAN-DATE CHAT TRANSCRIPT
FEBRUARY 14, 2015

Rickyg9999: u there??????

Rickyg9999: hello????

Rickyg9999: why aren't you responding?

Jeremyinsf: hey bud, sorry. kinda swamped here.

Rickyg9999: omg your there. it's been a month!!! where have you been?

Jeremyinsf: tax season. I'm an accountant.

Rickyg9999: you don't do accountant stuff all the time though?

Jeremyinsf: sorry, dude. just been busy, like I said

Rickyg9999: my spring break is next month, I've been making plans

Jeremyinsf: what sort of plans?

Rickyg9999: to come out and see you dummy ;-)

Jeremyinsf: oh, ok

Rickyg9999: unless you wanna save me the money and come here ;-)

Jeremyinsf: really busy few months, I'm serious!

Rickyg9999: I'm thinking of dropping out of school, just working

Jeremyinsf: what? no. you can't do that. you gotta stay in school. you gotta finish. you only have a few months left, right?

Rickyg9999: the teachers aren't teaching me anything, just sit there and look at us like we're all a bunch of idiots and everyone here is so lame I don't know how much longer I can stand it, maybe not even another few months

Jeremyinsf: you'll get through it

Rickyg9999: thanks, you're the only person who understands me I think

Jeremyinsf: I would suggest you reach out to some people there

Rickyg9999: and say what? people here are not smart

Jeremyinsf: I wish I could help, but I'm across the country you know

Rickyg9999: I know, that's a problem, that's why I'm trying to fix it

Jeremyinsf: I just don't want you to do something you'll regret

Rickyg9999: what does that mean???

Jeremyinsf: nothing. it's just that coming out here to visit by yourself is a big deal. if you don't tell your mom? that's huge. She'll call the police. it could turn into a mess.

Rickyg9999: I don't care about the mess I just can't stand it here anymore my mom doesn't care anyway

Jeremyinsf: I'm sure that's not true

Rickyg9999: she goes to work then comes home and talks to me about being motivated in school then goes on about how she thinks our lives are about to change, like for real I mean every day she says this! I'm serious she thinks she's gonna be famous or something

Jeremyinsf: she works to support you, you have to remember that. being an adult with children is not easy.

Rickyg9999: she's like everyone else in this town thinking they deserve to be something else and thinking the future's gonna be totally rosy cuz they have some get rich quick scheme or some dumb shit like that

Jeremyinsf: that's common there?

Rickyg9999: omg totally

Rickyg9999: like my neighbor's dad keeps talking about opening some business with specialty coffee and not like Starbucks but like with crazy flavors like fruit and meat and popcorn flavors and everyone's like gross!

Rickyg9999: but he's convinced it'll sell and he'll become like a billionaire

Rickyg9999: this guy is such a redneck too, always spits, like any real business person could ever take him seriously

Rickyg9999: my god

Rickyg9999: anyway my mom probably knows I'm not happy here surrounded by all this so maybe at first it would be shocking to her but I would send her an email and tell her I'm ok and then when I got a job there I would call her and tell her I'm staying

Jeremyinsf: so this isn't just a visit now?

Rickyg9999: more I think about it I don't think I can do this anymore, be here with these people

Jeremyinsf: let's think about this logically

Rickyg9999: ok

Jeremyinsf: first, what is it specifically that you hate?

Rickyg9999: I told you the people are stupid

Jeremyinsf: and I tell you that everywhere you go you'll meet stupid people. narrow it down.

Jeremyinsf: tell me what it is exactly you hate about your surroundings

Rickyg9999: I dunno. teachers are dumb, my classmates are dumb

Jeremyinsf: too broad

Rickyg9999: I don't now what u want me to say

Rickyg9999: know

Jeremyinsf: talk about one person you think is dumb

Rickyg9999: ok god there's so many

Jeremyinsf: one person. name him or her.

Rickyg9999: ok this girl Claire

Jeremyinsf: ok. what is it you hate about her?

Rickyg9999: I dunno, I thought she was my friend

Rickyg9999: we message each other sometimes but I can tell now that it's an act

Rickyg9999: she's stupid like the rest of them

Jeremyinsf: what specifically has she done to make you think that?

Rickyg9999: I dunno, she's just stupid

Jeremyinsf: ok contact me when you have more

Rickyg9999: no wait

Jeremyinsf: ?

Rickyg9999: ok so I tell her that Wesley and me are kinda tight and she responds saying I need to be careful, and I was like what?

Rickyg9999: like she's saying that someone like him would never hang with me

Jeremyinsf: why would she say that?

Rickyg9999: he plays a lot of jokes on people and he's just known as a troublemaker I guess, I dunno.

Rickyg9999: he jokes around with the teachers and the principal and they let him get away with things is what people say

Rickyg9999: his family's rich

Rickyg9999: they wanted to send him to private school somewhere but he didn't wanna go

Rickyg9999: anyway he's been asking me lately to go to the Meadows, that place I told you about, and he is very sincere with me and always nice likes my posts on Facebook and stuff

Rickyg9999: him and me are like the same, misunderstood. better than the rest of the idiots here

Jeremyinsf: and you think he's gay? and likes you?

Rickyg9999: I dunno

Rickyg9999: there aren't a whole lot of places for gay guys to be themselves here so maybe he just wants a friend who won't be judgy, I think he knows that's me

Rickyg9999: I'll be honest I'm starting to really like him, like I have really strong feelings and I think he's feeling the same but he can't admit it cuz he's in a different friend group who doesn't really like me

Rickyg9999: anyway I thought Claire was different but I guess she's not since she doesn't even think Wesley would want to be friends with me which is messed up

Jeremyinsf: well, if he's considered a troublemaker, maybe she's looking out for you?

Rickyg9999: that's just his reputation

Rickyg9999: he's not really like that he's a nice guy and just thinks this town sucks, like me

Rickyg9999: maybe we'll go to San Francisco together lol

Jeremyinsf: so you think he's in love with you?

Rickyg9999: I didn't say he was in love with me but maybe, who knows?

Rickyg9999: and like I said I feel like we understand each other are compatable and we could really get along together

Jeremyinsf: you feel love?

Rickyg9999: honestly I think about it, us together. I think he thinks about it too

Rickyg9999: and I'm not gonna turn down something wonderful. cuz I want it and deserve it and everyone else has it except me

Rickyg9999: that's why I wanna come out to San Francisco too just to hang out, see other people, maybe not even think about Wesley! haha

Jeremyinsf: I think you should really think hard about what you're proposing

Rickyg9999: all I do is think about it, I can't wait to get out of this shithole

Rickyg9999: I don't need much, maybe just a place to stay for a little while

Jeremyinsf: just think about it for a bit, ok?

Rickyg9999: I'll stay out of your hair totally ☺

Jeremyinsf: sorry, bud. gotta run. meeting.

Rickyg9999: you are soooo busy huh? meetings on Saturday even

Jeremyinsf: yeah, it's that time of year

Rickyg9999: ok well I'll let you know my plans very soon, maybe I should get your phone number so we can text and not just meet on here?

Jeremyinsf: I'm in the process of switching phones. mine got stolen. long story.

Rickyg9999: oh that sucks, well ok

Jeremyinsf: later man

Rickyg9999: ok bye

Jeremyinsf has closed his chat window.

JEREMY LITTLE

It was late when she visited me the second time that day. She looked happy, the pregnant-and-shiny-faced happy that seemed only to occur on the threshold of labor. I'd seen it before on some of my friends—an aggressively brilliant sheen that filled each facial contour and sparkled the irises of the eyes. It made me slightly uncomfortable.

"Alyssa," I said. "Hi."

She put her hands on her hips. "Can I come in? For just a second?"

"Well . . ."

"Come *on*," she said. "Just for a bit."

"Okay," I said. I opened the door wider and closed it behind her. "Sorry for the mess," I said.

"What mess?" she said. "You call this a mess?"

"Just . . . sorry."

"It's okay. No worries. Seriously. I've been in messes. This isn't one of them."

"Well, thanks." I walked to the bathroom, filled two plastic cups with water, came back, and handed one to her. The longing I'd felt after the movie had evaporated; in its place was an itchy red anxiety.

"Umm," she said, taking the water and furrowing her brow.

"Sorry," I said. "I don't have anything else."

"It's fine." She sat on the bed, pulled her legs up, crossed them. She set the water on the end table, dug through her pockets, set her keys next to the water. I sat on the pink chair and rested my hands on my legs. I felt strange, like she'd just caught me cheating and the other woman had just fled.

"Gettin' some work done?" she said, looking at my notebook, which was closed.

"Yeah," I said.

"You don't use a computer? Like a laptop?"

"No."

"Well," she said, leaning back and smiling. "Guess what?"

"What?"

"I got a job here!"

"You did?"

"Yeah, like just right now. Out of the blue, Robbie calls me, then he doesn't even really *interview* me, just says I'll be great. Totally weird, but who cares. He probably just got sick of me hanging out all the time. Anyway, I'm real happy about it all. He wants me to start tomorrow."

"Tomorrow?"

"Yeah—that's what *I* thought. But whatever. I can do it. It's just training. I can't imagine the front desk will be that difficult physically, if you know what I mean."

"But still . . ."

"I'll be fine." She smiled. "So when are you leaving again?"

"Tomorrow," I said.

"Tomorrow? Oh god, that's awful. It's like you just got here."

"Have to get back. You know, work."

"Yeah, I guess." She sat back up. We looked at each other for a while. "You know," she said, "I don't really get you, but that's okay, I think."

"Not a whole lot to get," I said. "I think I'm pretty normal. Pretty average."

"Ha. You're anything but." She sighed. We sat in silence for a while. She took a sip of her water. The air conditioner whirred. "Can't you stay just one more day?" she said. "It'd be nice to know one of the guests my first day on the job."

I shook my head. "Obligations."

"You know, I feel like if you lived here, we'd really get along," she said. "Like we'd click. Like we could be good friends—coffee buddies or whatever. I just have a feeling. You're wicked sweet. Good kisser too, if I say so myself."

"Yeah . . . Alyssa . . ."

"You must think I'm totally weird, just barging in on you like this at night, and I swear, I'm not like a needy girl who reads into a kiss or anything, and I know you're leaving, so . . ." She sighed. "I was just happy about the job and all, and I knew you were here, and, well, here I am."

"I'm glad you came over."

"Really? You are? 'Cause seriously, I can't tell at all. You look . . . I mean, you seem different."

"Just a long day, I guess," I said.

"Ha! Long day watching *The Proposal*?" She laughed. "Like I said, I'm not clingy or anything. I just think it's funny how random people can sometimes walk into your life and you feel something for them. Like strangers becoming nonstrangers, that whole process. It's like at first you're all hesitant around them, worrying about saying the wrong thing or whatever, but then it slowly gets more comfortable and you can say and do whatever you want around them. It happened kinda fast with you, I'll be honest, but I think we have a real connection."

She bit her lip. I nodded.

"But like I said, I'm not clingy," she said, "and I won't be hounding you across the country for sure, but if you come back sometime, we can maybe have a drink or something, since I probably won't be pregnant again. I mean, I'm not planning on it or anything, haha."

"Even if you were—pregnant, that is—we could have coffee."

"Yeah, but seriously, I think one kid'll be fine for me."

"You never know."

"Oh my god, I can't even imagine."

Alyssa's generosity moved me. She was pregnant, single, wrapped in the thorny wire of her little brother's murder-suicide, responsible for a near-comatose mother, about to start a part-time job at a run-down motel, and still her thoughts were of me: a stranger, an inconsequence, a nobody. With a world of calamity concentrated in her swollen body, she'd dedicated time and heart to someone who'd most likely give her nothing in return, and this, to me, was remarkable.

"You'll be a great mother," I said.

This kind of generosity didn't happen back in San Francisco, at least not among my cohorts. My friends and I were grotesquely self-centered, so much so that we often had trouble sticking to one subject for longer than a few minutes. When we went out, we effected no sense of real kinship. Though we'd sometimes assert some drunken platitude-ridden speeches about camaraderie and everlasting friendship and the unyielding gratification of steady companionship, we were never completely, unobstructively genuine. And the distraction of our phones widened this gulf, creating a small group of human bodies moving around together without actually *being* together.

One time, I remember, we were having brunch outside in Noe Valley—Derek, Kyle, and me. It was one of those perfect San Francisco days, the kind where you only needed a sweatshirt in the shade. We sat at a table meant for two, so our knees brushed up against each other when we moved.

"He's so fucking full of himself," I said. "I don't know why I wasted two years of my life." Craig and I had been broken up for two months. It'd taken me that long to realize he wasn't coming back, and I was angry.

"Yeah," Derek said. "You're better off."

"Having perspective," I said, "it does wonders. All he talked about was technology! How it was so damaging to everything, how it was like the worst thing to ever happen to the human race. Blah blah blah. Get over yourself. Jesus."

"Yep," Kyle said.

"What a sad person," I said. "God, I can't fucking stand him."

The waiter came, set down our omelets, asked us if we needed anything else. We didn't. Before they started eating, both Kyle and Derek checked their phones. Derek showed Kyle a picture. Kyle laughed.

"How does anyone even get to be such a shitty human being?" I said, spearing a potato. "Thinking they're above everything, above living a normal life. God, I'm so fucking over it."

"Jeremy," Derek said, looking sideways at Kyle. "Listen—"

"All the shit I put up with. Him coming home so late, not telling me when he'd be home, not talking to me, rejecting me. Jesus."

"Jeremy—"

"Did you know sometimes I'd have to yell at him from a different room just to have a conversation, because he wouldn't be in the same room with me? How pathetic. God."

"Jeremy, listen," Derek said. I looked up from my food.

"Yeah?"

"You know we love you and everything, right? But we both just wanna eat, okay? Can we just eat?"

"And we think you need to get over it," Kyle said.

"Get over it?"

"Yeah," Kyle said, taking a sip of his mimosa. "Get over it."

"Get over it?"

"Did I stutter?"

"Oh my god."

Interestingly, Kyle had been the first person I'd talked to about the breakup. I'd gone to his apartment, sat on his couch, cried. He'd said the usual inanities—Craig didn't know what he was missing, I could do better, he never liked Craig anyhow, etc., etc., etc. And while I knew these words were stock and unspecific to me, they did provide a small comfort, so I thought, then, that maybe I'd misjudged Kyle, whom I'd always found biting and thickheaded.

After that initial discussion, I'd called him daily to chat. After a week, he'd said it was better to text, so I texted, and the texts soon went unanswered. We were at brunch that day, in fact, only because I'd been running errands and bumped into them on the street.

"This isn't something you just get over," I said, shoveling omelet into my mouth. "It's not like that. You both know."

"We've been in relationships, Jeremy," Kyle said. "We understand breakups."

"Breakups aren't all the same."

"Your relationship was only two years," Kyle said. "I was with Joe for eight. Derek was with Sergio for ten. We know how hard breakups are, okay?"

"I'm not gonna sit here comparing breakups."

"We feel for you," Kyle said. "Seriously. But having gone through it? Our advice is still to get over it."

"You don't have to do the tough-love bit on me," I said. "I'm getting over it. But saying it like that? Kinda hateful."

"Please. We've listened to you for two months."

"Anyway," I said, "whatever. Sorry to *inconvenience* you both with my life. Two whole months—must be *such* an imposition."

"Stop it," Derek said.

"Whatever," I said, looking away. "So . . . I'm chatting with this kid from New Hampshire on Man-Date. He's having a difficult time with coming out and everything."

They both stared blankly at me.

"I'm just saying, I think of other things besides Craig."

"Why are you chatting with a kid in New Hampshire?" Kyle asked.

"I dunno. He reminds me of me, I guess. You guys don't understand, growing up like that, but . . ."

"Don't be patronizing, Jeremy," Derek said.

"Craig didn't think the Internet actually helped anyone. But this kid—he has an outlet. If I'd had this outlet growing up, I wouldn't have been so freaked about the gay thing."

"So you're thinking of other things besides Craig," Kyle said, sneering.

"All I'm saying is that I'm branching out, using the Internet for good purposes."

"Well, good for you," Kyle said, sighing. He checked his phone, scrolled through some pictures, pushed his plate to the side, and showed us a video of a cat licking a dog's ear. I tried to laugh, but only a small cough escaped.

I couldn't find anything funny anymore. Everything reminded me of Craig, which meant everything reminded me of loss. And the only things that seemed to mitigate this loss were the excruciatingly dull conversations I had online. They were salving distractions, committed under the guise of purposeful resolve. I didn't *truly* care about Ricky Graves. He was, at first, just a way to pass time.

"I gotta run," I said, throwing a few bills on the table. They looked relieved. "Shit to do."

"Okay," Derek said. "I'll text you later."

"Yeah."

He didn't text for a week.

In the motel, Alyssa pushed herself off the bed. Her water remained untouched on the nightstand. "I guess I should go," she said.

"You don't have to," I said.

"Yeah," she said. "I want to get a good night's sleep. Try to be half-way functional for tomorrow, haha."

"Alyssa," I said, feeling a rock in my throat. "Listen, don't go yet. I have something to tell you."

"Yeah?"

"Hmm . . ."

"You okay?"

I walked to her, put my arms around her, and held her tight. She let herself be held. "I like you," I said. "I like you a lot."

"Okay," she said into my chest. She pushed me back. "What's going on?"

Her earlier pregnancy-luster had dissolved. In its place shone a partially obscured freneticism—a widening of the eyes and a pursing of the lips. I looked away. She'd turned cold.

"What is it?" she said, moving away from me, toward the foot of the bed. "It's something bad, isn't it? I can tell. It's like I can sense it now. Bad news."

"I don't want you to be upset."

"It *is* bad . . ."

"I just . . . I think you should know. I knew Ricky."

"You knew Ricky . . ."

"I mean, I never met him. We chatted online. For six months."

"You chatted online . . ."

"Yes. He chatted with me the day of . . ."

She stared at me. I couldn't look away.

"I needed to meet you," I said, my throat suddenly dry. "I know how it sounds, but I needed to get to Ricky in the flesh somehow. I needed . . . But I didn't expect . . ."

"What did you chat about? Did you *know*? Did he tell—?"

"He wanted me to come out here, asked me a bunch of times. I said no, then—"

"Did he tell you? Did he—?"

"I thought I could coach him through some stuff online. Maybe, you know, help him through—"

"Did you know?"

"No! He never told me he was . . . I would've stopped it, I swear. If I'd known, I would've been on the first flight out!"

300

"You could've stopped it? You could've *stopped* it?"

"I didn't know!"

"He asked for you, and you didn't come!"

"I wanna help you. Please. I can send money. If you need it. I can send . . . Oh god, this is coming out all wrong."

"Money? Are you fucking serious?"

"He loved you so much," I said. My heart stretched, burst, sprayed. "He looked up to you so much. He kept saying . . . and I thought maybe . . . this was the only way to connect, with you. Please, Alyssa. Please believe my intentions are good. I just can't seem to explain myself clearly right now." I walked to her; she stepped away and headed for the door.

"I'm going. I'm going right now," she said.

"Okay, but let me give you my number, okay? At least let me—"

"No. I don't wanna ever see you again. I don't wanna ever talk to you again."

"Here. I'll write down—"

"No."

"Wait. Can't you wait just one minute?"

She couldn't; before I could give her my contact information, she was gone, the door closed behind her.

BRAD "CORKY" MEEKS

This time at camp, Louis McGovern—a shithead destined for juvie—
well, he knew Ricky was terrified of almost all insects, so he got his
group of guys, including Mark McVitry, all together and they jarred up
a whole bunch of grasshoppers and brought them in their backpacks to
lunch. When Ricky wasn't looking, they switched his water glass with
one of the jars, opened the lid, and let 'em fly. Ricky didn't know what
was going on at first, but when he saw those grasshopper eyes starin' up
at him, he lost it, kept screeching something fierce, batted at his shirt,
his pants, his face. Everyone laughed. Seemed like centuries passed.
Sounds comin' from Ricky were like he was getting murdered. Everyone
else was howlin', even the girls. Us counselors had to get everyone out
of the dining hall. I wanted to squeeze Louis's neck, but his dad was the
biggest donor—pretty much kept Burroway afloat.

Once everyone went outside, Ricky ran back to the cabin, lay on his
bunk, and stared at the corner. When I got there, he didn't look at me.

"Ricky," I said.

Nothing.

"Ricky," I said again. "You okay?"

"Go away," he said.

"Listen," I said, sitting on the bunk opposite him, lookin' at his
back. "You gotta stop lettin' those guys get to you. They're just idiot
boys. Playing pranks. Boys do that all the time."

"I don't," he said.

"Well, maybe you should."

"No."

"You wanna turn around, buddy?"

He turned around. Face was red and caked with dried-up tears.

"Now stop that cryin'," I said. "Here, wipe your face."

He took a napkin from me and wiped his face. "I hate it here," he said.

"You hate it 'cause you don't actually *do* nothin'. I'm serious. It'd be a whole lot funner if you'd try to participate. Now I know camp maybe isn't the greatest place for a kid like you, but it can be a good place to be. You gotta just let it be good, I guess."

"What's that mean, a kid like me."

"You're better than those fuckheads."

"It's stupid here. I hate it."

I closed my eyes for a second. It was hard to look at Ricky and not see Alyssa sometimes. "Hey—I got an idea, okay? But we can't execute this idea unless you promise me something."

"I'm not doing any more archery."

"You don't have to. Though you're really fuckin' good at it."

"Then what?"

"Before we go there, you promise me you're not gonna let yourself be embarrassed again, okay? You gotta promise me if any of those shitheads play any practical jokes again, you just pick yourself up, dust yourself off, then tell yourself you're not gonna be embarrassed again. Okay? Say it. You're not gonna be embarrassed again."

"No."

"Ricky, say it. First thing, you gotta believe you can do it, so you gotta admit it. So say it. *Not gonna be embarrassed again.*"

"Leave me alone."

"*Say it.*"

"Fine. I'm not gonna be embarrassed again."

"Good, now one more time."

"Not gonna be embarrassed again."

"Louder."

"Not gonna be embarrassed again!"

"Okay, fine," I said, chuckling a bit, and he even smiled for a quarter of a millisecond. "So here's the deal. Everyone's got their fears, right? Everyone. Nobody's fearless, not even in the goddamn movies. So know what that means? It means your good friend Louis McGovern freaks out about *something*. And guess what? I know what the something *is*."

Ricky sat up. "What?" he said.

"You'll never fuckin' guess."

"What is it?"

I leaned in, looked behind me, made sure nobody was about to come into the cabin. Then I whispered, "Dolls."

"Dolls?" he said.

"Shhh. Christ. Keep your voice down."

"He's afraid of *dolls*?"

"His mom told me this before he came this summer. Said he'd just seen a movie or something, some horror flick, and couldn't get it out of his head, kept thinking all of 'em would come to life and kill him. She even had to put away some of her old collection or something, because he'd freak out. Said I should watch out for nightmares, talkin' in his sleep, and all that. Haven't heard him 'til last night—moanin' somethin' I couldn't understand, tossing and turning. Nightmare, for sure. Anyway, I didn't think twice about it 'til now. Hear what I'm sayin'? Tit for tat. Eye-for-an-eye type of thing."

"Huh?"

"What I'm saying, Ricky, is that something bothers you, you don't get embarrassed and curl up in a ball. You fight back, okay? Now I'll help you this time, but after, it's all up to you. Got it?"

"Help me what?"

"Christ, Ricky, do I gotta spell every damn thing out for ya? Listen, here's what I'm thinking: Tomorrow during our crafts time,

I take you to town, tell everyone you've got a doctor's appointment or something. We shop for some hideous fuckin' doll, maybe at Spencer's or something. Anyway, tomorrow night you bring the doll out and just go to sleep with it. You're gonna get some shit—teenage boy with a doll, gonna happen—but I'll try to make sure it's in check. And to be honest, some of the boys think you're a little off, don't understand you and all, so the doll thing might just be another weird thing you do."

"I don't get it. What's the point if it's in my bed and not Louis's?"

"I'm gettin' to it. Hold your horses." I wiped some sweat from my forehead. "Now Louis, knowing him, he'll play it cool for a day or so. Might even try to get people to make fun of you. But even though that might happen, you gotta realize you're in control, okay? 'Cause he'll be really afraid. Shivering and shaking inside, trying so hard to keep composure. Anyway, the next night, I'll stay up really late, wait 'til everyone's asleep, then take the doll and put it in his bed. We can sit back and watch the fireworks for a minute when he wakes up."

"But his mom, she'll—"

"You think he's gonna admit this shit to his mom?"

"Someone'll tell."

"So what if they do? There's no rule against dolls in the cabin. And you just say you dropped it when you got up to go to the bathroom. Simple as that."

"But his family . . . I mean, you could get into some deep shit, get fired."

"Not an issue. Seriously. You think I'm gonna be a camp counselor here for the rest of my life anyway?" My heart was beating wicked fast. I didn't realize how excited I was about it all 'til right then. "You in or what, Ricky?" I said.

So the execution? Totally fucking flawless. Couldn't have been prouder of the kid. We picked out the creepiest little doll. Looked a bit like Chucky but minus the scars and blood; its head even moved if you pushed a button. As expected, all the guys made fun of Ricky—called him a fuckin' weirdo and a sissy fag and a little girl—and I wondered if they'd crush him, 'cause they got bad, and I couldn't be around him like 24/7. But Ricky, man, he kept his head on straight, didn't let it get to him.

Also as expected, Louis McGovern was the worst, trying to rally everyone into a taunting frenzy, but we both noticed how he kept his distance, and a few times, I caught him staring at the doll, and the only word for his face? Terror. He didn't hide it well. Plus, I fuckin' knew. I had insider information.

Louis didn't find the doll in his bed 'til morning, which couldn't have been more perfect, since everyone had to get up for breakfast anyway. Ricky and me, we'd hardly slept the whole night, just kept watching Louis. And when it finally happened, when Louis screamed—high-pitched, like Ricky—and retreated so quickly to the edge of his cot that he fell off, well, that there was some poetic justice. And the other boys? They just stared, wonderin' why the hell Louis was freakin' out so bad, and after a full minute of these screams, Randy Bridge, shrimpiest kid in the cabin, said, "Jesus, Louis. It's just Ricky's doll."

Well, I made like I was angry, saying, "Ricky! You put your doll in Louis's bed?"

And Ricky said, "No. I must've just dropped it on my way back from the bathroom last night."

Beautiful. Awesome. Totally justified. But the look on Ricky's face? Not what I expected. I'd expected some laughter maybe. Maybe some contentment, satisfaction, smugness. But what I saw was menace. Like serious power trip gone bad. For a second, he looked like he was snarling, like some rabid animal, and his little chest was heaving up and down, up and down. I didn't like that look one bit, so I was relieved when it turned into something like sadness.

I went up to him and whispered, "You okay?"

He mouthed, *Not gonna be embarrassed again.* And this gave me the fucking chills.

So the summer after Ricky's shooting, during the week Alyssa's visitor was in the Springs, I hung out in my truck in the Full Monte parking lot after work. Creepy as fuck, yeah, but creepiness wasn't my intention. Much as I hated to admit it, her coming back to town stirred up all the old feelings I had way back when—love feelings, total sap bullshit. Wasn't jealous of this dude per se, but was still wicked protective of Alyssa, especially her being pregnant and everything, so I just wanted to make sure she was okay, just be there if anything went wrong. Well, anyway, that last night he was in town, she came out of his room crying, sobbing really, and I couldn't help myself. I got out of my truck and ran to her, and it was like she was expecting me or something, 'cause she didn't ask what the hell I was doing there, at least not at first, just let me hold her and sobbed into my chest.

"That fucker," I said. "What'd he do? I'll fuckin' kill him."

"Corky," she said, hitching and sniffing.

"Hey now," I said, feeling suddenly soft. "Hey now. It's okay."

"Corky," she said.

"What's wrong? What'd he do?"

"Nothing. Nothing. Nothing . . ."

"What?"

"I *miss* him."

"You miss . . . Oh."

"I miss him so much!"

"Ah, baby girl," I said, rubbing her back, "I miss him too."

I did miss him, but having her there with me, folded in me again, well, what I realized then was that I missed her more. All the shit I'd done with Ricky, with her mom, maybe even with Mark, it'd been to stay connected to *her*. 'Cause when she'd left, I hadn't been able to leave my apartment for a week. Hadn't known what to do without her. Big blank space, if you know what I mean. So I hung out with Ricky, even convinced Mrs. Graves to send him to camp, and rigged it so he was in my cabin.

"What are you doing here?" Alyssa said. She pulled away and looked straight up at me. The parking lot light kinda made her face shiny. I wiped her cheek. "You spyin' on me?" she said.

"Spyin'?" I said. "Of course not. Just saw your car . . ."

"It's okay. Not like I'm mad. I just . . ."

"Should get you home."

"I'm not sure . . ."

"Not sure what?"

She didn't respond. She looked up at me with wide eyes and grabbed her belly. "Oh my god," she said.

"What?"

"Didn't think *that's* what it'd feel like. Jesus. Like a pop."

"A pop? What's that mean?"

"Water broke."

"Water? Oh. Holy shit."

"I'm having a fucking baby."

"Jesus. Come on. I'm parked there."

I led her to my truck; she kept sayin' how the water kept comin' with every movement, and she didn't know if that was usual. Was so like her, not to prepare much—no classes or even books. She just let things happen, which wasn't always good. I helped her into the truck, got in, turned the ignition, and, of course, sputter, sputter, die.

"Seriously?" I said, trying again.

Nothing.

"Perfect timing, huh?" she said, wincing.

"Shit."

"Take my car," she said.

"Okay."

So I helped her back out, and I actually felt the fluid on her leg and I got freaked for a second, 'cause what if it was blood and not water? It was too dark to tell. "Gimme your keys," I said.

She reached into her right pocket. Her left pocket. "Oh, fuck me," she said.

"What?"

"I left my keys in Jeremy's room."

"What?"

"I just took 'em out, 'cause they were scratchin' my leg, and then I left—oh Jesus, Corky, this doesn't feel good. Can you . . . ? He's in room 5."

"Okay. You wait here. Don't move."

"Hurry!"

Not thinking, I banged as hard as I could on his door. Guess I thought the louder I was, the faster he'd be, but that wasn't the case. He didn't answer right away, so I shouted, "Hey! Hey in there! Open the fuck up! Emergency. Open up!" and I banged some more. Poor fucker was probably scared to death, maybe remembering me banging on his door last time, then screaming for him to get out.

Well, he opened the door, looking pale as fuck, and I barged in and said, "Where are they?"

"What?" he said. His voice was shaky.

"Her fucking keys!"

"Keys?"

"Where the fuck are they?"

He pointed to the end table, and there they were, so I grabbed 'em.

"Wait," he said. "Alyssa's okay?"

I didn't say anything, just barreled out, and once I got past the doorway, who did I nearly run into but Mark McVitry and Claire Chang. "Fuck!" I said. "What kind of fuckin' circus is this?"

"Corky," Mark said, "what're you—?"

"Don't worry about it," I said, running off, wondering how it was that those two just happened to be there, at the motel, at that time. *Screwing?* I thought. *Nah.*

Anyway, I drove fast as I could, and Alyssa was breathin' real hard, sweatin' too, and I wanted to tell her then that I wished she'd taken a goddamn new-mother class, like the type where they taught you how you were supposed to inhale and exhale calm. Once in a while she grunted and squinted, looked like she was pushing, and so I said, "Hey now. No, don't do that, wait 'til we're at the doctor's."

"Don't do what?" she said, high-pitched. "Fuck, Corky, can't you go any faster?"

"Just settle down. Think of a waterfall or a forest or something."

"A waterfall or forest? Are you fucking *serious*?"

Well, I got her to the ER finally, and I screamed at people just like in the movies. But what was different was that nobody was really scrambling; they were just going normal pace, getting her in a wheelchair, sending her off. They were efficient—have to say that—but I thought they'd be a little more aggressive and full of anxiety and whatever, yelling things over to each other about her vital signs and stuff. Way they were, Alyssa could've had the goddamn baby dangling halfway out and they'd've just been like, *Hey, is room 3 open? Not yet? Well, take your time, we'll get her there soon.*

This brunette at the desk smiled and asked me if I wanted to fill out my wife's paperwork, and instead of sayin', *She's not my wife,* I just let her give the papers to me. Nothin' wrong with me occupying some of my time with that shit, helpin' her out some, doin' what I could. And as I was writing down her address and phone number, it hit me that she was gonna stay. She was gonna raise her kid in El Monte Springs, she was gonna be *here*, she was gonna be *around*, and I couldn't tell you how much fucking joy that filled me with. I couldn't *tell* you.

I put the papers aside—couldn't really fill most of 'em out anyway—and called up Mrs. Graves. She answered on the first ring but said, "Corky, I'm busy now."

"Your daughter's in the hospital," I said, and as soon as I did, I felt like shit. I said, "I mean, she's having her baby."

"Oh!" she said.

"I'm sitting in the ER," I said. "No clue how long this'll take."

"I'll be right there," she said.

Thing about Mrs. Graves was that even though she'd been doing this whole watch-TV-and-mope shit since Ricky died, I knew that part of it was an act. See, when your kid dies, you can't immediately go back to being whatever cheerful person you were before—that'd just make you look heartless. It was almost *noble* to go a little cuckoo when that happened, 'specially the way it happened with Ricky. But Mrs. Graves? I'd known her for years. I knew it was killing her to do what she was doing, sitting around and mourning. Not to say she wasn't mourning Ricky nonstop, but this woman needed activity; this woman needed a *project*. Not once since I'd known the Graveses had I seen her watch TV, and now it was all she did.

About a month after Ricky's funeral, Alyssa not back from Boston yet, I went over to her house, just to check up. Cameras were all gone, of course—everyone'd already forgotten about our little tragedy, and that was for the best. She answered the door right away, which surprised me. I'd expected to just knock and go away.

"Hello, Corky," she said. Her face was sorta indented from not eating, but even so, she looked better than the last time I'd seen her. Still awful, but better.

"I just came to see how you're doin'," I said.

"Oh," she said. "Well, that's nice."

"Do you need anything? Was gonna go to the store anyhow. Thought I'd swing by and ask—"

"I need to go for a walk," she said. "You wanna take a walk?"

"A walk? Yeah. Sure. Let's walk."

Now El Monte Springs isn't really a walking town, if you know what I mean. People walked downtown sometimes, but even there, it was mostly cars, not foot traffic. Not that it *shouldn't* be a walking town—it has trees everywhere and some places are wicked pretty—but it just isn't. Lots of the roads don't even have sidewalks. Still, while I was takin' that walk with Mrs. Graves, I kept thinking it was a shame we didn't do it more—you know, walk. You notice things when you slow down like that. Like when we passed the Santangelos' place, I noticed all different types of flowers growin' right in their front yard. I'd passed by there millions of times in my truck, but I never knew how carefully they kept up their garden. Awesome dedication. And walkin' by Justice Park, the one-block patch of grass with the curvy slide and swing set, I noticed that someone had stenciled a heart with the initials J. R. and H. M. in the center. It was Jimmy Rodriguez and Hayley Monroe. I knew it.

Anyway, we walked up Van Buren, down Harvard Lane, down Juniper Street, past Fourteenth, Fifteenth, and Sixteenth, and ended up at Spring High, where all of us had gone to high school. Didn't know then that she'd meant to go there. Thought it was just another building on our aimless way, I guess, but once we were facing it, she stopped.

"This building hasn't changed since I went to school here," she said.

I admit, I felt a little self-conscious standing there. It was what creepers and perverts did. School was still in session, and the kids would be out any time. I didn't wanna be there when the bell rang.

"I remember his first day of high school, Corky," she said, still staring at the school. Through one of the windows, I saw some students looking bored. "I dropped him off right here. I felt this strange old feeling, like *How the hell can my youngest kid be in high school?* Alyssa was already gone, long gone, an adult. Well, you know. And I'll tell you, it's a strange thing to have kids that separate in age. I could go on. But anyway, on his first day of high school, I felt old, but I also felt proud, like I'd gotten one kid through all this shit and I was gonna get another one through. I felt like a top-notch mother. So I told him have a good day, and he didn't even look at me, just opened the door and said, 'It's gonna be fine.'" She sighed. "Well, I thought he was talking to me, so I said, 'It'll be more than *fine*, young man!' And he gave me the strangest look, like I'd just woken him up. It wasn't until I got home that I realized he was talking to himself, psyching himself up. I had no idea how hard school was for him."

"You can't know everything," I said. "You're just one person."

"And I was emailing with this woman—maybe you know her. Victoria Gorham. She's famous, and she'd actually *responded*. She encouraged me to write my story."

"That self-help lady? The author?"

"Yeah. So I wrote it, my story. And the whole time I had all these memories and I was trying to put them in some sort of order, and a lot of them had to do with me trying to figure Ricky out. Even when he was a kid." She brushed her hair off her shoulder and blinked real slow. "You know that the day of . . . the day of . . . before he . . . you know that he came to me . . . you know that he hugged me and said he was sorry?" She choked up. I touched her shoulder. "And what I was thinking was that I was experiencing a defining moment. A *defining moment*. You know how fucking *stupid* that sounds? A defining moment? That's what some idiot like Victoria Gorham would say." She wiped her eyes. "Oh god, Corky. I haven't slept in a month. I'm so tired."

"You should try to rest."

"I just keep having these memories. Piecing together what I did wrong." Wind rustled her hair. It moved in these small clumps.

"You didn't do anything wrong," I said.

"I didn't even know he *knew* about my gun! I'd never told him about it. I only got it because Alyssa was worried. She said—"

"It's okay, Mrs. Graves. It's all right."

313

"The house is too quiet," she said. "Ricky, he was never loud, but he was there and he made noise." She turned to me. Her eyes were red. "Corky, I know this is weird, and feel free to say no, but would you mind sleeping on my couch tonight?"

"On your couch?"

"Yeah, just for tonight. Maybe I'll cook something, I dunno. I'd just like it if it weren't so quiet."

"Sure, I can do that."

The bell rang. A few minutes later, we were surrounded by high school kids. I knew a lot of 'em, from town or from camp. They waved to me and threw uncomfortable glances at Mrs. Graves. When they walked past us, she closed her eyes again, and her face was all pain. I wanted to know what she was thinking, but I didn't ask. We stood like that until all the students disappeared.

She didn't cook for me that night. She just went straight to bed. I huddled up on the couch and watched some TV. Felt good to be staying at the Graves place again, even with all that'd happened. I smelled Alyssa on the pillows—I was sure of it—and it made me sleep good. Next morning, Mrs. Graves got up and made me some eggs.

EMAIL CORRESPONDENCE
FEBRUARY 2015

From: **Harriet Graves** <harrietgraves4321@ yahoo.com>

To: Victoria Gorham <Victoria@victoriagorham.com>

Date: February 25, 2015 at 2:30 PM

Subject: The View!!

Hey Victoria!! I just saw you on The View! Wow! You've really made it big time! Not like you weren't big time before, but The View is huge! And you hit #1 on the bestseller list with your new book? I'm so, so impressed!!! I think it's great that you are branching out with your subject. Didn't Whoopi say that was very difficult to do? That you were known as a self-help author and for you to write a more journalistic book about separated twins was really risky? I'm so proud that we're kindred spirits!

I know it has been a really long time since I sent you my beginning pages but even if you have looked at them you can just throw them away. I started all over and now have 50 full pages! Writing is a lot of work! I don't know how you manage to do it so quick!

Everything is good here. Ricky seems happier than the last time I wrote. He's still not socializing a whole lot, but there's something lighter about him. That's how I describe it. Like he moped around for a long time, but recently he seems happy. I've even caught him singing while he does his chores. I think part of it is that he has his own computer now (though right now it's doing something weird so he's going to the library, but this is temporary, of course). The computer is really nice! He brings it to school with him sometimes, but mostly just leaves it at home. He's on Facebook a lot, and I've checked out his account (he refuses to "friend" me, but he sometimes shows me pictures of people at school) and for the most part it looks pretty normal teenager. I mean, he's not posting anything nuts, and he's friends with Mark McVitry on there too, so I guess that's just how kids nowadays interact. I also got him an iPhone, so he's totally up to snuff with tech stuff. I think maybe that's why he was in such a funk for so long? He felt behind everyone? Now he can just look on his phone or computer and see what people are up to. I should've tried to get him connected earlier, I think. It's just income-wise, I'm no Victoria Gorham (hehe, just a little jab).

He hasn't dated anybody, but that's normal. I'll be honest, I'm preparing myself for a conversation that'll be harder for him than it will be for me. Haha maybe that can be part of your next book! Maybe how to tell for sure if your kid might be gay? Like signs? Or maybe the difference between curiosity and full-fledged gayness? I'm not sure. For some reason, it makes me sad, though I'm fully accepting.

I truly hope you're well. If you can, drop me a line. It would be great to hear from you.

Sincerely,
Harriet Graves

MAN-DATE CHAT TRANSCRIPT
FEBRUARY 28, 2015

Rickyg9999: hello

Rickyg9999: Jeremy?

Jeremyinsf: I'm here

Rickyg9999: I probably can't come to San Francisco, I checked and flights are wicked expensive, don't know why since it's not Xmas or anything

Jeremyinsf: oh that's too bad

Rickyg9999: you could still come here though, spring break is soon ☺

Jeremyinsf: you know I wish I could. work is hellish. can't possibly leave now.

Rickyg9999: you work too much ☺

Jeremyinsf: this time of year is bad. very bad.

Rickyg9999: maybe in the summer then

Jeremyinsf: should have more time

Rickyg9999: I'm really sorry about not coming out there now, just you know, money lol

Jeremyinsf: I understand

Rickyg9999: I'm going to the Meadows tonight!

Jeremyinsf: where?

Rickyg9999: you forgot already! see you need to keep in touch better like every Saturday like before ;-) anyway the Meadows is a place where people hang out here but it's not that cool or anything, never gone but now Wesley wants me to go

Jeremyinsf: oh yeah, Wesley, the guy who likes you, right?

Rickyg9999: yeah I mean I caught him looking again he likes me that way for sure

Jeremyinsf: well, just be careful

Rickyg9999: ok Dad. lol jk. you sound like Corky

Jeremyinsf: who?

Rickyg9999: never mind no big deal anyway

Jeremyinsf: so you're excited about going there?

Rickyg9999: it's ok kinda nervous really, I mean I've never done anything with a guy before. but I'm determined ☺

Jeremyinsf: that's right, you've never kissed a guy before!

Rickyg9999: I haven't, why would I? lol

Rickyg9999: but I'm sure he wants to

Rickyg9999: keeps saying real nice things to me and he's confused like me I guess but he's even more confused I think and that makes me feel more comfortable for some reason

Rickyg9999: I'd kiss you if you were here lol

Rickyg9999: it would be the first

Jeremyinsf: haha the first. why do people always remember their first? it's not usually the best.

Rickyg9999: who was your first?

Jeremyinsf: first kiss?

Rickyg9999: yeah

Jeremyinsf: first real kiss was this girl named Carly. high school.

Rickyg9999: I thought u were gay??

Jeremyinsf: haha I am. doesn't mean I didn't kiss girls before I came out and everything.

Rickyg9999: was it good? what's the difference?

Jeremyinsf: not sure. girls are softer I guess. no hair on their lips. lol

Rickyg9999: so it was good??

Jeremyinsf: yeah. not bad. but what I was saying was that first kisses are just not that great.

Jeremyinsf: like nobody knows what they're doing, so there's too much tongue or weird lip arrangement or teeth. just not good. lol

Rickyg9999: so your first kiss wasn't very good

Jeremyinsf: haha I guess not. but we practiced ;)

Rickyg9999: so you got any tips for me?

Jeremyinsf: for kissing?

Rickyg9999: yeah I'm nervous

Jeremyinsf: you'll be fine I'm sure. just don't use too much tongue haha

Rickyg9999: yeah ok

Rickyg9999: so besides your first girl kiss when you first kissed your first guy was it like you knew?

Jeremyinsf: like I knew what?

Rickyg9999: that you were gay

Jeremyinsf: I guess I knew before

Rickyg9999: wish you could be my first

Jeremyinsf: I think you'll have a good time. just be open minded.

Rickyg9999: this is gonna change my life

Jeremyinsf: it might

Rickyg9999: no, cuz I've already made up my mind that after tonight I'm gonna come out like to everyone, to my mom and sister and Corky and everyone and I'm gonna try to convince Wesley to as well, and fuck everyone if they have a problem with it we can just move to San Francisco!

Jeremyinsf: wow, that's huge!

Rickyg9999: I feel so free! seriously! and I'll be honest I think I'm in love with him, like really in love and I just see this becoming something really really good

Rickyg9999: god I'm so excited and nervous!!!!

Rickyg9999: I'm so glad I have you to chat with

Rickyg9999: otherwise I'd be totally a wreck and probably like make a total fool of myself maybe do something stupid like bite his cheek

Jeremyinsf: haha aim for the lips

Rickyg9999: so just cuz we're probably gonna be a couple doesn't mean I still don't think your awesome I really really really want you to come out here, maybe be in our wedding even ;-)

Jeremyinsf: hold up, you're thinking way too far ahead, bud. try to get past your first kiss before you think wedding ☺

Rickyg9999: I know, I'm just soooo happy! And if you were here, I'd be even happier!!

Rickyg9999: we don't even have to stay here we can go to Boston or Providence if you want me to give you a tour of New England haha

Rickyg9999: so if not for my spring break then this summer maybe but who knows, I might not even be here anymore! Maybe me and Wesley will elope secretly lol

Rickyg9999: well I'm gonna get ready for tonight wish me luck

Jeremyinsf: good luck! can't wait to hear how it goes

Rickyg9999: things are gonna change after tonight, I know it

Rickyg9999: talk to u later

Rickyg9999: bye!

Jeremyinsf: bye

Rickyg9999 has closed his chat window.

EMAIL CORRESPONDENCE
MARCH 2015

From: **Harriet Graves** <harrietgraves4321@ yahoo.com>

To: Victoria Gorham <Victoria@victoriago-rham.com>

Date: March 4, 2015 at 9:52 AM

Subject: (no subject)

Hi Victoria,

So I know your busy and everything and I've talked to so many people around here but I feel like you are the expert and we're kindred spirits and everything like you said and you know how much I admire your work so if you could please just give me a little advice. My son Ricky was the butt of a horrible prank and it went on Facebook and since then he either shuts himself in his room or screams at me and that look is back, the blank look I told you about. I've contacted the school principal and everyone's mom and the boys who posted it are suspended for a week but what good is suspension? Its just vacation for those boys. Oh man I am so angry, Victoria! And everyone around here just seems to want to say that it wasn't that big of a deal but it was a big deal it was a HUGE deal! I know it sounds weird but if you can just write back with one piece of advice I'd so appreciate it! I'm trying to stay calm and keep my son calm at the same time and trying to work and deal with the school administration and the parents of the kids (who were my friends by the way and are all saying it wasn't so bad!!) and I posted something on my Facebook wall the other day about how it is never okay to use social media to humiliate people and that just made Ricky even more upset so I deleted it.

What do you think I should do? Any bit of advice helps at this point. Thank you so much!

Harriet Graves

From: **Victoria Gorham** <Victoria@victoriagorham.com>

To: Harriet Graves <harrietgraves4321@yahoo.com>

Date: March 4, 2015 at 9:55 AM

Subject: Automated Response: Re: (no subject)

Hi there!

I'm on vacation and will have very limited internet access. For publicity concerns, please contact Rachel Viren at Rachel@victoriagorham.com. Thanks, and happy living!

All my best,
Victoria Gorham

From: **Harriet Graves** <harrietgraves4321@yahoo.com>

To: Victoria Gorham <Victoria@victoriagorham.com>

Date: March 4, 2015 at 9:59 AM

Subject: Re: Automated Response: Re: (no subject)

Seriously?

From: **Victoria Gorham** <Victoria@victoriagorham.com>

To: Harriet Graves <harrietgraves4321@yahoo.com>

Date: March 4, 2015 at 10:01 AM

Subject: Automated Response: Re: Automated Response: Re: (no subject)

Hi there!

I'm on vacation and will have very limited internet access. For publicity concerns, please contact Rachel Viren at Rachel@victoriagorham.com. Thanks, and happy living!

All my best,
Victoria Gorham

JEREMY LITTLE

Time slowed after the tattooed man left, muting the surrounding voices and covering the room and the interlopers in a light-blue haze; this happened often. The first time was in first grade, sitting at my desk in Mrs. Hartwig's class, looking at my spelling book and wondering why there was an *e* in "chimney" and not in "funny." Carefully, I copied the words down in the space given, making sure my letters hit the center dashed line when appropriate.

"Jeremy." I looked up. Mrs. Hartwig had black curly hair, and when she smiled, crow's-feet dug into her temples. "Think you forgot something."

I looked down at my paper. *Chimny*, I'd written.

She leaned over. "Which one of these words isn't correct?" she asked.

I pointed to "chimny." She smiled, then time slowed. Her fingers danced slowly around my workbook; the pink of her knuckles flexed and extended with laborious, concentrated control. Abby Johnson, the skinny black-haired girl in front of me, turned her head, looked over at Mrs. Hartwig, and frowned. When she blinked, her eyes closed for a full second. From the open window, a breeze came in, the blue-white wisps forming an army of shaky scribbles, and when an individual ribbon hit a person's head, it shattered into millions of sparkling dots, painting the room with windy glitter.

"Jeremy?"

I looked over at Mrs. Hartwig, whose wrinkles voiced concern. I looked down at my workbook and shook my head. I erased "chimny" and started over.

In the motel, the time deceleration lasted longer than ever before. I felt terribly stoned, like I'd eaten at a Chinese buffet laced with marijuana, and as the two teenagers talked to me, I saw words leave their mouths in a series of indecipherable glyphs, lines and curves and shapes that appeared in the air and hung, frozen. I stared for a while, then sat down, trying to shake the pressure in my skull.

"You okay?"

There was a boy and a girl. The boy was classically handsome: blond, athletic, eyes arranged in a slightly sexy droop. And the girl was pretty: thin, small-boned, shiny black hair pulled back in a tight ponytail. They looked like an advertisement for a skin-care product.

"Corky didn't hurt you or anything, did he?" the boy said.

"No, no," I said.

"Just heard some banging earlier."

"It's fine. I'm okay."

"What'd he want?" the girl asked.

"Someone left her keys."

"Alyssa Graves," the boy said.

"You know her."

"Everyone knows her." The boy looked at the girl, then back at me. "How do *you* know her?"

"We just met this week," I said.

"You're just visiting?" the boy said.

"Yes, just visiting."

"Um, why?" the girl asked.

"That's a very good question," I replied.

At the end of March, a few weeks after Ricky's murder-suicide, I was alone at the Midnight Sun, the video bar where I'd met Craig. It was a Wednesday night, and the place was dead, only a handful of people I faintly recognized clustered around the far end of the bar. When he walked in, he glanced at me, glanced away, then glanced back at me. He hesitated, stepped back, and I wondered if he might leave, pretending he hadn't seen me standing there by the entryway, nursing my drink.

"Hi, Craig," I said, trapping him.

"Oh, hey," he said.

After he got his drink, we talked for a few minutes about his life. He was seeing someone. Someone I knew vaguely—a friend of a friend of a friend, an older guy, ten years our senior, a bank manager who'd been married to a woman for fifteen years and had two daughters. They'd known each other long before I'd met Craig, had maintained a friendship through his divorce, and had finally, one night shortly after our breakup, gotten drunk and expressed feelings beyond friendship.

"Glad for you," I said, looking away. Six months had passed since we'd broken up, but the hurt had remained, and he knew this, given the number of times I still texted him. That he talked so effusively about his new boyfriend was a testament to his fundamental lack of empathy, his uncanny ability to understand people theoretically while discounting the complexity of their individual experiences.

"Well, I'll leave you alone," he said.

"Wait."

He hesitated again and looked at the group at the end of the bar, then at the door. The music, for some reason, wasn't the usual shout-invoking Top 40. It was electric-guitar-heavy, unusual for that particular establishment. I didn't recognize any of the songs. "I just wanted to ask why you're not answering my texts or phone calls."

"We broke up a while ago, Jeremy," he said, his face turning stern.

"I understand that."

"So that's why." He turned away.

"But Craig," I said. "Look at me." When he turned, I saw creases below his eyes. They hadn't been there before, I was sure. "I'm going to New Hampshire this summer," I said. "Just for a bit. I bought my ticket."

"Okay?"

"You heard what happened in that small town, El Monte Springs."

"I'm not sure . . ."

"Kid shot two kids, then killed himself."

"Oh, I did hear about that." He furrowed his brow. "And that relates to you how?"

"I'm going partly because of you. Because of what you said to me a while back—how everything's too easy, too convenient online. You said the Internet couldn't spur true altruism."

"I'm not following."

"You said that people would rather send an instant message than comfort someone in person. You said we didn't make real connections anymore."

He stared.

"Well, I might've fucked up a bit," I said. "I chatted with the kid online."

"What kid?"

"*The* kid. The one who shot the other kids. We chatted on Man-Date."

"Holy shit."

"And I should've gone out there when he asked."

"Jeremy. Jesus."

"'Cause I know how it feels," I said.

"Does anyone know? Can't you be implicated?"

"I know how it *feels*, Craig," I said.

"How what feels?" His face blanched.

"To need someone who isn't there."

His brow furrowed deeper. He looked at the door. "Oh," he said.

"Your theory," I said, feeling a sudden well of anger, "your tapestry of unanswered prayers, your overnight proselytizing, your oh-so-ambitious and impressive removal of technology from your life—all for the high-minded ideal of real connection. And me, with all my gadgets and electronic buffoonery, actually attempting a real connection . . . Do you get it? Do you get your hypocrisy?"

"The cops should probably be notified . . ."

"I was there! I needed you, and you left me!"

"Stop being melodramatic."

His face was stone. The group in the corner tried hard not to stare. They tossed us furtive glances.

"Here you were going on and on about how true altruism, true empathy, becomes synthetic online, how the convenience of typing a few words of condolence or a few lines of congratulations replaces the actual experience of those offerings, spouting daylong polemics on the destructive nature of computerized interaction, making me feel like an idiot for so fervently participating, like a follower, like a *loser*. And me, stupidly revering every word you said. Because it made sense, and it still makes sense, even today. I'm not denying that your words have legitimacy, but just like a slimy politician who presents ideas with unwavering conviction, you disappoint."

"I'm leaving now."

"None of us was ever *really* there for each other, electronically or otherwise. You weren't there for me. I wasn't there for Ricky. But the difference? You were right there, in the same fucking house!"

"So you wanted to break up with me," I said. "Fine. I get it. People drift apart. Couples split. Shit happens. But you with all your morality, your instruction, your sermonizing, your fucking condescension, you couldn't see—not once—that you pulling away from me was tearing me apart! You were *surprised* by my reaction. You couldn't understand why I was taking it so hard. You were completely blind. All you saw was weakness, someone who couldn't match your impressive withdrawal from society. You saw my failure as a character shortcoming, and you lost respect for me for being vulnerable and human. That makes you kinda despicable."

"You've been rehearsing this, haven't you?" he said, still looking away.

"You've made me a better person," I said. "But I'm pretty sure I hate you for it."

"Bye, Jeremy," he said.

He put his hand on my shoulder, grimaced, set his half-full drink on the ledge, turned around, and left the building. I felt once again devastated—seeing him leave in any form did this to me—but perhaps not as much as before, for I was able to turn to the group at the end of the bar, wave, and give them a really big smile.

The boy and girl continued to stand in my doorway after Corky tore out of the parking lot in Alyssa's car. They looked like a young couple on the verge of an amicable split, or more likely, two friends who'd just had sex for the first time.

"Sorry about the commotion," I said.

"I gotta get home," the girl said. She looked down at her bag, which bulged oddly.

"Me too," the boy said.

The boy squinted out at the darkening parking lot; the girl reached into her bag and shifted things around.

"Are you okay, Mark?" the girl said to the boy.

"I think I see him again," the boy said, still staring out at nothing. I started closing my door. "But he's faded, like blurry. I guess that's good."

"It's better," the girl said.

"Definitely better," he said.

"Let's go," the girl said.

"Okay," the boy said.

I shut my door, locked the dead bolt, and returned to my desk. Once my notebook was open, I wrote Alyssa the necessary instructions, ripped the page out, folded it in thirds, and stuffed it in an envelope. I'd at first thought I'd need a long explanation, that my tone necessitated remorse and apology, but after I'd revealed myself to Alyssa, I understood that I'd really done nothing wrong. Ricky, even in death—especially in death—remained a stranger, and to strangers I wasn't beholden.

Alyssa, on the other hand, was not a stranger anymore. I'd inserted myself briefly into her life, had interrupted her during a very vulnerable time period. So leaving her without contact information would relegate her to the same end—in my head anyway—as Ricky. With this in mind, I removed the letter from the envelope, and wrote my email address and Facebook and Twitter information. After that, I called the car rental place and told them I would be returning the keys earlier than planned.

MAN-DATE CHAT TRANSCRIPT
MARCH 7, 2015

Jeremyinsf: hey, man, what's up?

Jeremyinsf: Ricky?

Jeremyinsf: hey, u there?

Jeremyinsf: how'd it go??

Rickyg9999: I'm not feeling good sorry

Jeremyinsf: what's wrong, bud?

Rickyg9999: I'm tired

Jeremyinsf: you wanna chat?

Rickyg9999: no

Jeremyinsf: you need help? You know someone there who can help you out? what's going on??

Rickyg9999: you always ask that

Jeremyinsf: what?

Rickyg9999: you always say I need someone here and I always say that everyone here sucks and you say it again and again and its like you don't listen to me, well now I'm very tired of it all

Jeremyinsf: sorry, man. just trying to help

Rickyg9999: you could of helped before but now you can't, you could of come

Jeremyinsf: I'll come out there sometime, ok? I don't know when but I will. you got my word. soon as things settle down.

Rickyg9999: your never coming out here, and I'm never going out there

Jeremyinsf: you don't know that

Rickyg9999: yeah I do

Jeremyinsf: I'm serious about being busy! I know it sounds like an excuse, but it's really the truth. I'm up to my neck in work. I'm hardly even sleeping. only reason I'm on here is because I wanted to check up on you, see how your time was at the Fields.

Rickyg9999: god your pathetic

Jeremyinsf: what?

Rickyg9999: the Fields? What the fuck is that?

Jeremyinsf: isn't it where you went?

Rickyg9999: smh

Jeremyinsf: are u ok?

Jeremyinsf: what happened there?

Jeremyinsf: you can tell me

Jeremyinsf: hello?

Jeremyinsf: ???

Jeremyinsf: you got me a little worried

Rickyg9999: I did? how sorry I am for that

Jeremyinsf: sarcastic?

Rickyg9999: I know why you don't come

Rickyg9999: we don't know each other we never did we just typed and shared pics and

Rickyg9999: we've never met and that's fine, we never will.

Rickyg9999: I'm ok with that now, not like i ever really thought it was gonna happen

Rickyg9999: anyway was just hoping I guess but now it doesn't matter

Rickyg9999: I'm done lying to everyone and I'm done chatting with you

Jeremyinsf: hey—don't be like that

Jeremyinsf: Ricky? come on.

Rickyg9999: what? I'm learning the truth about everything and I get it now I get everything ok? so you can stop pretending cuz I'm through with it I'm through with everything

Jeremyinsf: do you wanna chat on the phone?

Rickyg9999: now? lol are you serious? We've been chatting for months and now you wanna talk on the phone??!?! I thought your phone was lost anyway, another lie. I'm not stupid, I know what's happening I know you don't like me and that's fine cuz we never met so why do we even chat? I don't know, it's stupid.

Jeremyinsf: if I didn't like you I wouldn't have continued chatting

Rickyg9999: whatever

Jeremyinsf: you sound very upset. I really think you should reach out to someone. maybe your sister? you really like her. what about your mom?

Rickyg9999: I hate when people say that, reach out, like what does that even mean? Who came up with that term reach out like what is someone supposed to do, just reach out and grab someone and tell them everything that's wrong with them?

Rickyg9999: It's so fake like when someone says thanks for reaching out it's like what the fuck are you talking about, are you some sort of robot? Just say I really loved talking with you or I really hope we can talk again or when can we meet? let's set a date but instead they say thanks for reaching out which means basically that the other person is in such a terrible position they literally had to reach out to someone just to get there attention

Jeremyinsf: sorry

Rickyg9999: I think everyone can just fuck off, to be honest I'm tired of it all

Jeremyinsf: I'm gonna get going. but really, I think you should talk to someone—a friend, your parents, your sister, anyone.

Rickyg9999: what do you think I'm doing now? OMFG just cuz we're not talking in person you don't think I'm talking like reaching out or whatever? I'm talking to you! right now!

Jeremyinsf: there's not a whole lot I can do from here

Rickyg9999: who says I need you to do anything?!?!

Jeremyinsf: I think it's better if you talk to someone in person, a friend or something

Rickyg9999: fuck, seriously?

Rickyg9999: I asked you so many times to come out here and you said you couldn't all the time and now I know you won't so it doesn't matter cuz I can't talk to someone in person cuz you won't come out here you understand?

Jeremyinsf: you have more than just me. I'm not a serious part of your life, really. just a chat buddy.

Jeremyinsf: Ricky?

Jeremyinsf: hey, you there?

Jeremyinsf: well I'm serious about you talking to someone. you need to get this all off your chest. you'll feel much better afterward.

Jeremyinsf: have a good day. ttyl

Jeremyinsf has closed his chat window.

ALYSSA GRAVES

Having a kid's obviously this humongous responsibility, and of course I'd thought about it a lot before it came out—the responsibility, I mean—but the moment I saw my kid, I stopped stressing, you know? I mean, look: I'd had this thing, this living, breathing thing inside me for almost a year, and even though I knew it was an actual kid, I didn't really think of it having a totally distinct face until it came out. I mean, it obviously had a face—it was a real child, not some alien!—but it wasn't something I saw daily, so I sometimes thought of it more as an idea, even when I felt it moving and kicking, and I mean, ideas were so easy to fuck up, so I'd get wicked paranoid about all the ways I was gonna disappoint it with my lack of responsibility and my ridiculously low income. But seriously, once it was out and I saw her little face and little hands and little legs and little feet, all those concerns disappeared, because I knew then that I really had no other choice but to go forward and be the best mother I could be, and if I fucked up, I fucked up—so be it. I couldn't obsess so much about the negative.

So.

My first thoughts postbirthing were about Corky. It wasn't like I wanted him there like a *boyfriend* or anything, but I just felt like he *should* be there, like he was the daddy or something though he obviously wasn't. So I just kept saying his name, and finally he came into my room and saw the baby. He had this moment where he couldn't move, just stood there staring at me with his mouth wide open. I was wicked tired, but I was still able to say, "I'm a mother now, Corky" before I kinda passed out for like five seconds. When I opened my eyes again, Corky was still there along with my mother, and my mother was rocking the baby in her arms. And I expected her to bawl or something, but she didn't; she just rocked it and made some weird baby sounds and giggled and made more sounds and finally gave her back to me and looked at me like she was really proud, which maybe she was. Corky didn't hold the kid, but he did touch it every once in a while, like making sure it was real or something, and one time he bent over and kissed it on the cheek and I thought that was real sweet.

Meanwhile, I was so exhausted I could hardly even move my legs or arms, but I still felt like this awesome feeling in my head, like a warmness, like when I was a kid, I carried around this red-and-yellow blanket with pictures of little pigs, and at night I wrapped myself up in it really, really tight and my mom called me her "de-Alyssa-cious burrito baby" and I just felt like with that blanket and my mom saying that, everything was superokay, not just okay, but like *major* okay, if that makes sense? Like nothing in the world could get at me, and if I wanted, I could just crawl into the blanket and disappear. Well, that was kinda what I felt like with my mom and Corky there and my new baby, like with this group together nothing could really get at me or anyone else.

When the nurse came, the feeling didn't really fade, which confused me a little because, I mean, she was just a nurse, not part of my family or anything, but I figured after a bit that maybe the feeling would stay no matter who was around, just so long as those three were with me.

"Do you want some pictures?" the nurse asked, and I said yes.

I looked so fucking gross in all of them, but it was okay; I still posted them, and instantly I got over a hundred "likes," which made me feel really nice. Sandra from the diner posted, OMG. MOST BEAUTIFUL FAMILY I'VE EVER SEEN. EVER. I responded, THANK YOU with a smiley face.

I decided to name her Ella, and both Mom and Corky approved, said it was a really pretty name. Corky asked why Ella, like what was the significance, and I just shrugged and said I liked the name. He gave me a few looks like I was crazy, like names should always have meaning, like his—Bradley—which was his grandpa's middle name but which he didn't even go by. (To this day, he thinks "Corky" is superior. Like I've only known him as Corky, so "Brad" sounds weird to me, but if I'd've been with him before he started with the nickname, I'd've said, *Jesus, no. Brad is fine.*) It wasn't like anything we argued about—it was my kid, not his; I could name her whatever I wanted—but sometimes he reminded me that "Alyssa" and "Richard" (Ricky) had family importance.

"Oh, it doesn't matter," my mom told Corky later. "A name is just what you're called. I only named them for relatives because I didn't have any real strong opinions on names back then."

So there. He shut up about the name after that.

Not like I was really even that irritated with him about it, because during that time, the time directly after I had Ella, he basically stayed with us for a week, sleeping on the couch and helping me with Ella on his days off, and after that, even when he slept at his own apartment, he came over all the time and helped me out. I told him he didn't have to—I was fine to do everything necessary or whatever, and Mom was all about helping suddenly, like this kid had revived her from her constant QVC watching—but he insisted, and my mom thought it was good of him, so I let him help out.

Well, I felt all right pretty quickly, and, again, I had a bunch of help, so in just like a couple weeks or so, I went back to the motel. Robbie was like, "It's good you had the baby before you started, since we don't have no maternity-type leave or anything."

"So if I'd actually *started* and I'd had the baby, you wouldn't have let me come back?" I asked.

"I'd've let you come back, but I wouldn't have paid you."

"Um, you didn't pay me anyway."

"Exactly."

I shook my head. "You don't make any sense."

"You wanna work here or what?"

I was gonna learn soon enough that he hardly *ever* made sense. He had all these weird rules that he couldn't explain very well, and every week there was a new note about some new mandatory duty, like one week we had to clean the bathrooms in rooms 5, 9, and 14—totally random—after the housekeepers, because, as he said in his note, *We must double-check everything!*

This was just one example. There were so many!

So thank god for Corky during that time. I mean, seriously, if he hadn't been there, I'd've totally lost it. I just couldn't deal with a completely insane boss and a new job and a new baby and a sort of "recovering" mother without another person to vent to. And he let me vent—kinda like old times—and when I was done, he didn't really say anything that went against what I'd said, just said that I needed to get it all out.

Well, this one day, after I "got it all out," he said, "I know you're under stress, but let's chat, okay?"

We were in the living room, and my mom was at work still and the baby was napping, so it was just us, and I felt really nervous, like maybe he was gonna say that he was sick of me whining, that I'd become too much, and that he was gonna stop being around all the time listening and helping out, or that maybe he was gonna go back to helping Mark McVitry (who, by the way, didn't really need any help anymore—he'd even gotten a part-time job with his girlfriend Claire Chang at the Yolo). So I tensed up all over and got ready to be really upset and disappointed.

"You know I have no problem helping you out, right?" he said.

"Corky. You don't have to. I'm sorry, I don't wanna make it like—"

"I know I don't have to. But I like it."

"Okay?"

"Anyway, I was just thinkin' that like maybe you and me . . ."

"You and me what?"

"Like maybe we could give it another go? Wouldn't be that much different than now, right? I mean. But if you're not into it, I get it. Won't affect how I help you out, okay? No pressure, expectations or anything."

And I felt so much relief and thankfulness—and also, yes, joy! Like I didn't know that that's what I'd wanted, but of course it was; it's what I'd wanted the whole time. So before he could say anything more, I gave him a huge wet kiss and we basically did it right there on the couch, and after, scrambling into our clothes (my mom was due home any minute), we were both giggling like a couple kids, because it was just so fucking *right*. I finally felt fully home!

"I'll tell you this, Alyssa," he said, buckling his belt. "Those years you were gone? Worst years of my life."

"Well, I'm not leaving again," I said. "Not unless you're with me."

High cheese factor, sure, but who cares. We were back in love, and when you're back in love after a really long time, you can say anything and do anything you fucking want.

Okay, so time passed and all that, a couple months anyway, and everything seemed okay—Mom getting better, Corky being amazing, me getting the hang of the motel—and then one week in September, I got two letters in the mail, one from Mark McVitry and one from Jeremy Little. They came within two days of each other, which was weird, almost like they'd planned it, though that was obviously not the case. I stuffed both of them in my desk drawer unopened. I let them sit there for a week until one night when both my mom and Corky were out, I pulled them out, opened them, put them side by side, took a deep breath, and looked.

Mark's was a drawing of Ricky. Ricky was standing in a forest at night. The moon was lighting only part of his face. It was hard to tell if he was happy or not because of all the pencil lines, but the dog in his arms—there was no doubt how *it* felt. He was licking Ricky's cheek and wagging its tail. Well, I mean, it had those lines that meant its tail was moving. It was seriously beautiful, like one of those paintings in a museum that you stood and stared at because you really wanted to try and figure it out, and it made me start crying. Not like a total flood or anything, just little streams that made me sniff a lot. Attached to the drawing was a green Post-it note that said *I carried this with me a really long time, but I thought you should have it now,* and I didn't know if Mark meant he carried the guilt or whatever, or if he physically carried the picture with him. Who knows. Either way, it was something wonderful. I put my hand all over it, traced Ricky's happy figure, stared at the dog. Who knew Mark could draw so well. Seriously, it was like a real piece of art. I put it away in my desk, then looked over at Jeremy's letter. It said:

> *Dear Alyssa,*
>
> *Please go to www.man-date.com and log in with the name Jeremyinsf and the password Racketsville555. Once there, find the "Conversations" tab at the top. Click on it. It should open up all my chat sessions with Rickyg9999. I will not be using this website anymore.*
>
> *I'd love if you came out to California for a visit. You can stay for as long as you want. I will make flight arrangements if you'd like. Open invitation. Whenever you'd like. Also, I was serious about helping out financially if you want. Please let me know. No strings attached, I promise. It would mean a lot to me, but if you're not comfortable, I understand.*

All the best with your future. I know you'll make a
great mother. I think you're remarkable, and I'll never
forget you, ever.
Jeremy
Email: JeremyLittle222@gmail.com
FB: facebook.com/jeremylittle066685
Twitter: jeremyinsf08

I read the chats right away and then, yeah, the floodgates *did* open;
seriously, I felt every emotion a human could feel, and in the end, I
actually felt *better*, like it was exactly what I'd needed to really dig deep
into this shit process of grief. I didn't, however, read the last chat session
right away, because it happened on the day Ricky died and I just didn't
know if I was ready to handle it. I sorta paced around my room for a
bit, checked on Ella, made myself a ham-and-cheese sandwich, ate half,
called Corky at work, called my mom's cell, made sure she was okay (she
was actually out with a friend!), called the motel to check on my schedule, checked my email, my Facebook, my Instagram, turned the TV
on, flipped through twenty channels, turned it off, then finally sat back
down, opened the Man-Date website, clicked on the Conversations
tab, and scrolled down to the last one. I took a deep breath, said a little
prayer, and read.

Man-Date Chat Transcript

March 14, 2015

Jeremyinsf: hey bud, you doing better?

Rickyg9999: I'm ok

Jeremyinsf: good, I was worried

Rickyg9999: thank you

Jeremyinsf: so you wanna talk about it?

Rickyg9999: I'm thinking a lot about my sister today

Jeremyinsf: yeah? what about her?

Rickyg9999: she's pretty amazing, outstanding really, just lets life happen

Rickyg9999: there was this one time when she was a teenager and I was still a kid

Rickyg9999: she got pregnant but had an abortion but before she did she came to my bedroom late at night and told me about it

Rickyg9999: about this kid she was gonna have and she kinda leaned in to me and said hey, you want a niece or nephew to play with?

Rickyg9999: and I remember saying that I wanted that, it would be nice

Jeremyinsf: but she had an abortion

Rickyg9999: yes, she had an abortion but I remember that she asked me about it and I was only like 7 or 8 or something. that's incredible, I love her.

Jeremyinsf: listen, I've been thinking. if you want, when you're done with high school and you wanna check out the Bay Area, you can stay here a few days, no problem.

Rickyg9999: you were always telling me to reach out to someone here, like a friend or my parents and I'm not close to my mom and I don't have any real friends, just have my sister, who's in Boston

Rickyg9999: and I miss her so much all the time cuz I mean she was mean to me a lot, sometimes ignored me with her friends but she was someone I admired and I can't say that for anybody else

Jeremyinsf: it's great to be close to your siblings

Rickyg9999: we've never been close

Jeremyinsf: I thought you just said . . .

Rickyg9999: don't worry about it

Jeremyinsf: so what do you think about that trip out here after graduation?

Rickyg9999: sure, sounds like fun

Jeremyinsf: great! just let me know your schedule.

Rickyg9999: I will let you know

Jeremyinsf: ok great, man

Rickyg9999: goodbye, Jeremy

Jeremyinsf: talk to you soon, bud

Rickyg9999 has closed his chat window.

Oh god. I was seriously paralyzed in my chair forever. Then suddenly it all hit me, and I fell on the ground, like my legs lost all their muscle or something, and I just lay there next to my desk for an hour, staring at the ceiling, sometimes shaking and sometimes just completely floppy like a jellyfish, and it wasn't until Corky knocked on the door that I finally found the energy to get up and face him and hug him tight.

"What's going on?" he asked.

I just motioned to the computer, pushed past him, and went down the hall to Ricky's old room. I reached into Ella's crib and put my hand on her small chest and felt it go up and down.

"Hey there, sweet baby," I said. "Sweet, sweet baby."

She was such a good kid, not a real bad crier or anything, and I saw her smiling a lot, like every hour, I swear, like she was totally happy with me and the world, and sometimes she'd make this noise, like a *yaaa*. High-pitched and totally content, like something you'd say after a really delicious meal or satisfying sex or just if you felt like the world was being good to you. When she did it, her eyes would get really lazy, like half slits or something. Corky thought it was a yawn at first, but then I actually pointed out her yawns and he was like, "Yeah, the other thing is happier."

"Sweet, sweet Ella," I whispered, putting my hand on her cheek. "What a crazy fucking world you've been born into."

She opened her eyes, looked up at me, searched my face for a good five seconds, then closed her eyes and kept sleeping. If it wasn't my own kid, I might've found it a little creepy, but I just figured she was dreaming or something.

"It's okay," I said, picking her up. I went to the rocking chair by the window. "You don't have to worry about it now. You just worry about sleeping. You'll have plenty of time to explore the world. Now you just sleep."

I put my hand on her head, listened to her tiny breathing, kissed her ear. It was so weird to feel that much for something so small, and all my life I'd been so anti all those girls in high school and at the diner who told me how having a kid was like the most important experience in their lives, like nothing compared, like a baby was like this life's purpose for a woman. I mean, that's what you were *supposed* to say, that's what *everyone* says, so *of course* you're gonna copy everyone and make your baby experience like the most meaningful thing or whatever. But sitting there in the rocking chair, looking out at my dark driveway, patting my little daughter's back, I thought how they weren't necessarily wrong: this *was* an important thing, me and Ella; it was a very important thing, but the most important? I'm not sure. Because Ricky, he'd been an important thing too, and I guess I hadn't realized how important he'd been until he was no longer there.

"It's you and me, girl," I whispered. "We're gonna get through whatever happens, okay?"

A little while later, Corky came into the room. He stood behind me, put his hand on my shoulder, and looked down at my daughter.

"I didn't read it all," he said. "I couldn't."

"It's okay," I said.

"Who's Jeremy in SF?"

"The guy at the motel."

"The guy at the motel?"

"My keys. The visitor."

"Oh." Then: *"Oh."*

"Yeah."

"Christ," he said. "We're never gonna be done with this shit, are we?"

"Afraid not," I said.

"But that's all right."

"Yeah."

Ella's breathing was interrupted by her tiny *yaaa* sound, only it was like she was still asleep, because it came out so soft, a whisper almost.

"You hear that?" Corky said.

"Yeah."

"Amazing."

"Yeah."

We went to bed an hour later. But before we did, I sat down at the computer and erased all of Ricky's Man-Date chats. Then I entered Jeremy's contact info into my phone.

ACKNOWLEDGMENTS

Thank you to my agent, Christopher Rhodes, and my editor, Vivian Lee, both of whom pushed me to see what this novel could both do and be. Thanks also to everyone on the Little A team for working so hard to bring the best possible version of this book into the world.

I am indebted to some superbly intelligent and insightful readers over the last six years: Jennifer duBois, Anna North, Kathleen Sachs, Henrietta Rose-Innes, Katie O'Reilly, and especially Edward Helfers, whose technical observations not only helped shape this novel but also sculpted my general approach to fiction writing.

For both financial and emotional support, I am grateful to the Iowa Writers' Workshop—particularly Connie Brothers, Deb West, and Jan Zenisek—the Michener-Copernicus Society of America, the University of Cape Town, UC Berkeley's Summer Creative Writing Program, SMASH at Stanford University, the University of Maryland's Professional Writing Program, George Washington University's creative writing program, and The New England House/Frills.

Keeping me sane through the whole process were some remarkably charitable friends and colleagues, namely Benjamin Hale, T. Geronimo Johnson, Akemi Johnson, Elizabeth Cowan, Nicole Fontaine, Jeff Kee, Beatrice Lazar, Jung Yun, Melinda Moustakis, Jennifer Chang, Lisa Page, Tony Willman, Gerry Stover, Michael Gray, Bill Gonzalez, Krys Lee, Imraan Coovadia, Viet Le, the OG Frills crew, Will Breedlove,

Joan Mooney, and Bernard Welt. Thanks for letting me babble and pontificate and be messy and boorish.

Thank you to my teachers: Ethan Canin, Elizabeth McCracken, Ron Hansen, Jim Shepard, Marilynne Robinson, Jim Ford, Gerald Shapiro, and James Alan McPherson, all of whom overwhelmed me with their vociferous dedication to both craft and human decency. Thanks particularly to Samantha Chang, who, for the last ten years, has told me to *keep going, keep going, keep going*.

Finally, thanks to everyone in my family, without whom nothing would be possible, and especially Tara, whose unwavering encouragement and support has sustained me throughout my entire adult life.

ABOUT THE AUTHOR

Photo © Tara Mattson

James Han Mattson was born in Seoul, South Korea, and raised in North Dakota. A Michener-Copernicus Fellowship recipient and graduate of the Iowa Writers' Workshop, he has taught writing at the University of Iowa; the University of California, Berkeley; the University of Maryland; the University of Cape Town; and George Washington University. This is his first novel.